RYAN PLUT

Heavy Cargo

First edition

ISBN: 979-8-9888043-0-7

This book was professionally typeset on Reedsy.
Find out more at reedsy.com

For Gordon Sullivan,

who "Couldn't put it down!"

Nursing sister
noun (British English)

a female nurse, sometimes of a high grade

— Collins English Dictionary.

Contents

Acknowledgement

A big thank you to my friends for the encouragement they offered, or who read early draft manuscripts and made valuable suggestions. In chronological order: Mr Gordon Sullivan (who, after reading my first draft, handed me $60 cash and asked for my first published copy); Sterling MacKinnon; John Hope; The Revd. Mark Rudall for editing an early draft; Wayne Breidford; my editor Julian Beecroft; the author Alaric Bond; my brothers Mark Plut and Jason Plute; and my wife Karen who produced the front cover and author website. If I have forgotten to include any person, my sincerest apologies.

1

A Search Concluded

She was old. Not ancient, just … 'elderly,' having been built in 1907, and now thirty-four years old. Ships that have been worked hard all their lives were lucky to reach forty when the owners, faced with rising costs of operation and falling returns on their investment, consigned them to the knacker's yard or sold them off to Greek shipping interests. The Greeks were only too willing to wring another dozen years out of them, before the Orthodox Church spoke the *Trisagion* service for the women dressed in black, who wailed for the sons who had perished when the antiquated ship went down off some Cyclades island.

Had she been lucky enough to have been built of British iron in any yard of the River Tyne, the Clyde, or even in Belfast, she could have been counted on for a half century of honest service. But she was not so lucky, having been built by the *Flensburger Schiffbau-Gesellschaft* in Germany, as the SS *Adelaide,* for service to Australia. After the Great War, she was taken by the Allies as part of war reparations and held at Swansea with seventy others, until they were parcelled out to any of a dozen nations whose shipping lines had been decimated. Yugoslavia had bid for her, but the Portuguese had got her, and her three sister ships.

Renamed the SS *Cunene*, they'd worked her hard, very hard, until 1936 when the refrigeration machinery they'd installed had failed and was removed. Bought by The Ellerman Shipping Line of London, she was renamed SS *Dominion Empress* and became a tramp: cargo as assigned, where assigned, anywhere she was told to go.

In September 1939, she was lying at Falmouth when Germany invaded Poland, and the entire British ship's company quit to enlist – officers and crew alike. There she languished for eighteen months, the grime of a wartime port coating her decks. The Ellerman Lines appealed to the Ministry of War Transport Office to assign a crew, but no one wished to work a thirty-four-year-old coal-burner, least of all one with a German profile.

And then a captain was found: Mallinson.

* * *

The shipping agent sighed in exasperation. His forehead cradled in his palm, he went over the figures yet again, but still was unable to focus on the task at hand. He tossed his pencil down in disgust and pushed the paper away. His main problem kept cropping up, crowding out all other efforts at conducting his normal pursuit of business.

Gurnam Singh was a slight man approaching middle age, nearly thirty-seven, with sunken cheeks accentuating a beak of a nose and thin lips, his large teeth protruding above a neatly trimmed jawline beard. He wore a Sikh's turban and a western-style linen suit and narrow black tie. Fourteen – no, sixteen – ships he had found over the past several months, though Sir Thomas had revealed to him that not a single master could be persuaded! Meijer was beside himself with anxiety over how desperate the situation had become, but refused to show it, projecting to the world his usual jolly demeanour. Singh knew better. He glanced at a folder then picked up his telephone and dialled.

The line was busy, always busy. He might have to pay them a personal visit this time.

The office was rather worn in a genteel sort of way, looking as if it belonged to another century. Indeed, it had been an office for decades. Even, some said, one of the most successful businesses in Singapore. It did not possess the clean spare lines of a modern European office, nor did it exhibit the fluorescent lighting over massive rooms typical of an American office. There was no need for ostentatious display, as it was not a place anyone would, or could, visit. No client ever came here, as Mr Singh did not permit it; any business requiring personal contact was conducted elsewhere. It was exactly the way he liked it. The office consisted of a tiny room, five storeys up, at the top of a twisted pathway of stairs accessed from the end of a dogleg blind alley. One might describe it as purposefully hidden away. You entered this alley by passing between a bank and an overseas cablegram office; the very reasons why Singh had chosen this location at all. The alley itself, too narrow for any car, was lined with fragrant noodle shops, spice merchants, greengrocers and bicycles. Above these were flats of mostly elderly residents, from which came the aroma of spicy home-cooked food. Laundry hung from lines between their balconies, reminding one of the prayer flags of Tibet.

Should you manage to make your way to the top floor, you would find the frosted glass window in the door proclaiming "Singh & Co., Shipping Agents, Est'd 1922" in gilt lettering outlined in black. This door now stood ajar, and the skylight was also open, the better to clear the heat from the room. The din of traffic below was only rarely loud enough to reach this high. The room held an oak swivel chair at a matching desk, backed by grey metal filing cabinets. Above these the wall held a calendar from a Chinese bank, showing a pretty woman reclining with a lute upon sacks of rice, and the month, October 1941. On the desk was a banker's lamp illuminating a few neat stacks of documents, a business card file, a telephone, an abacus and two hand-crank adding machines: one in pounds, shillings and pence and the other in dollars. The wall opposite the window accommodated a low table crowded with an electric kettle and a tea service on a battered copper tray. There was a water closet in a separate room, because this had once been a flat, just like those on the floors below. On a cabinet an oscillating fan stirred the air. A powerful telescope on a tripod was placed at the large industrial window at the end of the room, the only source of daylight other than the skylight. This permitted a view over the rooftops to the ships that swung at anchor in Keppel Harbour and for some considerable distance further out. The late morning sun now slanted in to illuminate the room, motes of dust drifting in its yellow rays.

Singh had only just returned the telephone receiver to its cradle when the door burst in, admitting a young Asian man, all out of breath. He wore flip-flops and dungaree trousers and was naked from the waist up except for an open leather vest – the back of it embroidered 'Double Eight M.C.' with a pair of dice each showing that number. His bronzed skin was wind-burnt and sunburnt. His black hair hung over his ears and a scar interrupted an eyebrow. Goggles hung around his neck and in his hand he held a leather helmet.

"Nguyen! What obtains?" Singh enquired in his slightly antique manner. This was his very best contact on the Malay peninsula. He could ferret out just about anything he was asked.

"Found one!" wheezed the younger man, doubled over with a hand on his knee. He waved the helmet as a signal to wait until he caught his breath.

"Impossible!" Singh replied, standing and waving a hand towards the telescope. "I know every ship out there. If there were a new arrival, I would be aware of it."

"Not ... here yet," he panted. "Loading ... American-built ... aeroplanes at ... Chittagong few ... hours ago." He coughed against his wrist. Singh went to the side table and poured tea for him into a stained cup.

"An American ship?" Singh asked, disappointed. He offered his visitor the stool from the telescope, the only other seat.

"No, that's just it," the young man said, sitting and gulping the tea. "It's British!"

"*British!* Are you certain?" He refilled the young man's cup, then perched on the edge of his desk, listening intently.

"My source tells me it's on its way here! The steamship *Dominion Empress.* Its flag is the Red Ensign, and it seems to have a British or Commonwealth crew, except for the usual Chinese. I'm told the master's name is Roy Mallinson." He finished off the rest of the cup and handed it back.

"Well done, well done!" Singh shook his hand. He went to the desk and produced a cash box from which he paid Nguyen the agreed amount. The young man tucked the cash into a leather wallet he brought from his back pocket, attached to his belt by a chromed chain, then left. Singh retrieved a bound volume from a filing cabinet and sat at the desk, leafing through it until he found what he wanted. He read for a while, stopping to jot down a few notes. Picking up the telephone receiver, he dialled and waited.

"Sir Thomas, if you please. This is Gurnam Singh." He tapped his pencil eraser anxiously on the book as he waited. "Ah! Your Excellency, I wanted to ... yes, my family is fine, so kind of you to enquire. I wanted to let you know I may have located another one. ... Yes, I know we thought we had exhausted all the possibilities, but it hasn't arrived yet. Due in a week, I expect, and it's British ... yes, British! ... The *Dominion Empress,* managed by the Ellerman Shipping Line of London, of which I am already a representative. I have her particulars here. ... Certainly, I expect I can visit you tomorrow." There was a pause. "Oh, and I should mention: her master's name is Mallinson. Roy Mallinson." He spelled it out, and there was a long pause. "I shall call Meijer for you, to let him know." Another pause. "Capital, sir, capital! See you then."

He rang off. Stepping to the window, hands clasped behind his back, he beamed a relieved smile as he looked at the view of the harbour. He bent to peer through the telescope. In a moment he returned to his desk, to make another call. He would need to compose a cablegram later to the Ellerman Shipping Company of London. Sir Thomas was correct: it would need to be worded carefully, very carefully indeed.

* * *

Sir Thomas rang off and sat back for a moment, his fingers steepled in front of him. He pressed and held a key on his intercom.

"Mrs Choy."

"Sir?"

"Please make inquiries about a British Merchant Navy master by the name of Roy Mallinson, due here in about a week." He spelled it out for her. "I don't know his age. Since he's almost certain to have been an officer at some time in his career, you may start by ringing Admiral Sir Geoffrey Layton at Sembawang Naval Base. I should like this information by tomorrow morning, by noon at the very latest. Also, please schedule an hour-long meeting for tomorrow afternoon, here, with Mr Singh and Mr Meijer. That is all."

* * *

Captain Mallinson glanced over the letter from Beryl yet again. She wrote that their handyman, Alec – Lance Corporal Saunders – had been evacuated by sea from Sfakia, Crete, narrowly avoiding capture in the attempt, but wounded anyway. He spent a month in Alexandria under a doctor's care. From 'Alex' they had shipped him home to convalesce.

6

He had arrived in Stowmarket 'only the week before', which had been nine weeks ago, to judge by the postmark on the envelope. Mainland Greece, and the island of Crete itself, had finally fallen to the Germans on the first of June. She described how Alec was still infuriated that the defence of Crete had been a first-class cock-up from beginning to end, due to stupid General Weston and 'that bloody dentist', Major-General Freyberg.

I must say something about Alec. He laid her letter down and began writing the next line of his reply, but then halted in mid-sentence, filled with irritation at the noise coming from without. How could he write, or even form a thought, with the infernal clacking of the steam-winch pawls to contend with?

With a bang the clattering stopped abruptly and the hissing became a roar. There was shouting. He made up his mind to have a word with Hamish. Capping and pocketing his fountain pen (a gift from Beryl) he carefully unhooked from behind his ears his gold wire-rimmed glasses and laid them upon the desk, then pinched the bridge of his nose. It was the eye strain again. Rising, he plucked the white cap with the Ellerman Lines cap badge from its hook and settled it on his head. He checked himself in the mirror. A framed portrait of His Majesty King George VI was screwed to the wall to the left of it; on its right was his framed Master Mariner Certificate: *Unlimited Tonnage, Foreign-going, Any Ocean.* Stepping into the corridor he made his way forwards, on the way glancing into the chart house on his left and then the wireless room to his right or, as "Sparks" preferred to call it, the "radio shack". Eugene, or Gene, was young, a third of the captain's age but rather capable, having graduated from Marconi's Wireless Telegraph Training College in San Francisco. Originally from a dairy farm in Oregon, and the only American in his crew, Gene was employed as a civilian contractor. The boy sat hunched at his set, headphones clamped upon his head, listening and writing intently. Mallinson did not disturb him but continued forward to the bridge. He stepped out onto the starboard wing and retrieved the smaller of the two megaphones from its bracket. On the number one hatch below, the roar was gradually subsiding amid clouds of steam vapour. *Something else must have broken. What can it be this time?* He raised the megaphone and shouted "Chief!"

Hamish MacCallan turned, cupping both hands behind his ears, and waited. Mallinson shouted, slowly, each word made distinct, "What is the matter?"

Chief MacCallan made his way up to the bridge wing where, with crossed arms resting upon the rail, he waited until the deck crew had finished closing the valves. The roar ended and the vapour drifted away.

"The bloody winch head has broken in two," he said.

"Can it be fixed?"

"I'm afraid no' without fixing our own lathe the first."

"Well, have you a spare cylinder cover, then?"

"Nae," he snorted. Taking the megaphone from Mallinson, he shouted to the deck crew, "I told ye, let that one doon with the brake, and be careful about it." They watched as the 5,000 lb aeroplane settled to the hatch cover, winch brake squealing in protest. The crew threw a green tarpaulin onto its canopy as others lashed it down to rings in the deck. Mallinson took the megaphone from him and replaced it on its bracket.

Mallinson was in late middle age, or so he liked to tell himself. His eyes were grey. He had a good head of grey hair that he combed straight back. His beard and moustache, neatly trimmed, were also grey. As was common in men his age, his ears were large and there were bags under his eyes. His nose was short and slightly bulbous at the end. His eyebrows were unruly and often raised, giving him the appearance of a surprised yet kindly grandfather. His Ellerman Lines Company peaked cap had long ago been salt-spray-washed, sun-bleached and faded, and was now comfortably shapeless, much like the man who wore it.

He also enjoyed a dram or two from time to time. He didn't exercise beyond what his job required of him: doing daily inspections the length of a 475-foot-long freighter, climbing companionway ladders and shouting commands for half the day. He had a touch of gout that flared up on occasion, but otherwise accounted himself in good health. He did carry a bit of weight; enjoying the varied foods of the countries in which he found himself was one of the perquisites of his profession. In his travels he had naturally mastered the art of using *hashi* – chopsticks. His fellow captains regarded him as odd, since they tended to keep to themselves in their own clubs, away from whichever natives might be about. Well, he thought them odd: hanging about in stuffy insular clubs, maundering on about this voyage or that, the same complaints about crews or officials repeated *ad nauseam* was not for Roy Mallinson, when every port his vessel touched presented something new to see, or taste. Consequently, in his long career he had managed to acquire 'acquaintances' but few he could account 'true friends.' Fortunately Hamish was one of the latter. He had known Hamish MacCallan a long time, both having worked for years, and often on the same ships, with Ellerman, a British line with one of the largest fleets in the world. Hamish was slightly younger than himself, and his curly ginger hair, the colour of a smooth single malt of the kind he enjoyed when he could get it, was gradually being peppered with grey.

The SS *Dominion Empress* lay in the Kallang Basin near the seaplane base, berthed starboard side parallel to the shore, at the end of a barge. One Buffalo sat upon the barge ready to lift. In the distance, a Fordson tractor was towing another, tail first, across Kallang aerodrome to the ramp at the foot of the barge. The grass aerodrome had no runway but instead was circular, permitting an aeroplane to land from any direction. A car honked faintly across the water. They both looked to the west where the city of Singapore lay bathed in the late afternoon light. Beyond the intervening water, flocks of seagulls wheeled and screamed above the waterfront restaurants. They watched as a Short Singapore biplane flying boat idled past a ship's length away, its triple tail sporting the markings of the New Zealand Air Force. Mallinson turned to the Scotsman.

"Can you do without it?"

MacCallan thought aloud. "Well, a derrick can lift the one, but two are needed to position it properly." He thumbed a pinch of tobacco into his pipe and patted his pockets for a match. "Perhaps they'll make us a new head, when we coal up."

"I'll ask the ship's agent when I see him." He did not add the thought that came to mind: *whenever he bloody well decides to show up.* "How many more of these are left to load?"

MacCallan glanced over the side. "Two," he said, and struck a match. Eugene appeared behind them, waving a flimsy and clearly agitated.

"Skipper!" he interrupted. The boy was thin, not at all muscular, his sandy hair always neatly parted. The unlicensed crew regarded him as somewhat of an intellectual and avoided him. It was true, he was an avid reader and not of comic books. His small library contained works by Bertrand Russell and David Hume, as well as Huxley's *Brave New World* and Darwin's *The Descent of Man.* Last month he'd been attempting, without luck, to find any officer willing to discuss Malthusianism. The officers tolerated his quirks with a smile. After finishing off Joseph Conrad's *The Children of the Sea*, the young man's current selection was *Heart of Darkness* by the same author. To the captain's mind, the boy seemed eager to experience life, but only through reading books, unaware it was all around him, if only he would look up to notice.

"It's in your hands, chief. Do what you can, eh?" Mallinson was grateful for the interruption, as he did not like the smell of tobacco of any kind. With Gene dogging his steps, he walked aft along the bridge deck and entered his quarters through the starboard door. The wireless operator was the only member of the crew allowed to call the captain

'Skipper', for two reasons; mostly because Mallinson couldn't stop him, but also, as a former Canadian, Mallinson knew it was in the nature of Americans to sound brash. He had decided just to tolerate it, though he did find the boy's language atrocious. Stepping into the captain's cabin, Gene held up the flimsy.

"Fuggin' Japs bombed Chung-Kiang. They're bombin' hospitals! Four thousand Chinks killed in a single air-raid shelter!" He scowled, "Whennerwe gonna do sumpin'? That's the capital, fer chrissakes! They're our ally, ain't that right?" Mallinson took the flimsy and glanced at it.

"Eugene, this was months ago," he said in admonishment.

"And they're *still* doing it! They're killin' civilians, burning down villages, taking the grain and food, starvin' 'em all. The Japs call it the 'burn-to-ash strategy.' This's been going on ever since Nanking. Remember *that*?"

"As I keep having to remind you, America is not in this war," Mallinson replied wearily.

"Yet!"

Mallinson sighed. "That's as may be, however—"

"Skipper, this's a British ship, and *you* guys *are* in this war." He sat in the armchair facing the desk, leaning forwards, elbows on knees, fists clenched. "The Dutch are in this war, the Norwegians are, even the goddamn Polacks are in this war!"

Mallinson ignored the young man's language. "Great Britain is not at war with Japan. For now, we are at war only with Germany. We are doing what we can, the best we can, when we can." He patted him on the shoulder "We're not the HMS *Repulse* you know, we're an unarmed Merchant Navy cargo ship and we have a job to do, as small as this may seem to you. If it means tramping from port to port delivering war materiel, well, that's important too. My advice, my boy, is to stay out of it," – he raised a hand to forestall an interruption – "yes, stay out as long as possible." He walked, hands clasped behind his back, to the porthole, looking out.

"You know, I was in the Great War, that 'war to end all wars'. I was older than you are now, but let me tell you something; I learnt young men like you think there is some 'nobility' in war, some 'romance' in fighting the big battles. This is not true. War is horrible and results in death all round and usually for no good reason." He turned to face the younger man. "Now, Adolf declares Germany needs its '*Lebensraum*', Hirohito wants oil and resources, and they justify their atrocities by proclaiming a 'Greater East Asia Co-prosperity Sphere'. But in the end their expanding empires will collapse in upon themselves. An empire subjugates weaker peoples to rob them of their natural resources. They never endure because the subjects always throw off the yokes of the rulers. This has happened with every Empire there has ever been and, for that matter, every one there ever will be. All those great civilizations that once surrounded the Mediterranean – and the Persians, and the Ottomans, and the Hapsburgs – they didn't last. Yes, even the British Empire won't last. Britain itself will carry on, but even now our empire can be seen to be fading, in India, in Africa, and even now, here in Malaya."

Gene stood and faced the captain. "Spoken like a true Canuck," he said bitterly. Mallinson scowled at this casual insult.

"What do you imagine will be the fate of your American Empire?"

"America doesn't *have* an empire!" said the boy, hotly.

"Oh no? Many of the islands of the Caribbean, many in the Pacific, the kingdom of Hawaii, the Philippines, what do you call them? America has appropriated over a hundred islands around the world." He held up his hands, "Yes, yes, I know you Yanks *call* them territories, but they're an empire nonetheless. I'll wager you've never heard of the 1856 Guano Islands Act? This ruling by your Supreme Court was said by legal scholars of the time, and I quote, to have '*laid the basis for the legal foundation for the U.S. Empire.*' Oh, don't look so surprised. Let me tell you, this is something that Canada will never do!" Mallinson handed back the slip of paper. Stepping to the starboard door, he wrenched it open, inviting the young man to leave. "Now, if you will just do your job, I think you will find that war will come to you, and sooner than you might expect!"

Gene struggled for a retort. He looked out the door, and his eyes grew wide.

"Skipper, look!" Mallinson did look, then dashed forward to the starboard bridge wing, followed by the young wireless operator. The deck crew below swarmed the bulwark.

Driving across the aerodrome, directly towards them, was an elegant grey and black car, a Rolls Royce Phantom III, its overlarge brass headlamps glinting in the late afternoon sun. It was followed by a covered green lorry, advancing slowly before rolling to a stop behind the car at the foot of the ramp to the barge. Mallinson couldn't help but wonder who owned such an expensive car. The uniformed chauffeur, a heavyset oriental chap in blue serge uniform and cap, got out, opened the passenger door and stood to attention. An enormously fat man in a black bowler and powder-blue suit emerged, followed by a much slighter man in a white linen suit, on his head a purple turban. This one carried a leather Gladstone bag.

"Har! It's Goering an' Goebbels it is, come to pye us a visit," said someone on the well deck below, just loud enough to hear. Mallinson blanched.

"You there! Lower the accommodation ladder!" he bellowed, without bothering with the megaphone, "… at the double, *now!*" He made his way down to the deck. The two men crossed the barge, skirting the aeroplane, and puffed up the accommodation ladder stairs step by step. The slight man was dressed in modern clothing, except for a foot-long ceremonial curved dagger at his belt. There was an iron bracelet on his wrist. He was obviously a Sikh. He reached the rail first and turned to wait for the other, who arrived somewhat out of breath. The Sikh turned and addressed himself to Mallinson.

"You are the captain? Captain Mallinson? I trust you are well, sir?" He presented a business card:

SINGH & C^O. Shipping Agents

Singapore, Malaya

There at the bottom of the card, he saw, was the company telephone and street address. He shook his hand.

"Yes, Roy Mallinson, and you are?" he said, his gaze turning from one to the other.

"Is there a place where we may speak," the agent said quickly, "... in private?" Mallinson became aware that the crew was listening intently. The Ministry of War Transport had assigned this crew to the ship just a few months ago and, with the exception of his chief engineer, most of them he still didn't know at all.

"My cabin. Right this way, gentlemen." Then, catching sight of the boatswain, he called out, "Oh, Mr Virtanen, will you tell the galley steward to bring some tea for our guests? My special blend?"

"Aye, sir," said the bosun. The three wound their way aft along the weather deck, up a companionway to the shelter deck, then navigated another companionway to the bridge deck and down a corridor to the captain's cabin. Mallinson shut the door and dogged all seven portholes, leaving the curtains open for the light this afforded. His cabin was oak-panelled, comfortable enough, indeed larger than most, being the full width of the bridge house. In addition to its starboard desk and lounge area, with its leather Chesterfield and two club chairs flanking a low table, there was an alcove berth with curtains to port. The large man remained standing while the Sikh set the Gladstone bag on the table and began unfastening the straps. As he did so, he spoke.

"Gurnam Singh at your service, sir. I am the local shipping agent representing the Ellerman Shipping Line here in Malaya." He handed over an envelope containing the ship's payroll in cash. Mallinson thumbed through it, counting, and locked it in the safe. A batch of newspapers and the post, tied with twine, was produced and handed to Mallinson. He moved the framed photograph of his wife to one side, then spread them on the desk. The *Straits Times*, the *South China Morning Post*, the *Hong Kong Telegraph*, the *China Mail*, and, many weeks old, the *Sunday Post* of Scotland and *The Times* of London. This last he slipped into his desk. He busied himself with putting his letter and envelope into a desk drawer and retrieving his glasses.

"And you, sir?" he asked the other man. The Sikh interrupted him.

"I'm afraid I am prohibited from naming my companion at the present moment. He is here only to observe. I do hope you will understand. The Ellerman home office has previously been apprised of his presence and concurs." His diction was excellent. Mallinson nodded. They shook hands all around.

"I don't see the *Tamil Murasu* newspaper. Did you not bring it?" he asked, "I like to see all my crew are kept informed. Many of the men are Chinese or Malay, or they're Lascars."

"So sorry. I won't forget again." He bowed.

"Please, have a seat," Mallinson said, indicating the chairs. He himself took a chair instead of the swivel at the desk. The big man sank into the Chesterfield with apparent relief, placing his hat beside him. His black hair was thin and combed over his pate, covering it rather unsuccessfully. His forehead glistened with sweat. His chubby face made his features seem small in relation. Singh reached into the bag once more and brought out a bottle of amber liquid. He handed it in apparent deference to the other man, who presented it, label first, to Mallinson. He spoke for the first time, in English, but by his accent

Mallinson could tell he was obviously Dutch.

"This is a gift for you, which we hope you will enjoy. A spirit much esteemed here in these many islands of the Dutch East Indies but still exceedingly rare to procure, even here." In a flowing red script, the yellow-foil label read, 'Exquise Oude Genever, Blankenheym & Nolet, Schiedam'. Mallinson thanked him and set the heavy bottle on the table to admire the label. He was aware Genever was a drink peculiar to the Dutch. Singh then arranged a number of official documents in a neat array on the low table between them.

"Do you have need of a doctor for the crew or for medical assistance of any kind?" he began. Mallinson replied in the negative, and uncapping his pen, signed the papers Singh presented, taking his own copy. He laid it to one side. Next, he verified that the amount was correct, then signed for receipt of the payroll.

"The lorry," Singh said, gesturing outside to the vehicle which had accompanied them, "has all the provisions and victuals you're going to need. Will you sign for them here ... and here, please?"

Mallinson did as requested, and stacked his copy with the other.

"What repairs do you need, if any?" Singh asked, and was told of the steam winch cylinder cover. Arrangements were made to have a new part made at the same time they coaled the bunkers and watered the ship the following day, tasks that were carried out by contracted stevedores, mostly Chinese. Singh had arranged a berth at the Empire Dock and asked whether tugs would be needed. Mallinson confirmed that they would, and then signed all the documents for customs and harbour services that Singh had drawn up, including copies for the Ministry of War Transport in Whitehall. Then the cargo was discussed, and how his own crew had unloaded it using the ship's own derricks; Mallinson made sure Singh realised that no charge was to be made for this labour. Then today they had finished loading these aeroplanes, for which again there should be no charge. Singh passed him a sealed yellow envelope. This was stamped with red ink in big block letters: 'Most Secret – Burn After Reading.' This contained his orders from the Ministry of War Transport. Mallinson opened it and read silently, lingering over the closing lines: '… are to steam westwards via the Cape of Good Hope to Southampton Water, course at your own discretion.' He slipped the orders and the envelope into his desk and locked the drawer. He would take them down to the boiler-room furnaces later today. Their business concluded, Gurnam Singh packed away his documents in the bag. He coughed, exchanging nervous looks with his companion.

"Would you agree a meeting to see some very important people who have expressed a desire to meet with you – personally?" The meeting would be 'on the QT', and to that end Singh implored him not to mention it to anyone. The captain agreed.

"Capital, sir! capital!" Singh exclaimed, much relieved. "Shall we say tomorrow at one, if convenient?" Mallinson smiled to himself. *I wonder where he learnt his English? It's so old-fashioned.* Remembering his letter, he asked that they meet in front of the post office less than a mile from the port.

"Where is that blasted steward?" Mallinson rumbled in irritation. He stood and started for the door but before he reached it, the door opened and a white-jacketed Vander Sluyt entered balancing a silver tray that held a porcelain tea service. Mallinson introduced him by name and sat again. The steward served the tea, then bowed and left, though not before Mallinson ordered him to tell the bosun that he wanted to see him now. The big man spoke for only the second time that evening.

"*Mynheer*, that man, he is not a Dutchman." Puzzled, the captain asked why he thought so.

"He observes the bottle prominent on the table and yet not a flicker of recognition. Genever is so rare in the East these days, a man can go months and find not a drop. Even our famous Raffles Hotel goes without." He took a sip of tea. "Do you know from where he is?"

Mallinson nodded, rose and went to his filing cabinet. "Martin Vander Sluyt from Heerlen, Kingdom of the Netherlands, so his papers say."

"Heerlen," he mused, "Not so far from Chermanny, hey? His accent also ... a little ..." The thought trailed off, and he shrugged. They sat and enjoyed the sweet tea, a blend called Rooibos he had obtained in South Africa six weeks earlier. Mallinson mentioned how the Australians called the Buffalo aircraft being loaded 'flying beer bottles' on account of their shape. Singh opined that Australians seemed to attach alcoholic references to everything. Then, to the disapproval of his companion, the Sikh confided that Singapore had a somewhat deserved reputation around the world of being such a fleshpot that it was well known among sailors as 'Sin Galore'. Mallinson chuckled, not letting on that he had heard it before. When bosun Virtanen appeared, Mallinson passed him the newspapers and post with instructions to parcel out the lot to the forecastle crew and the black gang – the stokers and firemen. Then he ordered that the crew should unload the lorry and he asked the Finn to "show these gentlemen the ship" before they departed.

He stored the gift bottle unopened at the back of his wardrobe, out of sight behind a wooden keg. Mallinson then sat at his desk and retrieved the letter he had started earlier. He re-read what he had written:

Thursday, 16 October, 1941, Singapore, British Malaya

    The Watermeadows,

    Stowmarket, Suffolk,

    Great Britain

    Dearest Beryl,

    I hope you are keeping engaged in your various endeavours while I am away. As you know, I was asked in December 1940 by the Third Sea Lord for Transport, Admiral Sir Bruce Fraser, that, as we are in desperate need of qualified merchant captains, he would count it a great favour should I desire to return to service. This you know. Now I have some news that may hearten you ~~ I have decided that after the present voyage I have done this enough. I cannot continue. I've been at this only eight months but already I am tired. Perhaps it is my age. Let me assure you it is NOT my health! I do hope you

He uncapped the pen and thought about how he should close. He continued the last sentence where it left off:

have kept an eye on Alec to see to my beehives (if he's feeling up to it now), as it seems I shall have need of them again. Give my regards to him but, please don't let him monkey with my trains (as much as I know he wants to). Indeed, you might lock the attic door for me.

We have recently been 'near' Calcutta, and you know I cannot now mention our next destination, but know that when you see me next, I promise you it will be retirement for us both, for good and all time.

He looked over the last line. He hoped the news might excite her, but it seemed to him to come across as rather bland. He thought a moment more, then penned a closing line:

I long to hold you in my arms again.

All my love, Roy

He knew this last sentiment wasn't really what he was feeling but, it would do: thirty-five years of marriage made some phrases sound banal no matter how they were expressed. Beryl would know what he meant. He folded the letter neatly and inserted it in the envelope. He sealed the flap and put it in the drawer.

* * *

The captain went to the wardroom for his supper. Jimmy, the cook, had laid on a joint of beef and roast potatoes with lashings of gravy and stewed vegetables. He found when he arrived, however, that he wasn't feeling at all peckish for anything as heavy as this. Instead he took a cup, a pot of tea and a pocketful of biscuits topside, all the way up to the compass platform, the square wooden house directly above the bridge; its sole purpose was to house a second compass that wouldn't be affected by the magnetism of the iron upperworks below, affording him a comparison with the compass on the bridge proper. There was a wicker table and chair in there. He poured a cup and sat. He took a sip, watching the city lights of Singapore wink on as darkness fell. No one would disturb him up here, which was just as well. He needed time to think.

The steam winch head bothered him. The fact was that minor things, and some not so minor, kept breaking. Ever since, it had all become such a cumulative headache. The SS *Dominion Empress* had not impressed him at first sight. He'd found her quayside in Falmouth Harbour, the ramparts of Pendennis Castle looming over her, on a blustery day in late February – the rain bucketing down, the wind slicing first from one direction, then another, and then not at all. Had she not been in such a decrepit condition, one could have said she had 'pretty lines'. The colours of the Ellerman Shipping Line could barely be discerned through all the filth; the hull, originally painted a dark grey, was now streaked with rust, the ventilators buff and white, a single funnel of buff with a black top and white dividing line, all now coated with grime.

There had been a lone elderly watchman aboard to guard against the bane of all laid-up ships: theft and fire. The man was in his eighties, an army veteran from the Boer War and damn near deaf. It had taken a lot of shouting and hammering on the hull plates with a brick that Mallinson had found to attract the man's attention. When he'd told the man the Shipping Operations Control Division of the Ministry of

War Transport had assigned him to take charge, the man couldn't leave fast enough. The fellow had told him the old ship was haunted, what with all the creaking and groaning and the other unfamiliar noises in the night. Mallinson had watched him limp away under his brolly, an oilcloth bundle clutched under an arm.

His first inspection tour had started with a quick turn about her decks, to ascertain whether any equipment was missing or glass broken. All was intact, a good sign. The hinged covers over the freeing ports were all either missing or rusted open. Rusted open was certainly better than rusted shut. There also were no rats nor mice: the rat-guards were still on the dock lines. He recalled that he had looked up her particulars: gross tonnage of 5,875 tons, able to carry 8,825 tons deadweight on a draught of 25 feet, three inches. Her length was 475 feet overall, with a breadth of 58 feet. There were five holds with two derricks apiece, all originally fitted with steam-powered winches, but at some time past the winches of the three aft holds had been repowered with electric motors. The decks in way of the passenger accommodations, the boat deck, and on and around the bridge, were surfaced with teak – a wood which had long ago fallen out of favour and now was usually only seen aboard yachts. An old ship indeed. All the cargo decks were of plain iron otherwise.

He'd taken a torch below into the engine room. There had been three feet of water sloshing about, in the engine room and in every hold, because the Chinese skeleton crew had left the hatches open to the sky. The steam-driven dynamo had been installed high enough that the water hadn't reached it yet. The high-pressure valve chest of the main engine had remained disassembled and open over the previous year. Normally this would produce mere surface rust and could be relatively easily sanded away, but the skylight had been left wide open and rain and snow had rusted the piston valve into its bore. The entire valve chest had needed to be replaced.

But it wasn't only rainwater, it was saltwater too. There had been a bad leak somewhere, probably from plates or rivets having started when, in July 1940, the Luftwaffe had bombed the tanker *British Chancellor* outboard of her. A narrow escape indeed. The skeleton crew had fled in terror, and who could blame them?

The captain poured a second cup, and dug another biscuit from out of his pocket.

There had been an odour that reminded him of a farmyard's stench – oh yes: sewage. There had been a broken drain somewhere, in all probability a legacy of that same bombing. There is nothing that produces a worse smell than a mixture of sewage and saltwater. He had also been alarmed to find that rivet missing, and the hole it had left was just three inches above the waterline, wind-driven waves already slopping through it. There was no power from the shore, so the electric bilge pumps were inoperable. Had he arrived a month later, he might have found her resting in the silt of the harbour floor, and who knew what damage that would have done to her machinery? He had caught it in the nick of time! Two months dry-docked had the workmen going over every rivet and seam with their pneumatic hammers. He'd made a nuisance of himself, getting in their way as he inspected every inch of the hull. The propeller was in good shape, and this was in all likelihood due to the many zinc billets having wasted to nearly nothing. He demanded their immediate replacement with new.

Of course, half the bilge pumps hadn't worked, as most likely sawdust from its final cargo of Norwegian spruce for the RAF had clogged the bilge strum boxes. Those had been cleaned out, and the few bad bilge-pump motors replaced. She still leaked, but at least the pumps were able to keep up with it now. Eventually she was slowly put to rights.

He'd been rather fortunate that Hamish had been available. His old friend had been chief engineer on the Ellerman Lines' SS *Lesbian*, but that ship had been seized in Beirut by Vichy French forces, and they'd scuttled her in the Med. On the bridge he'd seen evidence of just how elderly this ship really was; nothing had been added or changed here since she'd been built. There was no Asdic, no Tannoy, not even a Kent screen in the glass. There wasn't even any chair for the captain, nor one for the helmsman, as when she was built they expected that standing a watch meant exactly that – standing. The only controls were a magnetic compass in a binnacle, some voice pipes, and the engine order telegraph. He'd noticed an Anschütz & Co. gyrocompass, but it was broken, and since they were at war with Germany, replacement parts had been impossible to obtain. The helm wheel was a full six feet in diameter, above a grating to stand upon. The aft bulkhead supported a locker with cubby-holes for the signal flags, a slant-topped stand-up desk, an electrical panel, and a second doorway into the chart house. The sides of the bridge house were completely open, so a man could stride from bridge wing to bridge wing unimpeded: her Teutonic builders had expected that, if you got cold, you would throw on your greatcoat. He'd dashed out into the rain squall and looked up to find the twin loops of antennae which meant she at least had a radio direction finder.

His inspection tour had ended in the captain's quarters. It had a water closet holding (wonder of wonders!) an enormous roll-top bath supporting a convoluted Edwardian-era shower arrangement. This was indeed an old ship! It had doors port and starboard to the outside deck, and an interior corridor leading forwards. There was a 'head' off the corridor here for the use of the watch standers. This corridor contained a companionway to the deck below, and another up to where he was now sitting.

In walking about the captain's cabin his rubber wellies had squelched wetly in the carpet. He'd suspected a leak in the overhead, but his torch revealed the coffered ceiling to be dry. He'd found a heap of empty bottles of spirits and beer. No wonder the place smelt like a distillery next door to a brewery! This discovery, on top of all the others, proved the final straw. He had seriously thought about telephoning the Ellerman Lines Shipping Company head office and telling them he had reconsidered. Perhaps they could have handed him a desk job, to free up another man who might be eager to command. If not, going home to Beryl in Stowmarket was looking better all the time. But it was true, he hadn't wanted to admit defeat. At his letting bedroom at the Seaview Inn, he'd written to Ellerman, listing all the problems point by point, demanding in no uncertain terms the funds he would need and a free hand to do whatever was necessary, or else he would refuse the command forthwith! They had agreed immediately, of course, a measure of their trust in him, but also of the urgent need of ships. That carpet had been the first to go, taken out by the very next week. They had installed a handsome new carpet. It was dark blue, thick and had the Ellerman Shipping Company crest picked out in gold. Quite luxurious! He had also had the mattress replaced.

Captain Mallinson had finished off this cup of tea and poured himself another. He resumed his retrospective, reflecting that he had not been idle when it came to hiring crew, either. The very first he'd picked had been Jimmy, the cook, as his long-held belief was a well-fed crew was a happy crew. The news had flashed all along the waterfront haunts of Falmouth, Plymouth, Portsmouth and Canary Wharf. Just a few of the remarks he'd later been told about were: "Mallinson's back." – "Blimey, I thought he retired!" – "Cor! Yer havin' a giraffe!" – "Don't yer larf, I tell you it's true!" – "Better sign up quick-like now, afore he fills 'is roster." He smiled in pleasure at the memory. He'd discovered the rigid discipline of the Royal Navy was more resented than welcomed, and adjusted his world view accordingly. His officers were all licensed, of course, but all the rest of it, the saluting and the 'Aye, aye, sir!', had fallen by the wayside, becoming just 'Aye, sir' and sometimes just 'sir' – he did insist on the acknowledgement. His 'number one' was now called his first mate. These days he didn't have a quartermaster, but a helmsman. He didn't have any chief petty officers; he had a boatswain, a carpenter, a steward and a cook. There were no ensigns, nor midshipmen, just able seamen and ordinary seamen who turned to at any task he ordered. Many were often straight off civvy street and many had been rejected by the services for various, usually health, reasons, though he suspected one or two of the rougher-looking lads may have mustered out of Her Majesty's Prison Exeter on account of good behaviour. Although he suspected that, what counted as good behaviour on the inside hardly met the standard of good behaviour on the outside. He didn't even have a boy steward to lay out his uniform or bring him a mug of hot cocoa on the cold run to Halifax, and he found he didn't miss it at all. Five years of retirement had mellowed him for sure.

The only position he'd regretted being unable to fill was the ship's surgeon, but there was no sickbay anyway, so perhaps that would always have been a stretch. The last sign-on had been Eugene Graham, after leaving another ship at London because of fisticuffs with a fellow crewmember. A row he told me he had lost rather badly. The Ministry of War Transport had paid the boy's fare on a night express to Falmouth, on 17th August, for a pier head jump. When they'd finally been able to depart, the following day, they had steamed due west to try to catch Convoy OG-71 from Liverpool, bound for Gib. Fortunately, Eugene had maintained a watch, and when they were miles south of Bantry Bay, the boy had alerted him that they were steaming straight toward a massive battle involving a German U-boat wolf pack and the 23 merchant ships in that convoy. The Norwegian destroyer *HNoMS Bath* had been torpedoed first, before nine merchantmen were hit. The wolf pack had found the convoy because its two Irish ships had insisted on leaving their navigation lights on "because we're neutral" – what idiots! Worse luck, as a result of this disaster they'd been forced to steam eight thousand nautical miles independently all the way to Durban.

Mallinson finished his cup and felt the pot. It was still hot, so he poured another cup. He dunked another biscuit, his third. Oh, he did love sweet coconut! Dunking biscuits in his tea had been a pleasure he had had to forgo during the three weeks of mostly quartering seas they'd had to deal with on the way to the Cape, with little relief. Did they ever roll! There was some trouble about the suction intake for the main circulating pump coming out of the water, and the chief had taken aboard more ballast water to correct it. When off the Gold Coast of Guinea in Africa, the short swells had been more off the bow, and he had altered course into them in an attempt to reduce the roll, but this had slowed them down and so they'd had to resume their original heading. Still, many of the crew had been sick over the side.

Then the lights had flickered and gone out all over the ship, and he'd had to hold a torch over the compass for the helmsman. The dynamo had failed! Sparks had discovered a carbon brush had disintegrated so he'd replaced them all and, for good measure, had burnished the commutator with emery cloth. Still, the dynamo was the same age as the ship, so you couldn't fault German engineering!

One of the boiler water-level glass tubes had also ruptured. The engine room could be a dangerous place if you didn't know what you were about: a Chinese assistant was scalded by 375-degree steam as he shut its valves. This made it necessary for the engineers to depend upon the try-cocks for the water level. There were three of these for each boiler and, as each was opened, if steam escaped from either of the lower two, the boiler water level was much too low. Rounding The Cape the swells were steep-to, and the engineers had a time of it, throttling back every time the propeller raced as it lifted clear. They'd been fortunate to not encounter any greybeards, the Cape rollers that could capsize even a ship as big as theirs. Durban wasn't made on time, with the result that they'd entered the port just as Convoy CM-17, which they had hoped to join, was leaving. There they had coaled up, had the boiler glass replaced, and loaded South African troops into hastily installed bunks in the 'tween decks.

His nerves had been frayed from all the worry, and he had gone to a cinema to try to shake out the tension and relax. What a stupid film that had been, not diverting at all, in fact a total waste of his time.

They'd then been assigned to the WS-10B 'Winston Special' Convoy of six ships en route to Bombay, escorted by the cruiser HMS *Hawkins*. West of the crown colony of Seychelles they had suddenly been detached with new orders to proceed to Calcutta – independently yet again! – to load raw lead. His engineers had reported their lathe itself had broken whilst loading in India, so now they couldn't even effect their own repairs! Then the bosun reported that two of the seamen, Keith and O'Flannery, had each caught a dose 'chasing after crumpet' back in Durban! Mallinson had ordered them ashore to see a Hindi doctor. He remembered telling the mates at the time: "Calcutta! What the devil is the ministry playing at, sending us 13,000 nautical miles in seven weeks, and only one week of that under convoy protection? Do they think us expendable? This isn't doing my nerves a bit of good!"

Mr Morgan had assured him that "This is how it's done in these unusual times." Well, it certainly wasn't done this way during the Great War. From India it had been new orders to stop in Chittagong, Burma, before finally steaming here to Singapore.

I am so tired of all these breakages, all these problems! he thought. *When I reach England, I shall be retired again, and have no more need to worry about any of this!*

Mallinson finished his tea and touched the pot. It was cold. He gathered up his things and before leaving, from force of habit, he opened the hood of the auxiliary compass and was stunned to find it missing. That elderly watchman must have pinched it when he left. *That's what must have been in that bundle he was carrying!* Likely, it would already be in an antiques dealer's window or waterfront pawnbroker by now. He would make a note to get hold of another as soon as he got back to his cabin. He made his way down to the wardroom to return the cup and pot.

When he entered he found Eugene there, playing his music on the gramophone. *Ah, the perfect time to ask him about the tannoy.* This wasn't, it must be said, an actual Tannoy System obtained from the manufacturer. He had asked Eugene to source the parts himself and cobble it together, because of lack of time. But before he could speak, a crewman in a group across the room stood up, fists clenched.

"Crikey, wot's that bleeding earbashing?" he shouted.

Eugene looked up, startled. "Uh... it's 'New San Antonio Rose'."

"Who's singing?" yelled the crewman.

"It's Bob Wills and His Texas Playboys."

"That's a *bloke*? Stone the crows! Take it off!" Gene turned the volume down. The man sat back down again, grumbling.

"Are you making any progress on the installation of the tannoy?" Mallinson asked the wireless operator. Gene pointed upwards. A newly installed speaker hung near the overhead.

"Brilliant! It works?"

"No, I still need to wire it, but I need to buy some wire, and I still need to find a microphone." *Honestly, the boy has to be chased, if you want anything from him.*

"Wire and a microphone. How much?" the captain sighed.

"Five bucks oughta cover it." Mallinson picked out the coins from what he had in his pocket. "Here's two sovereigns." Perhaps the bit extra would help induce a bit of speed. Mallinson stopped to listen.

"What's wrong with that man's guitar?" he asked.

"It's a steel guitar," Gene replied.

"Yes, I know. I've heard Hawaiian music, but that doesn't sound like a steel guitar."

"It's an electric steel guitar."

Electric guitar? Mallinson shook his head in wonder. *What will these Yanks monkey with next?* Gene put his record back in its sleeve, and they left the room.

Not until Mallinson prepared for bed that night did the thought occur to him: *Vander Sluyt was tall, surely over six feet. Even though the portholes were shut, the curtains had been open, yet I didn't see him pass them by. He also hadn't knocked before entering. Had the steward been listening at the door? What had he heard? Perhaps I'd failed to notice him.* He shook his head and removed his vest.

* * *

Friday morning they had steamed five miles from the aerodrome, and now lay alongside the north quay in the Empire Dock. Ahead of them, a Dutch submarine also lay alongside, a welding torch flaring at its bow. At the south quay a BP tanker, the *Roumanian Prince*, oiled the new Dutch troopship SS *Klipfontein*. To the north the industrial port and, beyond, the business district of Singapore lay sprawled before them, the imposing green hill of Bukit Timah looming behind and, below that, the British barracks of Fort Canning. The city bustled with the noise of commerce: car horns, trolleybus bells, but dominant above all, the roar of heavy-goods vehicles. A steam locomotive reversed slowly across the waterfront and coupled to a carriage with a clang that was repeated at each carriage down the length of the train.

At noon, bosun Virtanen met the captain, who waited for him at the head of the accommodation ladder. He handed over a canvas bag containing the fractured iron cylinder cover. Mallinson instructed him to let the crew have a shore leave for the weekend beginning tonight, as they would be sailing next week. He left it up to him as to when each section could go. They stood together a moment longer, watching the progress of the loading. The dockyard Chinese wearing white dhotis, and coolie hats to ward against the sun, sweat running down their torsos making tracks in the coal dust, pushed wheelbarrows of coal up the ramps rigged to the coaling chutes open in the ship's sides. As each reached a chute, the coal was dumped, rattling down inside. He knew that a fine black dust would eventually coat the ship, so he hurried down the accommodation ladder to his appointment, eager to escape it. Not knowing how important these 'important persons' were, he had decided to dress kitted out in his old Royal Navy tropical dress whites.

Crossing the railway lines and leaving the gates of the port proper, he turned east at Keppel Road, passing many tattoo parlours, even more saloons, not a few bordellos and, although well hidden from the police, he suspected maybe an opium den or two. Or five. Turning left on Anson Road there was a surprising number of cars, mostly parked, and the ones that were moving had to contend with the occasional slow bullock cart piled high with sheets of black rubber. Soon he had left the sailors' district behind. Anson Road became Cecil Street, where he passed the Bank of China, then the French Banque de l'Indochine, which itself was next door to a branch of the Standard Bank of South Africa. Cecil Street turned into Collyer Quay, and at D'almeida Street was the impressive Oversea-Chinese Banking Corporation building.

He found himself walking among spice merchants' tables, and stalls hawking foods which he could not identify, but smelled delicious. He paused a few minutes to stand and eat some chicken satay on bamboo skewers, dipped in curried groundnut sauce, but ate holding it over the gutter so as not to stain his tunic.

He strolled past the Ocean Building, and the Alkaff Arcade with its Moorish arches and Mughal domes, and when he sighted Clifford Pier on his right, he knew he was close. There! The General Post Office in the Fullerton Building. A grey-and-black Rolls Royce ticked over at the kerb, waiting. As he approached, the chauffeur held open the door for him. He placed his cap on the seat and the canvas bag on the floor, telling Gurnam Singh what was in it, and saying that he was just going to post his letter. As he climbed the steps, he caught sight of the Chartered Bank of India, Australia and China behind the Post Office at Flint Street. *My goodness me, there are an awful lot of banks in Singapore!*

Considering he wanted Beryl to read his news at the earliest opportunity, he paid the extra thirty cents *par avion* rate to reach England. The letter would be taken on the recently inaugurated Pan-American Clipper flight, from Singapore to San Francisco, then on to London via Miami. He licked the stamps, carefully affixed them in place and handed the letter to the clerk. He returned to the Rolls. Settling in, he arched an eyebrow.

"What are they paying shipping agents these days?" he joked.

Singh raised the speaking tube and said, "Drive on." Not looking at Mallinson, he replied "Not mine. This is borrowed for the occasion." Mallinson then told of his discovery of the ship's stolen auxiliary compass, and asked Singh to find a replacement for it. The Sikh passed him a copy of the *Tamil Murasu* newspaper but said little as the Rolls purred away, and that was fine by him. *He seems preoccupied.* He reckoned the agent would be as close-mouthed today as he had been yesterday, and contented himself with watching the street scenes they passed by. The business district was left behind and they motored along a wide boulevard lined with tall royal palm trees. They crossed a bridge and skirted Fort Canning. Once away from the trafficked part of the city, Mallinson wound the window down to cool the interior. Soon they entered a residential area of black-and-white bungalows and Malay houses. Turning up Sophia Road they began to climb. For a time he noticed an ornate cast-iron fence painted hospital white and, beyond this, thickly vegetated botanical gardens. Mounted on the fence at intervals he saw square red signs printed in various Asian languages he could not read. The centre pictograph, however, of a man pointing a rifle at another with his hands in the air made their meaning clear: *not principally a garden at all.* They approached a gate on the left that matched the fence, opened by an attendant who had been waiting for them.

"This is the rear entrance, the better we be ... unobserved," Singh murmured.

The tarmacadam road continued to climb. The higher canopy consisted of various palms, some banana trees and the traveller's tree, *Ravenala.* Lower down were sago cycads, fishtail palms in profusion and, lining the road, the broad-leaf gunnera, a plant he recognised from gardens in England, interspersed with brilliant bougainvillea. A trio of elderly men wielding bamboo rakes paused in their work and bowed low as the Rolls passed. *Whoever lives here must be as rich as Croesus.* A troop of spectacled leaf monkeys worked at dismantling a stalk of bananas which had fallen in the gutter at the kerb. They scampered into nearby trees and screamed abuse at the car for the interruption. The varied smells of a tropical woodland assailed him; fragrant blossoms and rich earth, so unfamiliar after his months at sea. The road, its surface now changed to gravel, left the forest behind and emerged into an open area. Close-clipped lawns behind granite kerbs spread away to either side.

Ahead, through the windscreen, he saw they approached a white two-storey villa on the right in the Palladian style with a centre Porte-cochére. The ground floor had arches the length of the building shading a verandah, the first floor with Ionic columns supporting latticework screens in between. They stopped in the shaded portico and the chauffeur again held the door open for them. A pair of Malay guards in jungle-green shorts and slouch hats with puggree, the side pinned up, flanked the entrance and stood at ease, rifle butts at their heels, angled out with stiff arms and bayonets fixed. As he and Singh ascended the steps, the soldiers snapped to attention, holding their rifles before them vertically. *No doubt mistaking me for Royal Navy. This can't be a private residence, can it?*

They passed through the open doors into the cool interior, the white marble floors reflecting the glass-globed chandeliers hanging far above them. A smiling major-domo approached with hands clasped before him. Stocky yet well-dressed all in white, he had a pleasant demeanour, all the while displaying a gap in his front teeth. His black hair was parted in the centre and slicked down in a manner characteristic of a decade earlier.

"Welcome to Istana, gentlemen. Please, follow me." Singh and Mallinson were escorted down marble-floored corridors, the sound of their footfalls echoing back at them. Darkly polished wood doors with blistered glass panels in them stood open at intervals, exposing the din of dozens of women clacking away at upright typewriters; once he spied a silent teletype writer, sitting alone in its own room. The ringing of telephones within was nearly constant. Ovoid-bladed fans revolved beneath the high ceilings of each room. People carrying documents hurried past, ignoring them. Soon they were led up a stairway to the first floor. The corridor here was much quieter, its doors shut, its floors covered in rich Persian-style carpet runners. They passed a closed double door labelled 'Library' and a placard on an easel that read 'Private'.

They were admitted to a parquet-floored room, its walls a soothing cerulean blue, dominated by a heavy table of smooth polished mahogany with rosewood inlay and, around it, eight carved armchairs. Mallinson saw ornately gilt-framed portraits lining the room, between the egg-and-dart crown moulding and a frame-and-panel wainscoting painted white. A red-and-gold-upholstered French Empire recamier graced a wall near the door. A mahogany sideboard displayed an array of crystal decanters, and across the room from that stood a faux fireplace. Their guide departed. Singh threw himself into a chair at the far end of the table and sighed heavily, looking quite troubled. Seated at the table was the Dutchman from the previous day, who now rose and introduced himself. Shaking Mallinson's hand, he smiled broadly.

"Meijer, my dear sir. Marinus Meijer, managing director of the Nederlandsche Middenstands Bank here in Malaya. Have a seat, captain," he continued. "We are to be joined by others in a moment." Mallinson took a seat with his back to the bar. He glanced about the room, observing the portraits of men, some bearded or with muttonchop whiskers, some in frock coats, a few in uniforms with sabres. One slightly resembled Marinus Meijer.

"Nice place you have here," he remarked.

"You mistake me, captain! It is not I who lives here." Meijer responded, and sat. The door opened once more and a white-haired, patrician man of Mallinson's generation entered, followed by a young woman wearing a fetching cheongsam skirt and holding a clipboard. He wore a tropical white uniform jacket with a gold-threaded standing collar and epaulettes. At his neck he wore the 'GCMG' – the Knight Grand Cross of the Most Distinguished Order of Saint Michael and Saint George. He turned, signed the papers she presented him, and said, "Thank you, Mrs Choy," whereupon she left. The white-jacketed major-domo stepped in, leaving the door open. The man instructed the major-domo to serve whatever anyone might wish from the sideboard. He then approached Mallinson and introduced himself.

"So pleased you could attend. Shenton Thomas, high commissioner for British Malaya." They shook hands. "Welcome to Government House. What shall it be – whisky? Soda?" Mallinson nodded, at a loss for words. Thomas walked around the table shaking hands, then took the chair in the centre of the long side across from him, and next to

Meijer. A stack of manila folders lay prepared before him. The major-domo placed an etched crystal tumbler on a cork drink mat in front of Mallinson and poured two fingers of Johnny Walker Red Label followed by a squirt from a soda syphon. Gurnam Singh waved him off. He then poured the same for Thomas, and stirred a gin and tonic over ice for Meijer.

A man half Mallinson's age in British lieutenant's uniform and Sam Browne belt entered and shut the door. He threw himself down wearily on the recamier, a forearm thrown over his eyes. Sir Thomas ignored him for half a minute, then in warning said, "Freddie!" The lieutenant stood slowly, a hand pressing into the small of his back. Crossing to the sideboard he was handed a rye whisky neat, and took the chair to Mallinson's right. The major-domo departed. Twisting in his chair the young lieutenant offered his hand and introduced himself.

"Freddie Spencer Chapman, of the Seaforth Highlanders." He had a strong jaw, with a direct gaze and wavy brown hair that was parted on the left.

"Roy Mallinson." They shook hands. Then Sir Thomas spoke.

"Much to my chagrin, Freddie has been seconded to, how shall I put it, 'teach' at Special Training School 101. He has proved himself to be quite indispensable – if he would ever learn to follow orders!" Freddie grinned, clinked his glass with Mallinson's, said "Chin-chin", winked and took a gulp. Mallinson replied, "Cheers," and sipped his own. Sir Thomas asked about his hobbies and seemed delighted to learn of the finer points of bee-keeping. Next he spoke of how important the Malay rubber plantations were for the war effort. Freddie now regaled the room with tales of how he and his Sherpa, Passang Dawa Lama, had four years earlier been the first to reach the summit of the 24,035-foot Chomolhari in the Himalayas, from the Bhutan side, a feat never before accomplished. Sir Thomas then enquired after the state of his ship and cargo, to which Mallinson filled him in on how they had brought South African troops, and delivered 24 crated or partially assembled Curtiss model 75A-7 "Mohawks" from Chittagong, deemed surplus to requirements by the Royal Indian Air Force, for use by the Royal Netherlands East Indies Army Air Force. Subsequent to this they had only yesterday finished loading F2A-1 Brewster Buffalo aircraft from 453 squadron RAAF, who had found them slow and under-powered (and who vastly preferred their new Hawker Hurricanes). His bosun, Maakki Virtanen, had found these, and Mallinson had obtained permission from the MoWT to load them. The Finn was doing his utmost to aid his homeland. The Buffaloes were to be reassembled or reconditioned in England and flown to Finland; the country was in the middle of a war against the Soviet Union and were in desperate need of them. Finally, completing his cargo was a quantity of Hindustan lead and Malayan rubber sheets, and a minor amount of wolfram, destined for use in England.

Shenton nodded. "Ah, yes, the war. Have you heard what the Japanese have been up to in China?"

"Don't I know it," Mallinson replied, shaking his head. "My American wireless operator follows it avidly and badgers me at every turn."

"Yes," Meijer interjected, "we fear their next move may be into Burma and Siam, or even an invasion of the Philippines, although we can't imagine Lieutenant General MacArthur will tolerate *that* eventuality. Lord help us all if they ever reach Singapore." He shuddered, the flesh of his neck wobbling. Freddie now chipped in. "Yes, who can forget the catastrophes at Đồng Đăng and Lạng Sơn a year ago, September? The Japanese getting a foot in the door, just 6,000 of their troops allowed in as inspectors, so called, then last June more than 20 times that number invading Indochina. That's how these things always start, rather slowly, eh? Say, did you hear what MacArthur's wife said about his retirement five years ago? When he joined the

Philippine army, she remarked he had gone from being the highest-ranking officer in the American army, to the highest-ranking officer in a *non-existent* army."

Shenton chortled at that. "Yes. Now he's back in the American Army." He then turned to the captain. "So, I hear you have an American wireless operator, a Finnish bosun, and a Dutch steward. I would have thought that a British ship would have a British crew. Is this not true?"

"Well, all my licensed officers and engineers are either from Scotland or Northern Ireland. My Second Mate is Welsh, but as for the general crew, they seem to come from all over, and that does include England."

"Commonwealth countries, then?"

"Well, not necessarily. We've a handful of Australians and our cook is Jamaican. We do have over half a dozen Norwegians. As for the rest, the Ministry had to take what was available at the time, so we have a Pole, a Belgian, a Yugoslavian, even three Greeks and a Moroccan." The captain stroked his beard thoughtfully, and sighed. "Mind you, not all of them speak English, but they do their jobs well. We manage." Out of the corner of his eye he saw Meijer look meaningfully at Gurnam, who returned a slight nod.

"And you're Canadian," Shenton replied.

"*Was* Canadian," Mallinson corrected. A moment of uncomfortable silence was broken with a question. "Sorry, Sir Thomas, I have enjoyed meeting all of you today, but why is it I have the feeling that everyone but me knows why I am here?" Meijer, in the process of taking a sip, coughed and dribbled gin down his shirt. Freddie laughed aloud but covered it by tossing off his drink. Singh winced and looked to Sir Thomas, while Meijer rose and went to the sideboard for a serviette to blot his shirt.

"Please, call me Shenton." He cleared his throat, "The truth is, we..." and here he waved his hand to indicate everyone in the room, "have convened here many times in the last four months. As you may be aware, Gurnam Singh represents many more shipping companies than just the Ellerman Lines, and we have vetted one ship's master after another—"

"You are the last of seventeen!" Singh interrupted.

"Gurnam!" Shenton admonished him, then continued, "And we have vetted one ship's master after another, and not yet found the right fit. Either we couldn't trust the master, or the crew, or their managing directors turned us down flat." He glanced at a paper in front of him.

"We think you are the right fit, because of your record."

"Sorry, my record?" Mallinson repeated mechanically.

"Yes. You see, it seems in your long career as master of one vessel or another, you have never lost a ship." Here he referred to a paper from the dossier and read aloud. "At age nineteen you emigrated from White Rock, British Columbia, Canada, enlisting as a seaman in the Royal Navy. You spent sixteen years working your way up the ranks until the Great War when, as sub-lieutenant of HMS *Lizard* in the Aegean, you were brevetted commander when you took charge at the Battle of Imbros, forcing a Turkish battlecruiser ashore in the Dardanelles, name of *Yavûz Sultân Selîm*." He looked up from the sheet he'd been reading from. "Mentioned in despatches. Distinguished Service Cross. Impressive!" A murmur of approval ran around the table.

"That was a long time ago," Mallinson muttered. "Long time."

Shenton continued. "Five years later you left the service. Your brevet captain's rank having now been made permanent, you took command as master of the first of a number of merchant ships. Eventually, in 1936, you retired. And then you came back." Mallinson nodded at this. Shenton leaned forwards, forearms on the table, fingers interlaced, fixing him with a steady piercing gaze from under his brow. He spoke carefully and deliberately. "We have need of a ship to undertake a highly important and, shall we say, somewhat hazardous mission." Mallinson groaned inwardly at this. An image of Beryl greeting him at the garden gate entered his mind.

"Shenton, I have been given my sailing orders from Ellerman. My ship is fully loaded. As soon as we are coaled, I am steaming for England, and home!"

2

Demands Are Made

At a nod from Shenton, Singh removed a slip of yellow paper from an inside pocket and laid it on the table. Smoothing it out, he pushed it at Mallinson. It was from Ellerman in London. Mallinson read:

CABLE & WIRELESS LTD. CABLEGRAM
   To: Gurnam Singh & Co Shipping Agents Singapore
   RE: your request via mowt STOP mallinson is free
   to make own decision in this matter STOP if affirm-
   ative all expenses covered this office or mowt STOP
   Ellerman - - - - - - - - - - - - - - - - - - -161041

"It arrived yesterday evening, captain. Will you at the least listen to what these gentlemen have to say?" Singh pleaded. Mallinson finished his Scotch. He refolded and pocketed the cablegram, and sat back with arms folded.

"I guess it doesn't hurt to listen, as long as you keep in mind any decision is final and rests with me," he said. Meijer looked relieved. Freddie appeared at his side and refilled his glass. Shenton reviewed the papers arrayed before him, and began.

"We have recently learnt from the Greek ambassador to Great Britain that the Nazis had a plan to forge British five-pound banknotes and drop these over Britain to bring about a collapse of our economy. They called it Operation Andreas, and it started early last year. They were successful in duplicating our rag paper and produced near-identical engraving blocks. They even deduced the algorithm used to create the alphanumeric serial code on each note. When the ambassador apprised us of this, the Bank of England altered the codes and printed slightly different notes, and of course collected all the old notes!" He smiled. "The Nazi plan did not succeed. Marinus?" Meijer then took up the story.

"We, that is, the Dutch Government-in-Exile, have recently discovered the Japanese are attempting a similar plan here." He nodded. "Oh, yes, we have our ... spies and contacts. The Imperial Japanese Army has an organisation called the Noborito Laboratory. Since 1937, we think, this laboratory has been counterfeiting and distributing the Chinese yuan. Naturally, this has greatly affected the economy of the entire region; the contagion has spread to all of China's neighbours." Meijer paused and sipped his drink, to let this sink in. "We cannot, unfortunately, duplicate here the success of the British solution for many reasons; the Asian economy depends upon millions of tiny family-run shops, and these shops are run by people speaking a dozen different languages between them. The complexity of it all is enough to make your head spin!"

Mallinson nodded, puzzled. "How does all this spy-craft tie in to a need for my ship? Do you need us to drop an agent somewhere?"

Shenton resumed the tale. "Certainly not, nothing so prosaic. It seems there is nothing we can do about the thousand-million phoney Chinese notes floating around the region in as many different hands but it seems," – here he smiled and his eyes twinkled – "the Chinese are not stupid. In fact, all the countries of the region have long realised currency is just, well, paper. What's important are the securities backing that paper."

Mallinson frowned. "Sorry, securities? You mean stock certificates? Bonds?"

"No, Captain Mallinson," Shenton replied. "I mean gold."

"Yes, gold!" said Meijer. "The banks of all the countries in the region saw the threat posed by the advancing Japanese and, quietly so as not to start a run on the banks, began slowly moving their physical gold reserves away from the reach of the Imperial Japanese Army whilst maintaining a veneer of business as usual. And when I say 'away', that is to mean 'south', to here, in Singapore. I'm sure you can see, as a belligerent nation Japan will have a rather difficult time trading for what she needs in the new 'Greater East Asia Co-prosperity Sphere' by paying for it with insubstantial paper currency! Japan will need the substantive backing only gold can offer. How likely is it that China will relinquish its yuan and accept the yen? Or Siam ... excuse me, I meant Thailand ... do the same with its baht? Now it seems the Japanese may shortly be breaking out of China proper and, many think, may even be able to reach us here." A note of pride crept into his voice. "I have kept meticulous records, and been honoured with the duty of shepherding these reserves to a place of safety, so when all this unpleasantness is past, they can be returned to the original owners and all will be right with the world once again." *Spoken like a true banker*, Mallinson thought.

"Where is this so-called place of safety?" he asked. Lieutenant Chapman, having waited for this moment, blurted out the vital information: "The Perth Mint, Australia!" Mallinson rubbed his eyes and, crossing his arms, tucked his chin to his chest. Moments passed. No one dared speak. He caught sight of his unfinished drink and drained it.

"Why don't you," he ruminated, "just fly it down there?"

Shenton replied, "Why don't you fly your cargo of aeroplanes to where they need to be?"

"I've been told there are no pilots to spare."

"Exactly."

"Then surely a single KLM airlines DC-2 — even the Japanese wouldn't be stupid enough to shoot down a civilian airliner; it would be a worldwide scandal!"

"If we were to fly it down, they might suspect something when they noticed a fleet of aeroplanes ferrying it south. Also, a single elderly ship – sorry – is not likely to attract much attention."

Mallinson frowned. "A fleet? How much gold are we talking about here? I mean, physically."

"Freddie, you've been there. What would you say?" Shenton asked.

"Hmm. Well ... altogether, I'd say ... it's ... well, try to imagine a sentry box lying on its side," the lieutenant responded.

Meijer chimed in, "Roughly sixty-nine and one-half tons, by Troy measure, naturally. Put another way, it's nineteen million, four hundred sixty-eight thousand, eight hundred British pounds sterling, more or less."

"Great Scott!" The captain sat back, heavily, gripping the arms of the chair.

"You see our dilemma," Shenton said. It was not a question. "If we used KLM's newest acquisition, the DC-5, having a greater payload than the DC-3, it would still take fifty-six return trips."

Mallinson's head swam. He made some rapid conversions in his head; *nearly seventy-nine million Canadian dollars.* Shenton seemed to know this was exactly his thought.

"How many warships could they build with that?" asked Shenton, rhetorically. "Current intelligence tells us the Japanese are intending to make some kind of move before next April."

Mallinson brightened. "Speaking of warships, there's a Dutch submarine at the Empire Dock undergoing some repairs. Have you thought of sending it on that?"

Shenton nodded. "Not that specific sub, because it will be a while before it's available and we haven't the time, frankly. A submerged submarine will be slow, and extremely hard to control in terms of depth. We have looked into that idea, and our naval architects tell us that even with the ballast tanks fully blown, a submarine's reserve buoyancy will be marginal at best, meaning the entire voyage will need to be made on the surface. So, you see, no better than a surface ship, and actually slower."

"I see," Mallinson nodded. "But, what of a fast surface ship, say, a warship?"

Shenton began to answer, but it was Meijer who offered the response.

"Oh, no. Besides, this being a civilian operation, that is quite impossible, politically speaking. The difficulty was to get each country to agree to the scheme at all. You see, we as bankers were able to get some of the gold out of French Indochina prior to the Japanese invasion, but the Cambodians and Laotians distrust the French and the Vietnamese, the British rule Burma as a colonial power hated by their nationalists, the Chinese government is allied with the Americans and regard the British as imperialists, the Indonesians are agitating for independence from the Dutch and do not trust them, and Siam, or Thailand if you prefer, is suspicious of everybody. So the question remains: whose warship do you agree on? Now, in this part of the world, the Australians *are* trusted, but they have three cruisers and two destroyers in Australian waters, and all of them are in constant use and cannot be spared. Most of the Royal Australian Navy ships are in the Mediterranean assisting the British. No, the only way we could get any collaboration at all was to negotiate to use a non-warship, and one crewed by civilian volunteers from a mix of nations, to eliminate any collusion between like-minded individuals. Since the majority of shipping worldwide is British – 'Britannia rules the waves' and all that

– it was difficult enough to get them all to agree on that, but eventually we succeeded. The negotiations were a struggle, I can tell you."

"What of the Americans? You've said nothing of them," Mallinson asked.

"The Americans seem to be maintaining their position of strict neutrality."

"Seem? Since they've embargoed Japan's oil, I would think it would be in their interest to … to …" he trailed off. Meijer had wiped a hand over his face and looked embarrassed. The group shifted uncomfortably in their seats and looked to Meijer.

"Yes … well … this is a bit embarrassing," he said.

"Just a bit!" Freddie barked, amused. Shenton and Meijer scowled in his direction.

"Early on," said Meijer "we did approach Lieutenant General MacArthur personally in Manila. Our spies had informed us he has nineteen B-17 Flying Fortresses based there at Clark Field. Relieved of any bomb load the entire fleet could have delivered the lot in two trips. Although MacArthur was sympathetic to our endeavour, he denied us their use for the simple reason he needs them ready to repel any imminent strike. I personally don't begrudge him that decision. We then entreated him for the use of either their USS *Houston* or USS *Marblehead* or any one of a dozen of their fast destroyers, or 'four-pipers' as they call them, but he's army, not navy, and so deferred any decision to his President. I'm sure you must be aware their army and navy departments are constantly striving one against the other. Our envoy came back, a wasted trip. So I took it upon myself to write a short letter outlining our scheme, in general terms, to the Netherlands Embassy in Washington, asking them to approach the US Department of State for assistance. The reply was a long time in coming; it arrived as you left Chittagong. Our consulate failed to translate the letter themselves, instead giving it to the Americans still written in Dutch.

"The package that arrived here was comprised of four documents, the first being an American translation of my original letter. It seems their translator confused our mention of the gold being gathered from the 'nations of the Indies' with their own 'Indian nations', but then, instead of our request moving up the chain of command to the president, it trickled down to various sub-departments of their government. The next form letter from their Internal Revenue Service reminded us that tax will be due on the entire value. The next form letter from their Department of the Interior, and the final form letter from the Treasury Department, made the claim that any gold found on federal land is the property of the federal government, and will be expected to be turned in to the US Treasury."

"You must be joking!" Mallinson exclaimed. Gurnam, hearing this part for the first time, giggled nervously. Freddie rolled his eyes as Meijer continued.

"Not a joke, but the worst sort of bureaucratic bollocks-up I've seen in a long time. In the interim we have run out of time. As Gurnam has revealed, you are the last of seventeen captains we have interviewed. There are no more."

Mallinson shook his head. "Sorry, gentlemen but, no. I have my orders. My ship is fully loaded with war materiel desperately needed at home. Your fight is not my fight. Truly, I wish all of you well in your endeavour, but I will be steaming for home and retirement. Full stop!"

No one spoke. Meijer covered his mouth and gave a muffled cough. Everyone looked to Shenton.

"I was hoping it wouldn't come to this, but it seems we are left no other option. Have you ever lived in the States?" he began, selecting a sheaf of papers.

"America? Not lived, just visited. What does it matter?"

"I'm curious as to what you may know of the powers of the American President."

"Very little, as it happens."

"Have you ever heard of the 1917 Trading with the Enemy Act, banning shipments of arms to belligerent nations?"

"Yes. I believe Canada has something similar. Great Britain too, I imagine," Mallinson said, slightly defensively.

"Very well. The president has the power to issue what are termed executive orders, and he often uses these to make an amendment to an existing law. He may do this to circumvent Congress, or Congress may subsequently support his executive order, or the order can stand on its own. An executive order can also amend a previous executive order, and sometimes several executive orders all at once."

"Seems reasonable." *It doesn't seem reasonable at all. What is he getting at?*

"Now, Franklin Roosevelt has issued Executive Order 8785, amending the Trading with the Enemy Act. I have a copy here. You may find it of interest." Shenton slid a sheaf of papers across the table to Mallinson, who picked it up, looked briefly at the top sheet, and dropped it on the table. He fixed Shenton with a cold glare.

"Why don't you summarise it for me?"

"Captain, sir!" Singh admonished.

"Gurnam." Shenton held up a hand, "Very well." He referred to a sheet in front of him. "The 1917 Trading with the Enemy Act bans shipments of arms to belligerent nations. In April, 1940, following the Nazi invasions of Denmark and Norway, President Roosevelt issued Executive Order 8389 amending the Act, to freeze their American assets so Germany couldn't get at them. Then, in July 1940, after the Russian occupation and annexation of Lithuania, Latvia and Estonia, he issued an amendment to that order with Executive Order 8484, freezing the assets of those nations.

"Next we come to this year, and Roosevelt issues his Executive Order 8785, on 14th June 1941, and it is titled," – here he put a finger on the page and read it out directly – "'Regulating Transactions in Foreign Exchange and Foreign-Owned Property, Providing for the Reporting of All Foreign-Owned Property, and Related Matters'; which is long-winded and somewhat obtuse but, in a nutshell, it shut all German and Italian Consulates in the United States and froze all the American assets of Germany and Italy." Shenton looked up. "Follow me so far?" Mallinson nodded. Shenton continued, "Now, buried in this order is an amendment to his previous number 8484, and this expands a list of countries with which no one ..." – here he paused for emphasis and looked directly at Mallinson – "no one may conduct business. If you will refer to section 4305 in what you have before you, I think you will find it of great interest." Mallinson nodded, but there was a growing sense of unease in the pit of his stomach. He began to leaf through his document, and Lieutenant Chapman leaned over and helped him locate the proper section. There he saw a column of two dozen countries in alphabetical order, and circled in red pencil he read, 'Finland'.

Stunned, he said, "Finland is on the side of the Allies."

"Finland *was* on the side of the Allies," Shenton replied. "In June, Finland invited the Nazis into their country to fight alongside them against the Russians. They fight *with* the Axis now and *against* an Ally."

Mallinson sat immobile. He spoke slowly and thoughtfully. "As a subject of Great Britain, I fail to see how an American law has any power over me."

Shenton turned a page. "Your nationality doesn't come into play in this matter; when President Roosevelt issued his executive order, the aeroplanes you carry as lend-lease to an ally became lend-lease to a belligerent. This essentially broke their lease, and they reverted to being American property." Shenton nodded. "But you are correct. These laws have power only insofar as they can be applied. If you will turn the page, there is a section labelled 'Penalties.' Please read it."

Mallinson read he could face a fine of US $10,000 *and* ten years in jail if he delivered 'war materiel intended for a belligerent country'. This applied even if he delivered said materiel to an Allied country; if the ultimate destination was an Axis country, the penalties came into effect automatically. His eyes met Shenton's, who said pointedly, "How would you like to never again be able to land your ship in an American port?"

Mallinson shrugged. "After this voyage, I shall be retired. I doubt I will ever set foot in America again."

Shenton spread his hands, palms up. He said casually, as someone who knows he has organised and sealed a *fait accompli*, "The United States has extradition treaties with most countries. I can notify the Americans of your intended route. Should you ever stop in any country to re-coal, you may be extradited to face charges. In your deserved retirement, imagine never being able to visit the Continent ... or Canada." Shenton rose and made his way around the room to the sideboard. He poured himself another Scotch. On the way back to his chair he paused and looked down at Mallinson. "As the cablegram relates, you are free to make your own decision in the matter."

The hell I am. His attention was drawn to Mr Singh, who had a handkerchief out and was mopping his brow. Meijer sat with eyes shut; he may have been listening, or he may have been asleep. Freddie was leaning forwards, intent on what Mallinson was going to say next.

"May I suggest a possible solution that will solve both our problems?" Shenton asked. Mallinson thought about refilling his tumbler and decided against it. He wanted a clear head.

"Let's hear it," he sighed.

"You can offload the Buffaloes here, and any other war materiel—"

Mallinson, alarmed, said vehemently, "The southwest monsoon season ended in September, the northeast monsoon is due in mid-November. I am faced with a rapidly closing window and I must leave now!"

Shenton held up a hand, "Calm yourself, captain. It is only one recommendation. Well, we can give you an American flag and paint large American flags on your ship. This will take at most a day. As a ship supposedly from a neutral nation, they will not dare disturb you."

"There are a number of problems with that: the Yanks don't use Oriental or British crew, and many of our controls are still labelled in German or Portuguese, so if we're ever boarded it will be immediately obvious who we are. And Sir Thomas," Mallinson continued, "I trust you have never been a military man. According to the Hague convention of 1907, 'fighting while wearing the enemy's uniform' is a war crime. We are a British flagged ship, and our nation is at war."

"What you say is true, I have always been a colonial administrator," he said, adjusting the GCMG medal at his throat. "Well, how would it be if we ask Ellerman, or the Ministry of War Transport, to have them officially alter your ship's manifest to declare your cargo as destined for Australia, an ally of Great Britain. Will that suit you? Is it not a possibility, Mr Singh?"

Gurnam nodded enthusiastically. "Indeed so, excellency. It can be done tomorrow!" Meijer opened his eyes and sat up, beaming broadly.

Mallinson was elated, "My ship's manifest already declares my cargo as destined for an ally, but by way of an intermediary, Great Britain itself. Before I leave for England, I'll simply declare that they shan't be forwarded beyond Britain, because of the president's order, and that will be the end of it!" At this, Shenton was outwardly unperturbed, but Mallinson was alarmed to see, by a slight narrowing of the eyes and the set of his jaw, that the man had had enough of attempting to wheedle acquiescence from recalcitrant ship masters.

"We had hoped to gain your cooperation willingly, but now ..." He paused and sat up straight. He squared the papers before him in a neat stack. His voice became businesslike and official. "As governor of the Straits Settlements, and high commissioner for the Federated Malay

States, I have the power to deny you the right to leave Singapore. A telephone call to the harbourmaster and your ship will be impounded, for as long as I desire. My actions will be viewed as upholding the conditions required of the Trading with the Enemy Act and will be supported by His Majesty's Government. Make no mistake, I will use it. Now, Captain Mallinson, will you accede to our demand?"

Mallinson thought, but not about the question Shenton had posed. His mind was elsewhere: Beryl waiting for him at the garden gate. Britain was in need of the cargo of lead for ammunition, and rubber, and wolfram for God knows what. The Finns needed those aeroplanes. Maakki had made all the arrangements to find them and transport them. Beryl! Retirement! But Roosevelt's order! England! How he wanted desperately to be there!

Shenton continued in a tone that was not too stern. "You see, your mission will be one of actually helping the war effort an enormous amount, shortening the war possibly by years, but to an outside observer it will look as just another lend-lease delivery of aeroplanes. Then from Perth you can steam for home. What do you think?"

His shoulders slumped. When he spoke, it was with a note of resignation. "It seems I have been given no choice."

"Excellent!" Shenton replied ebulliently, with the air of an executive who had outfoxed a competitor, though this was hardly the case. "Thank you, Captain Mallinson, you are rendering a great service to Britain and her Allies. Freddie, will you act as liaison with our captain? I'll call the motor round for you." He pushed a button under the table, and the major-domo appeared. Mallinson, fuming at having been outmanoeuvred, was barely listening. The meeting disbanded, and Shenton disappeared. Shenton had not shaken his hand. *That might have been a good thing because I would likely have refused.* He told Singh he expected to leave the following Thursday, and would he please arrange for two tugs and a harbour pilot on the day, and pay the quayage on Ellerman's tab. Singh agreed. The group retraced their steps to the entrance, where Singh and Meijer departed in a black Chevrolet.

Mallinson was left standing with Lieutenant Chapman. After the cool interior, the sun beat down so bright it hurt the eyes. They wandered away from the building across the parkway, gravel crunching underfoot, and soon found the lawn. Unseen tropical birds whooped from the gardens. A pair of green and blue peafowl three dozen yards away screamed loudly. They paused at a shallow, round concrete-rimmed pool, orange and white koi circling lazily under Egyptian water lilies, a fountain at play in the centre. The whine of insects seemed unnaturally loud. He shaded his eyes and squinted down the slope of the lawn to a lake in the distance, where white swans stretched their necks and adjusted their wings. He wasn't cheered by the sight: he was in fact browned off at the treatment he had received. Freddie spoke first.

"Sorry about all that palaver. Rotten show, I must say, but I'm awfully chuffed you stepped up to the mark, eh?"

Mallinson dropped his hand and rounded on him, fists clenched. "You bloody fool! I and the men I'm responsible for have been press-ganged into a mission we don't want, in a direction we don't want to go, into an area filled with warships in a cat-and-mouse game we want no part of – and you're chuffed?! Bloody fool!"

"Steady on, old boy!" Freddie said, caught on the back foot now. But Mallinson was adamant.

"Had we been allowed to go westwards on our way around Africa there is nothing, absolutely *nothing*, out there. Our route would have been clear nearly all the way to England. We're an unarmed merchant ship," he fumed. ... "Unarmed!" he repeated.

"I may be able to help you there, captain. What arms have you now?

Peevishly, he said, "I have my Webley service revolver – oh, and my American wireless operator brought a twelve-bore pump shotgun aboard, which I locked away in my cabin. All of my officers have their own personal pistols, to guard against mutiny, you know."

Freddie laughed. *"That's it?* What say I have our boys fix you up with a British quick-firing 2-pounder. Jolly good, don't you think?"

"Twin?"

The lieutenant, embarrassed, replied, "No. Single-barrel."

"You want to fob me off with a water-cooled, pre-Great War relic?" Mallinson scowled, "Thank you, but no."

"Then, what say you to a 40-millimetre Bofors ack-ack gun? It's off one of our naval trawlers that ran aground at speed a fortnight ago off Pulau Seringat. Bad show, eh? A total write-off."

The Rolls Royce ghosted up, and they climbed in. On the way back to the port they agreed the gun would be delivered tomorrow afternoon.

Late the next day a flatbed lorry was waiting quayside, on its bed a Bofors painted navy grey. Eugene was climbing all over it as the agitated lorry man waved his arms and shouted. Not of the 'Chicago piano' type, it had but a single barrel; an early model. *Oh, well. Better than nothing, I suppose.* Lieutenant Chapman appeared at the top of the accommodation ladder and saluted the Red Duster at the stern. Mallinson, standing on the port wing, waved him up. He blew the whistle affixed in the lid of the voice pipe and lifted it.

"Second engineer, aye?" came the response.

"Mr Sinclair, will you tell the chief to report to the bridge?"

"Aye." The lid clapped shut. Lieutenant Chapman stepped onto the bridge and greeted Mallinson. In khaki uniform as the day before, today he wore a Wolseley sun helmet. They stood awhile discussing the weather, which was hot and muggy, and the nearby ships, but most especially what might be going on with that submarine. Soon enough,

Chief MacCallan arrived, but before they could get down to business, so did an excited Eugene.

"Skipper! Do we get it? Is it for us? It's a real beaut, isn't it? Can I get trained on it? I saw a plate that read '1933' – is that when it was made? All the plates on it are in Swedish!" he blurted out breathlessly.

"Gene, *calm*!" Mallinson admonished. "Gentlemen, this is Lieutenant Freddie Chapman. Freddie, this is our wireless operator from the States, Eugene Graham, and here's our chief engineer, Hamish MacCallan." Hamish gave a slight nod in the lieutenant's direction, as he puffed his pipe alight.

"Pleased ta meetcha, sir!" said Eugene, pumping Freddie's hand enthusiastically.

Mallinson put a hand on Eugene's shoulder to restrain him and said, "Now, Eugene, about training; if we encounter any ... difficulties ... I'll be needing you at the wireless, understand?"

"Ahh, Jeez ..."

"Excuse us, please, we need to discuss its installation."

"Yes, sir." Gene left, deflated. The group then walked aft, crossing the catwalk in single file. Standing at the base of the funnel, they spoke about the best place to site the gun. They ruled out putting it abaft the funnel because all the davits, lifeboats and ventilators were an obstruction. Equally, it could not be set ahead of the funnel, as the tall bridge obstructed it.

"And besides," Freddie said, "should there be any encounters, you chaps will want a clear field of fire as you scarper." Mallinson was fully aware of how it was done, but still, being reminded kind of rankled.

"What about on a bridge wing?" the captain asked.

"That only covers the ship on one side," said Freddie.

"Aye," said Hamish, "and I doubt the bridge wing will take the weight."

Looking aft, the view was over a veritable forest of planes. Two planes for each of four hatch covers, arranged side by side but nose to tail and wingtip to fuselage, to maximise the space. In between were crated aeroplanes, filling any available space. Descending the ladder to the after well deck, he asked Freddie if they would be assigned a Naval Auxiliary gun crew.

"No, but I'll show you how it operates."

"I'm knackered," Mallinson said. "See me when you're done here. I'll be in my cabin." He left the two of them to work out the details. He retired to his cabin for a bit of a kip, and lay down in full kit, without removing his shoes. He was awakened by a rapping on his door. How long had he been asleep? One hour? Two? He didn't know. He let in the chief and Freddie. They sat.

"Is everything decided then?" Mallinson yawned.

"Och, aye." MacCallan was pleased. The shipyard was to do the actual installation once the apparatus was aboard. The consensus was the best position was the stern, forwards of the auxiliary steering station. The advantage there was the sound-powered telephone from the bridge for the aft lookout that could be put to use. He asked the chief if it could be lifted aboard with the aft derrick, and got a positive reply. MacCallan then excused himself and left for the wardroom, as it was getting on for teatime. Mallinson told him he would be down directly, after he had spoken privately with the lieutenant.

When he was gone, Freddie asked, "So, this gold, you haven't said anything to your crew about it?"

"Correct, and I'm not going to, until I must," he sighed. He quickly looked about him to make sure the portholes were shut. They were.

Freddie was relieved, "Good. I want to know how you intend to take it aboard and secure it. What I mean is, well, some sixty-nine tons. How do you keep that a secret?"

"Where is it now?"

"We have it in London Good Delivery bars, stacked in a vault in a bank downtown, under 24-hour armed guard of the best available, His Majesty's Royal Gurkha Rifles."

Mallinson thought aloud. "It would be best to bring it aboard, all at once, under cover of darkness."

"You mean, in crates and lifted aboard by one of your derricks?"

"Hmm. That won't do. Once here we would have to open it and put it somewhere safe. Opening it will let the crew see what it is, and I don't want that. Can't leave it on deck. For one thing, there might be ... pilferage."

The lieutenant grinned. "I take your meaning. What do you suggest?"

"How heavy is one bar?"

"They vary slightly. Actually 400 Troy ounces ... is ... erm, just under twenty-seven and a half pounds?"

"What if we were to take ten ... no, make that nine bars, put them in a sturdy pine box with, say, a rope handle on each end ..."

"Yes! So it takes two men to lift it, preventing any one of them from carrying it away," Freddie said excitedly.

"That'll be 250 pounds, and then to disguise it, how about stencilling each box with 'ammunition'," Mallinson said exultantly. "Then Bob's your uncle!"

"Brilliant! Pine might be challenging to come by in these parts, but otherwise that's it!"

"Use whatever wood is typical for the region. Can you take care of all that at your end?"

"I'll hop to it. Let you know when you can expect it." They shook hands. Freddie rose to leave but then turned back. "Blast my eyes, I'd nearly forgotten! This is for you," he said, lifting two oblong tins from a shirt pocket.

Mallinson uncapped one. "Pens? Thank you."

"Not just any pens, mind you," he said, conspiratorially, and sat. "These are time pencils." Roy pulled one out and saw that each was a tube made of brass on one end, copper on the other, and with a screw in that end. Freddie continued, "We have thousands of them issued to us, so we can let a few go. They're used in sabotage. In Europe we give them to the Resistance. You may find a use for them. The boffins back in Blighty call it a No. 9 delay switch. Look, I'll explain how they work; inside is a lead alloy wire notched to a set diameter, the diameter setting the time delay. When you remove this starting pin here," – he pointed to it – "the wire is placed under tension by a spring, and it will gradually begin to stretch. After a certain time it snaps at the notch and allows the spring to propel the pointed striker to hit the percussion cap at the end of the brass tube, and that sets off the detonator. These are two-hour pencils, but of course that's just an approximation, could be a few minutes more, could be less, depending on the weather.

"Now, these in this other tin are No. 10 delay switches, and they're similar except there's no start pin, and it also has a glass phial of cupric chloride inside. You start this by crushing the copper section of the tube with your heel or a set of pliers to break the phial, which then begins to slowly erode the wire holding back the striker. In both versions you must pull out this safety strip here to allow it to work." He held it up, and his eyes shone. "Elegant, isn't it?"

Mallinson went below for his tea, and sat to eat with his chief engineer. When he'd finished, he stacked his tableware with the dirty plate at the end of the table and rose to go, but then hesitated.

"Oh, Hamish, before I forget, I've been given these things called time pencils and wanted to pass them on to you. Knowing how much you like fiddling with gadgets, I thought you might enjoy a bit of fun experimenting with them." He explained their operation. Hamish slipped the two tins into his pocket.

Sunday had been quiet. Monday, too, for that matter. The shipyard had finished welding the Bofors in position and adjusting it. Lieutenant Chapman invited Mallinson to join him as his guest aboard the battle-ship HMS *Prince of Wales*, whose executive officer was an old friend of his from his days at St John's College in Cambridge. Tonight, Tuesday 21st October, was Trafalgar Night; each year the commissioned officers of the Royal Navy celebrate the victory at the Battle of Trafalgar by sponsoring a dinner in the officers' mess. Mallinson declined, as he wasn't fond of idle chit-chat with strangers. Freddie then told him the 'special items' would be delivered the next night at dusk, and to have steam up ready to load them.

Mallinson spent Wednesday inspecting the ship making sure all was in good order. He spoke with Jimmy to see if he needed any last-minute items from the souk. He asked Sparks to listen for the weather report and transcribe it, then give it to the second mate. He told the second to expect it and to plot a course for Fremantle, Australia, leaving on the next afternoon's favourable tide. He visited the stern and adjusted the Red Duster, which hadn't been set exactly to the top of its staff. Examining the Bofors that now stood there, he found a plate which had been stamped '40mm lvakan M/36'. Eugene had been right, it was an early model; single barrel, air-cooled, manually stabilised, about the most bog-standard gun you could possibly get. Freddie had trained one of his deck crew in how to operate it, but Mallinson wanted others to know, too. He spoke with the bosun in the forecastle about that, and Sinclair, the second engineer, about steaming up, too. The ship was coaled and watered and ready to go. Satisfied, he remained in his cabin, transcribing log entries from the day log and finishing minor paperwork. When all that was dealt with, he read *The Times* for a short while. At 1700 hours, halfway through the first dog watch, he had his tea in the wardroom. His bacon butty was rather good. After 1900 hours, he went up to the bridge and looked down to see the bosun on the quay directing a lorry that reversed to number one hatch, forwards of the bridge house. An arc lamp had been rigged at the top of the foremast and directed at the foredeck, so their operations were on the fringe of its illumination. Nearby, dimly visible in the dusk, there were three more lorries, their loads covered by tarpaulins, and then armed soldiers standing casually against various dockyard godowns. In a corner three shadowy figures crouched behind a belt-fed machine gun covering the dockyard. He counted some three-dozen men in total. Cat-like, Lieutenant Chapman materialised at his elbow, seemingly out of nowhere, startling him.

"Sorry. Royal Marines Commando," he whispered. "Sir Thomas has ordered the dockyard shut until you leave." Mallinson shivered, even though it was quite warm.

"Not taking any chances, are you?" he replied, unsure of why they were whispering. Freddie chuckled softly.

"Watch." The tarpaulins on the lorries, thrown back, revealed eight enormous crates. The number three derrick was attached to a crate on the first lorry and lifted it aboard, setting it down between the number one hatch and the bulwark at the ship's side. The others quickly followed. The deck crew swarmed the crates and prised apart an end on each, revealing stacked wooden boxes with rope handles exactly as they had planned. At a command from the bosun, the serang called out, and pairs of Lascars began dragging boxes out, carrying and stacking them against the forward bulkhead of the midship house. The luckier ones claimed the use of the ship's single hand truck for this task. The captain and lieutenant descended to the main deck. The boxes had been put together with screws. Each had been stencilled in blue paint: 'Ammo, L/60 40×311mmR'. Freddie told him the marines would bed down for the night in the godowns until he steamed the next day, then slung his gear into an empty stateroom for the night. He went to the wardroom for his supper. Mallinson asked Freddie to tell the cook to bring his supper up to his cabin. When he had gone, he asked the bosun to secure a tarpaulin over the boxes on deck, and to have one of those boxes brought up to his cabin, with the proper type of screwdriver to fit. Later in his cabin he found the box and a screwdriver. He pulled the curtains and set to work unscrewing the top. Screwing wasn't the normal construction for an ammo box, as they were usually assembled with ribbed nails. He lifted out a heavy gold bar. He flipped the lid onto the box with the toe of his shoe, but it didn't land squarely. Placing the bar on his desk, it gleamed brightly in the light of the desk lamp. He put his glasses on and examined the bar carefully. On its top were cast the words, 'THE CHARTERED BANK OF INDIA, AUSTRALIA AND CHINA' and 'LGD', but next to that was hammer-stamped '403 oz.' There were marks showing year of manufacture, serial number, and a refiner's hallmark. He took a ruler from his desk. *10 inches by 3⅕ inches by 1½ inches thick.* This he wrote down. Its sides tapered towards the top. The door opened, and Martin Vander Sluyt backed into the room holding his supper tray. As he pivoted into the room the steward's head swivelled smoothly from Mallinson to the bar to the box and back to Mallinson.

"Do you never knock, damn you!" he shouted, flipping *The Times* newspaper over the bar. *Fuck, I didn't lock it.*

"Captain, sir, can you not see my hands are full?" the steward remonstrated. Mallinson blew out his cheeks.

"Yes, yes, of course, Mr Vander Sluyt, I'm sorry to have shouted." *Did he see it or not?*

"Your supper, sir," he said, briskly, placing the tray on the coffee table. *Not the desk*, Mallinson realised. As he was still holding the pencil and ruler, he held them up to view.

"I was just making some sketches."

"I'm sure they are nice, sir. Please, enjoy your supper," he said unctuously. He bowed slightly and left. Mallinson locked the door then sat in thought for a time, reviewing in his mind exactly what had transpired in those few seconds. Why hadn't the cook himself brought his supper, as he had asked? The cook would have knocked. *I'll have to lock my door without fail from now on.* Finally, he turned to eat. It was cold.

Sometime during the night, he rolled over and groggily punched up his pillow, having been awakened by a splash.

3

Replacements

Entering the wardroom the next morning for breakfast, Mallinson could hear pans clattering in the galley. The officers' wardroom was identical to the crew's mess, but a mirror image of it and on the other side of the galley. There was a series of deep square reliefs down the wall and at the room's end, each with its own porthole and curtain. These provided illumination for an oilcloth-covered rectangular table beneath, each flanked with bench seating. Really, the only difference was that the wardroom had a gramophone and a stack of 78s, while the crew mess had a wireless – and a dartboard over which someone had taped a 1938 *Time* magazine cover of Der Führer, a dart jutting conspicuously from his left eye. Three officers of the deck crew sat at a table in the far corner playing cards, a poster on the wall above them proclaiming 'REMEMBER THE ATHENIA!', with a silhouette of a ship in lurid red and yellow flames. On the wall opposite, another poster depicted Churchill giving his famous Victory sign, behind him a sinking U-Boat, and above his head the caption 'Where is Prien?' The gramophone was softly playing Helen O'Connell singing 'One Sweet Letter From You.'

He spotted Hamish spreading blackcurrant jam on a roll, a plate of bacon with eggs before him. Seated with him was Taffy, his second mate, a curly-haired Welshman from Swansea, a pot of tea between them, and a plate empty except for some crusts. His name was Dafyd Ap Morgan but everyone called him Taffy. Mallinson helped himself to coffee from the urn and sat.

"Good morning! Today we sail," he said, happily.

"Aye," said Hamish around a mouthful of roll.

"Yus," said the second, around his own mouthful.

"Mr Morgan, you plotted a course to Fremantle yesterday. What was the result?"

"Something like 2,400 miles. Call it a week and a half perhaps, depending on the weather. Sparks tells me the RAF aerographer's reports indicate there's a Tropical Storm Twenty-Five that formed yesterday over Palawan, with winds Force 11, heading west."

"Hmm. That's nearly hurricane force. Did he say due west?" Mallinson asked.

"Aye."

"Very good. It will bypass us well to the north. But best to keep an eye on it, eh? How are the winds here?"

"Force 1, barometric pressure 29.86 and steady, sir."

"Couldn't be better! Well, I'm famished!" Mallinson swivelled in his seat. "Steward!" he called out. The mate cleared his throat.

"The cook told me to tell you, our galley steward has jumped ship."

"Jumped ship? That's a serious accusation. How—"

"We've searched the ship and there's no trace of him. Also, one of the ammunition boxes has been tampered with. A screwdriver was found." The blood drained from Mallinson's face. He reached for his cup but saw that his hand was trembling, so placed it in his lap.

"Did he get it open?"

"No sir. Whoever it was left behind a Phillips screwdriver, but the screws are all Robertson-type square drive."

"Anyone else jump ship?"

"Just him, sir."

"I want you to report the steward AWOL to the Singapore Police! Oh, and I'll need to give you his identity papers from my files. They're likely false. I've a feeling we won't be seeing that thief again. And tell Mr O'Malley to run the Blue Peter up the fore-truck." This was the flag denoting they were about to depart.

"Aye, sir." There being no steward, the second took his mug and empty plate to the galley and left. The gramophone now played Benny Goodman's 'Blue Skies', and a minor argument had broken out among the card players. Freddie arrived, and Mallinson filled him in on the morning's events.

Freddie grinned mischievously. "Wonderful thing, the Robertson screw. If you're not expecting it, it can throw a spanner in the works." He chuckled at his own remark.

Jimmy, a string bean of a man originally from Jamaica, with a narrow bald head and pendulous lower lip, appeared with the captain's breakfast. A gold ring pierced one ear. His basso profundo voice belied his looks.

"Bloody stoo-hard. Nevah did like 'im, suh," he grumbled. The cook had been the very first of the crew to sign on in (as he pronounced it) 'Lun-doan Town'. Mallinson was always careful to provide good food on his ships, because a well-fed crew was a happy crew. Besides, it cut down on the number of rows. It had been Jimmy who suggested that if the captain wanted to sign on any more crew to a ship as old as this was, he had better change the watch schedule from a two-section dogged watch to a three-section dogged watch. Mallinson felt the man had been right on that point, because this allowed crewmen more sleep time – always popular! Breakfast finished, Freddie said he had to get back to his unit, "despite all the fun I'm having."

"I'll go into the city with you," said Mallinson, checking his pockets to make sure he still had Singh's business card. Freddie shouldered his rucksack and departed, striding to the dockyard gate, whistling. As Mallinson followed after Freddie, puffing to keep up, he took care to notice the ship's Plimsoll mark, denoting the waterlines to which it could be legally loaded. When they reached the trolleybus route, they parted. Mallinson thanked him for everything, Freddie wished him luck, and they shook hands warmly. The lieutenant then stepped back and gave the captain a crisp salute. Pleased, Mallinson returned it. *He didn't have to do that, I'm not Royal Navy now.* Freddie boarded the bus, and Mallinson went in search of a public phone box. He asked Gurnam Singh to cable Ellerman and the MoWT to tell them what had happened, and tell Shenton they were leaving as soon as Singh could find another galley steward for them. Singh agreed, but told him the Merchant Seaman's Hiring Hall was on Anson Road, only six streets from the port, and it would be quicker if he went there himself.

Singh was right; he found a Dane, Tord Andreassen, who was also a qualified baker. He told him where to find the *Dominion Empress*, and the Dane went off to collect his gear at his hostel on the way there. On the way back to the ship he told the Royal Marine at the port gate to expect the man, and gave him the name. When he arrived on the bridge, he found Eugene kneeling and drilling a hole in the deck with an egg beater bit brace. The crew was busy hosing the coal dust from the deck.

Hours passed and there was still no sign of the new steward. Mallinson was infuriated. They couldn't delay leaving to wait for him, as there would be extra charges if the tugs had to return another day, and everyone knew it was bad luck to leave port on a Friday. Mallinson went to the chart house to review the course. The second poked his head in.

"Tugs approaching!" he announced. Mallinson and the Second

stepped to the starboard wing to see two steam tugs entering the Empire Dock from Keppel Harbour, between its west and main wharves. These were the harbour tugs *Pengawal* and *Saint Breock*. They stopped below the bridge.

"Helmsman, take your post," Mallinson said, then told the third mate to sprint to the gate to see what, if any, hold-up there was. He picked up the megaphone and asked the tug if the pilot was there. A short man in a fedora waved, and Mallinson's crew dropped a rope ladder over the side. When he arrived on the bridge, the first thing he did was look at the Ellerman house flag at the masthead, a triangular blue pennant with the initials 'J R E' in white, and below that the white-and-red pilot flag. They tossed lazily towards the east. The second thing he did was ask, "Right-hand or left-hand screw?" "Right-hand," Mallinson answered. They discussed the procedures for getting underway. The man did not give his name.

"Call me pilot," he said, very businesslike. He wore a fedora to match his suit and a wide tie. *He must be sweltering*, Mallinson thought. The captain said his third mate was "still on the quay, and it might be a minute," and this clearly irritated the man. Mallinson crossed to the port bridge wing and looked down. His third mate was slowly coming up the accommodation ladder with the Dane draped on his shoulder. He dropped the man on the deck and left him there, running back to the gate and returning with a kit bag. When he reached the deck, Mallinson shouted to bring the accommodation ladder aboard. The first tug took a line from the bow, and the other took a line tossed from the stern. Mallinson stood at the engine order telegraph and rang for 'stand by', which was answered. Then he said, "Pilot, you have command."

The pilot, now in charge, called out, "Cast off all lines aft."

Mallinson picked up the telephone, selected the stern with a switch, and gave the order.

"Left full rudder, dead slow ahead," said the pilot.

The helmsman called out, "Left full rudder, aye!" Mallinson rang the telegraph, with each order being answered from below. Slowly the stern moved away from the quay. When it was aimed at the entrance channel, the pilot said, "Right half rudder. Dead slow astern. Cast off forward."

The helmsman repeated "Right half rudder, aye!" and Mallinson rang for astern. Again, he phoned the bow. Reaching for the cord, he gave three blasts of the whistle. This was the signal for the aft tug to take up the slack. As the aft bow spring line slackened, the dockyard crew lifted it and the breast line off the bollard, dropping both into the water, and the foredeck crew hauled them in. Slowly the trio moved down the fairway.

"A bit more helm."

"Aye." When the turning basin was a ship's length away, the pilot said, "dead slow ahead. Centre your helm." Never did he raise his voice.

"Helm centred, aye!" repeated the helmsman. Mallinson rang the telegraph. The deck vibrated underfoot. Gradually, the *Dominion Empress* slowed her movement astern until she was stopped. The tug *Pengawal* pulled to starboard and the *Saint Breock* pulled to port. Soon the ship was aimed at the dock entrance.

The pilot said, "Cast off all lines. Two blasts." Mallinson, reaching up, gave two blasts of the whistle. This signalled both tugs to cast off the lines. He watched his deck crew haul them in and flake them down. The pilot picked up the binoculars and, stepping out on the bridge wing, scanned both ends of Keppel Harbour for approaching traffic. The Singapore–Penang ferry SS *Kedah* was just passing westbound but was well clear of them. He ordered a turn to port at the harbour entrance as they exited the docks, and they went east with the two tugs flanking the *Dominion Empress* at each quarter, ready to rush in at the first sign of trouble.

"Half ahead," said the pilot, "helmsman, make your course 125 true.

Pass the lighted beacon number 6 close aboard to port. You'll need to stay clear of Pulau Brani Shoals to starboard."

"Half ahead," repeated Mallinson, and rang the order.

In a mile or so, when they were clear of the lighted beacon at Tanjung Pagar point, the pilot ordered, "Half astern," and Mallinson rang the order and echoed "Backing down." The vibration underfoot increased.

A tug came alongside. The pilot said, "You have command. Good luck!" He climbed down the rope ladder and jumped while the vessels still had slight way on. The tugs peeled away, saluting with their whistles. Mallinson rang for full ahead. Joining Reginald Wallace, his first mate, in the chart house, they reviewed the course yet again, agreeing to make for the Bangka Belitung Islands. From there they would transit the Java Sea on their way to the Sunda Strait. The ship's clock struck sixteen hundred hours, the beginning of the first dog watch.

"Shape your course eight five degrees true," he told the replacement helmsman as he returned to the bridge, then to the first mate said, "You have command, Mr Wallace." He ordered the pilot flag to be taken in, then went below with his third mate.

The Dane lay unconscious where he'd been dropped. His left eye was blacked, he had a swollen lower lip, blood in his blonde hair, and what was left of his shirt hung in shreds about his waist. This revealed three tattoos: an enormous three-masted sailing ship graced his chest; a topless hula girl in a grass skirt was on one bruised bicep; a red heart and the word "*MODER*" on the other.

"What happened?" Mallinson asked of the mate.

"Well, sor, the Royal Marine at the gate wouldna let him in, so he forced his way in. Then this happened." Mr O'Malley hailed from Northern Ireland.

"But I gave the man instructions to—"

"Sure, and there's a strict rule of no drunks in the dockyard," the third interrupted. Mallinson snorted.

"Leave him until morning, and take his kit bag. If there's any spirits in it, bring them to me. Have him report to me when he's sober." A few minutes later, Mallinson returned and handcuffed the man to a tank vent. He gave the key to the third. It wouldn't do, to have him roaming the ship when he woke up. Five hours later, when they had cleared the island of Pulau Mapur, the first ordered a change of course to the south, as planned. The tropical storm to the north had petered out within two days. The sea was calm now.

The next day, Mallinson had finished his daily inspection tour and was on the bridge during the forenoon watch when the third mate handed him a quarter-full bottle of Aquavit.

"How was it?" he asked. The mate made a face.

"'Twas weird, sor," he said. "Sure, and it tasted like bread, and not our own. Summat what the Swedes bake, belike." Mallinson took it to his cabin but, before putting it in his desk, had a taste for himself. *Not bad at all. I like it. What's that flavour it reminds me of? I can't seem to place it.* Before noon he went below for a light tiffin of tea, a sausage and a bap. The Dane was gone. He wasn't in the crew's mess either, and the cook was still upset. At 1200 hours he observed as the second and third mates made their noon sights from the bridge. Taffy was the first to finish while O'Malley still struggled. Standing over the chart the captain pushed the ship's copy of *Bowditch* aside.

"I'll plot it this time, Mr Morgan. Read it to me!" He took the dividers from the mate.

"Aye, sir," Taffy said, then announced, "Latitude one degree, fourteen point two minutes South," and the captain set the dividers to the proper position against the scale, stepped it off and pencilled a mark.

"Longitude one-hundred-six degrees, twenty-one point five minutes East," the Welshman added, and the captain repeated the procedure. He extended the tick marks until they crossed. When the third mate O'Malley arrived, his calculations agreed to within a few seconds of arc.

"Very good, Mr O'Malley," Mallinson teased him, "we'll make a second mate out of you yet!" He wanted to give the island of Pulau Gelasa, more than six hours away, a wide berth on the way to the Strait of Selat Baur, the preferred route in the Admiralty Sailing Directions.

"You should stay three miles to the west of that island," he told the second mate. Mallinson saw the wireless operator was on the bridge wing with the captain's binoculars, looking overhead at an aeroplane flying southeast. "Don't worry about that. It's the KLM flight from Singapore, going to either Surabaya or Semarang in Java," he told him. At the end of the afternoon watch, the third mate arrived on the bridge with the Dane in tow, who at least wore a new shirt.

"Come with me," Mallinson commanded, and the three of them went to his cabin. The third handed the captain's handcuffs and key back to him, and he locked them in the gun cabinet.

"Now then," he said, "How much had you to drink, after we left the merchant seamen's hall?"

"Vell, yust beer. A few … er … litres."

"And?"

"I bott a boddle of Aquavit."

"I can tolerate a man coming off leave a little 'squiffy', but I would have never signed you on had I known that you're a drunkard. Now it's too late and I've no choice. Do you know, I could clap you in the brig and drop you in any port without pay?" *No need for him to know we have no brig, or for that matter, a nearby port.*

Andreassen looked alarmed and said, "Yah, I yust vant to start … uh … *på god fod* … uh … on a good foot."

"Try harder. Can you do what we hired you for, or shall we take you ashore?"

"Nigh, I can verk ... I *vill* verk, yah," said the Dane, chastened.

"Good. As long as you understand it's against regulations for crewmen to have alcohol aboard ship during wartime." He had the new steward sign the ship's articles, and the third witnessed it. His identity papers were handed over, and the captain filed them. "You know, I do grant shore leave occasionally, and sometimes," he repeated with emphasis, "*sometimes*, because I once was Royal Navy, I might choose to issue a tot of rum, though it's not a usual thing." He reached into a drawer and held out the bottle. "Here, this belongs to you. Report to Jimmy the cook in the galley." The new steward left the cabin, closing the door gently behind him. O'Malley started for the door, but Mallinson held him back, saying "Wait a bit." A moment later the door was flung open and the steward stood there.

"Iss water!" he raged. He turned on his heel, heaving the bottle overboard as far as he could, and stormed away. Captain and third mate looked at each other and burst out laughing. Wiping away a tear, Mallinson said, "I may have to insist that Jimmy serve me personally from now on, but, boy, was that worth it!"

Sparks put his head through the open door. "Skipper, whennerwe gonna get schooled on this here Bofors?"

Mallinson looked to the third mate. "Who did Lieutenant Chapman instruct on that last day?"

"I believe Maakki Virtanen and the chief."

"Well, I guess there's no time like the present. Would you have the first hand-pick some of the deck crew that might have some aptitude for this, and meet me at the stern at 1700 hours, and MacCallan if he's not on duty."

"Aye, sor."

"And me?" asked Gene, hopefully.

"Oh, all right, and you. May I have my binoculars back, please?"

* * *

The sun blazed low on the western horizon, the distant low clouds over Pulau Bangka Island brilliant in colours of orange and salmon. To the north, some miles distant, a cumulonimbus cloud reared to 20,000 feet, travelling slowly to the west. The group gathered round consisted of the bosun Virtanen, six seamen from the deck department, Gene the wireless operator, the third mate O'Malley, the ship's carpenter Nowiczski, the second engineer Sinclair, and Mallinson. The Bofors stood looking naked, as the shipyard workers hadn't had enough time to install a gun tub. It did have a square shield in front offering some protection from small-arms fire. The bosun began by asking for volunteers to fill the pair of seats flanking the device. Sinclair took the right seat and an able seaman took the left.

"This is completely unpowered, except there's this 6-volt battery here that operates the trigger. Don't touch that foot pedal yet!" he admonished the seaman. "That's how it fires. This is capable of reaching an altitude of 23,000 feet, but don't do that. Wait for any aeroplanes to be below 12,000 feet or even much lower before you fire. All right?" There was a murmur. He had the engineer shift the gun from side to side using the two-handed crank in front of him, and explained how to aim with the large round pancake sight, leaving the gun pointed off the stern. He then had the seaman do the same with his two-handed elevation crank and sight, positioning the barrel to point horizontal. There was a discussion of how to lead a target so the victim would fly into the space the shells were passing through, and the shells would be passing through that space the moment the victim reached it. It was a bit tricky. Most of the shells for the Bofors had been transferred to steel lockers welded to the deck, but there was still a stack of unopened crates. A haphazard pile of empty crates lay nearby. Maakki unlatched a locker and held up a cartridge clip of four shells, telling each man to take a clip for himself.

"Whoever is the loader will be very busy. This is how you load it," he said, holding his clip above the rectangular slot in the top of the machine and dropping it in.

"Now, watch," he said, "Stephen, step on that pedal. There. That one." In two seconds four brass casings clattered to the deck out of a curved chute at the rear. It was loud. A second later, a geyser appeared a half mile astern. The off-duty Chinese firemen and Lascar coal-trimmers came boiling out of their quarters. Mallinson soothed them by waving his hands palm down and shouting in Pidgin English, "Makee Practice! Makee Practice! No can help!" A few of them remained on deck, to smoke and watch the goings on. Maakki then had a seaman load continuously, the others passing him cartridge clips one after the other, while the aimers practised tracking high-flying frigate birds. Of course, none were hit. They all took it in turns. Even the captain gave it a go. Gene was the last to try. As he began to climb into the left hand seat he glanced out to starboard.

"Sub!" he screamed, pointing. "Sub!" Two miles away the top of a black conning tower appeared awash in the placid sea. "Turn! Turn! Turn!" he yelled. He scrambled into the seat. The loader tripped. He dropped his clip. Others dug frantically in the locker for more.

"Gene, wait! It may be Dutch or Australian," Mallinson shouted. *Wait a bit. Oh, yes, the noon sextant sights.* He looked at his watch. *It's been five and a half hours since then.* He picked up the lookout's telephone to the bridge. The group waited anxiously, listening as he spoke. "Off the starboard beam ... two miles or so distant." Seconds ticked by as Mallinson waited for an answer. He hung up. "It's a reef. The mate says it's in the Admiralty Sailing Directions as Warren Hastings Reef." Everyone let out their breath. One man laughed.

"Can I shoot it anyway?" Gene asked.

"Sure, have a crack at it," Mallinson said. All his shots went high.

"Thought I'd do better," he mused, shaking his head.

Mallinson turned to the ship's carpenter. "What is this pile of boxes doing here?" he asked.

"Sorry. We left in such a hurry, the shipyard crew never cleaned up, sir."

"Well, can you do something with these?"

"Aye, sir. Ammo boxes can't be used for dunnage, but I'll find a spot for them." Later, after the group had gone back to their duties, the captain and the bosun were left standing together.

"There's one more thing Lieutenant Chapman told me, I think I should tell you – and only you," Maakki said.

"Oh, yes? What was that?"

"He said, having this thing is pretty much useless." He pointed to the gun. "It's really good for only one thing: to keep our spirits up."

Mallinson patted him on the back. "I know, son. I know."

4

A Breakdown And A Detour

When the island of Pulau Gelasa was off the port beam, the first mate had the helmsman hold to the same heading of 150 degrees true. The preferred course was to pass between the islands of Pulau Liat and Pulau Mendanau. Three hours later, after Pulau Gelasa had disappeared below the horizon astern and the island of Mendanau was to port, the first mate ordered a change of course, bringing the *Dominion Empress* to a heading of 215 degrees true. The Sunda Strait was now sixteen hours away. An hour and a half later, Mallinson was in his cabin, reading before going to bed, when the deck under his feet stopped its vibration. The telegraph on the bridge rang faintly. He stepped from his cabin onto the deck outside and padded forwards, noting on the way the darker bulk of a low island to port. The safety valve on the after side of the funnel blew with a roar, and he ducked involuntarily. *Boiler overpressure. Normal with a sudden shutdown.* He entered the bridge from the port wing to find the mate standing at the voice pipe.

"Why did you stop engine?" he asked.

"I didn't. The order came from below. I was about to find out why."

Mallinson stood by while the mate whistled the engine room. "Third engineer, aye," came the response.

"What's going on?"

The voice came back faint, "The condenser has blown a tube. Mebbe several. Don't know yet."

Mallinson nodded. "I'm coming down." Turning to the mate, he asked, "Where's the nearest port?"

"If we backtrack, the nearest are Tandjungpandan, Java or Palembang City, Sumatra, but we've too deep a draught to get into either of them. We'd need to anchor some distance offshore."

"What about that island there? Does it have a cove?"

"Not a chance. Completely surrounded by reefs."

"Do what you can to find a usable port. I'll be back shortly." As he left for the engine room, the bridge clock struck the start of the middle watch. It was midnight. Mallinson crossed the catwalk in darkness to the base of the funnel. As he opened the door to the machinery space, a gust of heat washed over him. Without the engine running, the silence was unnerving. He paused to get his bearings. He stood on the grating of a catwalk, the uppermost of four encircling the towering engine. The massive iron cylinder tops lay before him, below an overhead crane used for lifting them during repairs. Below him, faint yellow Edison bulbs hung about at ten-foot intervals to dimly illuminate the space at each level. To his left the grating disappeared in darkness, its bulbs apparently burnt out, on its way to the overhead funnel casing hatch. He stepped to the nearest bulb and turned it. It lit up. The next one did, too, and the next. He climbed a vertical ladder and pushed up on the overhead hatch. There was no need to strike a match for light, because the smell assailed him immediately. He shut the hatch and dogged it. Returning along the grating, he put the bulbs back the way he'd found them, and smiled in amusement. *Well, I now know why this is being kept dark.*

Ahead of him the stairs fell away. He descended past the enormous cylinders, and encountered MacCallan at the engineering desk on the same level with the Stephenson valve gear linkages. On the wall above the desk were arranged the mouth of the voice pipe, the prominent gauges for boiler pressure, feedwater pressure, intermediate receiver pressure, the low-pressure cylinder vacuum, and a clock. Hamish sat on his stool, his elbows on the desk, his head in his hands. Voices and faint clanking noises drifted up from below.

"Hamish, what's the story here?" he asked. MacCallan yawned, holding up a test tube to the nearest light bulb, and shook his head with worry. He pointed down through the grating at the engineers working below them.

"The condenser is shot. As ye ken, I make a salinity test every watch, an now we have salt in yon boiler feedwater."

"Salt! That's no good. We can't let that get into the boilers."

"Aye, well ye ken. We can steam with a wee bit o' salt in the boiler, and have been, but any more will make much trouble, and now we have e'en more. To fix the problem we'll have to bide a wee."

"How long do you reckon we'll have to hang about?"

"Well, to do what needs doing perhaps two hours, maybe three. We'll ken more when we gives it a dekko."

"What about the auxiliary condenser? Can we use that?"

"That's the problem. We haven't got one."

"No auxiliary condenser? How can that be?" Mallinson asked, in exasperation. Hamish sighed and explained how, when the ship was converted in 1923, the auxiliary condenser was used as a heat exchanger for the hold refrigeration. Then, when the hold refrigeration was broken and taken out in 1936, the auxiliary condenser had been taken out along with it.

"Blast! What can be done to get us going the soonest?"

"I might take the covers off, and bung a wee plug in, but it's temporary, ye understand."

"Let me know if you can do that. The mate may yet be able to find us a usable port." Back on the bridge, he found the first in the chart house poring over the charts, dividers in hand. "We're out of commission, at least for a while," he told him.

"The chart shows a depth of eight to ten fathoms, and that's true all the way to Java," the mate said. "The good news is, there's no wind and the current is setting us to the south-south-west, the direction we want to go, and there's nothing in front of us. Do we anchor?" he asked.

"Hmm, I think not. Let's drift awhile but have the lookouts keep a sharp eye out for other ships. Send a man to the bow to stand by, ready to drop anchor if we approach any land."

The first turned to an able seaman standing watch and ordered, "Run up the 'Not Under Command' flag and stand ready to trigger the lights at the first sign of an imminent collision." Then, turning to Mallinson, he said, "I think I've got something. The port of Merak in Java. It's on the Sunda Strait and less than a day away, due south."

"Distance?"

"Hundred and eighty miles. If that's no good, there's an alternative on the Sumatra side of the Sunda Strait but it's a longish way away — two hundred and forty-two miles. It's a large shipyard in the village of Panjang near Telukbetung in Sumatra. They may be able to handle us."

"We'll try for Merak first." Chief MacCallan arrived on the bridge. Mallinson turned to him. "What news?"

"Aye, it can be fixed, for now."

"How long will it take?"

"Three hours. I ken we'll make perhaps two-thirds speed. We'll no want to put a strain on it. When we reach port, we'll need some new tubes, to rod it out, boil it out, and get in new zincs, and soon."

"Thank you, chief. Well done." He addressed himself to the first mate. "At a reduced speed of, say, eight knots, that would be about twenty-three hours. Does that sound about right?"

"Yes."

"Good. Hamish, let us know when you're ready, and we'll get underway."

Two hours later the captain descended to the engine room, all the way to the bottom at the level of the crankshaft. It wasn't as hot as it had been before. The third engineer was directing two Chinese engineer assistants working to close up the condenser. Mallinson was amused to hear the assistants speaking English; not that they were, but that they did so with a Scots accent. In retrospect it seemed inevitable.

"Any luck?" he asked the chief.

"Aye, I stopped the raw water seacocks and drained the condenser to the bilge, took the covers off and filled it with water, an' observed what tubes leaked. Then stoppled 'em. We're putting the covers back now."

"I noticed an empty ammunition box at the engineer's station. What's that for?" he asked.

"Och, aye, the carpenter give it me. It be what we whittle the bungs out of." Mallinson observed as the third mate held the other heavy cover in place while the two assistants hand-threaded the bolts. They then went round with the spanner and tightened each in a peculiar pattern to keep from setting up any stresses. Hamish then directed the assistants to oil the feedwater pump, the crosshead slides, the main journals, and the piston rod pins, and top up the oil cups. While they did this, the third opened the raw-water seacock to the condenser, and they all climbed the stair to the engineering station on the catwalk above. The third then opened the cylinder drains. The chief opened the main stop valve and cracked the throttle handwheel. Hot water cascaded down the engine for a minute until it changed into jets of steam hissing from the drains, and piston rod glands. The group was engulfed in clouds of vapour. The third walked round the engine shutting all the cylinder drains, while the chief closed the throttle.

"Ready when ye are," he said. Mallinson blew the whistle into the voice pipe and the second mate replied, "Aye?"

"Ready when you are, Mr Morgan. Let's see how she does at half ahead, eh?" he said. The engine-order telegraph above the reversing wheel clanged from Stop to Ahead Full to Astern Full and settled on Ahead Half. The chief answered it in kind, and cranked the large reversing wheel to its stop against the engine. He opened the throttle hand wheel and, with a hissing of steam from a dozen places that may not have been tight enough, the great crankshaft rotated a quarter-turn and eased silently to a stop. The third engineer looked concerned at this.

"Well, chief, it looks like we'll need to bar it over," he announced with an air of confidence.

Hamish smirked at this.

"Ye didnae open the simpling valve, did ye?" he said, casually. The third smacked a palm on his forehead in embarrassment and, reaching up, turned a small hand wheel above his head. The crankshaft slowly began to turn over, gaining speed. He shut the valve.

The connecting rods, thick as a man's torso, flashed up and down, faster and faster, until the chief turned to the captain and announced, "Ahead Half."

"What revolutions?" Mallinson shouted.

"Forty!"

"Make it Fifty-three!"

"Aye!" He gave the throttle hand wheel a few more turns.

"Thank you, chief!" Mallinson checked his wristwatch. 0250 hours. He climbed the stairs to return to his bed. On the boat deck he crossed the catwalk to the bridge house and climbed the companionway. Making his way aft to his cabin he noticed a light coming from under the door to the wireless room. *It's the middle of the night, Eugene cannot possibly be working this late, surely?* He opened the door and peered in, then stepped inside.

It was a small room, but large enough to hold the L-shaped table of equipment. There was the transmitter with its microphone and transmitting key, the radio direction finder, and a box of tuning coils for the modern National HRO receiver. This last was still on, and the speaker at times emitted the familiar dots and dashes of Morse code. At night these were ordinarily meaningless chatter among bored operators on nearby islands, or else the weather reports.

A goose-neck table lamp illuminated a sleeping Eugene on a cot, a pasteboard box nearby filled with Popular Mechanics magazines. His dungarees, shirt and shoes lay heaped where they'd been dropped. Mallinson picked these up and hung them on the coat hooks. Even though he had his own cabin below, Gene often slept here, and Roy knew that the boy would be instantly awake if his ears detected any distress codes. He lay under a dark-green woollen blanket with the large letters 'U.S.' printed on it, a book open and face down on his chest. Mallinson gently eased the book out from under his hand. Gene smacked his lips and rolled towards the wall, hugging his pillow. This shifted the blanket and revealed two more books laying on the deck. Roy gathered them up and placed them side by side on the table to examine them. They appeared to be cheap grubstreet novels, but published in America.

The cover of the first showed a full-bosomed white woman in a jungle, her clothing tattered, an enormous boa constrictor wrapped about her torso, being rescued from the jaws of certain death by a white man wearing a pith helmet who was choking the life from the snake with his bare hands. A whip hung at his belt. The cover promised a salacious story. *Hmm, I'd no idea he read this type of thing.*

The cover of the next showed a similarly buxom woman, her platinum blonde hair in ringlets, the back of her wrist held to her mouth as if to muffle a scream. Again, the bodice of her dress ripped, an impossibly high slit in her skirt exposing a bare leg and midriff, and arguably a part of her bum. She lay upon her back, a whacking great ape with slavering fangs and red eyes looming over her. In the background, behind the same white man holding a shotgun, could be seen a line of black porters in full flight, their faces depicted as having broad noses and comically bulging fear-filled white eyes and thick white lips. Mallinson grimaced. *What utter rubbish! So much for Gene posing as an intellectual.*

But the final cover was the most lurid of all: an *extremely* well-endowed woman in no clothing whatsoever, jungle leaves in the foreground hiding certain bits of her from view, being held down by Japanese soldiers who crouched, simian-like. A repulsive, sallow-skinned Japanese officer loomed over her, his claw-like hands just opening the waistband of his trousers. This left no doubt as to what his intentions were. His slits of eyes were magnified by thick round glasses, and his lips curled back evilly to expose prominent oversize teeth. In the background other soldiers pinioned the arms of a white man, holding him impotent, unable to go to her aid. Roy shook his head in despair and sighed. He left the books on the table and switched off the lamp. *I really must find time to have a serious talk with Gene about the evils of racialism and propaganda, and sooner rather than later – before it takes root in his mind.*

Later that same morning he went below to the wardroom. Tord, the new steward, brought his favourite breakfast: bangers, eggs and toast. The captain thanked him, but took his time to carefully examine the meal after the man had left. Satisfied, he ate. At the beginning of the forenoon watch, having finished his daily inspection, he was on the bridge when they sighted HMS *Royal Sovereign* steaming on a reciprocal course a half mile off the port bow, northbound for Singapore. He called the wireless operator to the bridge because he knew Gene would want to see this super-dreadnought Revenge-class battleship, a stirring sight. At their combined speed they were passing each other at 30 knots. Everyone on the bridge stood silent as she passed, except the helmsman, who whispered, "Holy Smoke!" The deck crew working on the foredeck waved their caps in the air and cheered. Afterwards, Sparks returned to his room. A minute later he was back with a message in hand.

"Their operator told us a Jap sub was sighted 100 nautical miles east of Christmas Island nineteen hours ago."

"Transmitted in the clear?"

Eugene shook his head. "No, it was Morse. But they didn't mention us. It was a general broadcast."

"Did you answer?"

"No sir. Well, the mate did run up signal flags."

"Good. That's in the Indian Ocean, south of Java," Mallinson mused.

"Aye, sor," the third mate replied. "If they were following the *Royal Sovereign* they couldna hope to keep up with her. She can do nearly three times their speed."

"Let us hope that wasn't their intention."

"But, sor, if that sub was following her, we'll steam directly into their path! For safety's sake, shouldna we steam east, and around the Island of Bali?"

Mallinson shook his head. "The sub may have been motoring east itself. We don't know. Besides, going that way would add three days and over 600 miles to our trip. Because our condenser is playing up, we really need to get to a port, and the sooner, the better."

At noon the sextant sights put them at 4°30'S,106°36'E. Merak, Java was twelve hours away. Mallinson went to his cabin after checking the mates' calculations. Entering the head and sitting down he had time to think: *What if O'Malley was right? We're not technically at war with Japan but there's no telling what the Japanese may do, they're so unpredictable. But we can't know which channel that sub will take to go from the Indian Ocean to the Java Sea, or even if it will do that at all. An encounter with that sub might mean being boarded and searched. We can't have that. Worse yet, what if they decide to torpedo us unawares? After all, there were the* USS Panay, *the SS* Athenia, *and the SS* Robin Moor, *all of them attacked without any declaration of war.*

The door to the head was open, and he could see the 'Ammo' box still laying there, mere feet away. He had replaced the gold bar and screwed the lid down onto it. *If we are boarded and searched, how could we prevent the gold from being discovered?*

He could read the blue stencilled label on the box, and this brought to mind the empty ammo boxes he had asked the carpenter about. *If we're sunk, we might be able to get away in the lifeboats.* Slowly, a plan began to germinate. *Bali may be too far, but what about somewhere closer? I will need to confide in someone, someone with a technical bent.* He washed his hands and paused in the chart house on his return to the bridge, where the second mate, Taffy, was now on duty.

"We have ninety-six miles to go until we reach Merak, correct?"

"Aye."

"But Batavia is a similar distance. That's a city of half a million people, second only to Singapore in these parts. It's a bit out of our way, but I want you to lay in a new course for Batavia."

The second mate retreated to the chart house, emerging a minute later. "Steer one hundred and sixty-eight degrees. Any further west than that and there's a heap of reefs and skinny water."

"Helmsman, come to one six eight degrees!" Mallinson ordered. The

Helmsman repeated "One six eight degrees, aye," and spun the wheel. Taffy marked the time and new course in the day log. The captain blew the whistle down the voice pipe, and lifted the lid.

"Second engineer, aye!"

"Ah! Mr Sinclair, will you tell the chief to meet me in my quarters, please?"

"Och, nae. The chief's no' on duty now." Mallinson found it amusing how Sinclair lapsed into a Scots brogue, but only when in earshot of the other engineers.

"Oh, yes, of course. He has the dog watch today. Well, then, will you meet me in the wardroom at sixteen-hundred hours, when you're off duty?"

"Aye."

"What revolutions?"

"Still fifty-three, captain."

"Very good, keep at it." Turning to the second mate, he said, "Have Mr Nowiczski meet me in the wardroom at sixteen-hundred hours, and tell him to bring an empty ammunition box and lid with him." Turning to the runner standing at the after bulkhead, the second repeated the order. The ordinary seaman, a Geordie from Newcastle named Harris, trotted off to find Nowiczski, the carpenter. As the runner departed, Roy thought, *I really wish Gene would hurry up with that tannoy. All this would be so much easier.* He retreated to his cabin to sketch out his plan.

Most of the crew knew Nowiczski's story and were empathetic. He had owned a thriving furniture factory in Rzeszów, Poland, until 6 September 1939 when the Luftwaffe bombed the city for the first time, killing his wife and daughter and destroying the factory. The Wehrmacht marched in the next day, and he had been forced to masquerade as a devout Protestant until a winter's day early in 1940 when someone – he never knew who – had informed on him to the Gestapo. But he had been warned ahead of time by a "Good German" neighbour. It was too dangerous to attempt going north to neutral Sweden, so he had fled through the forested mountains of the neutral kingdoms of Roumania and Bulgaria, to the port of Thessaloniki in Greece, where he crowded into a ship bound for England and packed with refugees.

Nowiczski was frequently teased as a teetotaller – the best the crew could manage was "No-Whisky" – even though he ran a lucrative business with a pot still, hidden somewhere on the ship, though no one knew where. With this he blended two parts of spirits to three parts of whatever juice that came to hand. Among the seamen this was referred to as "panther piss". None of the licensed officers knew about it, and the unlicensed crew was careful to keep it that way. Jimmy the cook was constantly amazed at how much fruit juice this crew could burn through in a month.

Runner Harris descended two decks through 'Officer Country' and knocked on the carpenter's cabin door. Hearing no answer, he glanced in. Empty. He continued down another deck to the corridor outside the wardroom on the main deck. There he checked the duty board; Nowiczski was off duty and thus could be anywhere. Harris checked the wardroom and the crew's mess, before finding the cook's boy hunting through the pantry, and asked him if by any chance he had seen the carpenter. The lad darted his head out the door to make sure Jimmy wasn't near, put a thumb to his lips and, with a knowing wink, mimed drinking from a bottle. Ah! That's where he is. The cook's winger, as the boy was known, handed Harris a bucket of potato peels, turnip tops and beet scraps, and asked him to give it to Nowiczski. The boy's palm was regularly greased with a few shillings to make sure to not toss these scraps by the board. Harris went down the companionway to the deck below, taking it two steps at a time, and jogged forwards to the bulkhead of number one hold. He rapped the agreed signal on the watertight door and someone from the inside un-dogged it. He stepped through into the 'tween deck of the hold. It was a good thing this hold held only crated aeroplanes; once they'd tried another hold loaded with sheet rubber, but its pungent smell had nauseated them. Under a caged safety lamp on the wall, a rollicking game of acey-deucy was in full swing, below a pall of cigarette smoke. A dozen yelling men each held a glass or a fistful of notes.

"Ante up, ya sorry gits!" Hardcastle's voice rose above the hubbub. Somebody else shouted "Post!" and there were groans and laughter. A bloke could always play cards in the crew's mess for matchsticks, or pence, but this was where you could make, or lose, real money. At some time in the past these noisy games had been held in the paint locker, until the captain chanced upon it one day and read them the Riot Act for smoking in a compartment that was clearly labelled "*Nicht Rauchen! Feuergefährlich!*"

"Ya here fer the craic?" A torch flashed briefly in his face.

"Don't I wish! 'No-whisky' here?" Harris asked whoever it was had spoken to him. "The old man wants 'im."

"No-Nooky!" the man shouted into the darkness on the fringes of the light. "Oi! Yer number's up!" There was no response.

"Blimey, have a care, mate!" Harris said. "Don't ya know them Nazis killed 'is missus?"

"Uh ... No, I didn't – 'No-whisky'! Runner here for you," the man echoed. Nowiczski emerged from the darkness, vacant now except for the empty plywood bunks the South African troops had used. He cradled a canning jar in the crook of one arm. Harris delivered his message. Nowiczski held the jar up to the light and squinted at its orange contents, then handed the jar to the first man.

"I know how much is here, so none better go missing," he said.

"Never you worry none, me suspicious Pole. Any missing and I'll see ya get yer money."

Harris and Nowiczski stepped out of the hold into the light of the corridor, and the door was dogged behind them. Harris handed the bucket over, which was gladly accepted. Harris dug into his shirt pocket and shook out a black pellet from a matchbox, offering it to the carpenter.

"What's this?"

"It's 'Sen-Sen' – you'll need it if yer gonna be talkin' to the old man."

At 1555 hours the captain descended to the wardroom to find the carpenter was already there, a box and lid on the table. Mallinson asked him how many of these boxes he had left and was satisfied with the answer. He told him to store them away and keep them all in good condition, including the lids and screws, and dismissed the man. Nowiczski then joined a group of off-duty able seamen and ordinary seamen from the first section, lounging about in the adjacent crew's mess, reading comic books and waiting for grub. The Philco played dance music at a low volume, occasionally interrupted by a man speaking Dutch. The third section coming off duty began to stream in, and the room became noisy. Minutes later Sinclair, the second engineer, came in to take his tea before going off duty. Today it was roast lamb and mint sauce, with neeps and tatties. MacCallan and Sinclair had both been campaigning for haggis in recent weeks, but the cook wouldn't hear of it, proclaiming the dish "disgusting."

"Do we have any grey paint in the paint locker?" the captain asked.

"The stuff we use for the inside of lifeboats? Yes, I believe we do," Sinclair answered. They ate in silence, the second engineer occasionally darting a puzzled glance at the ammo box.

All Mallinson would say is "I have a project planned for you. We shan't talk here." When they had finished their meal, the captain asked him to pick up the empty box and said, "Follow me." Entering his cabin he was careful to lock the door, dog the portholes, and pull the curtains. "Give a hand here." They hoisted the heavy ammo box from the floor onto the low table, grunting with the effort. This ammo box was of slightly different dimensions than an actual Bofors ammo box. Mallinson measured the interior of the empty box and recorded its size. "Please, sit," he said, as he went to work with the screwdriver, "and tell me what you know of foundry work." This they discussed until the captain had taken out the last screw. It had been a required subject in engineering materials classes. Mallinson sat back. He related to the engineer all the events of that morning, the subsequent change in course to Batavia, his worries about the sub, and his worry they might be boarded or sunk, and then enquired, "Can I trust you with a secret? I mean a really enormous secret?"

"Aye. Though we'll be a crew for six months or summat, it's a good ship and a good crew. I hope to make chief one day, and with you as captain, I reckon I've a fair go. Aye, ye can."

"Good." Mallinson thought him sincere. He then sketched out for him the meeting at the Istana in brief. He told of the possibility of war between Japan and Great Britain, and the actual reason for the change in destination from Southampton to Fremantle.

"Our cargo is not primarily lead, rubber and aeroplanes. Now, it is … this!" he said dramatically, lifting the lid from the box. Sinclair sat speechless at the sight. He reached for it, paused, said "May I?" and, at a nod from Mallinson, lifted out a bar. Collecting his wits, he asked, "How much o' this do we carry?"

"Some sixty-nine tons. Not a word to anybody. The fewer that know, the better, understand? Not even the chief. Only you, and me." Sinclair nodded. "But," Mallinson continued, "we have to devise a way to protect it all should we ever be boarded, or sunk. So, here's my plan

..."

The captain and the second engineer talked through the first dog watch and into the last dog watch, formulating a plan and tweaking the details until every part made sense. When they parted, the captain said, "I'll square your schedule with the chief when you're needed. Remember, not a word!" Emerging onto the bridge before sunset, Mallinson had been there no more than a quarter of an hour before the lookout on the starboard wing hailed him.

"Sir, I'm not sure but, look there, broad on the starboard quarter," He handed his binoculars to the captain, "Is that a periscope wake, sir?"

Mallinson scanned the horizon in the direction the man had pointed, but the setting sun was making the water a blinding white mirror. *Was that the silhouette of a periscope? Was it?* His eyes burned from the glare.

The bridge telephone rang and the first mate answered it. "Aft lookout reports periscope wake on the starboard quarter! Ten thousand yards!" he shouted, and hung up.

Blast! "Action Stations! Douse the running lights!" Mallinson called. He handed the binoculars back to the lookout. The first mate flipped switches on the electrical panel and palmed a red, mushroom-shaped button on the aft bulkhead. A klaxon horn began blaring. Mallinson strode to the voice pipe, blew the whistle down it, and without waiting for an answer yelled "Flank speed, maximum revolutions!" The deck throbbed as their speed began to climb. "Keep an eye on her, son," he said to the lookout.

Everyone on the bridge went to the aft bulkhead and put on their Kapok life jacket and Brodie helmet. Mallinson's own battle bowler read 'CAPT' in white block letters. Sparks arrived, fastening his Kapok, and was told what was happening. He returned to his radio shack. Stepping to the starboard wing the captain shaded his eyes and looked aft. Seamen, some in nothing but shorts and vests, were scrambling aft on their way to the Bofors, ducking under and around the guy wires that restrained the aeroplanes. He silenced the klaxon. The captain and the first mate stood near each other and conversed quietly, so the others couldn't hear.

"How far?"

"Twenty-eight miles. Call it two hours, maybe less," said the first. The captain blew out his cheeks.

"Can we can outrun her, d'ye reckon?"

"We're loaded to our marks, and now doing nearly fifteen knots, fastest this old bucket has ever done. A sub does seven knots underwater so, yes, unless ..." He paused.

"Unless?"

"Unless it surfaces, then it's capable of nearly fifteen knots."

"Oh, boy." Mallinson mopped his brow and readjusted his helmet. "Let's hope it doesn't surface, and please don't call us an old bucket. The *Empress* may be listening." The first nodded and gave a tight smile.

"Sir, that sub is coming from the west. It may have been guarding the Sunda Strait. If we hadn't altered course to Batavia, we might have steamed directly into its sights!" Mallinson nodded and gave a shiver.

"Mr O'Malley thought the same and wanted me to change course to pass east of Bali. That's one reason why I did think to alter course." *It's astonishing to me how often unremarkable decisions like this happen in wartime, and often change the course of events.*

Thirty minutes passed. The eastern sky was a deep blue, nearly black, the western horizon a dull maroon red.

"I'm glad there's only a sliver of moon, so we're hard to see," Mallinson commented. But no sooner had the words left his mouth than a shell screamed past the *Empress* at bridge level a half-cable's length away on the starboard side, followed by the report a second later. The first answered the telephone.

"It's on the surface, dead astern. Five thousand yards," he said.

"Commence firing!" Mallinson ordered.

"Commence firing!" the mate relayed. The Bofors began a constant rate of fire.

"Raise the White Ensign, Mr Dunthorne!" Mallinson commanded.

"Sorry sir, the White Ensign? Who is Dunthorne?" Wallace asked.

"Oh! ... ah ... belay that order," he replied, self-consciously.

A shell screamed past the *Empress* a cable's length away to port.

"They've bracketed us. Helmsman, come left five degrees, now! Lookouts, inside quick as you can and hit the deck, *now!*" Mallinson ordered.

"Left five degrees, aye!" shouted the helmsman. The lookouts raced to the bridge and fell flat holding on to their binoculars. A helmet slid across the deck and fetched up against the bulkhead. A man crawled after it. Mallinson and the helmsman remained standing. The first dropped to his knees, still listening, and said, "They've made a slight turn to the east."

"Oh, he's a canny bastard, him."

"Sir?"

"He's going wide in an attempt to get a better angle at our port side for a torpedo. To keep him dead astern, he knows we must turn starboard, but if we do, it puts us into the reefs." In the next few minutes, they heard the sub's gun speak three times, yet only a single shell was seen to splash. There was a ringing clang to starboard, and the deck jumped. He looked and saw nothing obvious, until he noticed the bridge rail cap had gone. The captain took the telephone from the mate.

"Cease fire. The muzzle flash is revealing our position. Wait for them to fire first, then aim at their flash, but only one clip at a time, understand? Only one clip at a time!" He hung up.

"No! No! Go back! Stay here!" There was shouting coming up the companionway from below. The second mate appeared, wearing his pyjamas and a helmet, and reported a group of Chinese and Lascars had made their way forwards. "They're scared witless. The serang tells me a shell came through the steering flat and continued through their quarters."

"Anyone killed or injured?" Mallinson asked, alarmed.

"Fortunately, no, and we're still able to steer, so that's something. I ordered them to stay on the midship well deck for safety." The first mate then told the second mate to go to the chart house.

"I'll stay here in case the captain is … incapacitated." If Mallinson heard, he gave no indication. The second mate stood in the open doorway of the chart house, listening intently, and quickly sketched a pencil line on the chart for each course change, keeping an eye on the charted reefs to starboard.

"Helmsman," Mallinson ordered. "Come left five more degrees."

"Left five degrees, aye!" A half minute later a shell passed the bridge a hundred feet to starboard.

"Helmsman," Mallinson ordered calmly, "come right ten degrees."

"Right ten degrees, aye!" repeated the helmsman. The first silently marvelled at how coolly the captain gave his orders. A shell passed by, but far off to port. The Bofors fired a single clip.

"Helmsman," Mallinson ordered, "come left five degrees."

"Left five degrees, aye!" Then the sliver of moon was obscured by clouds, during which there was a lull in the firing. Each time this happened it was well and truly dark. Then the shells seemed to come every twenty or thirty seconds, and the captain continued to order seemingly random minor course changes, and for differing lengths of time. A shell passed through the compass platform above, and a shower of broken glass and wood splinters rained down on the number one hatch below. *Blast! I hope they didn't damage my wicker chair. I like that chair.* His first mate was looking at his watch, taking an interest.

"What is it you notice, Mr Wallace?"

"Rate of fire seems slow, sir."

"It is. They should be doing five rounds a minute or better, but it's dark, there's hardly any moon, and they're on a moving platform. And most importantly, it seems to me they're inexperienced!"

"Aye, you're right," said the first, "as are we."

Mallinson nodded. A shell whipped past the hull and raised a geyser that splattered the bridge windows. The Bofors spoke once.

"Helmsman, come left ten degrees! Anything else you notice?"

"They fire, and then when we fire, you immediately order a change of course ."

"Excellent! This means with their next shot, they're—"

Wallace interrupted, "Firing at our muzzle flash where our ship had been!"

"They've been aiming for our bridge or the steering gear. I now believe their intention is not to sink us, but only to disable us."

Ten minutes and twenty-four Bofors clips later, the lookout phone rang again. The first answered. Covering the mouthpiece, he said, "Lookout reports sub gaining on us, little over a mile distant now, but they haven't hit it yet."

Before Mallinson could give any order, or even blink, a shell came screaming overhead, followed by a deep boom rolling from shorewards. A geyser, grey in the thin moonlight, erupted a mile off the port quarter. Ten seconds later, another geyser at a mile and a half, and another report from shorewards.

The first listened. "Lookout reports it's going down, sir." A third shell whined overhead.

"That's a shore battery," Mallinson said. "From the sound of it, I could swear it's a six-inch. Quick-firing, too!"

The first shook his head. "I was here eighteen months ago. Batavia has no shore batteries. Both Fort Onrust and Fort Kasteel were demolished decades ago."

"Cease fire!" the captain ordered, and the first repeated it, then hung up. Gene appeared on the bridge, holding a flimsy, headphones resting about his neck. He gave the captain a rather perfunctory salute, which caught Mallinson's attention because it was so unusual for him to do so.

"Yes?" asked the captain, "Have you a message?"

"Nossir. I want you to know I sent this out, voice transmission," He read aloud: "Merchant ship inbound Batavia chased by submarine. Request immediate assistance."

"Well done, Eugene!" he said, impressed by the boy's initiative.

"This still doesn't answer who is firing," said the first.

"We'll find out when we arrive." Not until later, when they met a Smit Company diesel tug outbound to assist them into Tanjung Priok harbour, did the captain order, "Stand down action stations."

* * *

Sunday morning revealed them moored alongside, in the third inner basin a little astern of the auxiliary seaplane tender MV *Poolster*. The captain dressed in his dress blue uniform and, donning his Ellerman cap, went to inspect the damage. It wasn't too bad. The wooden cap of the rail on the after side of the bridge wing had been blown away, and there were pieces of it scattered across the deck. The riveted iron wall beneath, coated with thick layers of white paint, had a minor bulge at its top and a ragged split, but the rest appeared structurally intact. He asked the ship's carpenter to replace the cap, and also selected a certain piece of wood to save for him, as a memento of their escape. As the two of them stood discussing the repair, Mallinson sensed someone standing to his right. He turned to find a seaman staring at the damage. The man met his gaze and said, "Thank you, sir."

"Sorry?" Mallinson said, "For what? Oh! You're ..."

"Aye, sir. The lookout." The man put out his hand, and Mallinson shook it.

"Don't let it get to you, Mr ... erm ... ah ..."

"Langston, sir. Able Seaman Langston."

"Yes, of course. Things like this happen in wartime, you know." The man nodded, and turned to go. Mallinson was left thinking: *and sometimes they happen outside of wartime too.*

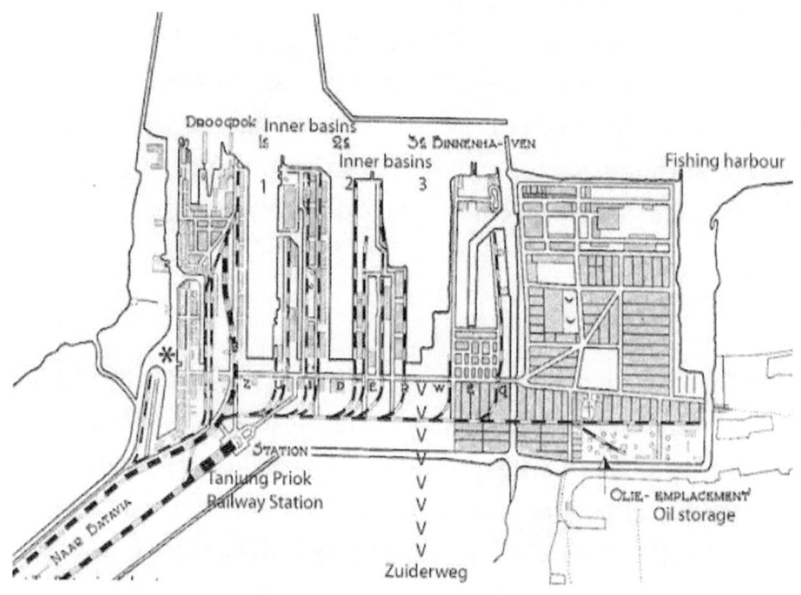

Tanjung Priok Harbour, Batavia, Java

He then led the carpenter topside, to review the damage to the compass platform. The shell had blasted a hole in the wooden bulkhead aft and gone out the front. Two windows were missing, together with the mullion between them. His favourite wicker chair and table were overturned from the blast but undamaged. The mate set a gang of ordinary seamen the task of cleaning the debris on the compass platform, the bridge and number one hatch. The captain and the bosun then went aft to inspect the damage there. One of the aeroplanes was missing its wingtip. They found a ragged shell hole through a bulwark, port side aft, but the ghastly realization was the same shell must have hit the corner of the Bofors's square shield first, as it had folded over. Mallinson set the third engineer the task of checking its alignment. They switched on their torches and descended below deck at the stern to inspect the steering flat, only to find the jagged hole in the ship's counter admitted enough light that they didn't need them. That shell had passed completely through the compartment and out the front, without touching the steam steering engine, as luck would have it. The bosun then ducked through the shell hole into the firemen and coal trimmers' quarters. Mallinson followed after, and found himself having to avoid a row of ducks hanging by their feet from a string overhead, and stepping around a pair of charcoal braziers, one holding a massive copper kettle in the centre of the compartment. This was new. Unlike the conduct on other British ships, Mallinson was perfectly happy to have the firemen and coal-trimmers eat in the crew's mess, but they still preferred doing things their own way. The serang conducted him through their quarters to the shell hole blasted in its forward bulkhead, in time for him to overhear a seaman standing outside remark to his fellow, "I fink this-here *shell hole* oughter be left, to clear the Chinese stink from this-here *hell hole*." The man laughed heartily until Mallinson put his head through the hole and glared, reminding him that without these Chinese this ship wasn't going anywhere. He told the bosun he would have this damage repaired, and gave him orders that this seaman be assigned the task of peeling potatoes for a fortnight in addition to his regular duties. As their inspection party stepped out through the forward hatch into the sunlight, the serang murmured to his fellows, no doubt translating what had been said.

They went forwards to the wardroom for breakfast. After his 'full English' breakfast, the captain used his binoculars to locate the KNIL cruiser HNLMS *De Ruyter* three-quarters of a mile away in the first inner basin. She was easy to spot, being much the largest warship in the harbour.

"I'm going over there," he told O'Malley, "and thank that gun crew personally for sinking that submarine last night. You know, I wouldn't be at all surprised if I find their turrets are directed by gun-laying radar!" He descended the accommodation ladder to the wharf. Since the walking distance to the cruiser was nearly three miles, he hailed a three-wheeled *becak*. The driver, who by his appearance was a Muslim, was a bit surly in his manner, until he discovered Mallinson wasn't Dutch, but British. All smiles then, he used a dirty towel to snap the dust off the seat. Raising the shade for him, he clambered on behind, and they were off.

The port seemed busy. They passed many godowns disgorging varied materials into waiting ships or lorries. When they reached the accommodation ladder of the Dutch cruiser, he instructed the driver to wait for him. Stepping onto the deck, he saluted the Dutch naval ensign at the stern. At the foretop above, a square red, white and blue tricolour flag with two six-pointed stars stood out in the fresh breeze. An armed warrant officer in the uniform of the Royal Netherlands Navy inquired what business he had there.

As he was explaining who he was, a man in an open-necked white shirt and blue serge trousers passed by, engrossed in reading a sheaf of papers that he was busy marking up with a pencil. Mallinson fancied he rather resembled the writer Noël Coward.

"Sir!" the warrant officer called, "This is the captain of yesterday's merchant ship, and he wishes to thank the gun crew for firing on the sub last night."

The man looked up briefly. "Oh, yes? Happy to help," he said, preoccupied with his task, but not stopping.

"Thank you for sinking it, captain!" Mallinson called out after him. Still deep in thought, the man stepped over the coaming of an open doorway and was gone.

"Sir, that wasn't our captain. That's Rear Admiral Karel Doorman. This is his flagship." Mallinson reddened. *Of course, that's his admiral's pennant at the foretop.* The warrant officer gave him instructions as to how to locate the gun crew below, but continued, "We fired on that sub last night, but we didn't sink it."

Brilliant, Mallinson thought, *that means it may be waiting out there, or it may be gone, we'll never know for certain.*

Before he left the HNLMS *De Ruyter*, Mallinson visited the engine room, where he found one of the engineers on watch. He asked if the man knew a company in Batavia where he could have some essential foundry work done. The man recommended *Jawa Gieterij en Machinefabriek* near the *Koningsplein Park* and provided him with the address. Mallinson thanked him and returned to the waiting *becak*, where the driver crushed his cigarette and pedalled him back to his ship. On the way, he stopped at the harbourmaster's office to gain permission to temporarily discharge a portion of their cargo here, and to arrange for shipyard crews to attend to their condenser, and also to weld patches over the shell–hole damage.

As prearranged, the second engineer met the captain in his cabin on Monday at 1000 hours. The captain had retrieved a bundle of cash from the ship's safe, and was thumbing shells into his Webley. Mr Sinclair was given a green canvas rucksack containing one gold bar and an amount half again as much of raw lead nodules. Mallinson checked the engineer had remembered to bring his personal pistol, an automatic of American manufacture and rather more modern than the captain's

Great War-issue Webley. Like the captain, he carried it in a shoulder holster under his coat. They descended to the wharf and walked south.

Batavia was not outside the port. It was, instead, eight miles to the west and the foundry was a further three miles south of that. They boarded a local train at the Tanjung Priok Station. At the centre of the Old Town they disembarked and crossed the street to De Javasche Bank to exchange their Singapore 'Straits' dollars for Netherlands Indies gulden. They walked a few hundred yards north past the courthouse and city hall to the British Consulate, where they sent a cable to Ellerman in London telling them where they were, and why, and describing Saturday's events. Retracing their steps, they boarded a tram and rode it south to the third stop past the city's Chinese Quarter. When the captain and the second engineer alighted from the tram at the enormous Koningsplein Park, Sinclair was startled to see a platoon of German soldiers in the park engaged in parade manoeuvres drill. The captain explained their 'coal scuttle' helmets meant they were LBD – the *Luchtbeschermingsdienst* – the City's anti-aircraft gunners. "They're Dutch," he assured him. A half dozen anti-aircraft howitzers were hidden beneath the trees. Imposing government buildings were clustered within the district west of the park. They left the park walking east. Entering a side street lined with sizeable buildings sided and roofed with corrugated iron, they easily found the machine shop within a few streets.

The foreman, a stocky, balding man with bulging eyes and a three-day stubble, wore overalls without a shirt. He spoke passable English but they were unable to determine his original nationality. He was glad enough to receive them once he understood they had a job for him. The foreman ordered tea be brought at once. They all repaired to the foundry's office as an overhead gantry crane slowly trundled away from them, carrying a colossal propeller to the other end of the huge room. Showers of luminous yellow sparks cascaded across the shop floor, as an electric grinder howled until the door was shut. They sipped their tea and, after exchanging some pleasantries, got down to business. The second engineer produced from the rucksack a quantity of loose lead nodules. After examination, they established the firm could indeed melt it and pour it to form a peculiar shape of ingot. Could they perhaps show the officers a demonstration of their skills? "Yes." Perhaps today? "Indeed!" The questions left unanswered were: how many ingots, and could they pick up the loose lead at the dock, and deliver the cast ingots covered by tarpaulins to the same, on wooden pallets ready to be lifted aboard? The foreman left the room for a minute. When he returned, the answer was "Yes," but then asked of them, in what particular shape? Here the captain rose and stood against the closed door to the shop floor. Unbuttoning his jacket, he nodded to the second engineer. Sinclair lifted out the bar of gold and dropped it heavily upon the table. It gleamed even in the dull light from the filthy skylight. The foreman gasped and his eyes bulged even more, if that were possible. Mallinson pulled his jacket aside to briefly reveal his Webley still in its shoulder holster. Then the foreman did something entirely unexpected: he laughed. Placing his finger to the side of his nose, he nodded at them and laughed again.

"I see what you do. You make the fake gold bars to deceive! Of course, you wish the *Politie* not to learn of this. I understand completely," he said, holding his hands up, palm outwards. Sinclair smirked. Mallinson buttoned his jacket. *He's assuming we're criminals. Well, let him think that.*

"Can you cast an exact copy of this bar? If the quality is good, there will be many more coming afterwards."

The foreman nodded, "But payment in advance," he insisted. The captain had anticipated this, even knowing the price was slightly more than he had been told was usual for this type of work, and a firm price was agreed. The man then shouted into the shop floor, "Lunch!"

and his workers downed tools and made for the exits. Mallinson had one more request to make of the foreman; could he perhaps gold-electroplate the finished ingots? He caught sight of the engineer standing behind the foreman and shaking his head while drawing a finger across his throat.

It took less than thirty minutes to pound a bit of fine-grained oiled sand into a shallow box and press the upturned bar into it, while the lead nodules melted in a cast-iron handheld crucible. Carefully the foreman lifted out the gold bar, and Sinclair replaced it in his rucksack. The foreman put on a leather apron while admonishing them to stand well back and not breathe in the deadly fumes. They both retreated to stand in the alley, watching through the open garage door as the foreman, wearing a canister gas mask, skimmed the dross off the molten lead.

Mallinson asked the engineer about his reaction to his request for electroplating? After all, they had plenty of gold, and the mission was so important that a little bit missing could easily be explained away.

"It's quite possible this machine shop will be unable to get the very dangerous materials necessary to gold-electroplate," Sinclair replied. "I mean a mixture of nitric acid and hydrochloric acid, or they might even use cyanide. Gold will dissolve in mercury but, again, very expensive and very dangerous, and probably unobtainable here."

The foreman poured the lead into the cavity. He came out to the alley and said they could return in an hour to handle the result, but before they left the man proudly showed of his largest crucible hanging from an overhead gantry. With a bit of time to kill, they found a nearby café and ate a lunch of *semur daging*, beef stew with rice. Walking away from the café the captain spied a temple of some sort. Before the second could restrain him, he dashed up the steps and burst inside. Sinclair trudged up the steps after him and entered to find a man in a turban addressing the captain.

"This is a Sikh gurdwara, *sahib*. I am the *ragi* here in this temple.

How may I help you?"

"The front of your building is all covered in gold!"

The man was perplexed and answered slowly, "Yes?"

"It's beautiful! Do you have any gold paint? I am in need of some."

Understanding now, the man's face brightened. "Ah! I see! Yes, thank you, it is most beautiful, *sahib*, but it is not paint. Our volunteers make it so with gold leaf."

"Oh." The second had him by the elbow and was tugging gently. Mallinson began to realise how he must appear to this stranger. The *ragi* spoke again, addressing them both.

"Are you hungry, *sahibs*? Our langar hall is serving food at this very moment, and all are welcome to partake. It is all free, there is no obligation. We serve all peoples."

"Thank you kindly for the offer, but we have only just had lunch," the engineer said. As they descended the steps of the temple, he casually remarked, "Gold leaf won't do, sir, you see—"

"Yes, yes, I know," Mallinson replied irritably. "Too much surface area, too much labour, and not enough time, eh?" He scowled at how stupid he had been. Sinclair assured the captain he would spend some time thinking on the problem and try to come up with some sort of answer. Returning to the foundry, they discovered the marks on the still warm ingot were legible enough. Ever suspicious, the foreman checked to make sure the notes handed him were the new issue, issued the previous year, showing *wayang* dancers – the Dutch Government had done this to appease the Indonesian nationalists, with their growing calls for independence; one couldn't be too careful, he said, what with the state of the economy these days. Arrangements were agreed to deliver a quantity of lead to the foundry's lorry at dockside the following day. They returned to the ship.

The next day at the end of the morning watch a shipyard lorry arrived with a crew to carry out the repairs to the condenser. The chief engineer and the first mate were off duty now, and Mallinson met them both in the wardroom. While they ate, Hamish reported fully one-third of all the tubes, more than a hundred of them, needed replacement, as the bad ones had been 'temporarily' plugged for years. This would take ten days, or longer. Mallinson was sick at heart, but tried his best not to show it. *We have been on this mission nearly two weeks, and repairs might take another fortnight, and we still have 1,800 miles to go to Australia, not to mention the 11,000 miles to get home to England after that. Blast!*

He asked the first to have a crew ready to offload some of the lead cargo into a lorry that would be arriving later that day. This would require two of the aeroplanes to be shifted to the wharf to gain access to hold number two. Hamish assured them there would be steam up in the donkey boiler for the winches. They stood to go. As they left the wardroom, Sparks stopped the captain and asked for permission to leave the ship to buy a microphone in the city. Halfway through the forenoon watch, two aeroplanes had been off-loaded to the wharf, and the number two hatch had been opened. An hour before noon a ten-ton Leyland Hippo three-way tipper lorry arrived – on its door a faded logo from some Australian company. Mallinson was astonished such a relic was still on the roads. So old it had solid rubber tyres! It looked beaten to death.

They set to work. Mallinson insisted his crew wear goggles and bandanna to cover their faces against the lead dust. His deck crew had rigged a clamshell bucket to the number six derrick with a trip line, and this was used to transfer the raw lead to the lorry. When the nodules were a foot deep, the weight limit of the lorry was reached. It departed and two hours later was back for another load. This continued for the rest of the day, and all of Wednesday and Thursday. Mallinson was worn out. *The foundry will need maybe two weeks to complete and deliver the work, and of course the condenser is being worked on at the same time. I need a rest. We all do. It could be the stress of encountering that sub is getting to me. Hell, everything since my visit to the Istana is getting to me. No, it isn't that, it's everything since leaving England. I should have stayed retired.*

The end of Thursday saw the last lorryload of lead depart the dock. The deck crew heaved the hatch boards of number two hold into place and hammered the wedges in tight. A gang of deck crewmen struggled to drag a tarpaulin over its hatch boards, and they stretched it tight and laced it down all around its perimeter. The captain's attention was drawn by Gene who had appeared on the bridge. The boy began stringing wires around the perimeter of the bridge to connect with new wires protruding up through the deck. He held up a metal box containing a toggle switch.

"Where do you want this mounted?" he asked, and Mallinson showed him. He screwed it to the forward bulkhead below the window and left. He returned in a few minutes with a microphone, which he handed to the captain. It was round, made of copper, mounted on an oak handle, and heavy. A flex of twisted cord covered in green fabric hung from it.

"Isn't it a beaut? I have it wired to speakers on the bridge top, facing forwards, facing aft, and in the wardroom and crew's mess! If you want to say anything, ya just flip this-here switch and speak," said Gene, as he plugged its jack into the box. Mallinson looked out the bridge windows at half a dozen deck crew in the forward well deck, beavering away at chipping paint off the bulwarks.

"Is it ready?"

"Sure! Go ahead!" He toggled the switch, and hesitated. *Oh, yes, it's October thirtieth, isn't it?* He cleared his throat and could hear it outside the open bridge.

"This is your ... erm ... the captain speaking." Gene reached up and repositioned the microphone a foot away from his face. "Ahh, ... since tomorrow is All Hallows Eve, and Saturday is All Saints' Day, I will," – he coughed – "I will be issuing your pay a day early. The crew will queue at the crew's mess beginning tonight at twenty-hundred hours ..." There was scattered applause from outside. He continued, "... and at noon on Friday, I will be granting shore leave until twenty-two-hundred hours on Tuesday, and ... " – whistling and cheering erupted throughout the *Dominion Empress* – "... you may find it wise to visit a bank tomorrow for the local currency." Mallinson hoped that last bit hadn't been drowned out. He toggled the switch off and handed the microphone to Gene, who hung it from a hook installed near the switch. "I have to say that works just fine," he said. "Well done, you." Gene grinned, happy to have done something right.

The queue snaked from the mess door, down the corridor, out on deck and around the bridge house. The captain sat at a table guarding the cash box, with his first mate at his side acting as the paybob. As the third mate controlling the door admitted each man, the captain had the man countersign the paybook and the first mate counted out his pay in pounds sterling. Each man then left the mess by the opposite door, and the next man was admitted. On the face of it, this was to prevent rows breaking out over the settling of gambling debts. Since a man who owed always had to queue before the one who collected, it didn't always work out. The captain reminded each man to visit a bank tomorrow to get gulden, or they might find they would be going nowhere until next week. He also reminded each man that he wanted them back onboard the *Dominion Empress* no later than 2200 hours on Tuesday, the fourth of November. Mallinson sighed. *The last thing I need is drunk sailors loose on Guy Fawkes Night attempting to build bonfires. That is, if any of them have any money left.*

A few minutes before the end of the forenoon watch on Friday, the captain stood on the bridge with third mate O'Malley. They watched the first mate and the bosun standing together at the head of the accommodation ladder below, trying to keep the horseplay under control in the hugger-mugger crowd of hands. Some wore khakis and some were in dungarees. A number of the latter even sported Aloha shirts. Those with hats wore flat caps, or fedoras jauntily tilted to attract the eye of the ladies, and one older gentleman even wore a bowler. A group of Chinese sat off to one side waiting patiently. On the wharf a gaggle of rickshaws and *becak* pedicabs waited with equal patience. There were even a few covered two-wheeled carts, each with a single mangy donkey. Their ears waggled as they shook their heads to drive off the flies.

"Who's on watch in the engine room?" Mallinson asked the third.

"I t'ink the second engineer is overseein' the work, sor."

"You have a skeleton crew assigned?"

"Aye, the first does; Chinese fer the most part, to be sure. They're to be relieved on Tuesday night when this group returns."

"Yes," Mallinson mused aloud, "won't we all be relieved when this group returns." He picked up the microphone and toggled the switch. "Remember, you are crewmen of the *Dominion Empress* but more importantly, in this foreign nation, you are representing His Majesty the King! I do not want to hear any reports of theft or vandalism, or there'll be hell to pay!" Someone on the deck below blew a raspberry. Someone else yelled "Bert! Archie!" Another man bellowed "Geordie! Join us!"

Mallinson sighed. The ship's clock struck the afternoon watch, and he said, "Have fun!" There was a general stampede and a scramble for seats, and the carts clopped off down the wharf amid a ringing of bicycle bells. The Chinese followed behind on foot at a leisurely pace. He switched off the microphone, and hung it on its hook. "Have you any plans, Mr O'Malley?" the captain asked.

"Only sweet fanny adams, sor. What do ye intend to do?"

"I don't know. I want to get away from the *Empress* for a time, mostly. Play it by ear, I suppose. What I really need is a rest. Get out of this bloody hot city, maybe find a small hotel in the countryside, eh?"

"Sure. See ye Tuesday, sor."

5

Departures

As before, Mallinson took a train into Batavia. He wore his civvies again, a herringbone Harris Tweed jacket with a matching flat cap, but this time he carried a grip with toiletries, a change of clothes, and his old Royal Navy dress whites and peaked cap in case the opportunity of a formal occasion occurred, wherever he happened to end up. His first destination was the British Consulate where he asked the desk clerk, a blond lad busy filling in a ledger, for advice on where to get away for a few days.

"What is it you want to do?" the clerk asked of him, without looking up from his task.

"I don't want to 'do' anything, but was thinking of a quiet hotel in an out-of-the-way village," Mallinson replied. The lad looked Mallinson over.

"An 'out-of-the-way village', as you put it, on Java you might find a bit boring," he said, and hazarded a guess.

"I'm going to say ... British Navy? Are you driving?"

"Yes, and no. Now I think of it, getting away from this insufferable heat would be nice." At this, the clerk brightened with the kernel of an idea. He disappeared and returned a moment later with a pamphlet.

"There you go: Bandung, on the Cikapundung River. At night it can get down to 66 degrees. They call it the Paris of Java." On the face of the brochure, the photograph showed a stylish woman in furs emerging from a parked limousine, a model from a decade earlier. In the background was her destination, the Hotel Homann, modelled after a Swiss chalet. Next door to this was a shop with a sign over its door: '*Glacier*' – 'ice-cream shop' in French.

"Thank you, m'lad, this will do nicely," he said, pleased that the young desk clerk had so intuitively understood his needs. He walked the few streets to the railway station and bought a ticket. He boarded the train and settled into a first-class compartment, after placing his luggage in the overhead rack. As the train jerked away, he reread the pamphlet; a hundred and eighty kilometres south-east by rail. On a plateau at an elevation of 768 meters. Surrounded by high mountains. To its north, intensive rice, fruit, tea, tobacco and coffee plantations. The view out the carriage window as it climbed was of mile after mile of rice paddies. Lines of women clad in blue dresses tucked into their belts stooped, shoulder to shoulder and ankle-deep in water, planting handfuls of grasses. The paddies then gave way to terraced plantations of tea. Six hours later, the locomotive huffing mightily on the steep stretches, and after halts in Buitenzorg and Soekaboemi, he arrived in Bandoeng, or Bandung, as English-speakers spelled it.

It was sunset, and the streetlamps were lit. He hailed a cab. This was definitely not a village. The look of the place was very cheerful. He then realised it was that way because of the proliferation of colourful neon signs. The driver easily located the hotel, which was well known. It did not look at all as pictured on the brochure; having been rebuilt in 1939, it was now a streamlined Art Deco. He ate his supper in the hotel restaurant and afterwards took a stroll through nearby Alun-Alun Kota Park. That clerk had been spot on: the evening was positively chilly. He slept that night more restfully than he had in a long time.

Early on Saturday, he woke to hear birdsong outside the open window, the slight breeze still cool from the night. The hotel had left him a *Java Bode* newspaper at his door. Dressed in his civilian kit again, he took his newspaper and went down to breakfast. The waiter confirmed his suspicions on the discrepancy in the brochure: the owner and his wife were indeed Swiss and had been hoteliers for many decades. The buttered toast and coffee were delicious. The jam pot was labelled *Himbeer* and turned out to be raspberry. His smoked kippers came prepared in the German manner with a dill cream sauce, fortunately served on the side, so he was able to ignore it. Tucking his paper under his arm, he went out to see what sights there were.

The city had a sophistication he hadn't expected. The colonial influences he did expect, but many Art Deco buildings had been introduced into streets of otherwise Neoclassical and even Gothic architecture – all influences imported from Europe. He strolled north on Braga Street and was amused to see the streetlamps in the daytime, each one topped by a cast-iron leaping tiger. This image was everywhere and seemed to be a symbol of this city. He turned left on Suniaraja Street, and left again on Banceuy Street. He had not walked for long before his gout started playing up again. Soon he recognised the park of the evening before. Grateful to get away from the ever-present crowded pavements and give his aching foot a rest, he settled on a white painted cast-iron bench under a shade tree. Uncapping his pen, he began to do the crossword puzzle, but soon moved on because many of the words were foreign to him.

There was, of course, the war news, but this he skipped over, not wanting to be reminded. There were the worker's strikes in Australia, and a photograph showed marchers carrying banners reading, '8 hours a day, for 8 hours' pay, 8 bob a day'. He reflected on how lucky he was, getting the repairs done in a nation where the labour rates were so much less. There were the usual announcements, which seemed to appear in every newspaper around the world, for Women's Clubs, a flower show, bingo and church events, and recipes. There were many advertisements for new fashions, for grocers and department stores, but he was looking for local events or tours. As for these, there was a tobacco plantation tour. *Don't need to see that.* He saw there was a thrice-daily bus to the tea and coffee plantations that left from his own hotel, as it happened. *That might be interesting to see, how coffee is produced. I'll do that, then.*

He folded the paper back on itself so the article was uppermost, and circled it. The day was getting hotter. *It must be up to the high seventies.* He stood and took off his tweed jacket, folding it over the back of the bench. He loosened his tie and rolled up his shirt sleeves. There was an advert for a cinema near the park showing a film, *Moon Over Burma*, produced in Hollywood. He had seen it some months before in South Africa. Rather forgettable, despite the presence of Dorothy Lamour.

There was a dance featuring a ten-piece orchestra the next night at the Officers' Club at the aerodrome west of the city. This caught his eye because he knew this particular Netherlands Air Force Base also hosted a contingent of the RAF. *I could do with some music and a drink or two.* He circled that too. He capped the pen and put it in his pocket.

Intending to leave, he folded his jacket over his arm and picked up the newspaper from the bench. A little girl squealed, and he looked around. Two young women, not little girls, had burst into the park at the opening in the hedge not fifty feet away, one chasing after the other. The first, her arms flailing, was twisting just out of the others reach. When they spotted him, they hauled around to a new heading and set a course straight toward him. They slammed onto the bench giggling hysterically, the redhead next to him, the blonde on the other side of her. *It's a good thing this bench is bolted down*, he thought. They were dressed identically in off-white knee-length, short-sleeved, belted dresses with buttons up the front, and wide-brimmed hats set at a rakish angle. They wore the white service Oxfords typical of nurses.

"Whooo!" said the nearest one, out of breath. She looked him over briefly. "Whatcha got there, pops?" She snatched up his paper.

"See here, young lady, let me have that back at once!" he commanded, reaching for it. She held it high above her head.

"Crikey, don't getcha knickers in a knot, mate. This here's Nancy, but you can call her Nants, and I'm Rebecca, but you can call me Becky. Whatcha readin' here? Coffee plantations? I love coffee! Wish we could afford a tour. Oh! Lookit here, Nants! The Bijou is showing *Moon Over Burma*! It has Dorothy Lamour in it! And Robert Preston! Dontcha think Robert Preston is so dreamy? We should see it! Ya wanna see it? Let's go tonight!" Nancy leaned in to see the paper. She didn't answer, so Becky turned to Mallinson. "You wanna see it?" *Like listening to a typhoon*, he thought.

"I saw it weeks ago in South Africa, and it wasn't at all good. Now—"

Becky's eyes lit up. She turned to the blonde. "Afrikur! Didja hear that, Nants? Afrikur!" He lifted the paper from her while she was distracted.

"Young lady, I am here on holiday," he said, stabbing the paper with his forefinger for emphasis, "and am just attempting to find something to do, so if you—" Becky's eyes followed his finger, where she saw the aerodrome dance circled.

"Yeah, ya been ta Afrikur. What are ya, some sorta pilot?"

"No, miss, I'm" – *Can't say "Royal Navy" as that isn't strictly true anymore* –"a sea captain," he finished, lamely. *Should have said "merchant mariner" even if they might not be familiar with that term.* Up to this point a whirlwind of chaos, all of a sudden she was quiet. She seized his arm so hard it hurt. She leaned toward him and her eyes were bright.

"A sea captain? Ya have a ship? Here?"

"Yes, miss, I am master of the steamship *Dominion Empress*, out of

London for Fremantle." *Aargh! Shouldn't have said Fremantle; 'Loose Lips Sink Ships' and all that.* He prised her fingers from his arm, and she released her grip. She shot a look at Nancy, who gave her a nod of encouragement. She turned back to him, her mouth opening as if she was on the verge of saying something, then shutting again. Her eyes searched his face and settled on his eyes. She seemed somehow older than before. Her breathing quickened. She opened her mouth again, shut it and froze, seemingly uncertain of what she wanted to say, her gaze never leaving his. *This is most unusual. I noticed when I reached the age of forty or so, women younger than myself stopped talking to me, actually stopped noticing me at all, as if I wasn't really there. Now, here is a young lady who is seriously intent on me. Most unusual, indeed.* His attention flickered to Nancy, who gave her shoulder a nudge. This seemed to break a spell. Becky dropped her eyes to the paper in his lap.

"Ya goin' ta that dance?" she asked.

"I was thinking about it, yes."

"I'll go with you," she said, deadly serious, "because we need to talk."

Good God, kids these days! "Miss, I really don't —"

"I'm going with you!" she repeated forcefully. "We got things to discuss!" Plucking the paper from his hand she read aloud, "Sunday, 7 p.m. No cover charge. Open to the public. Ladies must have escort. See?" she said, "Ya gonna be my escort! We're dancin'."

"I—"

"Look, pops, we're goin' and that's that! What's yer name?"

"Captain Mallinson"

"Yer *name!*"

"Roy Mallinson."

"Where ya stayin', Roy Mallinson?"

"The Hotel Homann."

A portly man in a plaid flat cap appeared in the opening of the hedge and began walking towards them. He wore braces and a flannel shirt. He had mutton-chop whiskers and a double chin.

"There you are. Let's go, girls!" he shouted. He clapped his hands.

"See ya at six sharp tomorrah, Roy!" The seriousness evaporated. They were girls again. She slapped the paper down on his lap, and they jumped up and darted away. Mallinson objected weakly.

"I hardly think any father would allow his daughter to—"

"Daughter!" Nancy exclaimed. "We ain't no *daughters*. We're nursing sisters!" Becky turned around to face him and, bending over, cupped a hand under a boob and jiggled it at Roy.

"Nursing sisters!" she repeated.

"You're incorrigible!" Nancy shrieked, and slapped Becky on the bum. They turned and ran away. Roy's mouth hung open; the stunned look on his face made Becky turn back round again.

"Crikey, it's fuckin' 1941, Roy. It ain't 1910, ya know. Lighten up, woodja?"

Mallinson spent the next few hours riding in an orange and silver late-model Chevrolet bus that took a dozen tourists to a tea plantation first and a coffee plantation after that. He visited their museums and saw the coffee roasting machines demonstrated. The coffee samples were aromatic and delicious. He was back in the city by early afternoon. He stopped by the hotel to change into lighter clothing, then went in search of a late lunch. He found it in a Dutch bistro by the river. A deck under an awning overhung the water and it seemed slightly cooler in this location than in the rest of the city. *At least I'm not roasting in Batavia.* Looking over what was on offer in the *spijskaart* he saw *bitterballen* with mustard, *erwtensoep*, Dutch beefsteak, *poffertjes* and *pannenkoek*. He chose the veal *bitterballen* and a half litre of *witbier*. Now that he was seated at a table and waiting for his meal, he had time to think. *This is my holiday. I don't want it stolen from me. I'm really looking forward to listening to a live band, being around military people for an evening, perhaps chancing upon someone I know, but now ... I don't want to not go. How can I go now and refuse to take her? That would be most unkind.* The food arrived. As he ate, he continued to ponder what to do. *What does she have to discuss that's so important ... important to her at any rate? I let slip we're going to Australia, and she's obviously Australian, so maybe she wants a passage home? Or maybe she wants to have an evening of music and dancing, and I happen to be a convenient companion?* For pudding he asked for *poffertjes* and, when it came, it was sprinkled with icing sugar and served with a demitasse of custard-like advocaat on the side. This Dutch liqueur he had never tasted before, but found that he liked it. He decided to put his problem with this Becky out of his mind and not think about it today. They would have a discussion and clear the air before they went anywhere tomorrow. Yes, that was it. The remainder of his day passed uneventfully. He visited a small museum and the zoological gardens. He arrived back at his hotel after dark, actually quite tired from his exertions all day, the gout in his foot troubling him. *I must have walked miles today. I'm not a young man any more. I shouldn't be doing all this.* He fell asleep on the couch, only moving to the bed after midnight.

On Sunday morning he awoke rather hungry, then remembered he had forgotten to eat supper the night before. Again, there was birdsong outside the open window, and again the breeze was still cool from the night. *I could get used to this.*

After breakfast he visited the city's botanical gardens. In the afternoon he took in a film, for the sole reason it was at an air-conditioned cinema. It was a new British comedy titled *Sailors Don't Care* featuring the actress Jean Gillie, who he remembered from her earlier film, *This'll Make You Whistle.* Strangely enough, after leaving the cinema, he couldn't remember much of the plot. As the day wore on he found, almost with something of a shock, that he was anticipating seeing her this evening. *Don't be a fool. She's young enough to be a daughter. It's only dancing and talk,* he told himself. He returned to the hotel for a nap. In late afternoon, after eating his supper at the same bistro as before, he carefully trimmed his grey beard and moustache. He had not brought his Merchant Navy dress blues, and anyway, this occasion called for something more impressive. Before he left Batavia, he'd had the ship's laundry wallah clean his old Royal Navy uniform, and he had it with him now. Donning his tropical dress whites, he inspected himself in the mirror: short-sleeved tunic with black-and-gold captain's epaulettes, white belt, shorts and knee stockings, white leather shoes. White peaked cap with scrambled egg and the Ellerman Lines cap badge. *Something did not look quite right.* He retrieved his Distinguished Service Cross from its case in his leather grip and pinned it in place. *There.* He combed his hair and beard once more. Descending in the lift, his cap under his arm, he emerged into the foyer precisely at six to find Becky and Nancy waiting. Nancy was wearing the same outfit as the day before, but Becky wore a sarong. They didn't see him at first, but then Nancy caught sight of him as he approached.

"Blimey! Have a 'Captain Cook' at *this* bloke, Beckers," she said.

"Don't you clean up nice!" said Becky.

"You look lovely, my dear," Mallinson said. He meant it, too, but she actually looked more than lovely. She wore a red hibiscus print sarong, the hem ending at mid-thigh. It left her shoulders bare and was almost backless. Evidently she wasn't wearing a brassiere, yet it appeared, as far as support was concerned, she didn't require any extra. On her feet were red peep-toe sling-backs. Even wearing these low heels, she was almost as tall as Roy. Her legs were tanned and muscular. With the exception of a few delicate wisps artfully arranged, her red hair coiffed atop her head exposed pearl earrings and a short string of pearls at her neck. She wore no lipstick, actually no make-up at all, that he could detect.

"Well, everything you see is borrowed for the occasion," she explained, slightly embarrassed. Mallinson saw the sarong had no pockets.

"Have you no purse?" he asked.

"No need for a purse, we're skint!" She shrugged. "No worries, mate, she'll be right. That reminds me, can you carry this for me, please?" She fished her identity papers from her cleavage where they had been secreted and held them out. Roy slipped it into his pocket. Nancy kissed Becky on the cheek, and whispered in her ear, to which the redhead giggled. Mallinson offered her his arm and Becky threaded hers though it. Nancy stood back and regarded the pair of them.

"Wish I had a camera. Have fun, you two. See ya later!" As they left the hotel he found himself giving her a sidelong glance because, somehow, she looked familiar to him. And then he placed it: she looked just like the screen actress Myrna Loy! The doorman whistled up a taxicab from the rank, a GM-Holden. Roy helped her in and climbed in after her. It was a modest car, so here they sat shoulder to shoulder.

"Aerodrome," Mallinson said to the driver. "What did Nants say?" he asked her, as they started off.

"Nothing," she replied nonchalantly. "Only, you know what they say about a man in uniform." She slipped her arm though his and hugged it to her. He could feel the warmth of her breast as it pressed against his bare arm. *Stop it! Stop thinking that way!* They rode in silence for a moment until he thought of a question.

"You've not mentioned your family name. What is it?"

"Oh! Sorry. Becky McKenzie."

"Well, Miss McKenzie—"

"Becky!"

"Becky, ... that man yesterday, in the park, the one with the whiskers. Not your father?"

"Mr Woodley? God, no!"

"So, a chaperone then?"

"No ... Yes ... Well, not really. Our companion."

"Our?"

"Shh, let's not talk about that now." Then a moment later, "Roy, how old are you?"

"Nearly fifty-nine."

"What about me? What do you reckon?" She squeezed his arm. Mallinson caught the driver looking at them in the rear-view mirror and listening, so he slid the perspex partition shut. The man resumed watching the road. *The older I get, the less I'm able to know another's age. But, with women anyway, it's best to err on the low side.*

"Thirty-one?" he guessed.

"You're so funny! Twenty-four."

He shook his head. *She was an infant when I was made a captain. She was entering college the year I retired. There was no need to clear the air here, no need for any discussion.* He heaved a sigh; unfortunately, he had done it aloud.

"Roy?"

"Yes?"

"No worries, mate. I know what I'm doing. It's just dancing and talk, ya know?" She snuggled closer. Her perfume filled his nostrils. As he later learnt, it was Evening in Paris, a scent he would come to adore.

They alighted from the taxicab, and Mallinson paid the driver. As they walked arm in arm through the car park towards the Officers' Club, Becky hauled him up short.

"It's Meara," she whispered in his ear. He looked round, but there were no other women within view. A group of Aussie servicemen loitered at the foot of the stairs having a 'smoko'. He and Becky waited to allow a group of civilians to precede them, then ascended the stairs and entered the club, the captain removing his cap and tucking it under his arm. A Netherlands military policeman at the door automatically repeated to each person as they passed, "No smoking inside, please". An Australian MP, a truncheon hanging at his belt, looked them over as they passed, then spoke in low tones to his younger comrade.

They saw the room was filled with men in the uniforms of all services and from a half dozen nations. As for civilians, there were a few men, but overall women roughly equalled the number of men in the room. They mostly stood in groups chatting, drinks in hand, but on occasion their voices were raised to be heard. A man nearby guffawed at another man's remark. The orchestra was on stage but had not yet started playing. The stringed instruments were tuning up. A clarinet tootled melodically. The pianist tinkled lightly on his keyboard. A trombonist practised a bar or two from a number he was due to play. A mirror ball hung from the ceiling, producing moving flecks of light that dappled the walls and floor. Mallinson could see the unoccupied tables were beginning to fill up. He took Becky's waist and steered her though the crowd to a round table halfway back from the stage, yet also at the edge of the dance floor. A candle in a glass bowl threw a pool of light next to a diminutive pot of violets. A young couple placed their jacket and wrap on the chairs opposite, nodded at him, and disappeared in the direction of the bar. He placed his cap on the table and held her chair for her, but remained standing.

"What would you like to drink?" he asked.

"Oh! Ah ..." She grinned. "A Singapore Sling, please." The captain approached the bar and waited while the servicemen ahead of him were served. He noticed the women in the room were dressed conservatively in skirts that covered the knee, and wore conservative shoes, and many had expensive silk tights, with a seam up the back. *Officer's wives, no doubt.* He ordered the Sling and a Dewar's Scotch on the rocks for himself, and paid. When he arrived back at the table the Netherlands MP was standing over Becky, a stern look on his face.

"May I help you?" he asked of the man. He set the drinks down.

"Your papers, please."

"Your papers, please, *sir*," Mallinson stressed, straightening an epaulette with its captain's insignia – one that actually didn't need straightening at all.

"Your papers, please, sir," the MP repeated. Mallinson produced Becky's and his own and handed them over. The MP snatched them from his hand and opened them briskly in a practised manner.

"How is it you know this young woman?" He directed this at Mallinson while at the same time regarding Becky with his head tilted back in a show of disdain. Mallinson thought for a beat. *He must have noticed our age difference. Do I say she's my nurse? Is that believable?*

"I'm his daughter," Becky said.

"Your daughter. What is her middle name?"

The Aussie MP, who had been observing from a distance, now stepped up.

"Is there a problem here, Lukas?" Becky was looking increasingly upset.

"*Jah.* This woman claims—"

"Meara!" Mallinson blurted. "It's Meara."

The MP compared the documents. "So it is. Why is her family name McKenzie and yours is Mallinson?"

"That's my husband's name," Becky interjected.

The Aussie smirked. "You don't wear a ring, *miss.*"

"He's *dead*, you cretin," she said, in desperation.

"What exactly is the problem you are trying to solve?" Mallinson interrupted. He was suddenly back in a similar situation he'd found himself in some thirty-five years ago. He was aware of 'the problem' all too well. The still smirking Aussie MP continued to ignore him.

"Yer not pulling the wool over *my* eyes, Sheila," he said, "there are women of certain classes of employment that we don't—"

Becky was on her feet instantly, her chair clattering over backwards, her fists clenched.

"Oi, tell yer story walkin', yobbo!" she snarled.

"Don't get sharp with me, Bluey," he barked, resting a hand on the handcuffs at his belt. The couple on the other side of the table left their drinks and fled to the dance floor. A man in a white uniform stepped into the midst of the group and, setting his drink down, turned to Roy with a question.

"Excuse me, but have we not met before?" He slightly resembled Noël Coward. The Dutch MP snapped to attention. The Aussie MP assumed the 'parade rest' position. Mallinson was greatly relieved.

"Admiral Doorman! So nice to see you again, sir. Yes, we have met. You rescued my ship from that submarine a week ago yesterday. Captain Roy Mallinson of the Ellerman Lines *Dominion Empress*." They shook hands. Mallinson turned and took Becky's hand, leading her forwards, taking the opportunity along the way to gently brush aside the Australian. "You remember my daughter, sir? Rebecca Meara McKenzie." Admiral Doorman took her hand and, bowing, kissed it.

"Charmed, Miss McKenzie. I do remember you. One of such grace and beauty does honour to our little backwater of a port." Becky had the presence of mind to curtsy. The admiral released her hand, straightened and scanned the room. "Please, enjoy your drinks. I believe the orchestra may begin playing at any moment." Turning to the Dutch MP and collecting the identity papers from him, he said, "Dismissed!" The man saluted and fled. He turned to the Australian MP and, with a baleful glare and a hard edge to his voice, ordered, "Pick up that chair!" Returning their papers, the Admiral held the chair for

Becky as she resumed her seat. He ordered the MP, "Dismissed!" and, after he had gone, confided to them, "We've had trouble with that one before. He's army," as if that explained it. Bending low, he whispered in her ear and then, collecting his drink, he returned to his table. Roy sat.

"What did the Admiral say?" he asked, as Becky watched him walk away.

"He said, 'I suspect you're not his daughter, but that is of no consequence whatsoever. Enjoy your evening.' What a noble man," she sighed. The young couple returned while whispering to each other, and sat. On stage a man at a microphone began to speak.

"*Mijn Dames en heren, mesdames et messieurs, bapak–bapak dan Ibu–ibu*, ladies and gentlemen, allow me to introduce to you the —"

"Now, what is it you're so eager to discuss?" Mallinson inquired, and took a sip of his drink. The band began to play 'Moonglow'.

"Oh, not now. Let's dance!" She pulled him onto the floor for a slow dance. His arms encircled her waist, and her hands were upon his shoulders. She buried her face on his chest, and he saw her shoulders shake.

"Are you crying?" he asked.

She looked up at him. "No. Laughing!"

"Yobbo?"

"It means someone uncouth and obnoxious."

"Well, you nailed that."

"No. No, I didn't. I would have to say, *you* nailed that," she said. The orchestra segued into the next number, 'Cheek to Cheek'. The Indonesian vocalist, crooning in English, was especially talented. They foxtrotted to 'Moonlight Serenade', 'Stars Fell on Alabama', 'Begin the Beguine', 'The Continental' and '*Bei Mir Bist Du Schoen*', which brought much applause from the Dutch present. When the orchestra struck up The Carioca, Roy pleaded for relief, saying the tempo was much too fast for him, and wouldn't she like to dance with another? A short Royal Netherlands marine standing alone at the edge of the dance floor overheard him and found an opportunity to ask her. Roy watched them move about the floor, but perceived that whenever the marine's back was to him, Becky's eyes were over his shoulder and on Roy. With amusement he thought, *Does he resent, or even notice, that her attention is not on him?*

Becky and Roy danced and drank through three sets, until the place shut down at eleven. They laughed and chatted all evening, although never about anything of any substance. Roy told her of their voyage since Singapore, the arrival in port and the submarine chase, and the admiral and his flagship. Becky told him of her grandparents' modest sheep outstation in the outback, where she had grown up after her parents died. When the orchestra later began to play slower songs, such as 'Smoke Gets in Your Eyes', 'Try a Little Tenderness' and 'These Foolish Things Remind Me of You', they slow-danced or waltzed to them. The mixed drinks she asked for were ones he had never heard of before, with names like the 'Hanky Panky' and 'Between the Sheets'. He related for her how Stanley, his father, a respected locomotive driver for the Canadian Pacific Railway, never really understood why young Roy hadn't wanted to follow on and do the same, but Roy said he couldn't be constrained to a set of rails. Instead, he had worked aboard a series of CPR coastal steamships, and that had sealed his love of the sea forever. His old man had passed away thirteen years earlier, oddly enough in the same year and month her parents had died, rather tragically in her account, in a motor vehicle accident. Becky spoke of going to nursing school in Sydney, and told Roy details of the jobs she had done before that. Later that evening Becky asked him to describe Beryl, just out of curiosity. Rather than try, he pulled an old black-and-white photograph from his wallet. A sunny day, Beryl wearing a long-sleeved blouse buttoned to her throat, and a long skirt, perched side-saddle on a beach donkey, the famous Blackpool tower and pier visible to one side.

"Here she is a few years after we married."

"Is that red hair I see?"

"Why, yes it is."

"Same as me!" she giggled. As he tucked the picture away again, he sighed to himself: *it used to be red. Beryl has never liked displaying bare arms or anything more than a bare ankle in public. I can't recall the last time I saw her in a dress. These days she usually wears trousers. Why have I not noticed this before?*

The penultimate musical number was 'Let's Stop the Clock (And Make Believe This Night Of Love Will Never End),' and the singer endowed it with real, poignant sentiment, although, it must be said, she was no Helen Forrest. They left the club during the final song, so they would not be stranded and have to wait. They stumbled into one of the waiting cabs and gave the name of the hotel. Having had so much to drink, they both nodded off. They were awakened by the driver standing by the open door, rapping his knuckles on the roof and saying, "*Burra sahib,* your hotel, *burra sahib.*"

Becky got out and helped him out, where they stood a bit unsteadily, gripping the door. The night was chilly, and she shivered. Mallinson asked where the driver could take her.

"Take me? Nowhere. I'm going with you," she said. He didn't argue. He paid the driver, and they supported each other up to his room.

Phew, it's a good thing this place has a lift. He wasn't exactly 'half seas over', it was just that his normal limit of two cocktails had been exceeded by two or three more, and many of those had been doubles. And he'd had a beer, possibly two. He couldn't remember how much she'd had to drink. The lift attendant focused on his task and otherwise ignored them. He had no trouble at all in finding the keyhole.

In the room he opened the windows for the fresh air, and that helped.

He flopped heavily onto the bed on his back, fully clothed. Becky took off her heels, and placed her string of pearls and earrings on the bedside table. He shut his eyes because the slow ceiling fan was making the room spin. She sat and pulled his legs across her lap. She untied his shoelaces and pulled his shoes off. Next she peeled off his stockings. She unbuttoned his tunic and helped him remove that and the vest. She struggled to unbuckle his belt, as it was quite tight.

"You know I'm married," he said, evenly.

"Yeah."

"Do you have a husband?"

"No."

"So, when you told that MP, 'He's dead, you cretin,' you were lying?"

"Oh no, he's definitely a cretin." His belt unfastened, she worked his zip down and began to tug off his shorts.

"I can get the rest of this," he said, sitting up on the edge of the bed, "Which side do you want?"

"Far side. Unzip me?"

By rote habit he reached for the bedside table lamp and switched it off. She stood. He felt for the zip. The sarong dropped away. She stepped out of her knickers, then pulled a few Kirby grips and shook her wavy hair loose. She lay on the bed and threw her leg over his. They kissed. He had never felt as old as his fifty-eight years, and as tired as he was at this moment. Still, this didn't prevent him from becoming aroused.

"Crikey, Roy, woodja look at you!" she exclaimed appreciatively, taking him in her hand.

"I've seen it. Becky, I have to say ..."

"Wanna getcha leg over?" she interrupted.

"Becky, to tell the truth, I don't have a 'safety' with me." She burst out laughing and buried her face in the grey mat on his chest. Her feet drummed the bed.

"Safety!" she squeaked, "It's called a 'franger', Roy! Whew! Thank god you didn't say 'French letter' or I swear I wooda pissed myself!" He had to smile at how she was always so very forthright. A moment later she continued, "Ahhhh, yer right, we had a skinful, didn't we?" She rolled off him and they lay facing one another. Her foot traced a path down the back of his calf. Hooking her heel under his foot, she pulled his thigh up between her legs. She reached down and gently nestled him into the hollow next to her belly, and gave him a final affectionate caress.

"Becky, for all your insistence we talk, we never really did."

"Mmm–hmm," she responded. Her breathing slowed and became regular against him. Soon, with her head on his chest, the sound of his heartbeat lulled her to sleep. He looked up to the ceiling in the darkness. *Beryl and I have not been intimate in more than three decades. We sleep in separate rooms. On the rare occasions we do sleep in the same bed, she won't allow me to touch her. It's almost as if we've become flatmates.* As she lay enfolded in his arms, her body yielding soft and warm against his, he buried his nose in her hair. The scent of her perfume lingered. He slept rather well.

He was standing on the bow of the ship for a reason he could not remember. There was splashing. He looked down over the rail, expecting to see a 'bone in her teeth', but the massive chain hung there, straight down from its hawse pipe into an ocean like glass. He opened his eyes then shut them again because the room was much too bright. He was having a dream but, curiously, the splashing continued. Carefully, he opened his eyes and looked up to the ceiling fan, which wasn't turning but then, thankfully, neither was the room. A nagging pain behind his eyes told him he may have had too much to drink. The splashing let him know that Becky was luxuriating in the bath. He prised himself painfully out of bed and gave his head a shake and at once regretted doing this. The splashing ended, and there was silence. He shut the curtains and then dressed, very slowly, in his tweeds. He took his Navy uniform that was folded over the chair, and hung it in the closet. Becky asked for her sarong, and he held the door ajar and passed it to her. When she emerged a towel wrapped her head, and her hands supported the sarong.

"Good morning! Ya know, Roy, ya coulda just walked in ta give me the dress."

"Good morning, Becky. Yes ... well, we're ... I suppose it's just that we're different generations."

"These are modern times, Roy, I wouldn't have minded at all if ya did! Zip me up?" He did, and she turned around to face him.

"Oh dear, you look awful!" she said with a sympathetic smile, and caressed his cheek.

"Bit too much to drink last night, I think," he responded morosely. As he brushed his teeth he watched her in the mirror, as she stood next to him using his comb on her hair. She seemed none the worse for drink. *I must be getting old. No, I am old.*

"Seems like I haven't had a hot bath in ages," she said as she fastened her earrings. "All we got for months were cold-water sponge baths from a bucket." *There's that 'we' again. Who is this 'we'? Does she mean Nancy?*

They went to find breakfast. The desk clerk recommended Maison Bogerijen, "because it has European ambiance," he said. They found the restaurant a few streets north on Braga Street, but then walked on a bit farther because Roy needed to find an *Apotheek* to buy a headache powder. The pavements were crowded with morning shoppers. The sound of many tongues, none of them English, reached his ears as they shouldered their way through the throng. As he paid the clerk for the powder, he thought, *What was it Hamish said, as we played at darts in that pub? Oh, yes, that's it: "never mix the grape with the grain, for it steals the keen dart from the bull." But, I didn't have any wine. Any I can remember drinking, anyway.*

Strolling back to the restaurant, they were standing on a traffic island in the middle of a busy junction, admiring a handsome white monument of four leaping tigers surmounted by a central clock tower, when Becky posed a question.

"How long are you here for, Roy?"

"I leave tomorrow."

She whirled around. "Tomorrah!"

"Yes. I must be back at my ship before midnight on Tuesday, unfortunately." Becky appeared disquieted at this news.

"Is that when your ship leaves?" she asked cautiously.

"Not at all. I'm having some necessary work done here." She relaxed. He smiled. *Well, this clinches it. She's going to ask me for passage back to Australia, and this will most likely include Nancy and this Woodley fellow. When she does, I'll agree.*

They entered the restaurant and Roy held her chair for her, as the waiter seated them near the pavement at a table with an umbrella. The waiter handed him the *spijskaart*. He saw the speciality of the house on offer was the *Rijsttafel*, so he ordered that for both of them. That and the delicious Javanese coffee, which the waiter brought immediately, along with the tableware, serviettes and a basket of dense crusty bread. Roy asked the man to bring him a glass of water, then swallowed the headache powder.

"Becky, tell me about yourself. It's exasperating that I know so little about you. Where do you come from? How is it you're here with no money? Let's start with you being a nursing sister – are you in the military? Is Nancy?"

"No, not military." Becky added a splash of cream and stirred an irregular lump of sugar into her coffee. She was quiet for a moment.

She sipped the coffee, composing her thoughts. When she spoke, it was as serious as he could ever recall seeing her. Her voice was controlled, a flat monotone. "Me, I'm from Wollongong, south of Sydney. We're civilian nursing sisters and are – were – assigned to work in the Central Hospital in Chung-Kiang, China, enrolled in an intern program. We arrived there in late August last year, and at the time we thought that the bombing the previous month had been the end of it. Then this year, I'll never forget, it was the fifth of June and they came again. Bombed us for three solid hours. It was horrible, just ... *horrible*." She grimaced at the thought. "Our hospital administrator, Mr Woodley, had taken a group of us out to lunch, and we watched as the hospital collapsed in on itself and buried all those people – patients, nurses, doctors, everybody. I saw fragments of babies in the street, there were burnt bodies, the smell was awful. I always thought the phrase 'gutters running with blood' was a figure of speech. It's not. We were too far away from the Jiaochangkou air raid shelter to reach it in time, and anyhow the streets were filled with rubble, so we all jumped in the river to escape the flames, but later we heard—"

"Yes, I know. Four thousand dead, or so I'm told. Let me tell you, you were lucky, very lucky." He reached across the table and took her hand as she continued.

"I saw people who couldn't swim drown right in front of me, and there was nothing I could do." Her eyes began to well up with the memory of it, and she swallowed. "Embers and ash fell like snowflakes." She jumped, startled, as a loud motorcycle passed by. "Well, when it had ended, Mr Woodley took us in hand, and using some of his own money, and some hospital funds, we ran away. We took trains until the tracks were destroyed, and then buses until the money ran low, leaving us with just enough to buy food, and then ... and then, we gone walkabout, ya see." She swallowed hard. "Walked with all the other million refugees." She blotted her eyes with her serviette.

"I am so sorry, my dear." He gave her hand a gentle squeeze.

"We ended up going to ..." she continued, but just then the waiter reappeared with an enormous tray, followed by another waiter and another tray. As the men proceeded to fill the table with many petite dishes of spicy foods, and bowls of rice, and ramekins of aromatic sauces, Becky's demeanour brightened considerably.

"I'm so hungry, I could eat a horse and chase the jockey!" she said. They tucked into the various dishes with enthusiasm. Once, after Becky had sampled a particularly delicious dish, she pushed it across the table to him and, with her mouth full, said, "Crikey, wrap your laughing gear round that!" Later, as they lingered over coffee and sugared *pannekoek,* he prompted her.

"So, you were saying, you ended up going to ...?"

"Oh yeah. Yeah, we walked until we were out of the war area, and then Mr Woodley had more funds wired from some church in Wellington, and that allowed us to take trains again. We went through, I don't know, either Siam or Burma, one of those, or maybe both, and ended up in Singapore – that's in Malaya."

"Yes, I know."

"So then, low on funds again, Mr Woodley visited ship after ship, any goin' ta New Zealand or Australia, begging for passage, but got no takers, ya see? Not that they didn't want to."

"Sorry, 'Not that they didn't want to'?" he said, confused. "I don't follow."

"Mr Woodley says one of those ship people told him that because their captain had refused to do something for some bloke, they had been denied permission to take any passengers with them when they left Singapore, by some Grand Nawab bureaucrat, name of Sheldon."

"Shenton."

"Yeah, that's it. Ya know him?"

"We've met." He couldn't let her see it, but Mallinson was smouldering with hatred inside, blind seething hatred for all the narrow-minded, jingoistic Colonel Blimp bureaucrats of the world. *When Shenton compelled me to take on this mission, I felt some obligation, some duty, to do my bit, but here are some hapless civilians buffeted by the fortunes of war who have no control over what happens to them.* He finished his coffee and pushed the cup and saucer away. The commis waiter came and cleared the table, giving him time to calm down. He waited until the boy left before speaking again.

"So, if you were unable to leave Singapore, how is it you ended up here?" She smiled at this, a part of the story she evidently relished.

"Mr Woodley saved our bacon. He found a troopship loading troopers going to Port Moresby. He put on his white hospital administrator lab coat and a stethoscope around his neck, we put on our nurses' kit, with our upside-down nurses watches pinned to it, and we simply marched aboard with all the other troopers, just as if we owned the place! No one questioned us until we were away, and by then it was far too late to do anything about little old us."

"You stowed away," he stated. She nodded, with a huge grin.

"What ship was that?" he asked, thinking he might have seen it.

"I don't know. Oh! Hang about! Our Nurse Kee took a photograph of us as we boarded. I have it in my room at the boarding house. I'll have to dig it out and show it to you sometime."

"So, you're not in Port Moresby now. How did you—?"

"When they discovered us to be civilians – I reckon this musta been nearly two weeks ago – they put us ashore in Semarang. We worked for a week at the Santa Maria hospital in Tjilatjap, then ended up here at the Bandung City Hospital, on a part-time basis. Mind you, it doesn't pay very well; they're overstaffed and they don't really need us. We make enough to eat and pay the tariff at the boarding house, but that's about it." *Let me see, three others she's mentioned so far: Nancy, this Woodley fellow and now this Nurse Key.*

"How many of you are here?"

"Eleven, and Mr Woodley." *So, twelve now. Still doable.*

"All of you are nurses?" She nodded. "I think your Mr Woodley should meet my wireless operator," he muttered under his breath, "They'd have much to discuss."

"Come again?"

"Never mind," he replied. "Oh, waiter! The bill, please!" He paid, and they left.

They were strolling through the city somewhat aimlessly, just window-shopping, when they found the day had become warm, actually quite hot. They decided to return to the hotel so that Roy could change into lighter clothing. On the way there they walked past a market, where Becky's eye was caught by a red-and-green display advert pasted in the window, the illustration of a little girl kneeling in front of a Christmas tree. The banner read: 'Drink Coca-Cola. So easy to take home the six-bottle carton.' She seized his arm.

"Oh, Roy, buy me some Coca-Cola! Please?" They left with a carton and an opener. Roy knew of this American beverage but didn't care for the taste of it.

As they entered the hotel room he said, "I'll go down and ask the maître d'hôtel for some ice."

"What for?" she asked, surprised.

"Your Coca-Cola. You don't want to drink warm Coca-Cola, do you?"

"No worries, Roy." She crossed the room to the water closet. When she came out, she found he had hung his tweed jacket and cap on the back of a chair, and was now relaxed upon the far side of the bed on his back, hands clasped behind his head. "How's the headache?"

"It's gone. The powder worked a treat! And the food helped a great deal, too." She placed her earrings and necklace on the bedside table, then took off her heels and lay down by his side, propped upon an elbow, her head supported on her palm.

"What about you, Roy? Tell me all about yourself!" He repeated essentially what Shenton had quoted from that dossier, but adding to it that he had married Beryl in 1906 when he was twenty-three years old. They had no children. Beryl had enjoyed raising a succession of moggies, but they had none now. They owned a lovely thatched and pebble-dash cottage they called "The Watermeadows" facing the green, just the other side of the River Gipping from the Pickerel Inn in Stowmarket, Suffolk. He liked to tend beehives, as a pastime. She liked to potter in the garden, and was an absolute green-fingered wizard with any vegetable. She was also much more involved with village activities than Roy. After he'd retired, he'd begun constructing a mountain diorama in their attic room for a Hornby Dublo electric train set, but laid it aside when he had resumed his occupation.

"How didja meet, you and Beryl?" Roy thought for a moment before replying.

"It was … 1905, I think, because it must have been three years after I had immigrated. I'd joined the Royal Navy as an ordinary seaman. I was stationed aboard a ship off the west coast of Africa—"

"You met Beryl on a ship?"

"Wait a bit! We were supplying Lord Lugard's forces as they planned to attack Kano, a town in the Sokoto Caliphate – that's in northern Nigeria – and had been delivering four 75mm mountain guns in support of our forces ashore. We hadn't known they – that is, the Fulani rebels – had any cannon, relics really, but when we got close enough inshore they let loose a fusillade that actually struck our ship! We were surprised, I can tell you. We hadn't known they were there. I caught a bit of shrapnel in my leg, you see, and couldn't walk at all."

"Oh, dear! What happened then?"

"I was invalided home, to some massive pile of a manor house in the North Riding of Yorkshire called Castle Howard, where the west wing had been converted into a temporary convalescence ward. That's where

I met my chief engineer, Hamish MacCallan. He was an engineer's apprentice in charge of the castle's boiler room, and when he came to the ward I was in—"

"Yes, yes, but Beryl?" she interrupted, "Was she your nurse?"

"No. Let me finish! She was secretary to Geoffrey, Baron Howard, and the man was writing a series of monographs on the limnology of the Scottish Lowlands, and she was typing up his manuscripts. I and others on the ward had made complaint that the rooms were too chilly, and Hamish had arrived to adjust the steam registers with Beryl in tow, as they were seeing each other at the time."

"Ooo, seeing each other. Did you and Hamish compete for her hand?"

"I don't know about 'compete' but yes, we were both interested in her. To my young Canadian ear her English accent sounded exotic, and I became quite attracted to her. She'd had a disagreement with Hamish, a minor argument really, nothing serious. After I was well enough to stand on my own, we ... well, we started walking out."

"Walking out? Is that what they used to call dating? Walking out? How quaint!"

"Up until that time I'd been bedridden, you see, and when I started walking again, I set my crutches aside and Beryl would hold my arm, for the support it afforded, and we would walk the manor avenue or circuits of the castle gardens. We made a game of it, to see how many more places we could visit with each passing day – the Atlas fountain, the Temple of the Four Winds folly, the lake, kitchen garden or the mausoleum, or the pyramid on Saint Anne's Hill again, and so on. And we'd talk. Once, we were caught in a sudden storm without coats and had to take refuge in the stables, holding each other for warmth."

"In the hay?" she laughed. "How romantic!"

"It was, rather," he reminisced, a faraway look in his eye. "Yes, well ... Hamish married a lovely highland lass some five years later, I believe." While listening, she had been absent-mindedly toying with his buttons. With his shirt unbuttoned, her hand had slipped inside, and now her fingertip traced circles around his nipple.

"Hey," she grinned, playfully, "ya wanna get bed-ridden?"

"Aren't you the clever one!" He smiled. Becky fixed him with a frank gaze. "Oh. You're serious?" he asked. She arched an eyebrow in reply. Hesitatively he asked, "In the middle of the afternoon?"

"Nothing wrong with arvo. Unzip me!" Sitting up and turning about, she presented the zip to him. He sat up and unzipped her. She stood, gave a shimmy, and the sarong floated to the floor. She turned about and took his hands, placing them on her knickers. He peeled them down, and she stepped out of them. Taking his head in her hands, she held his cheek against her belly and stroked his hair. His hands rose up the back of her thighs to cup her bottom. He gave her belly a kiss. His eyes shut, he nuzzled her curly hair, inhaling the intoxicating scent of her, and this brought arousal.

Then, taking his hands, she pulled him to his feet. She stepped back and, running her fingers through her hair, she turned for him, displayed herself to him, relishing his gaze. Her smile was brilliant. Her feet were small and delicate, the nails painted red. She had a thick mat of curly, ginger-coloured hair; the sight of her little belly bulging above this aroused him even more. Her waist met hips not particularly broad, although her bottom was pleasingly rounded, and this excited him, too. *How can any woman on earth be as beautiful as this?*

Then, her elbows held out at shoulder level, palms down, she began to twirl slowly about the room, dipping this way and that, a balletic dance to music only she could hear. Her breasts were high and fully round, yet they were not firm, as with each footfall they bounced with a silken ripple. Her aureoles were small, and the nipples stood erect, so he knew she, too, was as aroused as he. At the end of her final circuit of the room she stood on tiptoe, threw her arms about his neck, and with a heel kicked up, kissed him deeply and passionately. He returned her ardour.

"Becky, if you're looking for passage to Australia, there's no need to do anything at all to 'persuade' me. My ship has enough cabins to take all of you." She looked at him in surprise.

"Why, Roy, I'm insulted," she said, mock-seriously, "didja ever reckon that maybe I like ya?" She smiled up at him and then rubbed her temple against his cheek. He kissed her forehead.

"I'm on my way home to my wife. This cannot last."

"Roy, Roy," she implored, "I'm not asking for it to last." Her grey eyes gazed into his. "Do ya remember what I said, the moment we met?"

His brow furrowed, he concentrated, and it came to him. He quoted: "It's fucking 1941, it ain't 1910. Lighten up."

"The world is going to hell in a handcart," she said, "The Nazis hold Europe. The Japs are on their way. They're monsters, Roy, monsters! I've seen things that ..." she choked, then regained her composure and continued. "That Admiral bloke at the dance – if he hadn't rescued you from that submarine, you'd be dead now and we would never have met. On yer way home to England, ya might be torpedoed and never see yer missus, or this world, ever again." Her eyes glistened and she pleaded, "People gotta live for today, Roy – tomorrah we could all be dead." He nodded thoughtfully, and her words resonated for him – 'or this world, ever again'. Becky released him and giddily helped him as he shed his clothing. She bounced onto the bed. Drawing her knees up and apart, she held her arms up and her hands beckoned eagerly for him to join her. They made love all that afternoon. When Roy began to feel his age, she then made love to him, straddling him and rocking forwards and back, kissing him, caressing him with her breasts, covetously taking him into her mouth. They only stopped when they grew hungry.

Because Becky was wearing her fancy sarong, Roy dressed in his Royal Navy uniform again, but he left his peaked cap behind. It was only supper, after all. That evening, they chanced upon a restaurant he'd not visited before. After supper she insisted they go out on the town, and they ate sweet cakes, and there was ice cream in cones. Roy had never seen her so animated. As they strolled, one exuberant thought segued into another as she gave voice to her inner joy. She was constantly finding opportunities to touch him, taking his arm or hand, or stopping for a hug. And she also felt like dancing, excitedly pulling him into any club they encountered.

The fourth time she heard music, she dragged Roy down a narrow alley to a hole-in-the-wall club. It was entered through a nondescript door, beneath a neon sign of a purple cat with the words 'Hep Cat Gat' spelled out in orange – 'Gat' meaning 'hole' in Dutch. They stepped aside to allow a laughing couple to exit. Descending narrow stairs in a dimly lit concrete tunnel, ominously painted black, they passed a French tricolour flag on the wall, a Cross of Lorraine daubed in the centre – the flag of the Free French. At the foot of the stairway a thick steel door stood propped open against its strong spring, and Roy was alarmed to glimpse it pockmarked with dents. *Those are bullet marks.* Shouldering through beaded strings they encountered a beefy bouncer wearing a fancy homburg, blocking their way. Roy instantly recognised the bulge of a shoulder holster under the man's dapper suit coat. The bouncer looked beyond them, to see if any more like this one were following after and then, satisfied, waved them through.

The sight that greeted them was of a single snug room, painted entirely black. Seven tiny round zinc-topped tables, each with two or three chairs of the type Roy had last seen outside a Paris bistro. It had a high ceiling, a well-stocked bar with four occupied stools, and was kept dimly lit for intimacy. Each table boasted a drinks menu and a candle in a glass with a diminutive black shade, most assuredly for atmosphere, for otherwise it gave little light. There was a low stage a single step above the floor. There was no dance floor but they stayed anyway, taking a table at the edge of the stage, to listen to a jazz quartet of a piano, clarinet, saxophone, and trap set. The drummer had a vibraphone placed off to one side. The musicians wore identical suits, with shiny waistcoats that scintillated in the spotlights. The stage backdrop was a shiny curtain of deep electric-blue. Roy held Becky's chair for her, then went to the bar to order, where he spied a bottle of Macallan Scotch. *Hamish should be here.* He ordered a Macallan with a water back, in his engineer's honour. She had asked for the most outrageously complicated shaken cocktail, well, just because! (the damn thing had egg white and Chambord and brandy and cream and nutmeg and God knows what else in it.) Roy had a taste. It was delicious and silky smooth: a ladies' drink. She was startled, and slightly miffed, when the thin black woman who brought it sat and draped an arm across Roy's shoulders to engage him in a conversation that, on the face of it, went nowhere. With her other hand she brushed Roy's chest as she spoke, in a manner rather too familiar for Becky's liking. The woman was dressed the same as the band members. He then asked the woman if she could have the barman bring some Aquavit for Becky to taste. After she left, he explained what had been going on.

"Not to worry, my dear. She was only finding out why we're here, and coincidentally patting me down for any weapon. After all, I am looking quite official in my uniform, and surely you noticed we're the only whites in the place?"

"*Pour toi, ma chère,*" the woman said, as she set down a jigger of a tawny liquid. Becky thanked her, then timidly sipped it.

"Caraway!" she exclaimed. *Aha! That was it!* Roy knocked back the rest of it. The woman helped the drummer reposition his vibraphone, then left the stage. When the set started, Becky sat bolt upright in surprise. She grasped Roy's hand.

"What? What is it?" he asked, attentively.

"It's our song, Roy!"

"We have a song?"

"Of course we do, silly," she grinned. "'Moonglow', the very first one we ever danced to!" She stood and urged him out of his chair, and he rose reluctantly because he knew there was no dance floor. Still, Roy held her close to him in the triangular space between their table, the stage and the next table over. He moved her in tiny steps, trying to avoid bumping the shoulder of the man seated there, and not succeeding. The man's companion found this amusing. It seemed to Roy the other patrons did too. Becky hadn't noticed because her eyes were shut in contentment.

For nearly an hour they sat and enjoyed the music, which at times Becky declared was 'cutting-edge modern' and 'divine'. On occasion the session would end, and the musicians slip out the back for a smoke break in the alley. Roy went to the bar to pay the tab. When he returned he found the woman and Becky doubled over in paroxysms of laughter, snorting at some joke he'd been too late to hear. The woman stepped on stage to chat with the saxophonist. He asked Becky what they'd been laughing about. She giggled and wiped away a tear.

"Lorraine – she's the singer *and* the owner – thought that you're my father, but I set her straight: I told her you're a sea captain ... and also my lover." Roy rolled his eyes in embarrassment, compounded with a modicum of pleasure. "Lorraine left me these. She told me," – and here Becky essayed a passable imitation of the woman's accent – "Eet weel make enhance-mont of zee emotions *avec le sexe*." She pushed two hand-rolled cigarettes across the table at Roy. To Becky's astonishment he clapped his palm down over them in alarm.

"Do you know what these are?" he hissed.

"Of course! It's the 'dreaded reefer' they told us about in those scare films at school. What of it?" she said, flummoxed at Roy's reaction.

"I'll tell you later," he said under his breath, "Right now I have to find a way to rid ourselves of these." He scanned the room. The other patrons seemed intent on their own conversations. *What to do? What to do? Any one of these people might be the wrong person to have seen these.* As he worried, the remaining musicians returned from backstage. Roy detected the smoky-sweet odour of ganja from the nearest of them and was struck with inspiration. He looked around the room once more. The barman polished his glassware. The bouncer had detained a new customer at the door because the tables and barstools were full. No one looked their way. In one fluid motion Roy slid his hand off the table and the reefers fell at the feet of the saxophonist.

"I beg your pardon, my good man," Roy murmured, "But I think you may have dropped something there." The rheumy-eyed sax player caught the eye of Lorraine, and she nodded.

"Eees Oh-kay, *mon cherie*," she said, and winked at him. The sax man stooped to retrieve his instrument from its stand. As he clipped it into the harness around his neck, he scooped up the reefers and palmed them. Still bent low, he fixed a gimlet eye on Roy.

"I sees y'all be hep," he said hoarsely, "Much obliged, my man." Roy gave him a shallow nod.

"Becky, I think we should go now. I believe someone needs this table." He gulped the last of his black-and-tan stout, guided her past the bouncer, and they climbed the stairs to emerge into the cool night air. He let out a relieved sigh as he looked to the sky. His face was lit by the sickly glow of the sign, which was buzzing faintly.

"What on Earth was that all about?" she asked curiously, as he held her wrap open for her. They exited the alley and began to stroll towards the city arboretum. Roy asked her a question in return.

"Have you ever smoked that stuff?"

"No, but I had friends who did. Have you?" she asked, confident of his answer.

"Yes."

"You never!"

"Yes, in Canada, when I was but a lad of seventeen."

"Why, Roy, that's hilarious!" she exclaimed. Roy sighed. They crossed the boulevard to enter the park.

"Not when I tell you this: that was there, this is here. We are in a country that is overwhelmingly Muslim. They control just about every aspect of society here, and they absolutely do not allow illicit drugs into this country. Had I been caught with that in my possession I would most assuredly lose my job, and possibly go to prison, but as a captain in command of a vessel, they would confiscate my ship and everything in it, permanently."

"I had no idea!" she marvelled aloud.

"What's more, if they then convicted me on a charge of trafficking, warranted or not, it would mean the death penalty." She was silent for half a minute as they walked towards a fountain at play, then turned and gave him a hug. "It's all right, my dear," he said, "you had no way of knowing."

In a meadow beyond the fountain they happened upon an outdoor stage lit by torches that guttered in the gentle breeze. A Javanese *wayang gedog* play with live actors, not the usual wooden shadow puppets, was just beginning. They reclined upon the grass. Children sat respectfully with their parents and listened in rapt attention. There was a humble gamelan orchestra plus a drummer, a few gongs and a musician with a *rebab*, a violin-like instrument. The play was called *Smaradahana* – The Fire of Love – and, even though they didn't know the language, Becky was greatly affected by the story, which centred on the eventual marriage of Dewi Ratih, the Hindu goddess of love, and Kamajaya, the Hindu god of love. When the play ended, they continued their stroll, on past a lake, and found another tiny out-of-the-way meadow. Here they lay upon a grassy slope beneath the light of a full moon and kissed, and caressed, doing anything to hold at bay the unhappy world beyond.

Much later that night, in the moonlight streaming through the Venetian blinds, their lovemaking spent, he saw her rise and enter the water closet. When she emerged, he watched as she placed an empty Coca-Cola bottle into the rubbish bin.

"A trick I learnt from our Yank nurse," she explained.

* * *

"I must leave this afternoon," he said, as they breakfasted in the hotel restaurant, "most probably no later than five o'clock." She nodded, her face glum. "Shouldn't I talk with your Mr Woodley?"

"No, I can do that. I just need directions on how to find you."

"Can he afford the train tariff for a dozen people?" She hadn't thought of that. She would have to talk to Mr Woodley about the group's finances. While they ate, he had an idea; *Somebody should be suffering for this fiasco, besides us.* Saying nothing to her, he excused himself, telling her he would be back directly. Becky assumed he was going to visit the hotel's *Herren toilette* the other side of the foyer. There was a Western Union office across the street from the hotel, and he made for that. He sent a telegram to Gurnam Singh asking, no, *telling him* that he was to wire £500, or the equivalent amount in the Javanese currency, to him at the Hotel Homann, Bandung, Java, immediately, with no questions asked, and reminded Gurnam of the wording in the cable of 16th October, which he still had in his possession. Should Ellerman, or the Ministry of War Transport, balk, he could put it down to 'condenser repair, and the rescue and repatriation of a dozen Commonwealth medical staff'. He then returned to his breakfast.

He acquired hotel stationery from the Concierge. He wrote out detailed directions of how to find the *Dominion Empress*, and named the wharf to which she was moored. To this description he appended his full signature, including his rank, with instructions that the nurses be admitted aboard and assigned cabins the minute they arrived. On a second sheet he had Becky write out a list of all the nurses' names in full, including their nationalities, and the address of the boarding house at which they were staying. He reviewed it: four Kiwis (to include Mr Woodley), six Aussies, one Korean and a Yank. Both of these he pocketed.

"Becky, there is something else I must tell you." She looked up, quizzically. "I am the captain of a ship of many dozens of men, over which I must maintain discipline. To do this I must appear above reproach in their eyes. As captain, I must remain aloof from everyone except my officers. It is in this way that when I give an order it will be obeyed without question. When you arrive on board, you will be our passengers for the duration of the voyage. What this means is, you will each have your own cabin, and I, of course, have my own quarters on the bridge. So as to not interfere with our operations, all of you will be restricted to only certain parts of the ship, and this will *not* include the bridge. Do you understand?"

She nodded but also asked, "Isn't there a captain's table during supper? Where everyone socialises?"

He tried not to smile but failed.

"We're not the *Queen Mary*, my dear. I'm sure you'll understand when you see the *Dominion Empress*. I should warn you now: she isn't pretty." He briefly described for her, in layman's terms, the condition of the ship.

"So, are you trying to warn me that there's no lido deck?" she said with a pout, teasing him. He guffawed.

A few hours were spent wandering the city and strolling the pathway along the river. Becky commented on the varied floral displays, drawing his attention to little details he might have missed, and the trees around them were heavy and fragrant with blossoms. That afternoon they returned to the hotel.

Becky made love with a hunger that was intense, as if at any moment Roy might vanish from her arms. Later, as they lay exhausted, their passion sated, there came an insistent tapping at the door. Roy wrapped a towel around himself and answered it, but held the door open just a crack, as the pimply-faced hotel porter was shifting from foot to foot, trying to see past him into the room. He was told a courier was waiting for him at the front desk with an envelope, for which he was required to sign. He dressed and kissed her, saying he would be back straight away.

As he rode the lift down to the hotel foyer, he found himself lost in memories of his own distant past: as a seaman in the Royal Navy, drunkenly roaming a benighted back street of Rotterdam's Scheepvaartkwartier; egged on by his mates, his very first time had been with a 'sporting lady', much older and very bored, who reeked of cigarettes and stale perfume, tarted up with rouge laid on with a trowel. That experience had been rather a disappointment. But then, before his injury in Africa, he had been posted for a year aboard the gunboat HMS *Widgeon* on the China Station. There he had sampled the whorehouses in fetid villages on the banks of the Yangtze. Those women had been even more of a disappointment, as they had each silently and listlessly acquiesced to his attentions without showing the slightest interest. Had it been due to the language barrier? Who could say? Back in Britain, he'd pursued a posh English lass who had cruelly given him the elbow after a fourth date, without allowing him so much as a single kiss, and this after he'd exhausted his pay packet. He had boarded his ship for Africa penniless and disillusioned. And then there was Beryl. In 1911, when his ship had been stationed at Thessaloniki in then-neutral Greece during their national schism, he had been attracted by the beauty of the Greek women, but by then he was married, of course, and this had made him faithful.

But Becky was different. She was so unlike any woman he had ever known. She was playful, subtly assuming the role of vamp to amuse and arouse him. He found her exuberance exciting, exhilarating. She seemed to know, to anticipate, what he wanted even before he did. By her every sybaritic movement she made it easy for him to know, and to fulfil, her own desires. In making love she was always right there with him, and he with her, an unspoken meeting of minds as well as bodies. Moreover, she wasn't given to silence. Oh no, not at all! *Beryl was never like this. In Edwardian England proper young ladies were expected to "Lay back, close your eyes and think of England," and Beryl had certainly been a proper young lady. But Becky – Becky is a most improper young lady. She even has a petite tattoo – a tattoo! – and in a most private place. Hadn't proper English society deemed it illicit for a woman to have a tattoo? So I've always believed.*

The lift bumped lightly as it stopped, interrupting his reverie. The lift attendant opened the inner and outer doors. At the front desk he produced his identity papers, signed the courier's pad, and was given the envelope. He returned to the room in time to find Becky already dressed and inserting her earrings. He zipped her up. It was the expected 'letter of instruction' from Gurnam Singh to a local bank to disburse £500, in any currency required, to him personally. He slipped this into a pocket without divulging it. She was curious, naturally, but didn't press him. As they crossed the hotel foyer to the front desk to check out of the hotel, Becky handed the carton of unused bottles to the surprised, but grateful, hotel porter.

They strolled the city streets arm in arm as they made their way to the bank. Here Mallinson withdrew the money. Still at the teller's cage, he counted out and pocketed £200 to pay for the repairs to the condenser. He turned to Becky and gave her the remaining £300 and her identity papers, along with the written directions to the ship.

"Give this to your Mr Woodley. Do not lose it!" he warned her. "You are to tell Mr Woodley that these are my instructions to him, and he should follow them explicitly. First, he should use this money to treat you, all the nurses, to a magnificent supper. Secondly, he is to see that you are all supplied with clothing sufficient for an ocean voyage, as you can't be expected to go on wearing the same nursing uniform every day, as you have been doing. And third, you are to travel to my ship by train or taxicab, whichever he prefers, though he must understand I shall brook no objection to this. Are we clear?"

Becky nodded, and hugged him, blotting her tears against his tweed jacket. The teller, who had listened to this, wiped his nose and busied himself with his records. She folded the letter tightly around the wad of cash and pushed it deep into her cleavage and out of sight. They left the bank and walked to the railway station, where Roy bought his ticket to Batavia. As they stood in front of the open door of the train compartment, he embraced her. They kissed. The locomotive shrilled its whistle. Roy picked up his grip and heaved it into the compartment. He climbed in after it and shut the door. Dropping the window into its pocket by its leather strap, he took hold of her hand through the opening.

"Remember, you must be *at my ship* not later than on Tuesday next!" he insisted. A black-suited conductor nearby faced the locomotive to blow his whistle, waving a square flag off to one side.

"We'll be there!" she promised. The train started with a jolt and pulled their hands apart. As he watched her recede, she blew him a kiss.

6

Plan Of Attack

He awoke in darkness. He rolled over and reached for her, ramming his hand into the bulkhead rather painfully. *I'm in my cabin*, he remembered. He made a circuit of the cabin opening all the curtains, and daylight streamed in, then donned his dress blues. Upon entering the bridge he found First Mate Wallace being relieved by Third Mate O'Malley.

"How was your weekend away?" he asked the first.

"Just the ticket, sir. How was yours?"

"Well, I would have to say ... invigorating!"

"You look it. What did you do, climb a mountain?"

Mallinson snorted, then asked, "All crew get back all right?"

"Aye. Some more drunk than others, but only minor injuries. I'm going for breakfast."

"I'll be down in a moment myself," he replied. The first mate left. The two aeroplanes had been reloaded onto hatch number two. In their place on the wharf were two pallets, each wrapped in a tarpaulin.

"How was your weekend?" he asked the third mate.

"So-so, for certain sure," the mate said, and shrugged. His eye displayed the early signs of a shiner. Mallinson sighed. He had never understood any crew's penchant for getting blotto and finding a reason to fight.

"When did those arrive?" Mallinson asked, indicating the pallets.

"Both yestidday, sor. The lorry man told me they'll be coming at the rate of two a day."

"When today's batch arrives, hoist them aboard and put them port and starboard of the number two hatch. Do that every day until all of it is aboard."

"Aye, sor. What is it, sor?"

"Oh, ahh … just some of our lead cargo I've had reprocessed for … ahh … an Australian client that must remain nameless, for now." Mallinson went below to the wardroom for breakfast. He asked Jimmy to quarter a dozen limes for his own use at noon, and told him there would be twelve additional mouths to feed for the voyage to Australia. While they ate, he told the first mate about the dozen new passengers due to arrive. He asked him to have the engineers see to it that every shower and tap in the passenger accommodation worked and had plenty of hot water. He also asked him to make sure to have Einar, the cabin steward, freshen the sheets and pillows in all the passenger cabins, and hoover them all. The mate was to remind Einar these were female passengers – nurses – so cleanliness was paramount. His instruction was to overlook nothing.

Later that morning, shortly before noon, the captain ordered the bosun and an able seaman to follow him. In his cabin, he had the men pick up a keg from his wardrobe and carry it to the midship well deck. While that was done, he remained on the bridge. Switching on the tannoy, he announced, "D'ye hear there! D'ye hear there! Today is Wednesday, the fifth of November. I am minded that since tonight is Guy Fawkes Night, even though we are *not* a Royal Navy ship, to celebrate this event we will splice the mainbrace at noon! Clear the lower decks! Lay amidships to the well deck!" He toggled off the microphone. Lifting the lid of the voice pipe, he called out, "Splicing the mainbrace" to the engine room.

Even though it had been a rather long time since he had been in the service, this was one tradition he was unwilling to part with. He didn't do this daily, as had been the custom in the Royal Navy, just on certain occasions he deemed worthy. There was the pounding of many feet as seamen raced to retrieve their special mugs from their quarters. Mallinson made his way down to the midship well deck, where he ordered, "Stand easy, men!" There were few Chinese among the throng. The bosun, with a clipboard, stood at the scuttled butt, as it was known: a brass-bound wooden keg with the words 'THE KING – GOD BLESS HIM' hammered into it in brass. On the lid was carved 'Pusser's Rum, 96 ½ proof'. The able seaman stood ready with a tot measure of about two and a half ounces. Jimmy stood with a bowl of quartered limes and a bucket of water nearby. He had the same-size measure. As each man was checked off the bosun's list, he was given a tot of so-called Nelson's Blood. The cook then asked if he wanted an equal amount of water for a grog, or a lime, or both. Some did, some did not. When each man held his drink, the captain raised his own, shouting, "The King!" and in unison the crew roared in response, "God Bless Him!" They drank to the health of the King. Mallinson had the bosun and able seaman return the keg to his quarters. The cook griped a bit at what he was supposed to do with all these leftover limes, until carpenter Nowiczski pulled him aside and kindly offered to take them off his hands.

* * *

All day Thursday and Friday, work continued on the condenser. Pallets were lifted aboard and distributed next to the bulwarks. Late Friday morning, Mallinson plotted with Second Engineer Sinclair over how to disguise the real gold. They had planned to paint the gold bars grey, the same colour as the inside of the lifeboats, and then place these bars in the bottom of each boat so that it looked for all the world like normal ballast. It seemed to them your average Japanese sailor wouldn't know that lifeboats don't carry ballast. Then if they were stopped and searched, they had been counting on swinging the boats out to be unreachable and therefore overlooked. They wouldn't worry about Germans; they wouldn't search you, just sink you. On the chance that they *were* sunk, and were forced into the lifeboats, they could then take the disguised gold with them. But the flaws in this original plan soon became apparent; it wasn't so much the volume as the weight that was concerning. These boats were, after all, only wood. They were standard 1934 Monomoy-type lifeboats, 26 ft by 7 ft, but 2 ft 4 inches deep, with a centreboard, a rudder, and a lug-rigged sail and ten oars. There were six lifeboats, which meant they needed to distribute over eleven and a half tons of gold into each boat. Once the lifeboats were launched, none of the crew could board them without sinking them. It was a quandary.

Sometime during their planning session there had come a screeching of rending metal from a half mile away to the south. This happened so frequently in any shipyard, no one bothered to look up from their work.

After much discussion, they agreed the only thing left to do was to dump the gold bars into the number two hold and shovel the loose lead nodules over it. If the ship went down, well, there was nothing they could do about that. Perhaps, if they charted their location (and they survived), someone else could return after the war to recover it; that is, if it wasn't too deep, as even the best divers had their limits. After dumping the real gold in the hold, they would be left with some six hundred ammo boxes and forty tons of cast-lead ingots aboard that, if they were searched, would be a red rag to a bull that something was amiss. Sinclair wanted to simply dump the ingots overboard and burn all the empty ammo boxes, or else leave them all with someone at the port authority. Mallinson insisted that if any boarding party were to intensify their search, they might find the real gold and, unable easily to take it away, might then confiscate the *Dominion Empress* itself. His concern wasn't so much with the ship, as such, because the value of the gold was many times more than the value of this ship; he just didn't want his crew and passengers ending up in a Japanese prison camp or dead. No, he was of a mind to keep the lead ingots and to colour them gold and put them in the ammo boxes. Any search party expecting to find gold would then find the gold they were looking for. It would be a classic case of misdirection. Sinclair reminded the captain they still had no gold paint.

"Why don't we just melt a gold bar and dip the ingots?" Mallinson proposed. The engineer sighed.

"There's a slight problem of temperature. You see, gold melts at 1,945 degrees Fahrenheit and lead melts at 621 degrees, so your lead goes *phffft!*" he said, throwing his hand in the air to illustrate how it would vaporise.

"I see," said Mallinson, "but, surely we could buy some gold paint somewhere in this city and paint or dip them in that?"

"Gold paint is just real powdered gold in suspension. It leaves a dull finish that looks fake and fools no one. It kind of looks like brass in a way. To get a beautiful shiny golden finish you need to run it through an oven and heat it up." There was nothing the captain could say to this.

Shortly after noon, Mallinson was eating in the wardroom when the speaker overhead emitted a crackle of static and he heard the second mate say, "D'ye hear there! Will the captain please report to the bridge. Captain to the bridge." When he reached the bridge, Taffy pointed out to him a taxicab standing at the foot of the accommodation ladder. Another line of taxicabs trundled slowly down the wharf, four more in all. These taxicabs drew up in line behind the first. The captain patted his pockets until he found the list of nurses, which he gave to the second mate, instructing him to sign them in and assign them their quarters. He watched as the nurses emerged from the taxis, each one holding a valise. Their dresses were of various colours or patterns and styles. Below him, seamen lined the rail, whistling and cat-calling.

"You down there! Belay that noise!" an irritated Mallinson barked through the tannoy. A bewhiskered man who he assumed must be Mr Woodley arranged the nurses to stand in a neat queue, then went from taxi to taxi, paying each driver. Four of the taxicabs drove away. The mate, holding a clipboard, descended the accommodation ladder and approached Woodley, who handed him a sheet of paper. They chatted for a moment. Then they walked the queue of nurses together, as each one signed the clipboard. Woodley shook hands with the mate, then climbed into the remaining taxi. It motored off to the south. With the second mate leading, the nurses trooped up the ladder and disappeared into the ship's passenger accommodations. All of them were wearing hats, and none of them looked up. A handful held handkerchiefs. Five minutes later the second mate stepped onto the bridge and joined the captain, leaning on the cap rail of the bridge wing. Mallinson turned to him and chuckled.

"Not many Merchant Navy ships can boast of having such a first-class medical staff, eh, Mr Morgan?"

"No, sir," the second mate replied, his voice somewhat subdued.

"Where is Mr Woodley off to? Needing to buy some last-minute items, eh?"

"No, sir." The mate cleared his throat. "I'm sorry to report, Mr Woodley tells me a taxicab broke a kingpin crossing the railway tracks and stalled. It was struck by a locomotive. He needs to return to the scene of the accident and give a statement. The police are waiting for him." A frisson of cold ran down the back of Roy's neck. The mate continued, "I'm told the driver and two nurses were killed. He'll need the rest of the day to arrange for the disposition and repatriation of their remains. He tells me he must visit the consulate, and also find a funeral home." A lump rose in Mallinson's throat.

"Do you know their names?" he managed to croak.

"I left my clipboard below but, if I remember correctly, the driver is named Gesang ... uh ... Gesang Ajij and there's a nurse called Nancy ... something. If you wait a bit, I'll go below and check my clipboard." Mallinson felt light-headed. He could hear her voice clearly: '*or this world, ever again.*' He saw her in his mind's eye, as if from a train window, watched her recede from him, blowing him a kiss. His knees buckled and he sagged to the deck. The mate, alarmed, caught him under the arm and supported him. An able seaman dashed out of the bridge house, looking quite concerned.

"Blasted gout!" he exclaimed loudly for the benefit of those present, gripping his leg, "Help me to my quarters." He limped down the corridor on the arm of the mate. Once he was seated in a chair, the mate disappeared, returning a few minutes later with a nurse. Her eyes were red and puffy; she'd been crying, but had to carry on regardless. The mate held a chair for her, and she sat facing the captain. Mallinson introduced himself.

"I'm Nurse Wright, Captain Mallinson. Chief Nurse Virginia Wright. Gout, you say? Which foot?" She unlaced his brogue and removed it. Rolling up the trouser leg, she gently peeled off his sock. When she pressed the side of his big toe, he winced in pain.

"What time of day does this hurt the most?" she queried. By her accent it was quite plain she hailed from America.

"Anytime. Sometimes all the time. At times it keeps me from my sleep."

"Okay, this is what you are to do: twice a day, when you wake and before bed – and without fail – you are to take a half a level teaspoon of turmeric, or a capsule if you can get it of that spice, and wash it down with a teaspoon or more of apple cider vinegar in a cup of water. You should feel a reduction of the pain within a matter of days. You can take it anytime you need it. When the pain goes away, you can stop the treatment until you need it again. Got it?"

"Yes, thank you, Nurse Wright," he responded, "and may I express my condolences at the tragic loss of your nurses. I had the opportunity to meet Nurse Nants, and found her a quite charming young lady." He pulled up his sock. She stood.

"Thank you, captain, but it's Nancy, not Nants. You see, since we have – had – two Nancys, we call the younger one Nants to distinguish them."

Astounded, he asked, "Becky – Rebecca – I mean, Nurse McKenzie is all right?"

"Oh yes. The nurses in the accident were Nancy Hightower and Barbara French. Rebecca and Nants were in another taxicab." The second mate shut the door behind her as she left. He turned to the captain.

"May I say, sir ..."

"Yes?"

"You know, the Chinese have a proverb: *dǐng shì jì mò*. It means, 'It's lonely at the top.' You're a good man, Roy. What I'm trying to say is, you're only human."

"Thank you, Mr Morgan, it's good of you to say. I didn't know you spoke Chinese?"

"Just a few phrases, sir, picked up here and there."

* * *

"Have you come up with any ideas as to how we can colour the lead ingots?" the captain asked Mr Sinclair. They stood together on the catwalk that afternoon, where Mallinson had encountered Sinclair as he crossed.

The second engineer shook his head. "I reckon it's best to bring in an expert to solve this. Will you mind if I talk to the chief about it?""

Mallinson responded, "I've known him for years. Surely he can come up with something? That is, if he's not overwhelmed with directing the condenser work."

"Let's talk it over after supper. Shall the three of us meet in the wardroom at, say, half-five?"

"Very good. See you then."

A little after 1730 hours, the captain, chief engineer and second engineer sat together at a table in the wardroom, their empty supper plates stacked. Each one had his cup of tea.

"So, Mr Sinclair has explained our problem to you?" the captain asked his chief engineer.

"Aye."

"Have you come up with any ideas as to how we can produce gold-coloured paint, with the materials we have on hand?" he asked.

"Nae, it canna be done."

Mallinson went to get another cup at the urn. When he returned, Mr Woodley was standing there. The captain had found it necessary to assign the medical staff to the officers' wardroom, as it wouldn't do to have passengers, especially female passengers, eating in the crew's mess. Many of the ordinary seamen had been away from wives or girlfriends for as long as two years.

"Ralph Woodley," he said, shaking hands all around. "I cannot thank you enough, captain, for your generosity. It is much appreciated, very much appreciated indeed." As a New Zealander, the end of his every sentence had a rising inflection, as if a question was being asked. He sat without waiting for an invitation.

"Think nothing of it, Mr Woodley. I am so very sorry at the loss of your nurses. Are you finding your quarters adequate?"

"Kind of you to say. Please, call me Ralph. Yes, we're quite comfortable, thank you. I must share the water closet with Nurse Wright but, no worries, we manage. I take it our Miss McKenzie has filled you in on the details of our escape from China?"

"Yes, she has. It seemed quite harrowing, according to her description. I'm impressed that you were able to shepherd them all over such a distance as you did." Ralph nodded and waved a dismissive hand.

"So wot's the topic, gentlemen?"

Sinclair spoke. "Well ... uh ... Ralph, we've been trying to figure a way to make a mixture of paint that looks like authentic gold for a ... a project of ours."

"Welp, I can't help you there. Know nothing about it, y'see?" The door to the wardroom opened and five nurses filed in, chattering brightly. Woodley motioned them over. "Girls! Join us," he said. Sinclair sighed and wiped a hand over his face, resting his chin on the palm, elbow on the table. When they had all settled in, and introductions had been made, Woodley spoke again. "Girls, these men are discussing how they can possibly make authentic gold paint. Any ideas?"

"Use actual gold?" said Ruth, and tittered. Woodley was stern.

"Let's be serious here! It's a problem to be solved. Anyone?"

"Nope." "Uh-uh." "Not a clue." Ruth, Doris, Helen and Violet all shook their heads. Margaret said nothing, eyes downcast, her brows wrinkled in thought.

"Margaret?" Ralph prompted. She raised her eyes.

"Varnish," she said.

"Och, nae," said Hamish, "'twill be clear, an' ye canna mix paint in it. 'Twill make a splodgy mess." Sinclair nodded in agreement.

Margaret said shyly, "I was in a panto before Christmas, 1934. We had to make a king's crown look just right. We painted it black, and then covered it with varnish, mixed with red and yellow food colouring."

It was as if a thunderclap had struck. Hamish abruptly shouted, "Lord sakes, I'm an idiot!" A table of deck officers across the room looked their way. "Thank ye, Margaret, for solving a problem that had us all befuddled." Tord, the steward, arrived with the supper selection for the nurses, a pack of cigarettes rolled into the sleeve of his T-shirt. The nurses were impressed with his massive chest and biceps, and didn't bother hiding their admiration. Each with a hand covering her mouth, they all tittered as he flexed his arm to make the hula girl sway. The captain and engineers dawdled, finishing their tea, waiting impatiently for the nurses to finish their dinners. When Ralph and the nurses left, Sinclair bade Margaret stay.

"Margaret, do you happen to remember the formula, or the ratio, of the varnish you mixed?"

Her brows knitted, she frowned. Eyes squeezed shut, she recited, "Two ounces of varnish, eight drops of yellow, four drops of red, I think?"

* * *

Late Saturday morning, towards noon, Sinclair met the captain in the wardroom as he was tucking in to his tiffin of cullen skink.

"Here you are," he announced, handing him a sheet of neatly scribbled calculations written in a cramped style. At the top of the page was a dimensioned isometric sketch of a gold bar. The captain wiped his mouth with a serviette and took the paper, to read the final result outlined in a heavy rectangle at the bottom of the page: '5 quarts varnish, 1 fluid ounce yellow, ½ fluid ounce red food colouring.'

"Five quarts?" he asked.

"Yes. I expect we can grip them with some sort of device, and dip them," said Sinclair. "At twenty-seven pounds each, whatever we use must be robust. If we – *Jesus!*" – he jumped - "Damn, you scared hell out of me!" The steward loomed over them, his head tilted, trying to read the paper.

"*Unskyld* – Sorry. Dip vaat? Iss yoo ere vanting to grippe sommeting haaffy?"

"Yes. Very heavy," said Mallinson.

"I yust curious." He began to collect dirty plates, all the time continuing his attempt to read it.

"Mr Andreassen," Sinclair said, wearily. "We're attempting to dip some ... some 'blocks' that are very heavy into paint, to coat them. Unfortunately, we cannot handle them because, well, that will leave fingerprint marks in the finish. Do you see?"

"*Ja, jeg forstår.* Du yoo vant sommeting to eat?"

"Yes, please. The fish stew will do nicely, thank you." Collecting his stack of dishes, the steward returned to the galley.

"Did you see that?" said Sinclair, "How can anyone that fu ... uh, ... hulking big, be so silent? Damn!" Mallinson smiled.

"Now, back to the task at hand: we can't drill a hole in the ingots for a suspension wire because, well, that's not what ingots look like."

"Agreed. A dead giveaway that it's a fake."

"Could we maybe form some sort of basket out of wire, to dip the pieces?"

Sinclair shook his head, "Lifting them out of the basket will leave fingerprints in the varnish. Dumping them out will likewise harm the finish. Again, a giveaway that it's fake, if anyone were to examine it."

"Hmm-mm." The steward approached with the engineer's lunch and set it before him.

"*Kaffe* or tea?" he asked.

"Coffee, please."

They sat awhile thinking over the problem as they ate. Tord returned with a tray. Holding the tray in the palm of one hand, he transferred the items one by one from tray to table, announcing, "*Kaffe, sukker* and *mælk* ..." then, lifting the empty tray to one side, he revealed what he had concealed underneath. "und a paar oaf tongs." Cast-iron and scissor-like, it had curved arms with a single pointed tooth at the end of each, the pair facing together and the other end of each with a circular handle. They were surprised. This was exactly what they needed. "Where did you get this?"

Tord explained patiently, "Det ere eis-blokk tongs. Venn dis schippe vas build, she haff det eis-boxx. Det ere long gone now. Tongs be hang in pantry for thirty yahrs. So." Mallinson was impressed.

"Mr Andreassen, thank you. You have helped us a tremendous amount here!" Tord gave a nod and turned to go. He turned back around and stood erect.

"Kapitan Mallinson. I vant yoo to know I nott be drunkard, yah. I yust vant to haff vun last pull ov de boddle, bekoss I tink you be a tee-total mann, like all de odder Kapitans. I see dis is nott trew, yah."

"Mr Andreassen, I believe you. Good man!" The steward left. Turning to his engineer, the captain said, "First the varnish, and now the tongs. Well, that's sorted then!"

* * *

Mallinson had long since given up conducting a Sunday service when in port, because the men could find a church, or a temple, in town should they so desire. He was also wary of appearing to proselytize by conducting any service for men who didn't subscribe to that particular faith. The crew's working week was Monday to Friday and half of Saturday. When in a port, they had the remainder of Saturday and all of Sunday to themselves. When they had embarked, Mallinson had escorted Mr Woodley and Chief Nurse Wright around the ship, showing them the areas where they were allowed to go, such as the boat deck, and where they could not go, such as the bridge and the engineering spaces. He had opened the upper door to the engine room on the boat deck and stepped inside to show them the top of the massive triple-expansion steam engine, but they had not descended the stair. He'd also apprised them of the crew's schedule. The passengers, of course, were not held to any schedule. They could come and go as they pleased whilst in port, needing only to give their destination and sign the clipboard at the bulwark gate. He reminded them of the significance of the Blue Peter flag. This Saturday afternoon he decided to go into the city to run some errands. He waited until much of the crew had disembarked and then sought out Becky in the passenger accommodation.

The *Empress* had twelve passenger cabins. Each pair of cabins shared a water closet between them. The cabins were located on the weather deck, arranged six each, port and starboard, and between these were the uptakes for the boiler furnace exhausts. Similar to an actual ocean liner, their doors gave out onto a covered promenade deck, directly beneath the boat deck with its lifeboats. In practice, the boats could be lowered to the level of the cabins for the convenience of loading the passengers.

The entry in the passenger log told him Becky had been assigned cabin one, port side, forward. He knocked on the door but there was no answer. Nants had been assigned cabin two, starboard side, forward. He rapped on that door and Nants opened it. Before he could say a word, she grabbed him by the lapels and hauled him headlong into the room. Darting her head out, looking right and left, she quietly shut the door and locked it. She pulled the curtains.

"What is—?" The captain began.

"Shh!" Nants whispered. "Did anybody see you come here?"

"I don't believe so. Why?" She blew out a long breath.

"Nurse Wright gave us a stern talking-to about *fraternisation*," she said, spitting the word out.

"I'm sure she must have been referring to the unlicensed crew. As master of this ship, I'm allowed to go anywhere."

"Keep your voice down! Nurse Wright is from the States. She's very protective of us."

"I'm sure she is. Is she insisting you stay aboard?"

"No. We can go out. It's just ... she doesn't want us to fraternise with anybody," she said, with a sulk.

"Well, I feel like going to the market. Where is Becky?"

"On the dock, waiting for you."

"I see. Thank you, my dear, for the warning. Would you like to come with us?" he asked.

"Oh no, you two go have fun," she brightened, "but thanks for asking."

"Do you know which cabin is Nurse Wright's?" he asked, unable to recall.

"No."

"She shares a water closet with Woodley. Do you know which cabin he's in?"

"Sorry, no." Nants stepped out onto the deck. She leaned on the rail and casually glanced about, as if admiring what view there was. Flocks of seagulls lifted off from one guano-laden, corrugated-iron godown roof, only to wheel in a wide circle before alighting on another. He left, after they had ascertained that the coast was clear. In the pedal *becak* heading south, out of sight from the ship, Becky stepped from behind a godown and flagged them down. Today she wore a knee-length navy blue dress with large white polka dots, wide shoulder straps, and the square neckline set low that she tended to favour. While stopped for a minute, the driver raised the canopy. Overhead were low clouds. It smelled like rain was in the offing. They continued south.

"Where're we going?" she asked.

"Shopping. There's some things I need," he said.

"What things?"

"Turmeric spice, for one."

"Turmeric spice?"

"For my gout."

"Oh dear, you have gout?"

"In case you hadn't noticed, Becky, my dear, I'm old."

"I had noticed. I. Do. Not. Care." She kissed his cheek.

"Becky, perhaps I'm being dense here, but I don't understand *why* you don't care."

"Roy, darling, I like that you call me 'my dear'."

He shrugged, "Fair enough, but you should know, that's just the way my parents raised me."

She wasn't dissuaded. "I like that in a man. You know, boys my age are just ... well," – she paused, searching for the proper words – "well, they're immature, and they can be *very* crude. I like that you're a gentleman. I also like that you're a gentle man." They were approaching a crossroads. A moment later Roy saw the road rise ahead and realised that in a hundred yards they would cross the railway track where that accident must have happened. *I don't want Becky to see that!*

"Driver, do you know where the harbourmaster's office is?" he called.

"Indeed, *sahib*, I have taken you there before."

"Oh yes, of course. Please take us there again." The driver turned the *becak* to the right, and they continued westbound on Zuiderweg Road. It began to rain, a drizzle that would last the rest of the day. The driver handed an oilcloth blanket to Roy, who spread it over their legs. Roy explained this was the harbinger of the monsoon, and would become more frequent, and heavier, as November advanced. The rain pattered noisily on the cab's canopy above their heads.

"Becky, I've just remembered, it's Saturday afternoon and the harbourmaster's office is most likely shut. Driver, will you please continue on to Batavia?"

"Yes, *sahib.*"

"Is it painful, this gout of yours?" Becky asked.

"Oh yes."

"Driver!" she shouted.

"Yes, *sahiba?*"

"Where is the very best spice market in all of Batavia?"

"The Jalan Pasar Baru, *sahiba,*" he replied.

"Take us there, please!" she ordered.

"Yes, *sahiba.*" Batavia was a city of canals. Becky pointed out the boatmen poling barges overloaded apparently to the point of capsize, although they never did. She thought the donkeys pulling the ever-present carts were incredibly charming. She laughed at the sight of the naked brown boys squatting on the riverside quays, slapping laundry against the stones in the rain, their smiles brilliant as they looked up. The driver turned left into a wide boulevard. He kept far to the left because there were hundreds of cyclists all going faster than themselves. Six miles later they were dropped at the market's north entrance, a high stone arch with a tile roof, near its top a carved wooden and gilded banner proclaiming, 'Batavia, Passer Baroe, 1820'. Beyond it they saw a narrow pedestrian shopping street, fortunately roofed over, a third of a mile long and packed with hundreds of stalls.

"Here is Little India, *sahib,*" the driver announced. Mallinson paid the man, and they dashed for cover. They sauntered slowly, in no hurry, browsing from stall to stall. There were many fabric stores, identifiable by the word *Tekstil*, and clothes and shoes, antiques, jewellery, musical instruments, as well as many restaurants. A stall of bamboo and rattan cages proved to be a man selling parrots and cockatoos, which Becky admired. The rain drummed on the arched canopy high overhead. Becky pulled Roy by the hand into a *Tekstil* shop, to drape herself with a few yards of shimmering Indian silk in a purple and gold pattern, while the proprietor beseeched him to buy it; there was not another bolt of this in all of Java and who knows when, or whether, another might become available! Roy was forced to remind her the ship had no sewing machine, and gently eased her out of the shop. As they strolled down the centre of the street, Becky suddenly turned and embraced Roy. They stood this way for long moments, surrounded by shoppers bustling all around them, until Becky whispered, "I've missed you."

"I've missed you, too," he whispered in reply, and then everything was fine again, and they continued on their way.

Soon they chanced upon the first of many stalls of Indian spices, mounded colourfully in ranks of open burlap sacks. Roy bartered with the proprietor for enough turmeric to last him a year. It was as well he was unsuccessful, because there was a better bargain further along the street. He bought a pint bottle of apple cider vinegar. The red and yellow food colouring he needed was provided by a wholesale bakery. They simply could not find the wood dowels anywhere that he needed for his project. In the end, as a substitute, he had to settle for a bucket of marbles from a toyshop. There was a young man at a stall with wooden crates of books, and Becky surprised Roy with a pocket-sized Javanese/English dictionary. They strolled past ranks of tables, the young women sitting stoically behind, waiting for passers-by to take an interest in their wares. Their elderly grandmothers sat nearby rocking back and forth, their wrinkled faces nodding, laughing happily at nothing in particular. Their grins showed missing or blackened teeth. Roy found a bottle of Pikaki Lani perfume in a monkey-pod wood holder carved in the shape of a plumeria blossom. A silver-foil label on its underside read, 'John Oya, Hawaii'. *Becky will love this.* He bought it for her when her back was turned, and was pleased when she was indeed delighted with it. He looked ahead and could see they were nearing the end of the market. As Becky browsed a stall of handbags, Roy went on ahead through the vegetable market. Jimmy the Cook had asked him to find some horseradish for tomorrow's Sunday roast, and this he bought. At the far end of the street, near the canal, he encountered the meat market and was immediately sorry he had. There were the usual live fish idling in tubs of water too small for them, and pigs and chickens in cages, but he was horrified to see roasted bats (wings sold separately), rats-on-a-stick, broiled snakes and, most terrible of all, whole roasted dogs on tables, blackened and bloated, fangs bared in a forever silent snarl, right next to live dogs in cages awaiting the same fate. *What the hell? This is a predominantly Muslim nation; eating dog is* dilarang, '*forbidden.*' He dashed back and caught Becky in time to steer her away, without explanation. Becky showed Roy a delicately beaded handbag she fancied, and he bought it for her. The perfume bottle did fit neatly inside. In early evening, after a supper of chicken rissoles and rice, they visited a clothing shop in the process of shutting its doors, and Roy bought Becky a waterproof wrap for the return trip. He hired a donkey cart, knowing this would please her. They arrived at the ship at sunset in the middle of the last dog watch. Roy made a visit to the galley to give Jimmy his horseradish, warning him to make absolutely certain of the source of his meats while they were here, and telling him the reason why.

* * *

On Sunday morning, when much of the crew was either still in the city or asleep, Mallinson met his chief and second engineers at the forward end of number two hatch. The rain had ended in early morning, and the heat of the day made steam rise from the deck as it dried. They strung sheets and blankets on lines from the after side of the midship house to the wingtips of the nearest aeroplane. This prevented prying eyes from seeing what they were up to. They knocked the wedges out of the hatch boards of the hold. They shifted three of them, the most they could do because of where the tail wheel of the aeroplane rested, but it was enough. Then the ship's hand truck was used to wheel each box from the stack at the forward bulkhead of the midship house aft through the covered deck to the open number two hatch aft of the midship house. The chief had rigged an extension lead to an electric drill fitted with a Robertson screwdriver tip. This they used to back the screws out far enough to release the lid, yet still have the screws remain with the lid. They hoisted each box of gold to the rim of the hatch, and tipped the 250-pound weight of gold bars into the depression left where they had removed the loose lead cargo. Then, keeping each lid matched with its box, they stacked them aside. It was hot, sweaty work, for which the captain and chief were ill suited, but they kept at it most of the day. The chief was two years younger than him; Sinclair was twenty-nine. At length they all had their shirts off. Near the end of the afternoon watch, their energies flagging, they had all slowed down despite frequently swapping roles. The chief poured himself another glass of water from the pitcher.

"Och, my arm's aching. I'm exhausted," he said.

"I'm fair played out," said Sinclair as he towelled the sweat from his aching shoulders. The captain leaned on the edge of the hatch, looking at the heap of gold bars filling the void in the lead nodules below, and tried to catch his breath. Sweat dripped off his nose. *This is going to take days. I'm going to need the crew to finish this, because it's going to kill me.*

"Whadja do, boys? Rob Fort Knox?" Mallinson whirled. There was no one there. Sinclair and the chief checked outside the hanging bed sheets. There was no one there either. "Hey! Can anybody join in this gig? I could use a few more simoleons in my pocket!" They looked up.

Nurse Wright leaned on the rail of the boat deck. She took a drag on a cigarette and blew a smoke ring.

"How long have you been watching us?" he demanded.

"Oh, I don't know ... half an hour?" Mallinson cursed himself for a fool. He looked at the engineers and made a decision.

"Come on down, and I'll explain." Two more nurses appeared on either side of Nurse Wright. It was Nants and Becky. Mallinson threw up his hands and sighed.

"Are there any more of you up there?"

"No."

"Good. Come down, and I'll explain." Nurse Wright flicked her cigarette overboard.

"So, that's the story," he said, as he finished his explanation. "The monsoon will start in earnest any week now, and after we empty these boxes, they still have to be filled with the fake bars, and those are not even dipped yet. We are running out of valuable time." The four of them sat perched on the coaming of the hatch. Becky stood behind the captain kneading his aching shoulders. Nants stood, working to get the knots out of Sinclair. The nurses cast glances down into the shadowy hold where the pile of gold bars shone dully, the result of eight hours of back–breaking work. Nurse Wright shook a Lucky Strike out of the pack and tapped it on the hatch coaming.

"When are we leaving Batavia?" she asked. MacCallan, his pipe packed, dug a matchbook out of his boiler suit and lit her cigarette, then his own tobacco.

"I'd hoped to leave by Thursday next. The thirteenth."

"And you can't delay that?"

"It's bad luck to begin a voyage on a Friday."

"Huh." She exhaled a stream of smoke. "I wouldn't have pegged you as a superstitious man."

"Personally, I'm not, but crews have jumped ship, or mutinied, for less." Sinclair and the chief nodded agreement at this. "I've been working on getting the crew to trust me, but it takes time. We've been a full crew for less than five months, and I still don't know all the men."

"May I make a suggestion, captain?"

"Please."

"You need more people involved, to do what needs doing, in the time you have left."

"Well, yes, that's obvious," he said, "A single day's worth of this work has damn near killed us, excuse my French. But if we're stopped and searched, and a gun were put against a man's head, he might sing like a budgerigar to save himself, so the fewer that know about all this, the better," he said, jerking his chin at the hold.

"But, there are six of us now."

"Six? Oh no, I couldn't possibly allow—"

"Hold this," she said, handing her cigarette to Sinclair. She interlaced her fingers, palms together, and placing them near her cheek batted her eyelashes at Mallinson. Affecting the accent of a southern belle from the recent hit film *Gone with the Wind*, she drawled, "Why, Captain Mallinson, suh, ah do declare y'all are about to intimate we nusses are the weaker sex." She dropped the mannerisms. "And if you do, buster, you'll be sorry." She reclaimed her cigarette.

"You misunderstand me," he replied. "I'm only insisting you're our guests."

"Guests or not, we can pull our own weight," she replied. "We're not useless. Now, this is what's gonna happen; you talk that hunk of Scandihoovian muscle into doing the dumping. Betcha he can go all day long. We're gonna set up an assembly line, see? Nurse Margaret came up with the varnish idea. She can sit and stir the varnish to keep the colour mixed uniformly, and do it slow so no air bubbles are introduced.

My nurses will take the tarps from the pallets of lead and spread them on the hatch cover. I'm guessing you bought that bucket of marbles as support for the wet ingots, right? Throw handfuls of marbles on the tarps. A nurse can arrange three marbles on the hatch cover as a support for each wet ingot you guys bring to her. As each ingot becomes dry to the touch, it gets put in a crate. You got a bunch of empty crates sitting right here all ready. That's a good start. When a crate is full, a nurse can screw the lid on with the drill, got it? The only heavy work is the dipping and the dumping, right?" Sinclair nodded at this.

"Gold is, what? Seventy percent heavier than lead," Sinclair said. "If Mr Andreassen does it instead of me, that saves my back. When he completes the dumping, we close the hatch and no one sees it until Australia. Then, if we're seen by the crew while we do our varnish work, so what? It's just painted lead cargo to them."

"Yes. That's a plan, a good one. We'll do it!" said Mallinson. "I'll give the crew a shore leave until Wednesday night, to keep them out of our hair."

"*This* is why she's our chief nurse," said Nants.

* * *

On Monday, a delivery lorry stopped mid-morning, and the harbour-master boarded and asked Mallinson if he would be amenable to dropping two sacks of post, three parcels and a small crate at Christmas Island on his way to Fremantle. Its delivery was long overdue. Since that island wasn't out of their way, Mallinson had the crew bring it aboard. The crew, to put it mildly, was cock-a-hoop to get a second shore leave in as many weeks. The captain gave them their freedom until the night of the twelfth of November, and even gave an advance on their next pay packet for those who had spent all their money on their last leave. He then spoke to Mr Andreassen, who agreed to be included in their operation. After the crew had left the ship, Tord was brought a box with the hand truck and stood by as Sinclair wielded the drill. When a lid was off, he hefted the gold over the coaming and it thudded into the cargo below. Nants or Becky then inserted the lid diagonally into the box and took it away, stacking them on their sides. In this way they were able to empty a box at the rate of one every minute and a half, stopping for ten minutes each hour for a rest and refreshment. All the remaining gold was into the hatch by suppertime. Tord and Sinclair shifted the hatch boards into position and hammered the wedges in, lacing down the tarpaulin.

On Tuesday morning the repairs to the condenser were 'done and dusted' and the workmen packed up their tools and departed, after the chief had completed his tests. Then the group started on the dipping operation. It went according to plan. The older men followed each other in a continuous relay, carrying one lead ingot at a time from the pallet to Tord, where they set it upon a wood block on the hatch cover. Tord stood on the hatch cover. He gripped each ingot with the tongs on its long axis. Margaret sat and slowly stirred the varnish mixture in a roasting pan next to the block. She removed her spoon and Tord dipped and drained the ingot. He then carried it to where Becky was placing marbles, setting it down and returning to the pan. The hatch cover filled with row upon row of glistening bricks. Becky kept track of the rows, so they knew where to begin picking them up, when dry. As each row of dry bricks was taken to the boxes, they were replaced by freshly dipped bricks. Nants wielded the drill like a pro, snugging the screws down without overtightening them. It developed into a continuous conveyor-like operation. They left the last hatch cover-full of ingots there to dry overnight.

The next day, the operation continued and was complete by sunset. These were merely varnish-coated lead ingots, so the captain assumed it was safe to assign a handful of ordinary seamen the task of finishing the last of the carrying and boxing up, while Tord continued his dipping. These were the men who had straggled back to the ship early from their revelries, having run out of dosh. They didn't mind, as it gave them the chance to chat up the nurses. They later bragged of their good fortune to their comrades when they returned. The men naturally wondered what the captain was up to with this weird project, but in the end they couldn't figure it out. Tord and the nurses, of course, professed to not knowing either. Aware the word would spread anyway, Mallinson invented a story, telling them, "The varnish is being applied to protect the lead from corrosion," and it was all being done for "an unnamed Australian client". Because they now carried passengers, the captain ordered the bosun to conduct a lifeboat drill according to the regulations. Just in case they might be torpedoed.

* * *

Early on Thursday morning, Mallinson was greatly relieved to be finally underway. The *Dominion Empress* left port at 0500 hours and steamed due north for an hour. The sun was up by 0530 hours. Once clear of the islets and reefs off Batavia he had the helmsman turn west, passing south of Pari Island and also south of Pulau Tunda Island. At 1000 hours he ordered a course change to a heading of 228 degrees, to align them with the centre of the Sunda Strait between the islands of Java and Sumatra. He knew the farther south they went, the better. They were essentially attempting to outrun the Asian monsoon. There was the Indo-Australian monsoon, what Australians called 'the wet', but that usually didn't build in until late December into January, and then it stayed mostly in the north of Australia anyhow. They had left the last hatch cover-full of ingots overnight, and the captain was pleased to see the crew and the nurses finish boxing them up shortly before noon. As each box was completed, it had been stacked against the after bulkhead of the midship house with the others, and a number of tarpaulins were now secured over this. They were careful to arrange the tarpaulins with the golden varnish splatters on the inside, where they could not be seen. He ordered the ship's carpenter to stow away the now empty pallets and the few leftover ammo boxes. The noon sight put them in the centre of the Sunda Strait, the famous Krakatau volcano looming off the starboard bow. Mallinson played tour guide for a moment by calling attention to it on the tannoy. A skein of smoke drifted eastwards from its summit. Binoculars revealed dusty rockfalls on its upper slopes as it trembled. What a magnificent sight! Three hours later, after they had cleared the strait and passed Pulau Panaitan Island abeam to port, he ordered a course change to 171 degrees to set them on a heading for Christmas Island, nineteen hours distant.

At the beginning of the first dog watch Mallinson went below to the wardroom for tea. As he entered he saw the chief seated across the room and waved to him, then sat with Chief MacCallan and they ate together. When they had finished, MacCallan said with a twinkle in his eye, "Come up to my cabin, I've summat to show ye." Tord arrived to collect their plates. Just then the captain noticed a bit of a commotion happening in the adjacent crews mess. Through the connecting archway he could see dozens of Chinese firemen and Lascar coal-trimmers gathered at the cook's pass-through, their voices raised. He asked Tord if he knew what was going on.

"Yah, det ere Chinese mann, komm here for supper."

"Supper? Well, of course they're welcome but, I was under the impression that they preferred doing their own meals after their own fashion, and in their own quarters."

"Dis be trew," Tord replied, "I nott know dem so much, but dey haff komm here every night, only for to ask nossing but to haff our potatoes."

"Potatoes? Isn't a basic staple of their diet made up mainly of noodles?"

Yah, iss noodles. Dey vant potatoes now, buckets of peeled potatoes dey taking at supper. Dat crewmann, he be peeling potatoes haff de day."

"I'd no idea that Chinese even ate potatoes." the captain mused aloud.

"Oh, dey nott eat dem."

"They don't eat them?

"Bekoss dey be giffing dem to de carpenter, yah." Mallinson bit his lip to suppress a snort. *How very cunning*, he thought, *not so inscrutable as people make them out to be!*

"Tord, is the serang in there?"

"Yah."

"Would you ask him to come here, please?"

"Yah." He left. Hamish spoke.

"Roy, do ye think that's wise? Ye dinna want the man to lose face."

"Ham, it's fine. Not to worry," he replied. Roy was well aware that there was a hierarchy at play here, but felt he could smooth it over. It was usual for the serang to be seen to take orders only from the bosun or on occasion from the mates when the bosun was elsewhere. For him to be called before the captain was highly irregular. The room fell silent, and he became aware that everyone had turned to look as the serang glided across the room, his plimsolls soundless on the chequered linoleum. No member of the Asian crew had ever been seen in the officers wardroom, in memory. He stopped before the captain, tall and imperious, his long-fingered delicate hands clasped before him, and bowed. Not bowed, exactly, as he had only inclined his head ever so slightly. He stood, waiting, his mouth a grim line, looking down at Roy where he sat.

"Ah! ... Mr Chang, so glad to see—"

"Chinn."

Mallinson cleared his throat and began again. "So glad to see you, Mr Chinn." Beyond Chinn he saw the Asian crewmembers crowding the archway, watching. He knew the Chinese engineering assistants among them did understand English. He increased his volume. "I only wanted to say, what *magnificent* work your men are doing on my ship, really splendid! Top notch!"

"Thank you, captain." Another nod. Mallinson lowered his voice, to *sotto voce* level.

" ... and also to let you know that the crewman who was peeling potatoes – *that* man – ended his punishment yesterday. Different crewman today, if you take my meaning." Chinn's mouth changed ever so slightly, to imperceptibly become almost a Mona Lisa smile.

"Your meaning is taken, captain. Is that all you wished?"

Mallinson nodded, and raising his voice, repeated "Yes! Splendid work!" Mr Chinn gave a formal bow this time, and glided back into the crews mess.

"Roy, what in thunder was all that?" Hamish asked.

"Oh, yes, Ham, you weren't there, were you? Well, back in Batavia when we were examining the shell damage, we—"

"Roy, look!" Hamish interrupted, and pointed. Roy turned to see the Chinese filing out of the crews mess through its far door, but each one first paused in the archway between the rooms, to bow in his direction.

A few minutes later, the captain and the chief engineer sat in the chief's cabin, an ammunition box on the floor between them. Mallinson finished relating his story for Hamish.

"Now, what was it you wanted to show me?"

"D'ye rememburr the time pencils ye give me?"

"Why, yes. What did you think of them?"

"Well, I've a use for 'em. If the Jerries or the Japs ever board us, and take our gold, here's a wee surprise for 'em." He lifted the lid of the box and lifted out two lead ingots, to reveal a Bofors shell cradled within a nest of bars. Behind the base of the shell lay one of the time pencils supported in a crevice gouged from the lead, its end attached to the primer in the shell's base. Turning the lid over in his hands, the chief showed a hole had been drilled through the lid, and a short section of artfully whittled wood dowel projecting through it was positioned over the crushable end of the pencil. This dowel was held in place by a springy piece of flat metal. On the outside of the lid the dowel stood proud a quarter-inch and was painted blue, the same colour as the printing on the box, thus effectively disguising it. It was immediately obvious to the captain it was a bomb. In engineering terms, a very elegant bomb, too! Mallinson was nearly speechless in his admiration of it.

"Why, Hamish, this … this is ingenious! I see you simply push on the dowel, the dowel crushes the time pencil, and in two hours it's going to fire. And of course, since the brass shell casing isn't constrained by any breech, the explosion will affect everything around it. The box looks similar to any of the others. How many did you make?"

"Two. I kin make more if ye want. Just rememburr, wherever ye store this, point it overboard. Will nae do to shoot ourselves accidentally!" Hamish pulled the "safety strip", making it ready, and replaced the ingots and the lid, firmly screwing it down. Together they carried it down to the stack of the others and heaved this 'special box' under the tarpaulin next to its mate, and out of arm's reach. Hamish had thoughtfully marked the end the shell pointed to, and this they positioned to point outboard. Mallinson had Nurse Ruth fashion a warning sign and pin it to the tarpaulin. He saw it later. It read: 'Keep

Off Under Pain Of Death!' and she had artistically fashioned the letters with red paint to look like dripping blood.

7

Interlude

On Friday morning Mallinson was greeted on the bridge by the first mate, who gave his usual morning report.

"Revolutions eighty-five, course one seven one, temperature seventy-four, wind south-south-west, Force 4, barometer 30.06 and rising slowly, sir." At 0700 hours a spot appeared on the horizon ahead and grew as they crawled towards it. This proved to be the 1,200-foot summit of Murray Hill on Christmas Island. Three hours later, the third mate rang for Dead Slow Ahead as they approached The Settlement, on Flying Fish Cove. Mallinson didn't have a pilot chart for this island but saw a Norwegian freighter, the motorship *Eidsvold*, loading phosphate ore at the end of the conveyor gantry, and his binoculars showed her nearly down to her marks. He had to assume there was enough depth. They rafted to her after getting permission from her master, who joked to Mallinson that he was happy to have the *Dominion Empress* there as a buffer against any incoming torpedoes. Mallinson was a bit concerned as to how exposed the *Dominion Empress* was, until they learnt there was a six-inch naval gun emplacement in the hillside above the governor's residence. That put his mind at ease. The nurses and some of the off-duty crew watched the phosphate loading operation. The bosun detailed a trio of ordinary seamen to lug the post across the other freighter to the postmaster and his assistant, who were waiting for it with a handcart on the gantry catwalk. When they returned they had two sacks of post destined for Australia, which the captain accepted.

Mallinson stood together with Seaman Halvorsen, his galley steward Tord Andreassen, his cabin steward Einar, and the Norwegian master of the *Eidsvold*, Samuel Fridvold. As they chatted, catching up with the reports coming out of occupied Norway and Denmark, a runner appeared on the catwalk. When he arrived on the deck of the *Dominion Empress*, he tendered greetings to the captain from the British Commissioner of Christmas Island. An invitation was extended to his officers and passengers to dine at Tai Jin House, the governor's residence. All the nurses clamoured for him to stay – "Just for a day, *oh, please!*" – and he granted this, after having determined that Sir Shenton Thomas wasn't visiting. As it happened, the dinner to which they'd been invited was not until the following night, so he was forced to concede an extra day.

"I sure hope you like crab," Fridvold commented archly. "They got plenty here!" On that Sunday he planned to leave at noon, and it didn't seem right to rob the crew of their Sunday off. He remedied this by giving them their freedom for the remains of this Friday, for all of Saturday, and for Sunday until the start of the forenoon watch. *That should appease them*, he thought, and it did. The ship's company went into the village, where they found a pub. This generosity on the captain's part wasn't quite what it seemed; trade-union rules mandated that if they were at sea instead of in port during a weekend, the crew was to be paid overtime. Since they were in port he was, in fact, saving the Ellerman Lines the cost of some of that overtime, up until the beginning of Sunday's forenoon watch.

Much of the island was covered in tropical rainforest. Roughly triangular, at its furthest extent it was barely fifteen miles long. The locals told them of the freshwater springs, and the waterfalls. There were many caves, too. The red crabs the island was famous for were due to start their annual mating migration any day now. The locals also warned everyone about the blue coconut crab, also called the robber crab, so named because it liked to steal things. Anything at all. They discovered there was a cargo train on a standard gauge track that ran the length of the island, to the phosphate mines at its southern end. This tender locomotive was an 0-8-0 type and was affectionately called Old Number Six. The commissioner had thoughtfully laid on three passenger cars coupled to the locomotive's tender. Plans were made for excursions the next day. Everybody anticipated exploring what seemed to them a veritable paradise. Groups formed and plotted. Jimmy and Tord were prevailed upon to prepare basket lunches for each group.

* * *

Saturday morning dawned, and Captain Mallinson arrived late and boarded the first car to find it nearly full of his crewmen, nurses and a few townsfolk. The seats were of wooden slats painted green and covered with carved initials and graffiti, some of it quite obscene. He took a seat next to Nants and they looked out the windows, open to the breeze, while they waited.

"Where is Becky?" he asked her after a minute.

"Don't know. Is she in the other car?" Nants replied. He stood and, through the glass, saw her in the far end of the second car, gazing out.

"There she is!" He gave Nants's shoulder a pat. "I'll just go sit with her, yes?" Nants smiled and nodded. He made his way down the aisle but, just as he reached the door to the next car, it slid open and Nurse Wright stepped through. The locomotive whistle shrieked.

"There you are! Come with me! There's no time to waste!" She grabbed him by the hand and dragged him bodily off the train, as he looked back at Nants, who shrugged her shoulders with a look of resignation. "Hurry up! I convinced the engineer to let us ride in the cab! Run!" She hustled him forwards through clouds of steam, and they climbed up and stepped onto the footplate just as the locomotive wheels gave a spin before gaining traction. They crowded in and Nurse Wright leaned out the opening into the breeze, a hand clamping her hat in place, as they gained speed. They were told it had been built in 1931 in Bristol, England, especially for this phosphate company. She seemed fascinated with its operation as the driver explained each of its controls. She insisted the fireman give her a chance to shovel coal into the firebox, and he proclaimed her 'a natural at it'. To accommodate everyone, it chuffed its way to South Point and returned, multiple times that day. At certain sylvan places the train passed through glades of wildflower meadows, and the locomotive driver halted to drop off parties of ordinary seamen and nurses for their idyllic picnics. Nurse Wright seemed to have no objection as long as they were in groups. The chief nurse and the captain debarked into one of these meadows and strolled for a bit.

"Is Einar taking care of you?" he asked her. "Are the beds clean and comfortable enough?"

"Einar. I thought you described him as a 'dour Norwegian'. He has a lovely singing voice!"

"Einar? Singing? You must be joking!"

"Not in the least. He's a tenor. He sang a selection for me from 'Pear Giant'." Mallinson coughed and suppressed a smirk.

"*Peer Gynt* ... So, does your group have sufficient hot water from the showers? Have you any complaints?"

"We're fine, thank you. Let's hike!" she exclaimed. They found a well-trodden jungle trail and tramped westwards. Soon they were deep in conversation. She was twenty-seven, older than all the other nurses, but not by much. They spoke of the events driving them out of China. This was the first posting overseas, for all of them. Nurse Wright was surprised to hear that Roy wasn't a churchgoer. Nurse Wright – "Please, it's Virginia" – was from Charlotte, Clinton County, Iowa, near the Mississippi River. From the captain's description of his Suffolk countryside, she felt it sounded similar, but without Iowa's heat and humidity, of course. Her college major had been in nursing, with a minor in hospital management, which is how she had ended up working with Woodley. The conversation then turned to the various nurses' personalities. The trail began to rise steeply. They fell silent to conserve their breath. The susurration of insects only served to augment the still heat of the forest. The trees were sparse here and there was little shade, as the sun was directly overhead now. Even the birds were silent. They pushed through a thicket of screw pine trees and emerged onto a high rock outcropping. This afforded a view of Flying Fish Cove in the distance, and Roy pointed out the phosphate loading conveyor with its pair of freighters. She opened her ever present clutch bag to bring out a pack of Lucky Strike cigarettes. She lit one and stepped on the match. They shaded their eyes as Roy pointed out the few frigate birds wheeling high overhead. They both could feel the heat emanating from the surface of the bare rock, and Virginia commented on this. Then Roy remembered what had been lurking in the back of his mind.

"I want to thank you for your excellent diagnosis and prescription! Turmeric and apple-cider vinegar. I'm speechless. My flare-ups of gout have completely disappeared!" Virginia waved a hand in modesty.

"It's an old remedy. We nurses have been trained to work with any local herbs that come to hand, for those times when we find ourselves out in the boondocks. Most recently, I've been studying Jethro Kloss, the American, but we studied them all, you know; your English guy, Nicholas Culpeper, even as far back as Galen in the ancient world. You know that turmeric is native to India, right?"

"But, of course, India! Yes, I've noticed that whenever I eat curry, it helps the gout."

She quoted a passage to him: "The Lord hath created medicines out of the earth, and he that is wise will not abhor them." She took a drag and exhaled, then said, "I want to thank you for the ride home."

"Think nothing of it. Happy to do it."

"Also the huge gift of money you provided for our group."

"No problem at all, really. You could say it was my little act of revenge; it was meant to make me feel better and, by George, did it ever work a treat!"

"My God, that worked out to a hundred bucks each!" she exclaimed.

"You know, that didn't come out of my own pocket; the expense was covered by either the Ellerman Lines Steamship Company or else the Ministry of War Transport." She took a drag on her cigarette, and stood a moment taking in the view as she exhaled. When she spoke next, it was in a manner that was calculated to be nonchalant.

"You spent the day out in the company of Rebecca the other day."

"Yes, I did."

"What was it you were doing?"

"Shopping for the turmeric and apple-cider vinegar you prescribed. Also food colouring and marbles for, well, you know, that project of ours. Jimmy asked for some horseradish, too."

"You bought her a rainproof wrap."

"Yes. It was raining."

"And what a lovely purse you bought for her – that did come out of your own pocket."

"I thought she might need something in which to carry her share of the allowance." *Quite the nosy parker, aren't you?*

"Perfume, too. Imported from Hawaii, and *very* expensive."

"Well, yes, I suppose I did. I saw no harm in that."

"You left from Nants's cabin, too."

"Oh! – ahhh, – you saw that, did you?" he said, and saw her smile vanish. Her eyes grew narrow and hard.

"Uh-huh." She looked around her in all directions. They were indeed alone. She turned to Roy and, jabbing a finger at him with the hand that held her cigarette, demanded, "Are you fucking my nurses?"

Roy caught his breath. A whiff of smoke came with it. Doubled over, he gave a strangled cough and his eyes watered. Virginia slapped his back.

"Not helping," he managed to gasp. He spat, struggling to get his handkerchief out, then dabbing his eyes and wiping his mouth. "You Yanks!" was all he finally managed to say. He straightened, but was careful to stand away from the smoke.

"I'm concerned for them," she said. "I don't want to see Nants get hurt."

"What? Nants! Nants is ... I must be three times her age! Nurse Wright – *Virginia* – there is nothing, *absolutely nothing*, going on between Nants and myself."

"Oh. So it must be Becky, after all. I suspected as much. It is only Becky, right? No one else?" she demanded. Roy looked at her, aghast.

"Do you take me for a bounder?"

"Is this the price you extracted from Becky in order to take us home?" she said, icily. She flicked the ash.

"That is a base accusation, and I refuse to dignify it with an answer. I think you are labouring under a false impression; it was Becky that initiated this ... this thing, this ... tryst between us."

"A tryst! Is that what you call it? There's another word comes to mind," she said, sarcastically. She took hold of his hand and, holding it up before him, showed him his wedding band, then released him. She didn't need to say anything more. He looked about the rocky knoll.

"Please, let's sit." They found a seat on a nearby log. Roy pocketed his handkerchief. "I know, I mean I'm well aware. In a sense, it does bother me. It seems that my wife and I, we ... well, after a third of a century of marriage, it seems we have been living separate lives, under the same roof, for quite some time now." He continued, "You will need to excuse me, I am unaccustomed to speaking to any woman in this manner but, you should know my wife and I have not, as you have so eloquently phrased it, fucked in over thirty years."

Now it was her turn to be appalled. "Thirty *years*? Good lord! Why, that's longer than my entire lifetime!" she said, shaking her head in disbelief. "I can't imagine what that must be like."

"Yes, I had forgotten, myself, until Becky came along. I'm no trick-cyclist, but – sorry, that's navy slang for 'psychiatrist' – but with the current state of the world and the horror of what happened to all of you in China, I believe Becky is searching for, is needing, happiness in her life, and now for her, at her age, I suppose that means physical happiness. I'm an old man. Becky has told me she doesn't care. I truly don't understand why she doesn't care. I must admit, I am extraordinarily fond of her, but with the difference in our ages ..." He left the rest unspoken, and shrugged.

"I've gotten the impression she's extraordinarily fond of you, too," she said, thoughtfully.

"Becky and I have discussed all of this. I have let her know this cannot become lasting, and I believe she may accept that. In any case, since we left Batavia it may already have come to an end, sad as that may be for me to contemplate."

"Okay, point taken. Sorry I accused you." Virginia took a drag and exhaled. She was silent for a moment. "We were worried back in Bandung when Becky didn't come home for two nights. Nants eventually assured us that she was safe and in good hands."

"Eventually? Good for Nants."

"After all, Rebecca is an adult, I suppose," she mused. She flicked the ash from the cigarette. "Well, as long as you were taking precautions." She gripped his arm. "You *were* taking precautions, right?"

"What it was you taught her," he said, red-faced. *I can't believe I'm actually saying this, and to a woman I hardly know, no less.*

She stood and dropped her cigarette on the rock, stepping on it. He accepted her proffered hand and she helped him to his feet. They returned to the meadow to await the next passage of the train.

Another group of officers and nurses descended from the train and tramped eastwards amid Tahitian chestnut trees, strangler figs, screw pine and banyan trees. This group consisted of nurses Doris, Margaret, Ruth and Sue, First Mate Wallace, Third Mate O'Malley, Second Engineer Sinclair and Eugene who, while still a civilian employee and not an officer, was included because his expertise with the wireless was held in high regard by the licensed crew. Most of them were in their twenties, Wallace and Sinclair being the oldest at twenty-nine, the youngest being Eugene and Nurse Sue Kee, both still nineteen. The 'Dolly Beach Gang' (for this was how they referred to themselves when they spoke of it later) experienced one of the more extraordinary episodes of that day.

They emerged onto Dolly Beach. Some 150 yards long, it had brilliant white sand and was fringed by coconut palms. A freshwater stream trickled across it. They spread the blankets on a shaded patch of sand below a close-set pair of coconut palms, mere yards from the largest of many rock-rimmed tide pools. Out beyond the still waters of the pool, the waves rushed in and collapsed with a muted roar and a hiss. The tide was out. The onshore breeze carried the cool moisture and sharp tang of salt air, which they found refreshing. Margaret and Ruth each claimed a spot with their backs against a palm trunk for support. The officers and nurses kicked off their shoes, took off their socks and relaxed. Doris waded into the tide pool up to her knees before returning to the blankets. They picnicked on cold grilled chicken and an endive salad with cucumber, carrot shreds and salad cream; Tord had done a splendid job with the sweet fig-jam pastry afters. The meal finished, Wallace stood and announced he had prepared a surprise for them. He packed away the plates and cutlery, then from his basket he distributed mixed styles of glasses, culled from the bar of the governor's residence. He then produced a bottle of champagne, donated by the commissioner. This brought forth applause and peals of delighted laughter from the nurses. He held up a hand for silence; this wasn't the surprise.

He took off the bottle's foil and the wire bail. Withdrawing a bayonet borrowed from the residence armoury, he announced, "I'm going to sabre this champagne bottle open. Gather 'round, kids, we don't want to waste any!" They all knelt in a semicircle, their cups held out. This was a treat, a spectacle, they knew happened only in sophisticated circles, and they were eager to consider themselves as sophisticates. Wallace pointed the neck of the bottle away from the group and, with the rounded back of the blade resting against the shoulder of the bottle, slid it forcefully down the neck, catching it under the annulus. It took a number of tries until eventually the neck, with its cork intact, popped off. He held the bottle out so the cascade of foam could be caught, amid much squealing. Wallace filled all their glasses, but warned them to be careful of any shards in the bottom. First, they toasted the beauty of this place, and drank. Next, they toasted their impending arrival in Australia, and drank. Their drinks finished, he picked up the neck of the bottle and, demonstrating the form of a practised cricket player, hurled it far out to sea.

Nurse Margaret then invited Sinclair to cushion his head in her lap. Even though she wasn't a smoker, she pulled a Player's Navy Cut cigarette from his pack and placed it at his lips, lighting it for him. He thanked her for the varnish recipe and for all her help with 'the project'.

She fluffed his hair in an absent-minded manner as she listened to the others talk. The third mate cradled his head on the lap of Nurse Ruth, who followed Margaret's example and lit his *Craven 'A'* for him.

Her champagne finished, Nurse Kee stood and walked to the edge of the tide pool. She stood with her arms spread, the palms turned upwards. With her eyes shut, she turned to face the sun, soaking in its warm rays.

"Psst, you fellows, look!" O'Malley hissed. The chatter stopped.

"Is she praying?" Sinclair whispered to Margaret. She shrugged.

"Are Koreans animists?" O'Malley whispered.

"Animists?" Eugene whispered, "Izzat some kinda religion?" She then stunned the group by pulling off her sundress over her head and dropping it on the sand. As an Asian, Sue Kee did not possess the shame of nudity customary among the white race. She wore no brassiere; it was apparently not needed because her breasts were very modest in size, though her nipples were quite large and fat and brown in colour. She also wore no knickers, possibly because of the day's tropical heat. Propped upon his elbow, Eugene coughed as if he'd been kicked in the ribs and sat bolt upright. Margaret covered her face with both hands and lamented "oh no, Sue, no!" Sinclair, his eyes wide, looked to Wallace and muttered "Christ almighty!" Wallace, older and more worldly-wise than many of the others, regarded Sinclair with a shrug and a smirk as if to say, "Well, this is unusual!" Doris said nothing, but leaned forward to get a better view of a freedom that would never have entered her mind before today. O'Malley shook his head and gave a low "wolf whistle". Ruth scowled at him, stuck out her tongue, and punched his shoulder rather hard. He rubbed the soreness out of it.

Sue Kee stepped gracefully into the tide pool and playfully kicked water towards them, calling for anyone to come join her. The officers half-jokingly urged the nurses to join in the fun, but they alleged the water might be too cold. Doris began to stand, but Ruth took her wrist, restraining her with a frown and a disapproving shake of the head. Bending over, Sue turned about and searched the floor of the pool. They watched as she picked up and examined shells from the sandy bottom, holding them up to show them off to the group, before putting them back. Gradually, as their amazement subsided, they included Sue in their conversations as she sat immersed up to her ribs.

Eugene's eyes followed her every movement in fascination. The first mate snapped his fingers, attracting everybody's attention, and pointed at Eugene, who was blissfully unaware he was being silently mocked. Nurse Kee left the pool and began to stroll away along the strand. She had gone only a few paces though when she turned and, looking directly at Gene, asked him, "You walk with me?" Gene leapt to his feet. She presented him with a Tiger cowry shell, beautifully mottled a shiny brown. He admired it, thanked her, and put it in his shirt pocket. The wireless operator and the nurse strolled the length of the beach together, talking intently. Partway along the strand, Gene stopped to demonstrate for her his prowess at skipping stones. As they continued their stroll, Sue asked if Gene was an officer, and he had to admit he was not. She then wanted to know why he was always on the ship's bridge, and he filled her in on his duties at the wireless, but quickly saw that all his technical jargon was beyond her understanding. He didn't know how to describe it in layman's terms so he changed the subject.

"Where in Korea do you come from?"

"I don't come from Korea!" said Sue, "well, not that I can remember. I was just an infant when we left."

"You speak very good English!"

"Thank you. I live in California now with my parents." Gene stopped abruptly and turned to her.

"California! Really? I'm from Portland, Oregon. What town?"

"Um, ... Sacramento."

"Why, we're practically neighbours!" Gene was elated. Things were looking very rosy for him just now, but still, he had some questions.

"So, I gotta ask – and I don't mean to cause you any embarrassment or anything, but – why ... this?" and he swept his hand out towards her to indicate he meant her naked body.

"Embarrassment? Why would I be embarrassed?" For a moment she looked down to regard her own form, then shrugged in resignation. "It is what it is, you know? It's hereditary, I guess!" She sighed.

"No, no, no, not what I meant at all – I mean, take your clothes off in front of ... others. Other people."

"Nudity? There's nothing embarrassing about nudity!" She laughed, a hand covering her mouth. "Wherever did you get such an outlandish idea?"

"Uh ... Americans don't ... they just don't – how long did you say you've lived in Sacramento?"

"Well, we moved around a lot before we settled there." Gene thought she looked flustered. Sue then gaily capered into the foaming surf, and attempted to pull Gene in after her, but he broke away laughing because he was still clothed and wearing his shoes. She ran and plunged head first into an oncoming wave and swam for a bit. They then continued their stroll along the strand some distance apart. Gene watched her as she splashed through knee-deep water, only returning to his side when her path was blocked by sharp rocks, but by then he'd forgotten his question.

Upon the spread blankets with the others, O'Malley then remarked that their little *mise en scène* here was reminiscent of the famous eighteen-sixty-something painting by that French Impressionist fellow.

"What was it called? Oh yes, the 'Luncheon on the Grass' by Édouard Manet." He pronounced the name in phonetic English, and Margaret corrected him – "It's Man-*ay*" – remarking how that one painting was said to be the beginning of the Modernist movement. Ruth objected, saying that couldn't possibly be true, as it was really a classical subject founded on one by Titian, but influenced by Manet's admiration of the lack of perspective in Japanese art. Doris spoke little but followed the discussion avidly. Sinclair said he remembered seeing a print of that painting somewhere, but reckoned if they really wanted to 'accurately recreate' it now, all they needed was a second nude, and he looked up into Margaret's face, giving her a broad theatrical wink. "Oh, you!" she pouted, and lightly slapped his cheek. He laughed, and Ruth had to remind the engineer there was only a single nude in that painting. Wallace then described for them how the captain, whilst they were being shelled, had remained standing on the bridge coolly issuing his orders as they raced for Batavia.

"He jinked her left and right and left, as if our fourteen-thousand-ton ship was a bloody speedboat!" Soon the conversation flowed so freely, and was so relaxed, that no one paused when Gene and Sue returned, holding hands. Sue found the sundress where she'd dropped it, shaking the sand out and slipping it on. Gene, not having any trunk to lean against, sat cross-legged on the blanket. Following the example set by his elders, he invited her to make herself comfortable with her head pillowed on his thigh, and she accepted. Gene and Sue joined in the conversation with the others. He buttoned the flap over the shirt pocket that held the shell and then, casually, let his hand fall, to rest very lightly upon her breast. Sue did not brush him away. Gene was thrilled when she intertwined her fingers with his and held his hand there. The group was well aware of the flirtation developing between the youngsters, but paid it no mind, no doubt remembering their own salad days. After a few pleasant hours had passed, the surf began to threaten their little enclave. The group decided to depart, but Wallace discovered a robber crab had made off with one of his socks. He groused of it on the return tramp, moaning of a blister forming on the back of his heel.

That afternoon as various groups returned to The Settlement, they reported having looked into a number of caves no one dared enter, because the nurses were afraid of unseen bats. The captain and Nurse Wright, with a few of his officers, climbed the hillside to the naval gun emplacement above the governor's residence. They were dismayed to see the Indonesian gun crew did not keep it in good nick, though it was still serviceable. Mallinson noticed Nurse Wright had a curiosity about everything new she encountered.

The dinner that evening was a very elegant affair. When entering the room, the nurses expressed an appreciation of the lovely crystal and silver table setting. There were even several candelabra. Alongside flutes of champagne, there were wine goblets of a perfectly acceptable 1938 vintage Australian Yarra Valley Chardonnay. The officers and nurses were directed to seat themselves alternately around the long table. Mallinson saw Nurse Wright seating herself at the far end next to Becky. Poor Becky. This forced Mr Wallace to sit next to the commissioner's nine-year-old daughter. Poor Wallace. Mallinson found himself seated next to the commissioner's wife, with whom he had few interests in common to discuss, other than the food. The captain was, however, pleased to overhear Mr Morgan quietly counselling Nurse Ruth in the correct usage of each proper utensil for its attendant course. He hoped his other officers were following the second mate's example. The commissioner then stood and rang a spoon against his glass. The toast he gave wished for a quick end to the war with Germany, and for them all, a safe journey to Australia.

The first course was, naturally enough, a local fish. This was followed by roasted chicken served with, to no one's surprise, crab Oscar *à la béarnaise*. There were jacket potatoes, and asparagus in maltaise sauce, and the pudding course when it came was revealed to be pears poached in wine accompanied by a cheese plate, followed by Java coffee. The evening's topic was world events or how even more Eden-like this island was against the backdrop of those events. Everyone had a comment about what they had done or seen that day. Someone had seen surf blowholes at the south end, the lovely Blue Grotto pool, the Hughs Dale Waterfall to the west, everywhere red crabs, secluded beaches, frigate birds, red-footed boobies, and so many blue coconut crabs that they didn't warrant a mention, except for, "My God, they climb trees … and they're enormous!" Wallace told of the sock theft, and that brought a chuckle and an "I told you so!"

No one mentioned Nurse Kee's tide-pool faux pas. By tacit yet common consent, the Dolly Beach Gang had supposed her to be having an entirely normal response 'for an Asian' to the beauty of her surroundings and let it go at that. While the pudding was being served by white-jacketed attendants, Captain Mallinson apologized to Nurse Margaret, and leaned forwards to catch the attention of Captain Fridvold, who sat the other side of her.

"I hear you attempted to hire away my galley steward. I'll have you know I don't appreciate that!"

"Yah, it vas for nossing. He turned me down flat," Fridvold complained with a shrug.

* * *

"Nurse Kee on the beach. Un-be-liev-a-ble!" said O'Malley, and he gave a whistle. Eugene and the mate found themselves together in the privacy of the library browsing the book titles. As they sipped their wine, the mate waxed effusive.

"The tits were nothin' special, but did ye see the size o' them friggin' nipples?"

"Oh, yeah, fer sure," Eugene nodded. He buried his nose in his glass, so he wouldn't need to say anything more, but the mate wouldn't let it go.

"I mean, have ye ever seen 'em so enormous?"

"No, I haven't." He was a bit unsure of whether he should be talking like this at all, but then realised he was out of his depth. He decided to just 'bite the bullet' and confess.

"I ain't never seen any woman naked before."

"Never?" the mate crowed, an eyebrow arched in surprise, "Mum's the word then, eh?" He sipped his wine. "Gene, me boyo, ye really are green! Normal wimmin got 'em no bigger 'an this, and they're pink!" he said, holding up the tip of his little finger, "Man, what I wouldn't give to put me mou—" He suddenly clammed up as he saw how this was affecting Gene. "Sorry. Ye got feelin's for her, huh?"

Eugene stared into his glass and nodded. "She's beautiful," he said, quietly. O'Malley clinked his goblet to Gene's and changed the subject.

"Sure, and ye walked with her down that beach. She mention anyt'ing to ye about why she did what she did?

"Yep, I asked her," Eugene said, relieved to talk of something he knew about, even a little bit. "She said where she comes from it's no big deal. Men and women bathe together all the time, and have for centuries. It has a special name: she called it ... uh ... lemme think ... *Kon'yoku* – she told me the word means 'mixed bathing'."

"Centuries, ye say?" The mate shook his head. "Who knew flippin' Koreans were so lackin' in moral teachin's?" It didn't seem to Eugene to be so immoral, but he kept that thought to himself.

After the meal, the evening wound down. The commissioner manoeuvred the two captains aside to quietly warn them that a *Kriegsmarine* merchant raider, the *Steiermark*, was rumoured to be operating somewhere between India and Western Australia, and was purportedly disguised as a Dutch merchant ship, the *Kormoran.*They believed it to have sunk perhaps eleven ships already.

"The British code name for it is Raider-G, and should you encounter it, we'd like to know," he told them. When they returned to the table, he invited the men to retire to the billiard room for glasses of fine port or brandy, and games of snooker. Nurse Wright refused to hear of a men-only event and insisted on bringing her nurses in as spectators. She made quite the impression by laying claim to a bourbon, neat, and running the table in the only frame in which she took part. That is, after the rules had been explained to her.

8

Encounter

Sunday was uneventful. The chief began to raise steam early. Breakfast was the usual, except there was a dollop of cold crab salad on each plate. Some of the crew walked into The Settlement to attend church services. The officers and crew went about their routine tasks before departure, and Mallinson made his usual daily inspection of the ship. They left as planned, exactly at noon. The passengers lined the after rail of the boat deck and watched the island recede. For them this was a bittersweet moment. They were leaving behind a tropical paradise yet Australia, and home, lay ahead. The *Dominion Empress* steamed on, taking a heading of 165 degrees. Flocks of seagulls had wheeled and screamed after them but, finding no food coming from this ship, soon returned to the island. The sky to the south was a brilliant blue. The northern horizon was a mass of white puffy cumulonimbus calvus clouds, their undersides flat and grey, the interval between them and the sea hatched with rain. But she was well out from under it, and getting further away with each passing hour. The third engineer said the condenser was 'tickety-boo' – indeed, performing better than it ever had. Many of the nurses requested permission of the captain to walk circuits of the deck. The women had dressed in printed cotton or rayon dresses, and sported white-rimmed sunglasses under their kerchiefs as they exercised, as if this was the four-stack Cunarder RMS *Aquitania* in peacetime. The crew blasting the phosphate smuts from the deck with steam lances and fire hoses stood aside for their phalanx as they strode rapidly past in single file.

The sun approached the western horizon, the distant clouds tinted a light yellow shading into a yellow ochre. In a few minutes it had turned a salmon-orange, and the passengers could watch the orb of the sun without having to shade their eyes. Soon it had dipped below the horizon, the western sky now a red fading to deep maroon and then to black. Stars appeared, more and more of them, until the Milky Way blazed a trail across the sky. First Mate Wallace was climbing the stairwell from the engine room, where he had obtained that evening's test results of the boiler-water alkalinity and its salinity. These he had to record in the ship's log on the bridge. He also needed to tell the captain that the shaft was out of alignment and pounding. The black gang had taken out some bearing shims and tightened it up at Batavia, but it was still pounding. The chief was recommending new Babbitt metal be poured into at least two of the shaft bearings when they finally reached Fremantle. At the top of the engine room stair, he stepped outside and paused, waiting for his eyes to adjust to the darkness. The sky was ablaze with countless stars but they afforded little light. He checked the luminous dial of his watch: *2100 hours. I know this ship well enough, I can find my way to the catwalk without waiting.* He started forwards and blundered straight into a bevy of nurses admiring the stars. After they realized who he was, they surrounded him closely, to plead with him.

"We don't know anything about constellations, please show us how to see them, please?"

It occurred to him then: *I guess I can spend a few minutes, the log can wait. I'm a shoulder-to-the-wheel type, but other things matter just as much as my career. I really should pay more attention to the lasses. I'm twenty-nine, after all, and not getting any younger.*

There was no moon at all, or else it had not yet risen. As his eyes gradually adjusted, he could barely make out the mass of the funnel, lifeboats and ventilators, but only because their blackness had blocked out the multitudinous stars. He pointed out for them how to find the constellation Crux, the Southern Cross, as well as a few others not seen in the northern hemisphere. He explained how to align two bright stars in a constellation, and then by counting off the distance between them in a certain direction, there would be the next constellation! They ahhh'd and murmured as each new constellation was revealed to them. They surrounded him closely, each in turn laying a cheek against his shoulder, trying to sight down his arm as he pointed aloft. He couldn't see their faces, but recognised their voices as the nurses from the Dolly Beach Gang, plus a number of others. As he spoke by rote memory about the stars, another part of his mind was busy evaluating each nurse. He recognised the voice of Doris, *not my type, and anyway she's seeing the carpenter*; and Margaret, *a knockout, but she and Sinclair are kind of involved, I think*; and there was Virginia, *I don't want to live in America, and she's too much invested in her career, much like myself*; there was Violet, *gorgeous, but much too tall*; and that Korean nurse, Kee, who pointed to the Pleiades constellation, but queerly insisted on calling it 'Subaru'. *Beautiful in an exotic way, but far too young for me and, in any case, the wireless operator is pursuing her, and I never interfere with another man's business. I have my principles; only unattached women for me,* he reminded himself.

One by one they drifted away to their beds, until he found himself standing alone in the dark with a nurse who leaned with her back against the rail, elbows upon it, one heel hooked on the lowest rung. *Was she in my group of stargazers? I can't tell.* He casually leaned his back on the rail next to her. It was much too dark to see her face, so he leaned close.

"Good evening, Miss …?"

"McKenzie. Becky McKenzie. Didn't I see you when I boarded the ship?"

"Oh yes, Nurse McKenzie. Yes, you might have. I'm the first mate, Reginald Wallace."

"Reggie!" she repeated, her laugh musical. She stood up straight. "Well, first mate Reggie, I have a question!" He felt her slip an arm about his waist, and take the crook of his elbow with her other hand. She pivoted him around to face outboard, and pressed him up against the rail. Here they were hip to hip. *I'm mad keen for her, but ever since Batavia the ship is rife with rumours that she may be in love with the captain. The prudent course of action here is to stand off a dangerous shore until … until I learn more.*

He looked up at the stars, wondering what it was she wanted to know. With darkness all around them, seemingly surrounded by myriad stars, his world became etherealized. For a fleeting moment his mind conjured up an image of them lying close in a bed. In his desire for her, his thoughts had them floating together seemingly weightless in an otherworldly expanse, and they were awestruck by the beauty of the celestial realm. She rested her chin upon his shoulder, and when she spoke her breath was warm against his cheek.

"What is that?" she whispered in his ear. He returned again to what was, for him, firm ground. He forced the fantasy from his mind. His knees were weak. He swallowed.

"What is … what?" he whispered in return. Her hand slid up his back, between his shoulder blades to his neck. Gently but firmly her hand directed his gaze downwards.

"Down there," she whispered, "what is *that*?" The inky black sea hissed by unseen, three storeys below, and became a ghostly green as it left a glowing trail in their wake. He forced himself to hold his voice light and steady as he answered, so as not to betray his emotions.

"That? That is a type of phosphorescence known as bioluminescence. You see, there are organisms living in the water too tiny to see with the naked eye, and when the ship passes through the water it disturbs them, and they glow for a time." Regretfully, he gently freed himself. Nevertheless, it seemed to him that she perhaps withdrew her hand only reluctantly. "I hope you enjoyed my little tour of the heavens. It's quite late. I'll say goodnight, Miss McKenzie," – he held up the test result paper, despite her inability to see it – "duty calls, you know."

"Goodnight, Reggie," she replied warmly, "and thank you." He resumed his journey to the bridge, wiping a hand over his face as he drew a shaky breath, grateful it was too dark for her to see him do it.

"Revolutions eighty-eight, sir. Course one six five, temperature seventy-six, wind north-north-west at Force 3, barometer 29.96 and rising slowly. No clouds, but there's some sea haze, and we estimate visibility at no more than ten miles." It was Monday morning, and Mallinson listened to his usual morning report from the mate on duty. During the forenoon watch, Mallinson looked out on the starboard bridge wing to see an ordinary seaman with a can and brush at the aft cap rail. Ten minutes later he looked again and another was there with him.

"What are you doing there?" he called.

"Carpenter 'No-whisky' ordered us to give the new rail another coat of varnish, sir," said one.

"Very well. Carry on," he replied. Half an hour later he emerged from the chart house to find four crewmen varnishing the rail, and one was actually leaning on it. The bridge lookout was also there, binoculars in hand. He approached the group. Glancing into the nearest pail he found it empty. Irritated, he took a brush from the man and felt it. It was dry.

"What is going on here?" he demanded. The seamen looked at each other sheepishly but didn't answer. "Well?" One man's eyes involuntarily darted aft, then returned to the captain. Mallinson turned to see a group of nurses on the teak boat deck some forty yards away, each in a one-piece bathing costume with its attached short skirt – called a 'swimdress' – sunning themselves on towels. They had apparently considered themselves safe from prying eyes, as they were nearly surrounded by the davits, lifeboats, ventilators and funnel. Some of the nurses lay face down, but most lay face up with hats over their faces, all apparently dozing in the warmth of the sun. Violet and Becky, however, were sitting up with their backs towards him. Violet was applying lotion to the back and shoulders of Becky, who had rolled her bathing suit down.

"You are all on report! Get off my bridge!" he bellowed. They rushed to leave. "Not you!" he barked at the lookout, pointing. "Man your post! Pick up those cans!" A seaman returned to do that, under the captain's glare. The second mate, Taffy, wrote down their names. Being 'on report' meant the docking of a portion of their pay packet. When they had gone, Mallinson shook his head, leaned his crossed arms on the rail, and heaved an audible sigh. *God, how I miss her!* His first mate leaned on the rail to his left.

"Sorry, sir, did I hear you say 'miss her'?" he asked. Mallinson was startled. *Did I say that aloud?*

"Ah, ... oh yes, ... miss my missus back home in England, Mr Wallace." Second Mate Taffy appeared to his right holding a clipboard and a pencil.

"Your signature is required for the report, sir." The three of them watched as Becky, alerted by the commotion on the bridge, twisted about to face them and, with one forearm held up to her breasts for the sake of modesty, she waved to them exuberantly with her free arm, a brilliant smile lighting her face. Wallace's eyes widened and he caught his breath. Becky turned her back to them once again as Violet helped her cover up, pulling up her bathing suit and smoothing its straps over her shoulders.

"Blimey!" Taffy breathed. Mallinson signed the clipboard where he indicated, and the mate left.

"Mr Wallace."

"Sir?"

"You are to get some butcher's paper from the galley, and cover the aft bridge house portholes."

"Aye, sir."

"Yes you, Mr Wallace. Don't involve the crew; attend to this yourself."

"Aye, aye, sir." They watched as some of the nurses gathered up their towels and left, while others arrived to take their place. "Is that not Miss McKenzie there, sir? I mean the redhead."

"I am aware of the one you mean, Mr Wallace, and yes, it is *Nurse* McKenzie." The mate hadn't moved. "I mean *now*, Mr Wallace!"

"Yes sir, straight away!" The mate pushed off the rail.

"And don't be late for your noon sight!" he shouted after his retreating back.

The noon sight showed them at 15°07′ S, 107°00′ E. The third mate reported a distance of 302 nautical miles travelled since the previous day.

Little more than an hour later one of the lookouts shouted, "Aeroplane approaching, three points abaft the port beam!" The second mate snatched up the tannoy and shouted, "Action Stations!" He jumped for the button on the aft bulkhead, and the klaxon began sounding. The captain arrived on the bridge with Eugene hot on his heels.

"What is it?" Mallinson asked.

"A biplane. Single engine, sir," he replied, adjusting his binoculars, "distance approximately no more than ten miles, I'd say. It might be one of ours – not sure." Mallinson looked aft at the seamen rushing toward the Bofors. He looked down at the boat deck for a moment. Nurses were scrambling to their feet, snatching up towels, mouths open in screams drowned out by the klaxon. He recognised Chief Nurse Wright among them, standing out in a dress, pointing and herding them all across the catwalk to safety.

"One of ours? Let me see." The mate handed over the binoculars.

"I've not seen one of those before, but that's a torpedo underneath. No, wait ... not a torpedo, it's a single centre float and ... outrigger floats under the wing. It's definitely a seaplane, but not a Seafox." Everyone put on their helmets. He silenced the klaxon. Mallinson and his mates stood on the port bridge wing. For several long minutes they watched apprehensively as it grew closer, its drone ever louder. "Tell the gunners to hold their fire unless it tries a bomb run; they'll know what that looks like when – sorry, if – it happens." The mate did so, and the plane began the first of several anticlockwise circuits of the ship. Coloured a dark green, the red 'meatball' outlined in white on the side of its fuselage confirmed the plane as Japanese, with machine guns fore and aft. They could see a pair of bombs, one under each lower wing. His gun crew was cranking madly, trying to keep it in their sights.

"D'ye think they'll do anything, sir?"

"Hard to tell. I mean, we're not at war with Japan, but who the hell orders an observation aeroplane to carry bombs?" The ill-tuned radial engine's exhaust rapped and sputtered as the pilot held the aeroplane to something above its stall speed. It had two open cockpits. Through binoculars they could see the pilot and observer wore fur-lined leather hoods as protection against the propeller's slipstream. The observer was diligently filming them with a handheld camera. The occupants' goggles glinted in reflected sunlight. As it approached the ship's heading again, it banked steeply towards them, the exhaust note increasing to a roar. It was clear they intended to pass over the ship from straight ahead.

"Hard to port and hold her there!" Mallinson shouted. The helmsman grunted as he muscled the wheel around. Thoughts flitted randomly through the captain's mind: *Are they planning to strafe the ship? The right-hand screw will help our turn, narrowing the available target, though not asking Freddie for a Lewis gun when I'd had the chance was definitely a blunder.*

"I really, *really* need my shotgun," Eugene complained loudly, to no one in particular. The ship turned agonisingly slowly to port. The Bofors began to bark, firing forwards above the ship's starboard deck. The seaplane approached at mast-top height. One of its bombs detached. It seemed to fall so slowly, and wobbled as it arced downward. All except the helmsman dropped to the deck, bracing for an impact. Mallinson ducked his head involuntarily as he watched the bomb cross the ship in front of the bridge windows. It cleared the ship's far side by mere yards. The explosion raised a formidable geyser that rose up higher than the bridge house. It hung there for a moment, then collapsed aboard. A woman screamed. A loud crash emanated from the direction of the stern and the Bofors stopped firing. When the seaplane was two ship lengths away, everyone stood. They all watched in amazed silence as its wings waggled and the other bomb dropped away. This explosion raised a tall fountain and, as the water cascaded back toward the ocean, a beautiful rainbow appeared for a moment.

"Helmsman, resume your heading," the captain ordered. The ship had now steamed in a complete circle.

"One-six-five degrees, Aye!"

"Jay-suss! 'Twas a near t'ing," O'Malley exclaimed, gripping the rail and crossing himself. "'Twould've blown us all to smithereens, near like." He lifted a silver chain out of his shirt and kissed its Saint Christopher medal. Mallinson looked down to see Virginia sitting on the well deck, drenched with seawater that even now cascaded from the freeing port. With her hair plastered down and fists clenched, she turned the air blue with curses he had only heard as a cadet from the mouths of sergeant majors. The seaplane had flown off in the direction from which it had come, becoming a speck that soon faded into the sea haze. Standing at the aft rail of the bridge wing with his mates, like them he shaded his eyes and stared aft, to see from where that loud sound might have come.

The after mast between holds number three and four held derricks and winches. Over hatch cover number four were two derrick booms. When not in use these heavy booms were usually stowed horizontally above the hatch cover in crutch supports at their ends. But since two aeroplanes now occupied each hatch, the booms had been suspended above them, hanging by their lifting cables from the mast truck. One boom now lay fallen across this hatch, crushing its two aeroplanes. A long cable hanging from the mast truck whipped back and forth as the ship rolled, at times slapping against the mast. The mates conferred among themselves and came to the conclusion that one of their own shells must have parted this cable.

"Stand down Action Stations," Mallinson ordered, and his first mate announced it on the tannoy. They watched as the gun crew threaded their way forwards past the wreckage. Virginia had vanished. They all went to the bulkhead and hung their helmets. The captain mopped his brow with his sleeve, and settled his cap on his head.

"Sir," Wallace said, "do you want me to speak to the gunners about the damage?"

"There's no need, Mr Wallace," he replied, "They were doing their best in the circumstances, and they were following my orders. In fact, tell you what, send them to the crew's mess and ask them to wait for me there. I think it's important we praise their efforts, despite the outcome, for the sake of upholding morale, don't you think? Detail a gang to secure that winch cable. Too bad about those Buffaloes: like as not, they've been done."

"Sor, d'ye t'ink yer after pitchin' 'em overboard?" the third mate suggested.

"Best leave them be, Mr O'Malley. They may have some salvageable parts, eh?"

"Sir, why would they jettison those bombs?" asked a mate. "It makes no sense. We're not at war with Japan, and we're not a warship." Both lookouts nodded in agreement.

"Well, Mr Morgan, I have to say those bombs *were* intentionally released but, for whatever reason, perhaps corrosion or a faulty mechanism, they jammed or stuck, resulting in a delayed drop. You saw them shake it loose, correct? Mr Wallace, I want you to log this in detail, because when we reach Australia, it's my intention to make a full complaint about their actions to their embassy *and* the Australian Foreign Office. It is now my belief the pilot may have been intending to provoke an incident!"

Since there had been an actual explosion close aboard, he felt it wise to dispatch Mr O'Malley, instead of a seaman, to reassure the passengers. The runner he sent instead to the engine room to alert the engineers to check for any leaking plate seams, and to show them where to look. It had been that close. In the crew's mess a few minutes later, the bosun had assembled the gang of six seamen who had handled the Bofors. They sat nervously and awaited the arrival of the captain. When he arrived, the first mate was with him. They all stood and the bosun introduced the men, pointing at each one in turn.

"This here's Able Seaman Wilson, and Halvorsen, and this is Ordinary Seaman Woodcock, and Howland, and O'Flannery, and Keith."

"Stand easy, men. You are not in any trouble, far from it," the captain said. " I just wanted to tell you what a fine effort that was. In my opinion you are improving! I want to remind you all that you don't need to crank it around so furiously. Remember what Mr Virtanen taught you; how you're supposed to 'lead' a target to have it 'fly into' your shell's path."

"Aye, sir," was mumbled out in a relieved chorus.

"That winch cable will need securing, of course, and you may volunteer for that detail, if you wish. I'll leave the arrangements for that in the hands of Mr Virtanen here. Before I dismiss you, have you any questions?" The men looked to one another, not wanting to be the first to speak. They shuffled their feet, eager to be out of there.

"Aye, sir." It was OS Keith. "What about the petrol, sir?"

"Petrol? What petrol?"

"From the aeroplanes, sir. The bleedin' 'atch is soaked with it, sir. It's run all over the bloody deck, it 'as."

"Do you think you might have mentioned this before now?" Maakki burst out. Mallinson called for calm, and turned to his mate.

"Mr Wallace, what cargo have we in hold number four?"

"Rubber, sir."

"So if the aviation fuel were to catch fire and burn the hatch cover through—"

"We would be unable to put it out. Once on fire, rubber will burn uncontrollably. It would definitely be the end of the ship, sir."

"Mr Virtanen, is the aft lookout a smoker, by any chance?"

"Mr Finleigh? Aye, sir, I believe he is," replied the bosun.

"I'll call and tell him to put it out," Wallace said.

"You'll do no such thing, Mr Wallace. That telephone is not to be used. Is anyone here a non-smoker?"

"Aye, sir, I don't smoke," said OS Howland, raising his hand.

"Then Mr Howland, you are the new lookout. You are to relieve Mr Finleigh, and tell the Chinese to douse their cookers and any other open lights at once, and not to smoke *by my orders*. Go now, and run!"

Howland sprinted from the room. "Mr Wallace, tell the chief to cut all electrical power aft of amidship. Announce there will be no smoking anywhere on this ship until I say so, under pain of death. Use those exact words! Break out the fire hoses. I want that petrol hosed off and the aeroplanes kept under a constant spray until they stop leaking. We'll drop them over the side when it's safe. You are dismissed!" Wallace jerked a thumb to the door, and the bosun gave the order. The group scrambled to obey. Wallace ran to the tannoy and voice pipe on the bridge.

Tuesday was also not uneventful. The captain allowed any smokers to light up, as long as they stayed forwards of the anchor windlass. The day passed for the most part as had the previous days. Some, but by no means all, of the nurses sunned themselves on the boat deck. Each helmsman on his four-hour watch held to their heading of 165 degrees, the same as all the days before. The noon sight put them at 19°45′ S, 108°20′ E, and the mate reported a distance of 289 nautical miles since the previous noon sight. Mallinson was pleased. Lunch was routine, then afterwards the captain rang for stop engine. The chief powered up the winches and the deck section dropped the two damaged aeroplanes in the drink. They took only minutes to sink. Tea that day was also routine. Mallinson spent a pleasant hour afterwards, napping in his wicker chair up in the compass platform. The carpenter had done a magnificent job of work restoring the damage the shell had done. When he returned to the bridge, his spirits appeared visibly buoyed, even to the mates. He expressed his opinion they would make Fremantle without further incident. The crew said that the Philco in the crew's mess was now pulling in ABC station 6WF in Perth. Reception was spotty but getting stronger. It was good to hear English spoken again, instead of all that unintelligible Dutch. He had Gene take a bearing on this station with the RDF for the benefit of the mate navigating. At 1320 hours the telephone rang.

"Aft lookout reports smoke on the horizon," said the first mate.

"Where away?"

"Aft. Dead Aft."

They both watched pensively through binoculars. It gained on them rapidly.

"Damn, she's fast," Mallinson said. "We're doing twelve knots, she must be at eighteen. Warship d'ye reckon?"

"No telling," said the first, adjusting his binoculars. "She's still hull-down. Sure is pouring on the coal, though. Look at that smoke."

"Hmm. Warships don't use coal these days, they're all oil-fired steam turbines as far as I know. The fast ones anyway."

He watched a moment more, then said, "Better safe than sorry." He picked up the tannoy and announced, "Ship approaching. Gun crew lay aft. D'ye hear there! Passengers shall remain in their cabins until further orders." Hanging up the tannoy, he said, "Helmsman, come to one three two degrees!"

"One three two degrees, aye!"

"This puts us on course for Carnarvon, the nearest port," he explained to Wallace, "No need to reveal our true destination to anyone. There's no need to reveal our true speed, either. Ahead two-thirds!" he called out. The telegraph clanged. The *Dominion Empress* slowed. Striding to his cabin, he strapped on his Webley and retrieved Eugene's shotgun and a box of shells. He picked up his copies of *Brassey's Naval and Shipping Annual 1934* and *Jane's All the World's Ships*. Returning to the bridge he found all of his officers armed. He placed the books on the slant-top desk at the bulkhead. He gave the shotgun to Gene with orders to stay out of sight, not to fire unless ordered, and then only if he had a clear target. Gene sat cross-legged with his back against the bridge wall, feeding shells into his pump shotgun's magazine. His hands were shaking so badly he dropped a few.

"What news?" Mallinson asked Wallace, who had his binoculars trained.

"She's hull-up now. It's black."

"Not grey?"

"No, black. Short, squat funnel, two masts. She's got king-posts fore and aft, and is wearing the Dutch Civil Ensign."

"Is she making her number?"

"No, sir."

"Then run up our signal flags, and signal them to do the same." The first nodded to the able seaman, and the man turned to the flag locker. Mallinson raised and adjusted his binoculars, saying, "A merchant ship. I don't think she's coal, that smoke is not dark enough. With that speed, I reckon she must be diesel-electric. Is it the *Kormoran* raider they warned us about?"

"No telling until she's closer," the first replied. They were at 12,000 yards now. The mate watched as the other ship's flags rose.

"Pip, King, Queen, Ink," he intoned aloud. Mallinson quickly leafed through his books.

"P–K–Q–I; it's the Dutch merchant ship *Straat Malakka*." He picked up the telephone to the gun crew. "It's a merchant ship. Stay alert. Do not fire unless fired upon first." He hung up. "Gene, did you hear that?" The boy nodded. The *Dominion Empress* maintained her reduced speed, and in half an hour the *Straat Malakka* glided up, fifty yards off the starboard beam. Mallinson could clearly hear the rumble of cavitation as she momentarily reversed to slow to her speed.

"Hear that, Wallace? She is diesel-electric," he said. Wallace nodded. She was much longer than the *Empress*. The Dutch captain stood on his port bridge wing and waved his megaphone above his head. Mallinson picked his own up.

"Ahoy, *Dominion Empress*. Kapitein Frank. What cargo you?" floated across the intervening water.

"Ahoy, *Straat Malakka*," Captain Mallinson shouted. "Captain Mallinson. Raw lead and rubber. What cargo you?" he called.

"Rubber. What destination you?" *Well, the man sounds Dutch, anyhow.*

"Carnarvon, Western Australia. What destination you?"

"Melbourne, Victoria." Mallinson nodded, but then thought of a different question.

"Captain Frank, from what port did you depart?" By his startled expression, the Dutchman had not expected this unusual question.

"Singapore!" Frank replied, after a moment. "What port you?"

"Batavia."

"Kapitein Mallinson, I warn you now: there is a German raider reported in this area!"

"Have you seen it?"

"*Nee*. This is only rumour."

"Many thanks! God speed to you, Frank!"

"God speed to you also, Mallinson!" The *Straat Malakka* turned away, on a heading for Cape Leeuwin. Mallinson leaned on the bridge rail and watched her depart, scowling. *Blast! There goes a merchant ship, and out of Singapore, too! A fast ship, with speed half again as much as ourselves. Sir Thomas could have quite easily put the gold aboard her, and with a better result all around. We would have been on our way home to England weeks ago. Blast it all!*

Having resumed her former speed, the *Straat Malakka* was soon over the horizon. The first mate leaned on the rail next to him.

"Sir? Is there something the matter? You look troubled."

"Oh, hello, Mr Wallace." *Should I tell him my thoughts? That would mean letting him know about the gold. Best not.* "Nothing of any importance. I'm just thinking."

"Sir, when you spoke the other ship, did you notice anything unusual?"

"Unusual? No."

"I did. Two things: their Plimsoll mark was high out of the water, so they must not have been carrying the cargo they claimed."

"And the other?"

"There were a lot of men on the deck faffing about, doing things."

"So?"

"So, none of them had anything in their hands. They weren't carrying anything, pushing or pulling anything, it was just ... activity for the sake of activity."

Mallinson gave an involuntary shiver. He ordered the gun crew recalled and sent the able seaman to reassure the passengers. The captain ordered a course change to a heading of 158 degrees, and rang the engine order telegraph for Ahead Full. As he did so, Eugene appeared on the bridge.

"Skipper?"

"Yes, what is it, Gene?"

"I heard a voice message, transmitted in the clear."

"What is the message?"

"I don't know, skip. It was in German, and the reply was in Jap."

"Did you get an RDF fix?" he asked, apprehensively.

"No, it was much too short for that, only half a minute. But I clearly heard the word 'empress'."

Blast! Mallinson ordered the helmsman to begin a zig-zag course, centred about a base course of 158 degrees true. Remembering the seaplane incident, he told his first mate to spread the word; none of his officers were to put away their weapons. He wanted them all armed until they reached Australia. Mallinson ordered Mr Sinclair to see to it that the six-volt battery of the Bofors was fully charged.

Wednesday was uneventful, for the passengers anyway. Ralph Woodley pestered the engineering section until they invited him below for a tour. Some nurses sunned themselves, some exercised as before. On the bridge it was different. Every sense was heightened. The lookouts constantly scanned the ocean. Gradually, as nothing developed throughout the day, the crew began to relax. Perhaps it had been a Dutch merchant ship after all. The radio message might have been a mere coincidence, or the signal may have been reflected off the atmosphere from some far distance. Who really knew? The captain stood at the bridge rail as he gazed aft at the nurses on the boat deck. Becky wasn't among them today. Aft on the hatch of hold number four, now empty of the aeroplanes it had once held, he noticed a gang of deck crew had formed a work party. What was it they were doing? It couldn't be that winch cable, as for that they would need to be in port. It was mid-morning anyhow and time for his daily inspection tour of the ship. He collected his pencil and clipboard from the bridge desk, and pocketed his torch. Half an hour later he stepped over a tangled mass of fire hoses heaped on the deck, adjacent to the after mast, to find a dozen men struggling with the massive tarpaulin that was used to cover the hatch boards. He recognised Able Seaman Langston there.

"Mr Langston!"

"Sir!"

"Are you the leading seaman here?"

"Aye, sir."

"What is it you are doing?"

"Beggin' yer pardon, sir, we be hunder orders from Mr Wallace, sir, and yer 'ave ter ask 'im, sir." *Bloody hell, the man just used three 'sirs' in one sentence. Something fishy is going on here.*

"But I am asking *you*, Mr Langston."

"Well, I'm not at liberty to say, sir."

"You may rest assured that I *will* ask him, Mr Langston. Carry on!" He made a note on his clipboard and continued on his way to the stern.

The noon sight put them at 24°11′ S, 110°13′ E. After the mates had made their comparisons, and plotted the course, the captain called Mr Wallace to one side and asked about the work party. The mate glanced at his watch, and smiled.

"Meet me on the midship well deck at 1430 hours, and I'll show you. I hope it'll please you, sir." A blanket of Stratocumulus stratiformis clouds filled in at 3,000 feet. It was hot and muggy. The wind direction was from aft, and at the same speed as the ship, so the air on deck was still. This only made the humidity all the more oppressive. The nurses on the boat deck had apparently gone below. Mallinson was waiting on the well deck at 1425 hours when the mate arrived.

"Follow me," said Wallace, mischievously. They walked aft past holds number two and three, as the first mate explained the progress of the work: the crew had lashed the broken cable to the mast as a temporary measure; then they had used the operational derrick to set the other boom back in its own crutch, after which they'd done a 'Maggy Miller,' – trailing the petrol-soaked tarpaulin in the sea to give it a good rinse.

"Oh, is that what Mr Langston was doing, then?" asked the captain.

"You'll see." The gang of crewmen lay sprawled on number three hatch in coils of fire hose, exhausted but happy, as they reviewed their accomplishments. As he approached hold number four, he was forced to watch his footing, because he had to step over a mound of fire hose still lying piled on the deck. He was on the verge of reprimanding Mr Wallace for it when he became aware of a strange sound. The sound of squealing. He looked up and was astonished. The two booms were splayed out horizontally from the mast in a V-shape, and supported in their crutches as normal. A hatch board spanning them completed a triangular frame some six feet above the hatch, and the work party had put the tarpaulin inside this. It was folded over and hung down the outside, its edges tucked underneath. The sides bulged from the weight of water inside.

"You may recall, sir, when you regaled us with the comment Miss McKenzie had made? We used the fire hoses to fill it with seawater," Wallace explained. The gangway, a metal ramp with a single rail, the other having been taken off, now spanned the booms. Three nurses stood there in their swimdresses. Sue and Virginia launched themselves into the pool. The heads of half a dozen nurses popped up, and their forearms dangled over the boom.

"Thank you for the lido deck!" Becky called out, "We love it!"

"Not my doing. You must thank Mr Wallace here!" the captain responded.

"Thank you, Reggie!" she called out, and threw herself backwards with a splash. He turned to Wallace.

"Really? Reggie?" he asked sardonically, an eyebrow raised, "Not 'Mr Wallace'?"

"Yes, well ..." The mate blushed and turned to the crew on the number-three hatch. "Thank you, men. Well done!"

"Oh, we already got our thanks," said Ordinary Seaman Woodcock, as he lay in a coil of fire hose with his hands behind his head, watching them frolic. The others murmured concurrence. Nurse Doris had remained poised upon the gangway, well aware she was being observed and enjoying the moment. The captain and the first mate walked back to the bridge. Mallinson expressed his thoughts: the lido pool had been an excellent venture. Perhaps, if they were going to carry passengers as a regular occurrence in future, they might want to cater to their wishes; was there enough room between the lifeboats and the funnel to paint a shuffleboard? Just how wide was a shuffleboard, anyway? They might want to carry steamer chairs as well, and then of course, they would need blankets for those chairs. Small wicker tables for their tea! Einar could possibly teach himself how to mix cocktails – if only from a book. He was sure the expense wouldn't be all that great. He would mention this to the Ellerman Lines staff captain when they got back to England. They were so close to Fremantle now that time itself seemed to slow down. The afternoon watch dragged by, as did the first dog watch. At 1703 hours, the first mate had command. Mallinson was on the bridge and thinking of going below for tea.

"Captain!" came a shout from the wireless operator. Mallinson and the first looked at each other in alarm. Eugene never called him that. They both sprinted for the wireless room to find Gene at his desk, headphones discarded, scribbling furiously on his notepad. The loudspeaker was emitting a series of dots and dashes. Mallinson caught the Morse code Q-Q-Q-Q, the distress call for a merchantman under attack from a raider. Gene tore it off and handed the flimsy to the captain. It was the *Straat Malakka*.

"Plot these coordinates," he ordered the first, who left for the chart house. At 1705 the same message was repeated. "Maintain a watch, Gene, and let us know of any developments," he said, and then followed. When he entered the chart house, the first was bending over the table, pencil and dividers in hand.

"It's right in front of us. We're steaming directly to it. Do you want flank speed?"

"No. That just gives us an extra few knots. There's nothing we could do for them anyway," he sighed. "Maintain zigzag course and speed." They returned to the bridge. At 1730 hours the sky ahead erupted in continuous flashes beyond the horizon reflecting off the underside of the clouds. A distant thunder-like rumble rolled over them. A group of nurses led by Nurse Wright appeared on the bridge, their eyes wide and full of fear. They watched in fascination and horror, clinging to one another, except for Becky who stood near the captain's side.

"What is that?" whispered Nurse Wright. The first was about to escort them below when Mallinson stopped him.

"It's a battle, likely involving the ship we met yesterday." At 1750 hours, the thundering ended abruptly. A continuous glow to the south led Mallinson to explain.

"It's likely a ship on fire. You should go below. Isn't it time for your supper? I'll take you down." He shooed them off the bridge and followed. "Call me on the tannoy if you spot anything," he muttered to the first mate as he went. The captain ate with them in silence, as they pushed their food around the plates, each lost in their own thoughts. They had been steaming for home, yet now it seemed they were approaching the war, not leaving it behind.

"See," Becky said, smiling weakly, "I was right about there being a captain's table where everyone socialises." Ralph Woodley entered. He collected his supper and sat.

"Stood on the bow and watched thet. Rather a cracking show!" he enthused. No one replied. Nurse Wright shot him a filthy look, which he seemed not to notice. Back on the bridge, Mallinson relieved the first so he could go get his supper. They plodded towards the glow relentlessly, hour after hour. The glow ahead was continuous until 2200 hours and then became intermittent, until midnight when it ended. It was after midnight, at 0030 hours, when a flaming explosion erupted some distance ahead. Taffy had come on duty at midnight. He sent the runner to fetch the captain. Mallinson appeared on the bridge wearing his robe, pyjama bottoms and carpet slippers. Taffy filled him in, and Mallinson listened, his eyes still bleary from being suddenly woken up. They steamed on for the next two hours. The telephone rang. Mallinson answered. He listened and hung up.

"Stop engine. Forward lookout reports debris in the water." Taffy rang the engine room. They drifted forwards in silence as they lost way. Mallinson stepped to the port bridge wing and switched on the searchlight there. The third mate O'Malley joined him, also wearing his pyjamas. They scanned the surface all around the ship.

"There!" The mate pointed. They drifted among flotsam in the water.

A door. Many lifebelts. Then another door. They illuminated a yellow rubber life raft, deflated and downside up. A life buoy floated by, the lettering on it reading 'HMAS SYDNEY'. Sticks of wood, sometimes whole panels. A whole crate. There were uniformed bodies, too, floating face down. And at least one shark, its fin carving the surface as it cruised. Very odd, there was half a burnt wing of a British seaplane, its roundel uppermost. As they watched, it sank out of sight. Eugene joined them on the bridge, also in pyjamas but barefoot and rubbing his eyes.

"What is it?" he yawned. The ship was now stopped.

"Take a look, Gene," Mallinson said. "This is war." He illumined a blackened Carley float containing a number of burnt bodies in *Kriegsmarine* uniforms, and a dead Chinaman without an arm, half his chest open, white ribs splayed upwards. His eyes were open and staring at the sky, and his bald head was thrown back. This position would have left his mouth hanging open, if he'd had a lower jaw; but that, too, was gone. Gene's face turned ashen. He sank to his knees and retched. Taffy remained expressionless. He had seen death before.

"Sir. Something over there." Mallinson swung the beam about. Two white lifeboats, both crowded with men, were tethered together and bathed in the glare. The name on the nearest read 'Kormoran' and in the bow a white-jacketed officer stood, shielding his eyes from the glare of the searchlight. Mallinson picked up his megaphone.

"What is your name, sir?" Mallinson asked.

"*Korvettenkapitän* Theodor Detmers." He dropped his hand. It was Frank, the captain of the *Straat Malakka*.

"They're squareheads. Do we pick them up?" the second asked.

"Do you wish to come aboard?" Mallinson asked through the megaphone.

The *Kapitän* bent low to hear what another sailor said. He straightened up.

"As you Englishers are saying, sod off!" He raised two fingers up.

"There's your answer," Mallinson said to the second mate, before raising the megaphone.

"Why did you not sink us when you had the chance?"

Detmers sat with his back turned. He didn't answer. Mallinson replaced the megaphone on its bracket.

Gene stood, unsteadily. "Do I transmit their location?" he asked hoarsely.

"No, I don't want to reveal ours," said the captain. "Maintain radio silence. Helmsman, resume a heading of one five eight degrees. Dead slow ahead until we're out of this flotsam, then resume a zigzag course. Lookouts, keep a sharp eye out for any Allied survivors." The telegraph sounded.

Thursday morning revealed a placid Indian Ocean, with not a breath to ruffle its surface. A long slow swell had built in from the north. The *Dominion Empress* rose and fell on it for interminable periods as she proceeded south. The sun beat down so hot that to stand on the metal parts of the deck without shoes was painful. The sky was a brilliant blue. It hardly seemed credible that the events of the previous night had happened. Yet they had, and all now assumed their way ahead was clear. In the event, they hadn't seen a single survivor of HMAS *Sydney* nor, for that matter, any bodies. The noon sight put them at 27°13′ S, 112°43′ E.

"The current must be setting us to the east," the captain opined. He had the first mate check his calculations, then ordered a new course of 152 degrees. They were close to the end of their voyage. He could feel it in his bones. He expected to warp into the quay in Fremantle at 1600 hours on 21st November, twenty-eight hours from now. He warned the port-side bridge lookout they would be coming abeam the

Houtman Abrolhos Island group sometime that afternoon and to let him know when it was sighted. The crew was anticipating it too. An air of palpable excitement filled the ship. Ralph Woodley and the nurses had had the laundry wallah clean all their civilian clothing the previous day, before packing it all away today. The nurses resumed wearing their nursing kit for the arrival. On the bridge all the officers were relaxed, now that they knew the fate of the *Kormoran*. At 1413 hours, the starboard lookout yelled, "Periscope wake off the starboard bow, 8,000 yards!" Mallinson snatched up his binoculars and trained them. It was indeed a periscope. The *Dominion Empress* was travelling faster than it was, and on a parallel course. *Is it Australian? We are obviously both on course for Fremantle.* He watched it carefully. Slowly the *Empress* caught up with it. *If it is Australian, why isn't she already on the surface? Could it possibly be Dutch?* When it was abeam, and still 8,000 yards distant, it began to surface. The upper half of a conning tower emerged. A figure appeared and fixed an aerial.

"Message coming in!" shouted Gene down the corridor. The rest of the conning tower emerged, and it surfaced completely, accelerating and matching speed with them. Mallinson's binoculars revealed a man on the tower looking at them also through binoculars. A puff of blue-black smoke told him they had started their diesel to charge their batteries. On the side of the tower he saw some sort of a white mark. It looked to him like a capital T with the top bar slanted to the left, followed by the numeral '123'. *Must be Japanese. At this distance if we swung to ram it, it would still take twenty-one minutes to close with it and by then he'd be out of range or submerged. He's a crafty devil, I'll give him that!*

He watched as tiny figures raced forwards and pulled the cover off the barrel of its foredeck gun. He picked up the tannoy and announced "Gun crew lay aft. Wait for my orders."

"Skipper! Message!" Gene called out again. The captain motioned for the first to follow, and they went to the wireless room. Eugene took off his headphones and switched the output to the loudspeaker. It was most definitely Japanese.

"I don't speak Japanese," the first said. "I have no idea what they're saying."

"Nor do I," said Mallinson.

"Skipper, there is someone on board who does speak Jap. I've been chatting up Nurse Kee, that Korean nurse. She speaks it," Gene said. Mallinson rolled his eyes in exasperation.

"Well, go get her, boy, there's no time to waste!" Gene sprinted off down the companionway, taking the steps two at a time, returning in less than a minute with Nurse Kee. Mallinson had not made time to meet all of them, and this was his first time encountering Nurse Kee at anything other than a distance. Mallinson took one look at her fringe of straight shiny hair, black as jet, framing a heart-shaped face, the creamy complexion, the demure lips, the brows perfectly formed. He had to admit to himself, she was beautiful. Flawlessly so. *Something doesn't look quite right here.*

"Come to my cabin, now!" he ordered. He strode off down the corridor. Entering his cabin he turned to find Gene close behind, leading the nurse by the hand. *I didn't mean Gene, too. Oh well.* As they stepped into his cabin, Gene placed his hand on the small of her back.

"This is Sue Kee. She's from California!" His hand remained upon her waist, and she did not object. She stood shyly, hands clasped, her eyes downcast. The captain began to question her.

"Do you speak the Japanese language, Nurse Kee?" She seemed taken aback by the question.

"Yes," she answered shortly, with a nod.

"We need someone who can translate Japanese into English while listening to the wireless. Do you think you can do that for us now?"

"Yes."

"Live with your parents, do you?"

"Yes." Her eyes remained downcast.

"Nurse Kee, from what city in Korea do your parents come?" She knitted her brows, and bit her lip. Roy and Gene waited, but her answer was not forthcoming.

I'll need to make something up, Roy thought.

"Your parents hail from the major seaport of Ping-Pong, yes?" he prompted her.

"That's it!" she said, with relief. Gene's forehead wrinkled and he looked confused.

Hmm. I need to try a different tack. "Where in California?" he asked.

"Sacramento."

"Sacramento! Such a beautiful place," the captain mused aloud, "I'll bet your parents have a wonderful view of all the freighters at anchor in the harbour."

"Yes, they do," she replied. Eugene's eyes widened in alarm.

"What is your full name?"

"It is Susan Kee."

"But what is your *real* name?" Eyes squeezed shut, her lips compressed, she began to cry, silently. Mallinson produced his handkerchief and gave it to her, but placed a reassuring hand upon her shoulder.

"Your given name is Suki, isn't it?" he said with care. She dabbed at her eyes and nodded, and her voice came in a whisper they could barely hear.

"Suki Higashikokubaru." Gene's eyes widened. His hand dropped to his side. He took a step back. Uncertainty and shame chased each other across his face. "Oh, *please*, do not tell anyone," she sobbed into the handkerchief.

"Do the other nurses know?"

"Yes, of course, they all do. *Please*, I like being a nurse, oh, *please*," she sniffled.

"Then your secret is safe with me" – he shot a look at Sparks – "and you! It's safe with you, isn't it, Eugene?" Gene swallowed. He looked at her, and it seemed his feelings of a moment ago had evaporated.

"Yes, sir."

"Tell no one, Eugene. I'd like you to work with Suki translating what is coming in. You can do that, can't you?" Suki looked hopefully at Gene, but he looked away. Keeping his eyes on the captain, he nodded.

"Good. Off you go then, and Gene ...?"

"Sir?"

"I want to sit down with you later and talk about this. I'm serious." *This will serve as a lesson for the boy, that a government ruling a people doesn't necessarily represent the views of the people ruled. She seems a nice young woman. I hope he can overcome his prejudices.*

"Yes, sir," he nodded. They returned to the wireless. Mallinson and the first mate stood by and listened. Eugene sat at his desk and wrote out what Suki said. She stood listening to the chatter coming from the loudspeaker and her soft voice intoned: "... your ship ... now ... prepare to ... be boarded in ... the name ... of His Imperial Majesty Hirohito. Do not use ... your transmitter. Stop your engines. ... if you ... do not you will ... be fired on. Stop your ship now. Prepare to be ..."

"Message just repeats, skip," Gene said. Suki stopped talking.

"Suki, say this: 'We will comply.' No, wait! Say instead, 'We will *obey*,'" Mallinson instructed. She bent to the microphone and spoke a phrase. The torrent of Japanese issuing from the speaker suddenly stopped. Taffy stepped into the room holding open the captain's *Naval and Shipping Annual*, and announced, "Found it!" Mallinson took it from him and read aloud selections to the others.

"KRS Class ... crew of 75 ... built 1927 ... a copy of an obsolete U-boat ... minelayer converted to be a seaplane refueller ... four torpedo tubes." He clapped the book shut and handed it back. "To the bridge! Suki, continue your work. Eugene, keep me informed."

"Helmets, everyone!" Mallinson said, as he entered the bridge. He went to the telegraph and rang the order for Ahead Two-Thirds.

"Suki? What the hell?" the first mate queried the captain.

"Not the time right now. I'll fill you in later." He switched on the tannoy microphone.

"Helmets on! Muster Stations! Deck section swing out lifeboats, port-side only!" Leaving the voice pipe open and holding the microphone of the tannoy close to it, he ordered "D'ye hear there! We are about to be boarded by the Imperial Japanese Navy. Do nothing, I repeat, do nothing to anger them. Keep your hands off your weapons. Obey all orders. Speak only when spoken to."

"Six thousand yards and closing," the first mate announced and lowered his binoculars. "I don't understand why they didn't torpedo us. It's obvious to them we carry aeroplanes."

"I don't know," he shrugged. "Perhaps they're out of them?"

"Why have you not stopped us?"

"Oh, ... well, ... this prevents them from turning towards us without falling behind. You can't torpedo a ship you're not facing." The first nodded and raised his binoculars. The sub's foredeck gun spoke and a geyser erupted off their stern.

"Four thousand yards," the mate announced. Mallinson rang the order for Ahead One-Third. The *Dominion Empress* continued to slow. The foredeck gun spoke again, and a geyser erupted off the bow.

"My God, they're bad shots," Mr Morgan said.

"No, they're not. It's deliberate. They're demonstrating they could place a shell straight through this wheelhouse if they so wanted. Now, if they *did* turn towards us, that would be a threatening move on their part, and I might then be forced to turn away to present a smaller target to them. Then it becomes a running gun battle, and nobody wants that. At night without a moon is one thing, but in broad daylight is another matter entirely. Their five-and-a-half-inch gun against our little anti-aircraft Bofors? It's no contest. I have no intention of letting this ship become a floating abattoir."

The first nodded. "Fifteen hundred yards," he announced.

"What the fuck is an ahh-bat-war?" Morgan asked Wallace.

"It's French for slaughterhouse," said Wallace.

"Good to know." A shell screamed straight over the top of the bridge. Mallinson rang the telegraph for Stop Engine. The deck stopped trembling. The *Dominion Empress* drifted, losing way. The submarine closed with them on a converging course, matching their speed all the way. Gene appeared on the bridge with Suki a few steps behind him.

"They told us to take their lines, and bring everyone on deck." He handed his code books to the third mate, who stood there ready with a weighted canvas sack. O'Malley slipped the books into it and tied the drawstring tight. He flung it over the side opposite the sub. Suki gave the handkerchief back. Mallinson went to the voice pipe and ordered the engine-room crew, the firemen and the coal-trimmers to come topside. When the *Empress* was finally dead in the water, the submarine approached and, scraping along the hull, stopped with the conning tower adjacent to the aft end of the midship house. Malodorous fumes of diesel wafted over them as its exhaust burbled. The sub was half the length of the *Dominion Empress*.

Mallinson announced on the tannoy. "D'ye hear there! Clear the lower decks! All personnel, I repeat, all personnel! Deck crew shall take their lines and make secure." He ordered his officers, Gene and Suki to follow him. They all went below to the deck adjacent to the conning tower. He saw with satisfaction there were two shell holes in the top of their conning tower fairing. *So we did hit them after all. This must be the same submarine that pursued us into Batavia.*

He told Suki to ask what the commander wanted. The man pointed and spoke. Turning to Mallinson, she said, "He say: you make bridge here now." There occurred a conversation in Japanese. "He say: You bring all person on deck. Hands on head, no person hold any weapon. A person hiding is shot."

"Suki, respectfully remind him that Great Britain is not at war with Japan."

Suki spoke a long phrase, and got a one-word answer: "Yet." Mallinson frowned, remembering Eugene's answer to him from weeks ago, and nodded. He then repeated what the commander had ordered, nearly word for word. He sent others to comb the ship for latecomers. As everyone appeared on deck he arranged them in lines, the civilians seated on the starboard side of number two hatch, the dozens of seamen ranged against the starboard bulwark, his licensed officers and engineers standing at the port bulwark. He sent crewmen Finleigh, Keith and Halvorsen, along with the bosun, to lift a hatch board specifically from hatch cover number four, the one with the lido pool, and bring it to the conning tower. Soon this hatch-cover plank, little more than a foot in width, spanned the gap between the ship and the conning tower. Japanese sailors lashed their end down on the conning tower, letting the other end scrape back and forth on the deck through the open gate in the bulwark, as the ship and the boat rolled with each swell.

Some two or three dozen sailors boarded, and as they did they fixed bayonets on their Arisaka rifles. They wore khaki short-sleeved shirts and knee trousers, with white socks and plimsolls. They fanned out to guard their prisoners, rifle butts to their shoulders, aiming at first one, then another. One nervous finger and someone was going to die. A few went aft to where the Oriental crewmen sat cross-legged or lay sprawled. Chinese were routinely taken to serve on Axis ships. They had no choice and were resigned to it. In fact, such was usually their lot but, this being a submarine, there was no room for them and they knew it. All they could do was await their fate, whatever it might be. They knew that – and this was their hope – although Japanese considered other Asians as lesser than them, they were still Asians, after all.

The last to board was the Japanese commander. Mallinson and Suki met him at the end of the plank. The man was young, less than thirty. He was short – well, tall for a Japanese anyway. His billed cloth cap sported the anchor and lotus of an IJN officer. He wore an impeccable khaki uniform which, unlike his men, included long sleeves and his trousers were tucked into knee-high black leather boots. There was a Nambu pistol in a black holster on his belt. Holster, belt, and boots were polished to a high shine. Unusually for a Japanese, he also sported a moustache – a Ronald Coleman moustache. He spoke; Suki translated.

"Helmets off. Put weapons on deck now." He did not tell them his name. Mallinson ordered it so, and each man placed his helmet downside up in front of him. The officers unbuckled their weapons and laid them on the deck in front of them. Mallinson unstrapped his shoulder holster and followed suit. A Japanese sailor, a rifle slung over his shoulder, went down the row of crewmen, nesting the helmets in an unwieldy stack in his arms. His rifle sling fell from his shoulder to his elbow, the rifle butt dragging behind him. He laid it down and continued his task. Mallinson saw an ordinary seaman fidgeting and eyeing the weapon. *Don't … Don't be a fool …Don't be a fool.* The commander barked an order and a sailor ran to pick it up. *Phew.* The commander whipped off Mallinson's helmet and rapped him on the head with it, as punishment for not obeying his order. It was placed on the sailor's head as he took his stack of helmets to the sub.

The captain then followed the commander as he strutted along the lines of men. They paused in front of Mr Andreassen, and the Jap took his cigarettes from his sleeve and pocketed them. Even though the captain knew that Tord was capable of lashing out and snapping the man's neck as easily as a twig, the Dane stood there impassively, examining an interesting rivet-head a few feet away. When they reached Eugene, the Jap paused and glanced up and down the line of men, then spoke.

"He say: where is this man's pistol?" Mallinson saw with alarm that the boy had not brought his shotgun with him. *In blatant disregard of my orders. How do I fix this? Oh, well ... I'm going to have to apologise to Gene for this later, but here goes.* He screwed up his face into a mask of rage, and snarled.

"*Mister* Graham! You are not an officer! What are you doing standing with my officers?" Eugene looked startled but failed to move. "Get over there with the crew where you belong!" The captain raised his hand as if to strike him, and the boy ducked and scurried across the deck, bent low. This must have had the intended effect, for as Suki translated his words, the man nodded and continued down the line; surely, here was a man who knew how to control men. Three more sailors scuttled down the line, one collecting weapons and piling them in the arms of the other two. These were taken to the submarine. As the weapons departed, the sailors aiming their rifles at the crew visibly relaxed. The commander pointed at four sailors and then fore and aft. The sailors jogged away. Minutes passed. A sailor appeared on the bridge wing overhead to shout something down at them, then disappeared. There was a single gunshot. One by one the sailors returned. The last to return bowed abjectly to the commander and murmured a phrase. When he straightened the commander slapped him hard across the face, and the man bowed multiple times whilst crying and backing away. The commander ignored him.

Suki translated: "Is this your entire crew?" *Everyone is here. No one is missing. That shot must have been an accident.* Mallinson spoke the single word of Japanese he did know.

"*Hai.*" – yes.

"Take me to your office." The man's lips barely moved when he spoke. They went, with Suki and an armed sailor, up to the captain's quarters. The gun cabinet stood open and empty. The commander demanded the captain open his safe. He pulled out handfuls of paper and threw them away until he reached the payroll cash box, which he cleaned out and pocketed. He then opened every cabinet and door. He went to the desk and pulled each drawer out, pawing through them and dumping the contents on the floor, then tossing the drawer across the cabin.

"Where are your code books?" he demanded. Mallinson answered, "In the ocean," and Suki translated this. The commander was angry, but managed to control it. Hands on hips, he looked over the mass of papers on the floor. Spying an object, he picked it up, examined it, then put it in his pocket. *It's the Robertson screwdriver. Why does it interest him?*

The four of them stepped into the wireless room where the commander lifted the lid of the transmitter. He pulled out a valve and smashed it to the deck. Next, they stepped into the chart house where the man pawed through their stack of charts. Selecting half a dozen, he rolled them up together and gave them to the sailor, and they all returned to the well deck. Then, through Suki, the commander made a demand that astonished him: "Where is the gold?" *He knows about the gold? How is this possible?* When Mallinson answered, Suki told the commander what he had said.

"I don't understand. We carry only these aeroplanes, as you can see." The man regarded him with obvious contempt, his head tilted back with half-closed eyes, judging him. He shook his head in disgust. Turning to the sailor on the conning tower, he barked a command. The armed sailors on deck laughed. The sailor on the submarine bowed twice and scurried below.

"Tell me what he says, every word. Quietly," Mallinson whispered to Suki.

Suki whispered in return, "I want him up here immediately." Minutes passed and the commander paced, growing increasingly irritated. Finally, the sailor reappeared. He bent over and helped another climb out of the hatch.

It was Martin Vander Sluyt, his former galley steward. Vander Sluyt mounted the hatch board and, arms extended for balance, crossed to the *Dominion Empress*. He was more than a head taller than even the tallest Japanese, and he had a sticking plaster on his forehead. He stopped in front of the commander, threw his arm out and shouted, "Heil Hitler!" The commander grimaced. There was a conversation between them in Japanese, Vander Sluyt's halting and crude, the commander's rapid. Suki translated for the captain in a whisper.

"Put your arm down, you moron. I don't subscribe to your cult worship. This man says there is no gold. Well, is it here, or is it not here?" Vander Sluyt lowered his arm and bowed.

"Yes, yes ... there ... is gold ... I have not lied. Follow me!" He dashed forwards to the well deck, followed by the commander, Roy, and Suki. "I saw it myself, right here against this wall." He touched the bulkhead with both hands spread, as if willing it to magically open up and reveal its secrets.

"This mission has cost the Imperial Navy an enormous expense in fuel and time and manpower that I, personally, have vouched for."

"It is here ... I tell you ... truthfully."

"I will not be pleased if all this effort is for nought."

"You have searched the ship? It is here, I know it ... hidden in ammunition boxes ... with square-drive screws in the tops ... just as I told you." The commander turned to his sailors and spoke.

Suki whispered, "He has ordered half these men to search the ship for boxes of ammunition." Fourteen sailors gave their rifles to their companions and ran forwards and aft. Mallinson asked for permission to have his men lower their arms, if they sat. The Jap nodded, and the captain bellowed the order. The crew shook out their limbs and sat.

The officers lowered their arms but remained standing. The nurses, seated on the hatch, did not have their hands on their heads; it was clear they were not considered a threat. Everyone waited without talking. Since both vessels were lashed together and dead in the water, they had gradually rotated, lying ahull to the swell, so as each swell of the Indian Ocean passed under both ships, the submarine's conning tower rocked to and away from the *Dominion Empress.* The hulls groaned as they ground together. The scraping of the plank end was extra loud. All the sailors returned empty handed, except for two from the Bofors. When their crate was prised open, it was seen to hold only Bofors shells. Another arrived and said something while pointing aft. The commander ordered them to follow him. Vander Sluyt, Suki and Mallinson walked in single file aft to the tarpaulin-covered stack with its sign. Vander Sluyt and the commander stood together to one side, Suki and Mallinson together to port of them. Becky was seated with Virginia at the forward end of the line of nurses on the hatch cover, and mere yards from Roy and Suki.

"What is the meaning of this sign?" Vander Sluyt demanded of Mallinson.

"It's ammunition. Very dangerous." Vander Sluyt struggled with the knots in the ropes. At a word, a sailor cut them with a bayonet. He whipped back the cover.

Suki translated: "See! Blue printing! This is the gold! Pull one out now!" Two sailors struggled to drag the topmost box, as heavy as a small car engine, off the stack. When it was free it fell and, as it hit the deck, there was a cracking sound. They stepped back into formation and were handed their rifles. Vander Sluyt bent over the box and spoke Japanese.

Suki: "Square-drive screws! This is it! What did I tell you?" The commander said something and, reaching into his pocket, produced the Robertson screwdriver.

Suki: "So you did. I found this in the captain's office. Open it!"

The captain grimaced, and thought, *He has the screwdriver. I should have hidden it. In a minute he'll have it open, and if he scratches the surface it will all be over. I have to distract him, but how?*

Vander Sluyt's hand extended, and as the Commander's hand held out the screwdriver, they bumped and it was fumbled and dropped to the deck. It spun in place. They both started to bend over to retrieve it, nearly colliding, then straightened up, the commander clearly irritated. He put a hand on Vander Sluyt's chest and gave him a shove, and he stumbled backwards, falling against the crates. This was the opening Mallinson needed. He fell to the deck, extending his leg as hard as he could. The screwdriver skittered and bounced and rolled across the deck and out the freeing port. There was a splash. Suki helped Roy get to his feet. The commander's eyes had followed the screwdriver's progress, and now he turned to Mallinson and said something in Japanese, and grinned.

Suki translated: "You English think you are so clever. So very clever. I will now show you clever!" He pulled the Nambu from its holster and cocked it, his eyes never leaving Mallinson's. Vander Sluyt stepped rapidly away. Becky screamed, "No!" and broke away from Virginia. In two strides she was in Mallinson's arms. Suki quailed and hugged them both. The commander took aim and squeezed the trigger, blowing a corner off the box's far side. Stepping up to it, he stomped down on the damaged side with his boot heel and the entire long side folded down. The ends of nine bars gleamed from the interior. A wisp of smoke arose from a splinter that stood up from the deck. Mallinson was far beyond caring about any damage to his teak.

"There, there, it's all right," he said, soothingly. "Suki, you need to release us, so Becky can go sit down." Becky returned to her seat, still shaking, silently wondering at how in the world Roy could maintain his composure. Virginia Wright took her in her arms and soothed her. Roy gripped Suki's arm tightly to himself as she trembled. Vander Sluyt up-righted the ship's hand truck and scooped up the box, trundling it over to the hatch plank. When he arrived he found the hand-truck wheels were too far apart to both fit on the plank. The commander shouted an order and the same two sailors jumped. They each took hold of a rope handle and, hoisting the box with difficulty, began to inch their way across the plank. Halfway across, the weakened box disintegrated and the bars cascaded into the sea, clanging off the hull of the submarine. The commander shouted abuse at them. The sailors discarded their box fragments and ran back to formation. One bar remained on the plank. Vander Sluyt walked out onto the plank and picked it up. Holding it clutched to his chest he turned to face them, and his eyes were bright and shining.

"This one is mine!" he said, in English. The commander unleashed a torrent of rapid-fire Japanese at Vander Sluyt, screaming so much that saliva dribbled from his chin. Suki tried her best to keep up with it for the captain.

"... insane ramblings about Hitler! The never-ending drivel from that fucking *Mein Kampf*! You halfwit! I've had all I can take of you! Now that we have the gold, I've no more use for you, you imbecile! I hope you're reincarnated as lichen!" Vander Sluyt's mouth hung open. His Japanese wasn't good enough to understand everything that was hurled at him, but he sure caught the gist of it. The commander shot him in the arm, and Vander Sluyt grimaced in pain. He opened his mouth as if to speak, but the commander shot him through the knee, and he toppled off the plank still clutching the bar, a look of pained astonishment on his face. His cries of "*Hilfe! Hilfe!*" rose ever more frantically, ending in a high-pitched scream that was cut short as the next long, slow, swell of the Indian Ocean passed under the *Dominion Empress*. The commander walked to the ship's bulwark and looked down. He spat. Some of the Japanese sailors applauded. The entire ship's company had watched this happen. Even though the man was a Nazi, the nurses recoiled in shock at the wanton cruelty of the man. Mallinson said nothing, preferring to wait for the man's temper to cool. The commander holstered the pistol. Calmly, he shook a cigarette from the pack. A sailor rushed to light it, and the commander snatched the man's cap off and wiped his chin with it, then gave it back. His eyes narrowing, he scanned the exposed ammunition boxes, counting, looking over at the conning tower of his submarine, calculating. When he had finished half the cigarette, he nodded. He turned to his sailors and began giving orders.

Suki whispered: "You! Get the grappling hook! You nine, continue guarding the prisoners! All the rest of you, take these boxes to the submarine. You will lower the boxes down the hatch with the grappling hook and stow them in whatever space you find." The sailors jumped to obey. Soon they had dragged enough boxes off the stack to create a 'stairway' to the top. It was unmistakably hard work for these slight men. Two of the more robust sailors climbed the 'stair' and dragged the first of MacCallan's special boxes down its slope to the bottom. They dragged the second special box down and across the first, then stepped on them as they climbed again.

Mallinson groaned inwardly. *Oh great, they activated Hamish's improvised bombs. They'll detonate in two hours.* He pulled back his sleeve and looked at his watch. Three in the afternoon. They had until five o'clock, give or take. A hand seized his wrist. The commander spoke.

"He say: that is a nice timepiece. Give it to me," said Suki. Mallinson unstrapped it and paused to read the inscription on its back: '*To my forever love.*' He handed it over. The Japanese put it on and admired it. He blew cigarette smoke in Mallinson's face, then flicked the butt overboard. Roy held his breath, and succeeded in not giving the man the satisfaction of seeing him cough. The captain now decided the moment was right to act.

"Honourable sir, There is no need for your men to work so hard. May I suggest you allow us, your prisoners, to load these boxes onto your boat?" He addressed the commander in as formal and respectful a manner as he could muster. Suki translated. The sweaty sailors within earshot paused and listened hopefully.

"I suggest you open your torpedo loading hatch. My men can use our derrick winch to position our gangway from our ship to your deck. The boxes will slide down by gravity to your deck. My crew is expert at handling these boxes. The work will go much quicker."

Suki finished translating. The commander stroked his moustache with a forefinger and thumb while he thought. Mallinson had the idea that perhaps the man didn't want to 'lose face' by having his own men do nothing.

"Your men can redirect each box into the torpedo hatch as it arrives at the bottom of the gangway. They can stack them in your torpedo room." The commander walked to the side of the *Dominion Empress* and stood, judging distances from bulwark to sub deck. He hesitated.

Perhaps I need to sweeten the pot, give him something that will tip him over the edge. "After you depart, we will launch our lifeboats and scuttle our ship for you. You will not even need to waste an expensive torpedo on us." *You have no torpedoes left, you bastard, and I know it.*

Slowly, the man nodded. He made a comment, which Suki translated as: "This I so order. This woman will tell me all what you say." The relieved sailors wiped the sweat from their faces and buttoned their shirts.

"Chief, restart the donkey boiler!" Mallinson bellowed. "Deck section, rig the gangway to the aft sub deck! Mr Andreassen, assist the deck crew. Start bringing these ammunition boxes to the gangway. Passengers and non-essential crew shall board the lifeboats now!" Suki stood near the commander murmuring in Japanese. The chief went below, followed by two armed Japanese. The mates began organizing the seamen's activities. Soon the gangway, taken from the lido pool, was lifted and positioned near the aft torpedo loading hatch of the submarine. That hatch now stood open. Some of the Japanese sailors had been ordered to go to the sub's torpedo room to receive the boxes. The captain and the commander watched Tord place the first box at the top of the ramp. It slid to the bottom, where a sailor stopped it with his foot. Four other sailors dragged it to the open hatch and tipped it in. With an easy shove it slid down the greasy chute into the hull, all by gravity. MacCallan's special boxes were included somewhere in the third row to be taken.

Having had to lift the gangway once, to complete the task at the forward torpedo hatch, the loading was now complete. The gangway had now been stowed on the starboard deck. Mallinson asked the third mate for the exact time, and was told "Sixteen forty-three hours" – seventeen minutes to five o'clock. The last of the Japanese sailors had boarded their submarine. As the commander and Suki Higashikokubaru stood facing each other, he heard the Commander repeatedly barking something at Suki, and Suki saying what sounded like "Eee-ay" to the commander, repeating this same word frequently, and more stridently with each reply. Mallinson did not know the Japanese language.

"What are you saying?" he asked her.

"*Iie* means 'no.' He orders me to board his submarine. He believes me to be a slave of barbarians. He thinks he is rescuing me."

"Tell him you are not a slave, and you want to stay here, on this ship." Suki translated this. The commander's face flushed red. A cord stood out from his neck, and his clenched jaw worked. Livid with rage, he spat in her face. The gob of spittle hung from her left cheek below her eye. She stood rigid, eyes shut, fists clenched at her sides. Mallinson gave the man a sour look. He dug in his pocket for his handkerchief. Taking her face in his left hand, he gently wiped it away. She opened her eyes.

"You should not have done that," she said.

"Why do you say that?" he asked.

"Because now he believes me to be your concubine."

"Screw what he thinks," he said, then quickly added, "don't translate that." In a few minutes, Chief MacCallan was in the engine room building pressure in the main boilers. Mallinson had quietly passed the word that the gun crew was to make their way aft. The commander stood in his conning tower. When he had asked for his watch back, the man had only laughed. The submarine's deck was near awash with the extra weight. There was no one manning the foredeck gun because with any more speed they might have been washed overboard. Wherever this sub was going, it was going on the surface. The sub banged and scraped forwards alongside the *Dominion Empress*. The captain and his officers watched it leave from the bridge. Once clear of the ship, the submarine began to veer to the right. It kept on veering. Soon it had turned through a half circle and was still turning. The sub was 2,000 yards distant, and nearly in line with the *Empress*. A mere 40 degrees more would do it. At this distance there was zero chance a torpedo could miss.

"The Jap bastard is going to torpedo us anyway," the first mate said, stunned. "We're a sitting duck." Mallinson picked up his binoculars and focused on the conning tower. He saw the commander standing with binoculars trained back at him. The third mate cranked the aft lookout telephone and screamed, "Open fire!" The Bofors began to bark. For the first time one of its shells scored a meaningful hit, as the seaplane refuelling tank at the top of the conning tower erupting in an aviation-gas-fuelled fireball. The commander threw up his arm to shield his face and ducked away. The captain lowered his binoculars, and looked at his wrist. There was no watch there, so he turned and looked at the ship's clock. The time was 1704 hours.

"I'm fairly certain he's out of torpedoes," he remarked, in as casual a voice as he could muster. He raised his binoculars. Then a muffled crack followed by a loud boom sounded across the intervening water, and a tongue of flame a hundred feet tall erupted from the conning tower hatch. A second explosion, and the submarine split apart, a third of the way from the stern. Mallinson watched as the half with the conning tower rolled over, pitching the commander headlong into the sea. The two parts of the sub upended and vanished beneath the surface within seconds. "I might have been wrong about that, eh?" he told the first. "Log this, and the time and location, will you?"

The lifeboats were still swung out, and filled with the ship's company. The captain ordered all but one of them stowed. That one was launched. They recovered seven survivors: six sailors and the submarine's commander. Roy retrieved his watch. It was still ticking because it was waterproof. He also recovered the ship's payroll from the man's pockets, and set one of the nurses to spreading the wet notes out in her stateroom to dry. The nurses dressed the sailors' injuries, mostly burns and lacerations, as they writhed in pain on the wardroom's tables. There was one broken arm. Mallinson was faced with the problem of where to put the survivors. He solved it by locking them in cabin one, port side, forward. This had been Becky's assigned cabin, so he solved that problem by having her move into his quarters with him. Still, he couldn't help but do this surreptitiously. Perhaps, if anyone noticed, it would be assumed she had moved into the cabin of another nurse. He suspected his relationship with Becky might have become an open secret among his officers, but he couldn't be certain. An able seaman stood guard outside the prisoners' cabin holding Gene's shotgun, which the wireless operator had hidden under his mattress. With so many bodies crammed into the small room it became very warm, so the porthole was left open. Roy had a chair placed outside this, and Suki sat there with a clipboard, transcribing everything she heard the prisoners say. He would later hand this over to the Naval Intelligence Division. The sailors were draftees who had not really wanted to be there in the first place. She related to the captain how she had to bite her cheek to stifle a laugh, when a sailor had called for the guard to show them how to use this non-Japanese toilet. No surprise there: Mallinson had ordered the pull-chain removed from its overhead water tank, so no one could hang themselves with it.

The *Dominion Empress* berthed at Fremantle Quay at 2150 hours on 21st November. Gene had replaced the broken valve from his hidden hoard and radioed ahead, so a unit of the Australian Army Third Corps was waiting to guard the ship. The prisoners of war were escorted down the accommodation ladder to the waiting MPs. The captain reported the last known location of Theodor Detmers with his lifeboats, and told of the Japanese commander's cold-blooded execution of Martin Vander Sluyt, recommending a charge of murder be levelled against the man. He gave a statement to the press, and many of his officers were interviewed too. When his passengers and crew disembarked the next morning, there was a contingent of reporters there as well. Blue flashbulbs popped. A band was on hand to play *Advance Australia Fair*, and *God Save The King*, and in that order.

Two days later Marinus Meijer struggled up the accommodation ladder holding a Gladstone bag, followed by the local shipping agent. He had flown in on the first available Qantas Empire Airways flight after Gurnam Singh had notified him he had received Mallinson's cable. They sat in the captain's cabin. As was usual, the local shipping agent brought him the payroll for the ship, a bundle of post and the local newspapers for his crew. Mallinson was astonished to see a photograph of himself on the front page of *The Mirror* shaking hands with the director of the Perth Mint, albeit below the fold. He hadn't remembered doing that. There was a photograph of a group of his passengers disembarking the ship. The headline and the subhead were somewhat sensationalist: 'Anglo-Canadian Sinks Jap Sub!' and below that, 'Merchant Navy Master Fools Jap With Ruse To Take Bomb!' *Who writes these things? I wonder if Reuters will reprint this in England? Will Beryl see this?* He skimmed the story and it was substantially correct, but there was no mention of the gold. Another story was headed: 'Minister of Foreign Affairs Shigenori Togo Demands Explanation'.

After the captain had signed all the requisite papers, he had two more requests to make of the agent: he wanted transcontinental railway tickets to Sydney for his medical staff passengers, paid for on the account of the Ministry of War Transport. The shipping agent had grumbled a bit but acquiesced when shown Ellerman's cablegram to Gurnam, who he knew professionally. The other request was for the agent to find him a new third mate. The agent agreed and departed. The man did not know about the gold, and it had not been declared on the ship's manifest. Marinus Meijer then locked the door and seated himself on the Chesterfield. The captain took the opposite club chair, and broke the seal on the bottle of Oude Genever to celebrate their safe arrival. He poured two tumblers, neat.

"It seems," Marinus said, "that your record of never having lost a ship remains intact! Tell me all the details you couldn't reveal in public," he implored. They clinked glasses and drank. Mallinson told the entire story, including finding the nurses, but not mentioning his actual relationship with Becky. Meijer hung on every word. When he was finished, he showed Marinus the Nambu that Able Seaman Halvorsen had taken from the commander. After two hours immersed in saltwater, it had refused to fire. The commander had refused to be taken aboard the lifeboat, so they had waited him out until he was tired, then dragged him aboard. He had been weeping with the shame of being captured.

Meijer polished off his drink and exclaimed, "Gad, sir, a cracking yarn indeed. If I were you, I'd see that George Cukor receive a script in a fortnight! I see Beryl being played by Elsa Lanchester, and the chief nurse played by Greer Garson, and that nurse, McKenzie, being portrayed by Glynis Johns. What a Hollywood epic that would make!"

"Glynis Johns? I think not. No one else will do but Myrna Loy," Mallinson chuckled, before asking, "Had you someone in mind to portray myself?" He performed what he imagined to be a dashing grin in the manner of Errol Flynn.

Meijer regarded him critically. "Hmm. What say you to … Nigel Bruce?"

"I would say: 'You must grow a beard if you want to play me!'" Meijer then dragged his Gladstone bag over and opened it, producing a single sheet of ornately illuminated parchment.

"I have discussed this with my colleagues and we have come to an agreement. May we present to you this acknowledgement." Mallinson took it from him and, tilting it to the light, silently began to read its calligraphy in the florid language usual in these kinds of presentations: "By These Presents, WE, the Undersigned, Make …"

"That's really just a lot of legal Mumbo Jumbo," the banker interrupted, "to permit us to award you this." He pushed the bag over on its side then lifted the bottom to tip a heavy gold bar out onto the table. "Well done, captain! We are all of us appreciative of the danger you put yourself through!"

"Why, Marinus, thank you," he said, warmly, "This is *most* unexpected and appreciated!" But privately he corrected the Dutchman's choice of words: *of the danger* you *put* me *through!*

9

Command Performance

The next morning Captain Mallinson was rather late for breakfast. The crew remarked on this. He had his breakfast with Nurse McKenzie. The crew remarked on this also. When he did arrive on the bridge, later than was usual for him, he used the tannoy to call all of his deck officers to report to the bridge and wait there until called, but his first mate was to report directly to him in his quarters. The crew remarked on this as well. First Mate Wallace found the other mates standing on the bridge when he arrived, and asked if either of them knew what was going on. They were as puzzled as he. Making his way down the corridor, he flattened himself against the wall to let Jimmy pass by carrying a wad of cash for the next fortnight's food allowance. The mate stepped into the captain's cabin. The captain was there, looking into a drawer of his filing cabinet. Beyond him Wallace saw the bed-curtains of the alcove bed neatly arranged, and the bed neatly made. *This is odd; it's always left in disarray.* He took another step forwards into the room but then stopped, uncertain of what to do because the captain had a guest. He assumed the stand-easy position, hands clasped behind his back, and awaited the captain's instructions. Miss McKenzie lounged upon the Chesterfield. She wore a knee-length felted skirt of hunter green, while the captain's crisply starched linen dress shirt that she wore was buttoned only carelessly. Her arms were spread wide upon the back of the sofa, so the shirt was stretched taut and its few fastened buttons were straining. She'd rolled its sleeves up above her elbows. Her wavy red hair tumbled loose upon her shoulders. Her feet were bare, and she had rested them upon the low table, crossed ankle over ankle. She was concentrating intently on flexing one foot around in a circle. When she noticed him standing there, she laughed delightedly and smiled up at him. His heart was pounding so loud in his chest, he thought for certain it could be heard on the bridge.

"Roy, Reggie's here!" she exclaimed.

"You wanted to see me, sir?" Wallace said.

"Yes, Mr Wallace, do come in," the captain said, not looking up.

"Roy, Reggie is the one that showed me the stars last week. It was *so fascinating!*" she bubbled.

"Showed all of you the stars! All of the nurses the stars! The constellations!" Wallace was quick to clarify.

"And he was educating me all about bio-essence—"

"Of the ship. *Bioluminescence* of the ship – of the ship's wake!" He grimaced when he thought of how idiotic this must sound.

"Entertaining the ladies, eh, Mr Wallace?" Mallinson said, as he flicked through the contents of the drawer, "Good, good. Have a seat, have a seat." To Becky he said, "My dear, would you mind pouring our drinks for us, please, while I finish up here?" An open bottle of an amber spirit and two empty glasses had been set on the table. Wallace occupied a club chair. Becky rose and bent over the table as she poured out a tot for each of them. She handed a glass to Wallace with another smile, and then reclined upon the rolled arm of the sofa, tucking her legs under her and smoothing the skirt down. Having found the paper he was looking for, Roy read it for a moment then filed it away again. Wallace watched as he then searched through the drawers of his desk.

The desk. There is something different about the captain's desk. What is it? Ah! The framed photograph of his wife is gone, nowhere to be seen. That's odd. The captain then occupied the other club chair, and placed a yellow envelope, a stack of newspapers and a bundle of post tied with twine upon the table. He raised his glass.

"Drink up!" he exhorted. They clinked glasses and drank. The captain paused and looked into his glass as he swirled its contents. It seemed to Wallace that he was in a reflective mood this morning. They sat in silence for a time, and then the captain stirred himself. "I suppose you're wondering why I called for you. Called for you especially."

"Aye, sir, it had crossed my mind."

"You may dispense with the 'sir'. Just call me Roy."

"Aye, sir ... erm ... Roy."

"Well, let me start by saying this: I'm an old man and I wish to put my affairs in order." Becky put her bare feet on the floor and, with her forearms on her knees, leaned forward, listening intently. This put her décolletage in Wallace's direct line of vision. He found this distracting. He struggled to focus on what Roy was saying to him.

"Sorry, your affairs in order? Are you ill, sir?"

"Huh? What? No, nothing of the sort! Fit as a fiddle. Only thinking about the future."

"That ... ahh ... sounds quite ... ahhh ... sensible, sir – I mean Roy!"

"Becky, would you excuse us, please? There is a matter of a private nature I wish to discuss with Mr Wallace." She rose languidly and sidestepped the low table. As she passed behind the captain's chair, she placed both hands on his shoulders and planted a kiss on top of his head. Roy took her hand and gave it a squeeze. "Buttons, my dear!" he admonished her, with a twinkle in his eye. "Need I always remind you, don't forget your buttons!" With her back against the door jamb, she glanced back at Roy as she fastened a couple more buttons, before pulling the door shut behind her. Roy watched after her longingly until she left the cabin. Wallace realised his mouth was open, and shut it. As the door swung away from the wall, a valise that had been placed behind it was revealed. The penny dropped! *That's the valise I saw her with, when she boarded in Batavia! That kiss ... the neatly made bed ... wearing the captain's shirt ... the missing photograph of his wife. So, the rumour must be true: she and the old man are lovers!*

Roy then raised his glass to Wallace in a silent toast and took another swallow, and Wallace did the same. The captain then gazed into his drink, tilting the glass and watching the reflected light dancing in its ripples.

"Oh yes ... affairs," he muttered, and cleared his throat. "As I was saying," he continued, "I wish to put my affairs in order, so what I mean to do is ... that is, what I am proposing here is ..." He paused, seemingly finding it difficult to choose the proper words, but then, with his demeanour kindly and rather avuncular, he continued, "I wish to give her to you!"

"Gi-gi-give her to me?" Wallace stammered. He hung his head and the blood pounded in his ears. He felt dizzy. For a moment Roy's voice faded away and, when it returned, he heard him say with concern, "... quite all right? Is the drink too strong for you?"

"No, sir."

"Well, do you want her? If not, there may be others interested."

"Is this why you called for all the officers?" he asked, stunned.

"Naturally, I'll talk to them in turn," Mallinson said, "but I wanted to hear from you first. Speak up man!" Wallace could hardly credit he was actually hearing this. *A man I've looked up to for the better part of six months, but to hear him speak about her in this way is destroying everything I admire about him.* He sat up straight on the edge of the seat, and gulped down his drink. He set the glass down on the table rather too hard, startling even himself, and erupted.

"Sir! This is most improper!" He glared at the captain, his voice rising, "I will not tolerate hearing of her being given away in such a cavalier manner," he barked, "or at all, come to that!" He threw himself back into the chair, shaking with the emotion of his outburst, surprised he had even had the cheek to raise his voice to a superior officer. Roy regarded him with his forehead wrinkled, eyebrows raised, slack-jawed in astonishment. As was typical of the man, when he spoke his voice was even and measured.

"Mr Wallace, there's no need to get all shouty," he said. "Have you never desired your own command?"

"My own command?" Wallace parroted.

"Yes," Roy replied, annoyed. "What the deuce do you imagine I've been talking about?" Wallace flushed as red as a lobster. *Did the captain pick up on my mistake? I'd better say something, and quickly.*

"I've always wanted command of a ship, more than anything in my entire career, Roy."

"You hold a valid master's ticket, do you not?"

"Aye, sir, I do."

"And you've accrued the required sea-time?"

"Aye, sir, since Singapore, I have."

"Well, Mr Wallace, in my considered opinion you are more than qualified. I can recommend you for the command and, providing Ellerman Lines concur, the *Dominion Empress* is yours, if you want her." He refreshed their glasses.

"Thank you, sir!" he said, gobsmacked at his luck.

"Roy. Call me Roy. Captains are usually on first-name terms. You are entirely welcome, Acting Captain Reginald P. Wallace. Now, let's wet a stripe, shall we?" They clinked glasses and drank. "I can take you down to the officers' club in town and introduce you to the other captains, if you're so inclined."

"I'd like that, Roy."

"What does the P stand for, anyway?"

"Purefoy. Reggie Purefoy Wallace."

"Hmm, ... a 'Slayer of kings'!" Reggie rolled his eyes at this remark.

"Like I haven't heard *that* before." They sipped again. The mate felt his face returning to normal. "This gin is good, but an odd colour," he said.

"Not gin, Reggie, but barrel-aged Dutch genever," said Roy. "It was given to me as a gift. I like it, too, and that reminds me: I should tell you that Carpenter Nowiczski keeps a small still aboard with which he makes his Polish vodka. He hides it atop the engine-room fiddley between the inner and outer funnel casing. The crew is unaware I know this. They cut it with pineapple juice and are careful not to imbibe too much, so I don't find out, and that's the way I like it. I'd rather it be that, than to have them sneak the stronger stuff aboard, or squander all their pay on drinking binges ashore. As acting captain you may deal with that as you like, but my recommendation is to leave it be, unless it gets out of hand, of course. Here are the newspapers, and this bundle here is the post for the crew. Give them to the bosun to distribute for you. And these," he said, holding out the yellow envelope, "are your steaming orders. They are private and addressed to me but, as you can see, I have not opened them. You may do so at your leisure. When the time is right, I'll sit down with you and go over the books, discuss the procedures, hand over the keys to the desk and other such compartments. You may move in here in December." Roy looked about the cabin rather wistfully, it seemed to Reggie. They chatted a few minutes more, until Roy shook Reggie's hand in congratulations and asked him to send in Second Mate Dafyd Ap Morgan. The new captain would need a new first mate.

At noon Mallinson announced on the tannoy, "D'ye hear there! Clear the lower decks! All crew lay amidship to the well deck!" They arrived in short order, a handful among them holding their special mugs, and were disappointed to find no keg present. The captain stood silent on the catwalk above them, regarding them benevolently, and flanked by his bridge officers. A murmur arose among the jostling seamen. When it had died away, Mallinson announced that he would be "on the beach" effective the first of December, less than a week away. Retired! No! A groan arose. He then introduced Acting Captain Wallace, the new first mate, Morgan, the new second mate, O'Malley, and told them there would be a new third mate joining them, Fred, an Australian whose most recent job had been as first mate on the tiny Fremantle cross-harbour passenger ferry: no doubt they had already met him, or at least seen him. When he had finished speaking, there was silence, then one by one they came to attention and saluted until the entire mass of men were saluting. Captain Mallinson acknowledged their salute with his own, before quickly excusing himself. It wouldn't do to have the crew see him get emotional. He would later confess to Becky how much he had been affected by this outpouring of respect.

That very afternoon the captain visited an overseas cablegram office. The message he sent told Ellerman Lines his first mate was qualified to take command, and would they please confirm. He would be resigning as captain effective 1st December 1941. He would take his final pay from the cash on hand in the ship's safe and, if they would be so kind, he would appreciate it if they would please restart his pension, which had stopped when he had taken on the position. The Ellerman Lines Shipping Company confirmed Reginald within hours as a Brevet Captain, pending his eventual arrival in London.

Epilogue

Mrs Velma Mermod was a stout lady who wore dresses that were too tight and with a low neckline which she always covered with a protective hand, as if she wished the neckline might be a tad higher. The other hand fluttered about to punctuate her manner of speaking. She called everyone "Dearie" without exception. She showed Roy and Becky a one-bed walk-up on the top floor of a block of flats on Little Marine Parade in the seafront village of Cottesloe. The place was furnished in a spare Polynesian style with two chairs of rattan upholstered in light blue and a low table of bamboo in the lounge. The fabric of the purple Chesterfield couch was a tad threadbare but, no matter, the bed was comfortable. The kitchen held a table of chrome, its Formica top a riot of faded colour, with a drawer underneath and three mismatched wooden chairs. Cabinets painted sea-foam green and a refrigerator and hob of white enamel completed the layout. There was no oven. The kitchen and the water-closet floors were black-and-white checkered linoleum, and a few of the tiles were curling at the edges. The rooms smelled faintly of elderberries, which the landlady told them was the former tenant's perfume, assuring them it would soon dissipate. There was no telephone, but there was a cabinet Zenith wireless. A glass door gave out onto a balcony and a view of the ocean. Anyone else might have described it as outmoded, but to them it felt homely. They loved it.

Chief Nurse Virginia Wright and Eugene Graham announced that, as Americans, they wished to treat the nurses, officers and engineers to the holiday of Thanksgiving. Unfortunately, no grocery or restaurant could be found with the requisite cranberry sauce, yams or turkey, and it was the wrong season for pumpkins for the pie, more's the pity.

They celebrated instead on Thursday 27th November with a Thanksgiving barbecue in the garden of the flat. There were Boston baked beans, collard greens, potato salad, and large juicy steaks, and Virginia had even baked some cornbread, because a large cast-iron cooking pot with a lid had been found in the cupboard. Mr Andreassen surprised them all by sending along a steamed plum pudding from the ship. He was practising for Christmas, less than a month away. There was a galvanized steel tub filled with ice and bottles of Kalgoorlie Bitter and Hannan's Lager. Hamish made sure that everyone held a bottle, then announced to the throng that Roy was due to celebrate his fifty-ninth birthday near the turn of the year, and toasted his health, and embarrassed him by starting a round of "For he's a jolly good fellow" to which everybody joined in.

The meal was followed by a swim at Cottesloe Beach. The nurses wore their swimdresses. Violet threw off her dressing gown to reveal a new two-piece swimming costume (without a skirt!) that scandalously exposed her navel. It was a good thing there were no constables about or she would have been arrested on a charge of public indecency. The young mates and engineers had not been prepared, but made the best of it by stripping off down to their boxer shorts and dashing into the surf, whooping and hollering. They seemed unaware that white boxer shorts, when wet, hid nothing. The nurses coyly didn't tell them. While the youngsters rough-housed, Hamish and Roy stood on the beach having a chinwag, this being their last day together. Becky and Virginia watched from the water as a bespectacled man wearing an old-fashioned blue woollen bathing costume, his hair greying at the temples, approached Roy and chatted for a minute. As the two women walked up the beach towelling themselves dry, they saw the man shake Roy's hand, turn and walk away.

"Who was that fellow?" Virginia asked when they arrived, tossing her towel about her shoulders.

"Oh, he had heard we had a skirmish with a submarine and a seaplane," Roy replied, "and that we had brought you nurses here. He wished to thank me for it personally. He lives here, and asked me to visit him and his wife tomorrow evening to tell them all the details. A rather pleasant chap, name of John Curtin." At the mention of this name, Becky choked.

"Strewth! You are bloody joking! Not John *Curtin?*" she squealed, "*The* John Curtin?" She hopped with excitement. The Yank, the Englishman and the Scot all looked at each other, not beginning to comprehend what she was on about. Unable to contain herself any longer, she burst out, "He's only the bleedin' prime minister of Australia!"

The party changed into dry clothes at the flat. That evening, the group walked the three-quarter-mile distance to the tram station to return to the ship. Roy took the opportunity to wish Hamish MacCallan, Captain Wallace and Eugene all the best, and shook their hands. He and Becky wished them well, all the mates and the engineers, and they hugged all the nurses, too.

The following afternoon, Ralph Woodley, Virginia Wright and her nurses boarded the transcontinental train for Sydney. That very evening, Roy and Becky walked to 24 Jarrad Street and spent an hour in the company of the prime minister and his wife Elsie, who served them each a lemon squash, as John had given up alcohol since being elected. Mr Curtin was apologetic that he couldn't spare them any more time, as he was currently in a rather tense negotiation with President Roosevelt for more assistance. At present, he was engaged in writing an article for publication in the *Melbourne Herald* called "The Task Ahead," in which he planned to announce that "Australia looks to America." Mr

Churchill had been told of this, and was not best pleased. Mr Curtin was keen to hear Roy's impression of the Japanese commander he had personally faced. When Roy had finished, the prime minister asked if he thought it might be accurate to write, "We Australians face a powerful, ably led and unbelievably courageous foe", and Roy had concurred with that view.

Nurses Sue Kee and Doris, and Eugene, sailed aboard the SS *Dominion Empress*. Suki had resumed going by the name Susan Kee from California, the name on her false identity papers. Mallinson finally revealed the truth to Captain Wallace, who was understanding and promised to keep her secret. On Saturday afternoon Roy and Becky stood on the balcony of their flat and watched the *Empress* steam away to the west-north-west, until she was lost in the glare. Becky cried a little, but Roy hadn't been her master long enough to form any lasting fondness for the old tramp steamer. He found he was somewhat disappointed that Wallace hadn't revealed to him their next destination.

Now it was only the two of them. The summer weather was glorious, hot and dry, and the sea temperature perfectly warm. They did the marketing, and cooked and cleaned, and ate, and she did the laundry, and he hoovered the flat, and they made love and did everything married couples do together that he had been missing all these many years. Becky made certain there were always fresh flowers in the vase, and at some meals he lit the two candles on the table. A thing Roy enjoyed was that Becky might invite him to join her in the bath or shower – this had begun when she'd discovered his Edwardian tub aboard ship – which often led to more lovemaking. They were extraordinarily happy together. She had easily knocked twenty years off his age. She let him know it was as if she had known him forever, and that's the way he felt about her, too. Oftentimes they might have the same thoughts, finishing each other's sentences. *Comfortable* with each other, that was the word for it! He now saw Becky as somehow calmer and more mature. She appeared to his eyes rather different from the young woman who had snatched a newspaper from his hand on that park bench seemingly an epoch ago. A feeling of wonderment washed over him; *had our condenser not played up, had I not altered course for Batavia, had I not decided on a short holiday, had I sat on a bench in a different park, none of this would be happening. If, if, if.*

Roy and Becky were laying in each other's arms late on the morning of 8th December, when the music programme was interrupted by reports of the capitulation of Thailand and the undeclared attacks by the Empire of Japan on Singapore, Hong Kong and Pearl Harbour. On that day, Great Britain, the United States and the Netherlands all declared war on the Empire of Japan within hours of each other. Australia declared on 9th December. This was it: they were now A World At War. He read to her the newspaper details of the epic battle which had sunk the Australian light cruiser HMAS *Sydney*. Half a dozen ships, including the RMS *Aquitania* which had raced at flank speed all the way from Singapore, had searched for survivors. Of the 645 aboard, there had been none. Detmers and his crew were now POWs, having been captured, parched and starving, wandering in Australia's outback.

He could have made the trip home to England at any time, with many train journeys and multiple aeroplane hops from continent to continent, perhaps interspersed with some sea voyages in slow freighters that, in truth, he had no desire for during wartime. He found he was content, yes, quite content to wait. To wait for some sign. But the overt sign seemed never to be there.

Becky and Roy took to swimming in the ocean across the road at Cottesloe Beach nearly every day, and sometimes they enjoyed swimming at the freshwater Crawley Baths in Perth. They enjoyed walking the city, seeing its sights and museums. He took her out to eat at various ethnic restaurants to introduce her to the foods of the world. They began going to the theatre in Perth to see stage plays. Becky loved going to see the films at the local cinema, as did Roy. As a girl she had assiduously attended all the film showings of the silent-film sensation Theda Bara.

They occasionally rented bicycles, and also a cuddy-cabin sailboat in which leisurely hours were spent on Melville Water. He showed her the rudiments of sailboat handling, describing for her the interaction between the sails and keel to make the boat sail upwind, or on a broad reach. She was thrilled, on a windswept day, when he gave her the tiller as they scudded across the bay wing-and-wing. One time they made a meal of the Scotch eggs he had prepared, and then napped in the cockpit in each other's arms as the little craft gently rocked at anchor in the warm sunshine.

Near the end of the month, he looked up from working out their finances to hear her merrily singing snatches of popular songs from the kitchen as she cooked. When she did this, it made him feel very happy and contented.

Late one morning Becky found a tiny, jet-black moggie lost and mewling in the garden and took it in. The poor thing was ravenous, so she fed it titbits of meat from their lunch sarnies. The little fellow was quite rambunctious and delighted in pouncing on Roy's shoelaces, so she named him Aglet. Roy was pleased to see her so happy. He thickly layered some newspapers under the washbasin for its convenience. That night it chose to sleep in their bed, curled against Roy's neck. The next afternoon a man from a flat on the ground floor at the rear, who said his name was Mavrodopoulos, knocked at their door and demanded its return. Roy assured her they would be able to get another one from a pet shop.

They were invited to numerous parties and dined and danced. When it became apparent they were going to be much in demand on the holiday social circuit, Roy bought Becky two evening dresses, one floor-length off-the-shoulder in purple satin, the other knee-length in rose red, and also a few pairs of espadrilles, as well as some nice heels of her very own. Since this was sunny Australia, Roy chose to buy a new charcoal grey Stetson fedora, instead of a trilby, and a new suit to match which, surprisingly, had no trouser turn-ups nor pocket flaps, all the mode that year because of fabric rationing. He sported a black bow tie. The guests at these parties pressed them to relate the stories of their escape from submarines, and from China, and they obliged. They did the same as guests at official dinners throughout December. They were introduced to the lord mayor of Perth, Thomas William Meagher, and met the premier of Western Australia, John Willcock, as well as too many officers from every branch of the services. Some of these men had never been to war in their careers, and wanted to know how he had managed to sink a submarine, and from an old merchant ship, no less. Since the gold had been safely delivered to the Perth Mint, they included in the telling what they had done to disguise it on board. He was careful always to give full marks to Hamish for the timely and brilliant invention of the makeshift bombs, and to Lieutenant Freddie Chapman for giving him the "time pencils" that made them possible. At Christmas parties, and at a New Year's Eve celebration, their oft-repeated stories inevitably became somewhat condensed in the telling.

There began a time whenever they arrived at yet another dinner party, at yet another grand manse, and Roy told the major-domo their given names, that the man might announce them to the assembled gathering as, "Captain Roy Mallinson, Royal Navy (Retired) and Mrs Rebecca Mallinson," and they did not bother to rectify his mistake. After departing one of these dinners, whilst waiting for the taxi, Becky hugged Roy close and whispered in his ear, "When I hear that said, I feel so pleased, my heart just swells like it's fit to burst!" Roy, for his part, knew precisely what she meant.

It was only a week later that he read of the torpedoing of the Norwegian motorship *Eidsvold* as she departed Christmas Island on 20th January 1942. He was relieved the crew of twenty-six had made it ashore unharmed. The naval gun emplacement on the hillside had been of no use at all. He was astounded at reports that, when the Japanese Navy had arrived in force, the Indonesian gun crew had mutinied and killed their British officers! Barely a week after that he read with dismay that the Japanese had bombed Tanjung Priok Harbour, Batavia. He followed the newspaper reports with discouragement, as island after island fell to the unstoppable Japanese. He stopped relaying to Becky any news of the war, so as not to upset her.

In mid-February Japanese forces attacked Darwin, Australia in a raid on a scale larger than the one at Pearl Harbour. Roy and Becky sat listening in trepidation to the familiar voice of Prime Minister Curtin speaking on the wireless: "Damage to property was considerable, but reports so far to hand do not give precise particulars about the loss of life. The government regards the attacks as most grave, and makes it quite clear that a severe blow has been struck on Australian soil." He switched it off. Still, Roy needed to keep track of what was going on, so he asked to borrow Velma Mermod's Austin Saloon so that he could drive down to the harbour and speak with those coming off the refugee ships that were arriving more and more frequently. He gave Mrs Mermod's telephone number to the harbourmaster and asked the man to let him know when each refugee ship was due to arrive. On one such day he was notified the Dutch coastal motorship *Janssens* was entering the port after a harrowing open ocean journey from Tjilatjap with a damaged rudder, to disgorge six-hundred civilians from a dozen nations, including the survivors of HMAS *Perth* and the USS *Marblehead*. From one of these Americans, an officer named Goggins, he learnt that Admiral Doorman had been killed in a naval engagement north of Surabaya, Java. His flagship, *De Ruyter*, had been torpedoed in the last week of February. The officer told him Admiral Doorman's last transmission had been, "Do not stand by for survivors! Retire to Batavia!" Others said that, as rumour had it, Lieutenant (now Captain) Freddie Spencer Chapman had disappeared into the Malayan jungles, to wage a guerrilla war against the Japanese with the support of Communist Chinese partisans, and that Sir Shenton Thomas, with his secretary Mrs Choy and her husband, were now in a Japanese prison camp. Roy did not tell Becky about Admiral Doorman.

On 15th March a convoy of troopships from Colombo, British Ceylon, escorted by the County Class heavy cruiser HMS *Cornwall*, arrived in Fremantle to disgorge more than 10,000 troops. Roy was on hand to meet it and, having briefly served in the *Cornwall* in 1931, was invited to visit aboard. His old friend Dunthorne told Roy that ABDA, the combined American–British–Dutch–Australian forces of South West Pacific Command, had ceased to exist. Three weeks later Roy read that the *Cornwall* was sunk on Easter Sunday and over a thousand men spent thirty hours in the water before being rescued. Mr Dunthorne was not among them.

One afternoon, while Becky was out doing the laundry in the room on the ground floor, Roy was standing at the window, gazing out at the Indian Ocean, mesmerised by the glittering silver of the waves. His mind was unfocussed, almost as if he was in a trance. *Beryl and I are no longer intimate. I can't recall how many years it's been since either of us told the other "I love you," in so many words. Our marriage long ago became, if not exactly dull, then at most commonplace and routine. In the years remaining to me, am I not deserving of some small measure of happiness?*

The next thing he knew, he was sitting at the kitchen table, a blank sheet of stationery in front of him, Beryl's fountain pen uncapped in his hand. Without consciously thinking about it, he had decided to write a letter to her, but he did not know what he wanted to say. Or might say. Or should say. Yet, at the same time, he also knew he still did love Beryl in some small way. His feelings were conflicted. *Perhaps if I just start writing, the words will come to me.*

He dated the letter, and wrote 'Perth, Australia' and then their Stowmarket address. He wrote the word 'Dear' but when next he began to write "Beryl" nothing appeared on the page. He shook the pen. He could feel there was ink sloshing within it, but the pen refused to write her name. He licked the nib and tried again, but the paper ripped. He looked in the drawer for another; it was the last sheet, there were no more. *Was this the overt sign? Was this fate telling him to stay with Becky?*

The door opened and she entered, gaily humming a tune and carrying a basket heaped with wet towels. He rose and quickly dropped the torn paper into the bin. His fleeting urge was to drop the pen in after it. Instead he went to the bedroom, took his leather grip from the wardrobe and opened it on the bed. He put the pen in it. He sat on the bed a minute more, anxiously twisting his wedding band around on his finger, thinking, *Becky must know how much I love her. I must browse a jewellery shop or two at the end of April when I visit the city for my annual check-up. Only when I've a proper ring in hand will I ask her. I don't think she'll be surprised.*

With difficulty, he slowly worked the ring off over his knuckle and placed it in the bottom of the luggage with the pen. He thoughtfully shut the grip and returned it to the wardrobe. When he turned about, he found her standing in the doorway to the bedroom. *Had she seen what I did?* He went to her and tenderly took her in his arms. Her eyes searched his face.

"Darling? What is it?" she asked.

"Oh, just thinking how lucky I am, to have you in my life," he replied. They kissed, then carried the towels to the balcony and together began pegging them on the lines to dry.

A week later on a Sunday afternoon, 12th April, they had just finished lunch. Becky put the dishes in the cupboard after Roy had dried them. The wireless was playing orchestral swing music being broadcast from a hotel in downtown Perth. He leaned back upon the Chesterfield, his feet propped on the bamboo table, the Sunday edition of *The West Australian* newspaper open to the cinema section. He smiled up at her as she handed him an open bottle of Swan Export Lager. She snuggled up to him, her head on his shoulder, as they discussed what film to see later on. There was a comedy, *Come Up Smiling*, or else an action drama called *Wings of Destiny*. It had earlier been decided that tonight's restaurant was going to be that new little French café in the Leederville neighbourhood they had spotted from the electric tram. The schedule for tomorrow included a visit to a pet shop. Becky was overjoyed to be getting a moggie of her very own!

A knock on the door was followed by the landlady, Mrs Mermod, continually calling, "Mr Mallinson! Oh, Mr Mallinson!" *What now, isn't the rent paid for this month? It can't possibly be a refugee ship this late. Didn't they stop arriving weeks ago?*

He set the beer and newspaper down and they both went to answer the door. Velma was in a very agitated state, more flustered than was usual for her. She said the harbourmaster had just been on the blower with a message for him: the *Queen Mary* had arrived in Fremantle harbour last night! The ship's schedule and route was never publicised; it was going to depart today, bound for Britain, and in less than one hour! Her car was in the car park ready to take them now! Hurry! Hurry!

A cold hand took hold of Roy's heart and squeezed. He thought he would never again be able to take another breath. In a single sentence, the world he had meticulously constructed for them had come crashing down. *All of it has vanished in an instant. My design to write to Beryl with an explanation, my intention to speak to a solicitor about a divorce, my desire to ask Becky for her hand. It seems the decision has been thrust upon me. What a fool I've been!*

He asked Mrs Mermod to wait outside for him and shut the door. He took Becky in his arms and, with a shock, she realised that what they had both ignored was here.

"Oh no," Becky whispered. "Oh no, no, *no!*" she wailed. He held her tight as she wept. He whispered it was for the best; their age difference was far too great, in ten or fifteen years he would be dead, and then where would she be? A widow at thirty-five or forty. Before then his health might fail, and she would be trapped in the prime of her life, caring for an invalid. They had known each other nearly half a year; it seemed to both of them a lifetime and yet, also all too short a time. They each told the other "I love you" for the last time. The stark reality of their predicament was more than he could bear and he sobbed too. He held her face and covered it with kisses, and the kisses were wet. Hurriedly he emptied the wardrobe and threw his things into the grip. At the open door he turned to her. *I can't have her in the car with me: Velma thinks she's my daughter.*

"Becky, stay here. The rent's paid to the end of the month. Here's the key. Velma, will you take Becky to the train when she goes?" Velma drove him to the waterfront at breakneck speed, her old Austin's tyres squealing at the corners. In the mirror she noticed him wiping his eyes with his handkerchief.

"Oh, now, Dearie, I know how tough it is to send a daughter off to university," she blethered on. "Why, last year my lad went off to the University of Melbourne and he ..." Roy shut his ears to her nattering.

He boarded 'The Grey Ghost', as the great ocean liner was now known, and was surprised to find Virginia Wright aboard. She had embarked in Sydney. They stood together at the stern, searching the shoreline as it receded, but could not even find the village. Roy knew Becky was there somewhere, standing at the window, watching him depart. Without warning he collapsed to the deck, a hand gripping the rail, and burst into tears.

"Roy! You okay?" Virginia asked with concern. He looked up into her face.

"I didn't think to get her address," he cried.

"I don't know it either," said Virginia, sadly. She took hold of his left hand to help him to his feet, and that was when she noticed the wedding band missing from his finger, and she knew, yes, she knew then what his intention had been. A thought occurred to her.

"Say, don't big boats like this have radios? You know, so that tycoons can contact their stockbrokers?" Roy wiped his eyes on the sleeve of his coat.

"Yes! Yes, they do!" He pulled his wallet from his coat pocket and dug frantically through it until he produced a scrap of paper. He held it up and crowed "Velma Mermod's telephone number!" He dashed forward, Virginia trotting along behind, until he reached the wireless room. The uniformed technician sitting inside saw him coming and jumped up to shut the door, but Roy got there first and jammed his foot against it to prevent its closing.

" 'ere now, none o' that! Civilians ain't allowed—" the man grunted, as he leaned against it. Virginia arrived a moment later and joined Roy and together they succeeded in forcing the door. They stumbled into the room as the technician gave up. The man listened wearily as Roy blurted out his request.

"See here, I'd like you to call the Fremantle harbourmaster, and have the man call this number. He's to ask for the address of a young woman there named Rebecca Meara McKenzie. Please."

"Sorry, sir, it's not possible."

"But you don't understand! This is highly important! You must do this before we're out of range!"

"This ship is under orders to maintain radio silence, sir. There's nowt can be done." He'd been making this same reply to passengers for over an hour and was sick of it.

"I met Commodore Sir James Bisset as I boarded. I'll speak to him! He can override—"

"No, sir. It's wartime regulations, y'see."

"But I'm a captain! Surely one captain can listen to another captain!" The wireless officer looked Roy up and down, as he stood there in his tweed suit and flat cap. Virginia recognised the doubt on the man's face and spoke up.

"He is! This is Roy Mallinson, captain of the steamship *Dominion Empress*, so you had better believe him!" At the mention of the name, the man stiffened.

"The *Dominion Empress*?"

"Yes!"

The man turned to his desk and idly flipped through the pages of his radio log, and then paused. He looked up.

"Of the Ellerman Lines?"

"Ellerman! Yes! Yes! Ellerman!" Roy affirmed fervently.

"The one wot stopped a torpedo three month ago?"

"Torpedo!" Roy replied, stunned.

"Aye, sir, ... in the Med 'tween Cyrenaica and Malta. Third January it were. They were under attack by one o' them Eye-tie motor torpedo boats."

"Did she sink?" he asked, suddenly despondent. *With a cargo of lead she must've gone down in minutes.*

"Couldn't say, sir. The transmission cut off sudden-like, right in the middle of a word, as it were. I believe she said she were afire. Was she carryin' explosives?"

"No."

"Well, that's a comfort—"

"Rubber. She was carrying rubber."

"Oh."

"Were … there any … survivors?"

"Sorry, that's all I know. We 'eard no more from 'er arfter that, sir." The man shut his logbook and shelved it. Roy's shoulders sagged. *First Becky, and now Hamish, gone. … Sinclair, Wallace, Taffy … Tord and Jimmy … Poor Eugene, so eager to experience 'the war' – what a waste!*

Virginia clutched his arm, and he could feel her trembling or, perhaps, it was him. They spoke of his grief over the coming days. He felt as if a hollowness had opened in his chest, an emptiness nothing could fill, and finally he admitted to her that he had never foreseen how such an empty void could form and yet, for him, become such a heavy cargo.

At stops in Cape Town, and Rio, and in New York City, where Virginia disembarked, he made frantic trunk calls to Velma that were not picked up, and eventually he gave up, knowing that Becky would have left Perth on the train at the end of April anyway. Naturally, his call to Beryl in Stowmarket went through without hindrance. He finally reached Greenock, Scotland on 16th May 1942, where Beryl met him at the dock. They had been apart for fifteen months. He told her how the watch she had gifted him had been "briefly owned" by a Japanese submarine commander. She had indeed received his airmail letter from Singapore, and had seen that Australian newspaper story, as it had been reprinted here. He finally was able to recount for her the story of the delivery of the gold.

In 1947, Roy received a letter from Ellerman Shipping Lines. When opened, it held another sealed envelope addressed to himself, from Eugene in the States. This contained a one-year-old cutting from *The Oregonian* newspaper, announcing the marriage of Suki Higashikokubaru to Eugene Graham. There was a black-and-white snap of them taken on Malta, as seen by the buildings in the background. A second cutting announced the birth of a seven-pound six-ounce baby boy. They had named him Roy Graham. Eugene's typewritten letter described what had happened after leaving Fremantle: after a stop in Aden to coal up, and Christmastime in 'Alex', they'd taken a torpedo in line with the bridge, and another in hold four, while attempting to deliver her cargo of aeroplanes to the island of Malta. The entire ship's company had survived, rowing four lifeboats into Marsaxlokk Harbour, under the command of Captain Wallace. In a postscript pencilled on the back of his letter, Suki thanked Roy for 'having had the talk' with Eugene. (Others had later told her the tale of how Gene had refused to leave the ship until he had found and carried her, unconscious, stepping into a waiting lifeboat as the ship foundered under them on an even keel.) Gene's letter continued: the ship's company had arrived back in England in January 1942. Gene and Suki had every intention of continuing on to his family in Portland, Oregon, but her real nationality had been discovered! To save Suki from incarceration in an American internment camp, they had fled in the middle of the night, smuggled to neutral Ireland in the lugger of a sympathetic Irish fisherman. There they had spent the remainder of the war posing as 'married American expatriates' in the riverside village of Foynes, County Limerick, while Gene supported them with his job as a radio-telegraph operator at its transatlantic flying-boat port. In an effort to reinforce their disguises he had even bought fake wedding rings.

Roy and Beryl deposited the gold bar in the Stowmarket branch of their London bank. A portion of it he used to build a modest steam launch that he would potter around in, sometimes from King's Lynn out into The Wash, though most of his trips departed Ipswich down the River Orwell and up the River Stour to the villages there. He made elaborate plans to steam across to Ostend or Dunkerque with Hamish, but it never happened. Once, he took Beryl to Brightlingsea, but she had always felt ill at ease whilst in a boat. There was the time when he and Hamish had steamed up the River Blackwater all the way to The Jolly Sailor pub in Heybridge, to dine with Freddie. They drank pints of bitter, or scrumpy cider, and swapped war stories until the end of the bank holiday. They'd been impressed by his little steamboat.

Early in 1953, for her Coronation Honours List, the Queen invested Roy with the title of Knight Bachelor, and his name was duly entered in the rolls of the Imperial Society of Knights Bachelor. Without his knowledge, the government of the Netherlands had put his name forward, and Prime Minister Churchill had verified the truth of the supporting affidavits for Her Majesty. Sir Roy and the Lady Mallinson were rather overwhelmed with the honour.

Beryl Mallinson outlived Roy, who passed away in 1966 two days shy of his eighty-third birthday. She never discovered, nor ever asked, why he had named his boat *Becky*.

Glossary

Some words defined:

Advocaat: an alcoholic beverage flavoured with eggs (Dutch)

Apotheek: a pharmacy, apothecary

Aquavit: a strong alcoholic beverage popular in Scandinavian countries

banger: a type of British sausage

bap: a bread roll or bun

Blighty: slang term for Great Britain

boffin: a scientist or technician

Bowditch: a navigation reference book

Chambord: an alcoholic beverage, raspberry flavoured (French)

craic: a party (Scottish)

godown: a warehouse

haggis: a Scottish dish of boiled oatmeal and organ meats

Istana: 'palace' (Malay)

souk: a food market

moggie: a cat, usually but not always feral

neeps and tatties: turnips and potatoes (Scottish)

Nicht Rauchen! Feuergefährlich!: No Smoking! Flammable Material! (German)

Rijsttafel: literally 'rice table', a dish popular in Indonesia (Dutch)

serang: the 'boss man' of Asian crewmembers

spijskaart: a menu (Dutch)

tiffin: lunch, a word borrowed from Hindi

A Typical Watch Schedule

A typical Merchant Navy watch schedule:
  2000-0000 First Watch
  0000-0400 Middle Watch
  0400-0800 Morning Watch
  0800-1200 Forenoon Watch
  1200-1600 Afternoon Watch
  1600-1800 First Dog Watch
  1800-2000 Last Dog Watch

About the Author

My journey to becoming a novelist has been a life-long one. I've always thought I had a novel in me, but never had the inspiration (or the time) until I retired. I spent a few years in the US Army as a mechanic, stationed in Germany. After this, I began my career in transportation design, working as a project manager until I retired in 2010. Casting about for something to do, I became a member of the Northwest Steam Society, and also the Steamboat Association of Great Britain. A life-long boat owner of both power and sail, my "retirement boat" is a steamboat I built myself. I love travelling, having visited Greece, Britain, Japan, Ireland and most recently, Malta and Croatia. Oftentimes, this has given me inspiration to write. I've been told more than once "your novels read like an old black-and-white film." I take that as a high compliment.

Ryan Plut is 67 years old and lives near Seattle, Washington State. He holds dual Canadian/American citizenship. He is married to Karen (Keefer) Plut. They are child-free, but have raised many "kids" who meow.

You can connect with me on:

🌐 https://www.ryanplut.com

Subscribe to my newsletter:

✉ https://www.ryanplut.com/contact

Also by Ryan Plut

HEAVY CARGO is my first novel. THE BELFAIR PINCH is the sequel to it. THE BITTER PIT OF THE CHERRY is the third in this loose trilogy.

The Belfair Pinch

IN YUGOSLAVIA OF JANUARY 1942 a civil war rages; factions of royalists, communists, and fascists are either fighting or collaborating with each other. To the Allies fighting the wider World War this fractured country is an unknown cipher. Captain Reginald Wallace of the British Merchant Navy is in Egypt after the SS *Dominion Empress* was torpedoed out from under him. He begins a torrid affair with Millicent Featherstone, the General's clerk.

But he's tapped to be a temporary SOE agent for a single short mission: very simply, he's to be dropped into occupied Yugoslavia to retrieve the HLV BELFAIR, a neutral Swedish-crewed ship stranded there. Millie eagerly awaits his return.

Things never do go as planned, do they? In Yugoslavia he becomes enamoured with Pavlina, a gorgeous assassin on the run from the Nazis. But Slavic commanders have ordered their female partisans to never become pregnant, or the <u>man</u> will be executed. Now what's a fellow to do? Well, *first*, get the ship out! Easier said than done when the ship is under 24 hour guard by the German army.